LIP READING

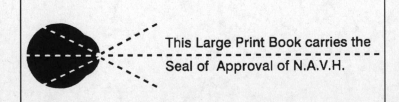

This Large Print Book carries the
Seal of Approval of N.A.V.H.

LIP READING

HARRY KRAUS

THORNDIKE PRESS
A part of Gale, Cengage Learning

GALE
CENGAGE Learning

Farmington Hills, Mich • San Francisco • New York • Waterville, Maine
Meriden, Conn • Mason, Ohio • Chicago

GALE
CENGAGE Learning®

Thorndike Press® Large Print Christian Mystery.
The text of this Large Print edition is unabridged.
Other aspects of the book may vary from the original edition.
Set in 16 pt. Plantin.

LIBRARY OF CONGRESS CATALOGING-IN-PUBLICATION DATA

Kraus, Harry Lee, 1960–
    Lip reading / by Harry Kraus. — Large print edition.
        pages cm. — (Thorndike Press large print Christian mystery)
    ISBN 978-1-4104-7895-5 (hardcover) — ISBN 1-4104-7895-5 (hardcover)
    1. Medicine—Research—Fiction. 2. Medical research personnel—Fiction.
3. Large type books. I. Title.
PS3561.R2875L57 2015
813'.54—dc23   2015001823

Published in 2015 by arrangement with David C Cook

[signature: Kraus, Harry]

Printed in Mexico
1 2 3 4 5 6 7 19 18 17 16 15

For Samuel Kraus.
Thanks for being such an encouraging
first reader.

ACKNOWLEDGMENTS

Stories are never written alone. Thanks to Susan May Warren and Jim Rubart for their help in brainstorming this plot. Thanks also to Kris, whose eyes always catch the details that I miss. Thanks to Dave Lambert, faithful editor and friend. We've been together since *Could I Have This Dance?* and although I hate your laborious edit suggestions, you make me better and I thank you on behalf of all my readers.

1

Kibera Slum, Nairobi, Kenya

With fluid dexterity, Rebecca Jackson, PhD, flattened the border of her upper lip with the tip of her lipstick. This wasn't just any lipstick. But then, this wasn't just anywhere. She was an ocean away from the cutthroat, high-stakes world of pharmaceutical manu-facturing, where she competed to create the world's next wonder drug.

Her location: Kibera, an inner-city Nairobi slum, home to two million sweaty inhabi-tants, a population of poor yet colorful Ken-yans who seemed little distracted by the equatorial heat.

Her lipstick: L'Absolu Rouge by Lancôme Paris. She preferred the Daisy Rose shade and the fact that it offered some protection from the sun, SPF 12.

But she didn't wear it for protection. She applied it, just as she had a hundred other brands, to cover up a cosmetic flaw, the result of a surgical error.

Twenty years earlier, seventeen-year-old Becca Jackson had wrestled with a surgeon through an intoxicated haze. In a small-town Virginia hospital, the doctor did the best he could under the circumstances, putting together a puzzle of skin that used to be her finest feature — her full and pouty lips. She didn't remember vomiting on the surgeon's shoes — something her mother had told her about the morning after that horrible, horrible night — but she didn't regret doing it.

There is one cardinal sin in lip repair: a failure to match up the red-white border at the edge. The vermillion border. It was a word she'd learned at age seventeen and one she whispered every day as she learned to apply makeup to cover the one-millimeter offset in the border, the red lip color jutting just that tiny amount into the pale skin beneath her nose. Even a small irregularity at the edge of the lip catches the eye and causes it to fixate on the imperfection. She knew this all too well.

Her cameraman Rich, a twentysomething man who looked at home in an olive-green T-shirt and jeans, appeared in the mirror. "Dr. Jackson, please. This is the fourth time you've adjusted your lipstick. You look fine."

"I haven't been outside without lipstick in twenty years," she muttered.

"This is Africa. The spot calls for a natural look anyway."

"I don't care for my natural look." She paused and placed her index finger over a small bottle of perfume and touched the finger to the skin just under her nose. "It smells like a sewer out there."

"I'd be careful to step over the little stream in front of the door," he said. "I think that's where the smell comes from."

Opium had been her signature fragrance for as long as she could remember. It was an Yves Saint Laurent perfume known for advertisements using naked or nearly naked women in front of shadowy backgrounds. She held up the bottle so that Rich could see the label. "Can you believe I was held up in customs for this?" She laughed. "As if I was really carrying drugs or something." She put the perfume back into her leather Tano designer handbag. "I had to spray the fragrance just to convince the idiot," she said. "What a waste."

"Let's go," he urged.

She turned in the mud-walled little school-turned-dressing-room. "I'm right behind you."

"Watch your step."

She stepped into the muddy, rutted, and unpaved street. Along both sides, vendors hawked everything from toothpaste and hair products to displays of shoes laid out in neat soldier rows on the ground.

Her team had assembled a semicircle of uniformed school children who were to be playing a game behind her as she slowly walked down the street toward the camera. The concept was simple: talk casually about the work Jackson Pharmaceuticals — JP — was doing to combat the devastation of AIDS.

But after three hours of trying, everything she'd done had come off as mechanical and plastic. The goal was to help salvage JP's sagging public image and boost the sales of her new autobiography, *Pusher: Confessions of an American Pharmaceutical Giant.*

It wasn't until the team was about to call it a day that Becca did something she'd thought was off camera. She joined a group of orphans playing a hand-slapping game that involved a rhythmic recitation about African women washing clothes. Becca joined the game, slapping the hands of a little Kenyan orphan and stumbling to keep up with the words.

Afterward, as she strolled back toward her team, the director, a stern man by the name of Lane Buckwalter, cracked his first smile of the day. "This is good. I say we trash the walking casual explanations and just show this. We'll hire a professional to do a voiceover about Jackson's newest AIDS drug."

Becca was surprised when she saw the clip. "What — you were filming?"

The cameraman smiled. "Every second."

The media representative from Becca's publishing house agreed. In their joint agreement to finance the campaign, JP and Putnam had agreed to tag the ad with the cover image of *Pusher.*

Mr. Buckwalter wiped his brow and looked at the sky. "Dinnertime. We need to get back to the hotel."

Becca nodded and looked at Rich. "Can you get my bag?"

"Sure."

She lingered in the street while the team packed the equipment into the back of a tan Land Rover.

"Dr. Jackson?"

She turned to see a dark-skinned African. She was just beginning to recognize the characteristics of the different tribes. He appeared to be Luo, with full lips, a broad nose, and teeth that seemed extra white against his skin.

"Could I get a picture?" he said.

"Sure," she said, smiling. She appeared to have a fan even in remote Africa.

"Just step over here," he said, leading her to the edge of an alley. "I want to get you in front of the sign of our little clinic."

She stepped into the alley and smiled as he held up a silver digital camera.

"Cheese," he said.

She obeyed just as arms closed around her from behind. She tried to scream, but a strong hand clamped over her mouth. Kicking, she was dragged into the alley and out of view of her team. She feared rape and robbery. She wanted to say that she had money in her handbag, but she'd left that back in her makeshift dressing room and she couldn't say anything with the hand over her mouth.

Within seconds, she was tossed into the back of a windowless van, where she stared into the barrel of a handgun. "No noise!" the man said. She heard tapping on the side of the van. The vehicle lurched forward and bounced along the rutted alley.

She understood. This wasn't robbery, at least not the type of street thuggery she'd imagined. This was kidnapping. She was a commodity, a research pharmacologist and the niece of the CEO and majority stockholder in a multimillion-dollar pharmaceutical company.

The van picked up speed. She looked at the back door, wondering if she could survive jumping if her captor was distracted.

After escape, which she quickly ruled out, her second thought was vain.

I left my lipstick in my bag.

2

Becca Jackson looked into her captor's eyes and pleaded. "I'm feeling sick."

He nodded. "I don't like riding back here either."

"I need a bucket."

The man handed her what appeared to be an old paint can. She clutched it under her chin as the van bumped and sped along. Retching, she deposited her lunch into the can. Several hours before, she'd enjoyed a local food known as *samosas,* small triangular fried-meat pockets spiced with *pili-pili* or pepper.

She wiped her chin and wished she hadn't eaten.

The man wrinkled his nose. "When we are free of the city, I'll let you sit up front where you can see. Have you been on safari and seen this great land?"

"Only Nairobi."

She looked at the man. He was thin and

wore a gray suit with a white shirt and a tie.

"You don't look like a kidnapper."

"I'm not." He offered a half smile. "I'm not a violent man."

"Then what am I doing here?"

"We want to give you an education."

"An education? I have a doctorate in pharmaceutical chemistry —"

"From Stanford University. Graduated with distinction," he interrupted.

"You've read my book?"

"Pusher?" He laughed. "Better than that."

"How do you know me?"

"I know all about you. I know about Camplex."

She took slow, deep breaths and tried to will her stomach to cooperate. Thinking about Camplex wouldn't help. Once upon a time, Camplex was intended to be Jackson Pharmaceuticals's next greatest non-steroidal anti-inflammatory drug. And it was. For a while. Until it became increasingly obvious that arthritis patients on Camplex were stroking out at a rate three times higher than expected.

Three times a very small percentage was still a small number, but the FDA didn't approve and yanked the drug from the market, putting a damper on the billion-dollar cash cow and blackening the eye of

JP in the public arena. Worse, when it came out that JP executives had managed to suppress the data for six months while sales of Camplex set records, JP looked even worse and paid a fifty-million-dollar fine, though that was chicken scratch in comparison to their income from the drug.

And it all happened under the watchful eye of Dr. Rebecca Jackson.

Now, it seemed that every time she turned on the TV, she heard another ad featuring a stroke patient in a wheelchair and a voiceover: "Have you or someone you love suffered a myocardial infarction or stroke while on the drug Camplex?"

The man no longer held a gun. Instead, he clutched only a white handkerchief for dabbing the sweat from his high forehead. "Did you know that your drug is still available here?"

"Really?"

Of course she knew. They'd unloaded several billion tablets onto sub-Saharan Africa just before the news of the complications hit the popular press in the US. She sighed. "What's the mean lifespan of a man in Kenya?"

"Fifty. Maybe fifty one."

"Exactly. The population here doesn't live long enough for the stroke problem to matter. What matters is that people who will eventually die of AIDS or malaria can get good pain relief from our drug in the meantime."

He nodded. It was a reasonable argument.

She repeated her question. "How do you know about me?"

He reached out his hand, an offering for a handshake.

She stared and kept a tight grip on the can.

After a moment, he closed his hand and rubbed his thumb over his empty fingers. "I am Dr. Jacob Opondo."

"You are a medical doctor?"

He nodded.

"So you know of Mopivadine."

"I am a doctor in Kenya. AIDS is our number-one killer. Of course I know of Mopivadine."

She smiled despite her circumstances. Mopivadine was an antiretroviral drug, the latest and greatest in an attempt to inhibit the reproduction of HIV. She was counting on Mopivadine to salvage the image of JP. "So you understand why we are so proud."

"Yes." He paused, shaking his head. "And yet you have reason for shame. That's why we're taking this little trip."

"So I'm not being kidnapped?"

19

"Depends on your definition," he responded coldly. "If you mean being taken against your will, then yes, you're being kidnapped. But I'm not asking for a ransom."

"What do you want?"

"I want compensation for the Kenyans who have suffered because of you. I want JP to change its course. Continue research but be culturally sensitive."

"Sounds like politically correct BS."

"Tell that to the children who die because of your trials."

"Hey, Mopivadine saves lives. It prevents maternal-child transfer of HIV."

"So you say."

The lack of circulating air and the bumpy ride combined to send her stomach into another fit of retching.

Becca pleaded, "I need to get some air."

Jacob opened a cell phone. In a moment, he spoke. "Pull over. I want to let the doctor ride in the front. I'm going to puke if she vomits again."

"Nice," she muttered. "Thinking of me like that."

A few moments later the van lurched to a stop and the back door opened. She stepped down from the vehicle and took a few slow, deep breaths. Just getting outside made her feel better.

As far as she could see were rolling plains of long grass. In the distance she caught her first glimpse of giraffe in the wild. She pointed.

Jacob Opondo smiled. "Never been on safari?"

She shook her head. "No. And this isn't my idea of fun."

"Try to enjoy it. What choice do you have?"

"I need to pee."

"You may." He pointed to a few bushes just off the road.

"Here?"

"You were expecting a rest stop, perhaps?" He touched a bulge under his jacket, undoubtedly a handgun. "Don't even think of running. You wouldn't last long out here. And the only ones interested in you would be the carnivores."

She looked around. Seeing nothing but waves of grass, she plodded off to a bush to squat. There, she considered the irony of her situation. Here she was, in some of the most beautiful unspoiled wilderness on earth, yet she wasn't free to enjoy it.

"The authorities will be looking for me," she said when she returned a few minutes later.

"But you won't be pressing any charges."

"That's crazy. You tackle me, throw me in the back of a van, and drive me off into the middle of nowhere, and you think I'm just going to forget about this?"

"Yes. After you see what I need to show you."

"What is it?"

"Patience. We will get there soon enough."

She looked at her watch.

Jacob gestured toward the driver, a muscular man with a shaved head. "This is Samuel Wanjiku."

Samuel nodded. "It will be dark soon. We need to prepare a camp."

Jacob said, "Daniel Saitoti is expecting us. We will stay in his *boma.*"

Becca felt her anxiety rising. "I can't stay out here. My things — I have a reservation, a hotel room in Nairobi."

Jacob didn't smile. "Be quiet."

Samuel looked at the sky and then scanned the landscape, a grassy plain dotted with acacia trees. "We'd better move."

At the equator, darkness pounced like a cat. There was no gradual darkening of the sky, no dusk to prepare her. The twelve-hour day ended, and the twelve-hour night began. The sun made a perpendicular dive into the horizon, and within minutes, the change was complete; light and clouds became darkness with the smudge of the Milky Way.

Even though the darkness had descended, Becca relished being out of the back of the van. She watched with interest as their headlights bounced ahead of their progress along a road that had become little more than a set of two parallel tire paths separated by a mound of grass. Several times she saw the shiny reflection of a pair of eyes just off the road in the grass. Were these the carnivores of which Jacob spoke?

A half hour into the night, they arrived at a small Maasai boma, three short manure-and-mud huts with thatched roofs. Daniel Ole Saitoti, Jacob explained, had a small hut for each of his three wives. Outside, a herd of goats and cows seemed to have freedom to move about. Surrounding the huts and the animals was a high fence made of thorny shrubs.

"It will keep out the leopards and hyenas," Jacob said. He held up his hand toward a man standing beside a small fire ring. "This is Daniel Ole Saitoti." He paused before explaining. "Ole means 'son of' in the Maasai language. Though I pronounce it *Oh Lee*, it is spelled O L E."

Daniel Ole was tall and wore a shuka, a typical tribal garment made of red-checked cloth. He held a staff in his hand, and when he smiled, he seemed to be missing several bottom teeth, creating two columns of white teeth with a gap in between.

"Hello," Becca said.

"Supa." Daniel held out his hand.

"He speaks only his tribal language."

Becca sighed. "So I can't ask him to rescue me."

Jacob cleared his throat. "Don't be a fool."

"My uncle will be sending a rescue team. We've got contingency plans for this sort of thing."

"Good. The media attention will bring millions to be moved by our plight." Jacob shrugged. "But it won't put JP in a good light."

She sighed. "Whatever."

"Two of Daniel's wives will sleep together tonight." He pointed to the second hut. "You can sleep in there."

He flipped on a flashlight and led the way. She ducked to enter the small hut. Inside, it smelled strongly of smoke. A small cooking fire on the floor provided the only light and warmth. Along opposite walls were two beds made of cow leather stretched across a wooden frame.

She began to cough. Her eyes watered. "I can't sleep in here. I have asthma. I don't have my inhalers, and the smoke —"

"Fine," Jacob said. "I'll sleep in here with Samuel. You can stay outside with the animals. I have a sleeping bag you can use."

They walked back outside, and two Maasai women approached with cups of steaming chai. Becca took one of the tin cups. "Thank you."

Before they ate, Daniel's youngest wife poured water from a plastic container over their hands so they could wash.

"Not so much," Jacob warned. "She carried that four kilometers from the well."

Becca longed for a warm shower and a change of clothes, but clean hands and a campfire would have to do.

They sat on the ground beside the small fire and ate a stew of cabbage in beef broth. Becca looked up at the stars, amazed. She'd never seen this many from her neighborhood back in Virginia.

Daniel talked, speaking in the Maasai language as Jacob interpreted. "This is our life, and we are proud of our connection with the land and our animals." Daniel pointed to a boy with a spear who stood a few feet away. "My son was circumcised at age thirteen, but I did not consider him a man until he killed a lion with a spear."

Jacob added his own commentary after

interpreting. "The Maasai are just about the last tribe to cling so tightly to the old ways." He smiled toward the boy with the spear. "He was circumcised without anesthesia, but I promise you that he could not cry out, for fear of shaming his family."

"Does he go to school?"

Jacob translated the question.

Daniel shook his head. "He learns all he needs to learn while keeping the cattle. How to hunt. How to provide. How to care for the animals."

"Sounds wonderful," Becca muttered. "What about the women?"

She could see by Daniel's big smile that he was proud of his wives and the stature they afforded him. "They are good to me," he said. "They were all circumcised to become women." He pointed to each of the three small mud huts. "They each built their own home."

Despite the vast open sky, the small boma smelled like a barn. "Do they need to keep the cows in here?"

Jacob nodded. "It is the only safe place in the wilderness."

He handed her a sleeping bag. The Maasai women laughed. Evidently only the young Maasai men slept out beneath the stars.

"And don't get stupid," Jacob said. "If you venture out alone, you will be someone's midnight snack. You won't last an hour."

"Convenient."

Jacob smiled — his way of saying, "Gotcha." He turned and walked away.

She unrolled her bag after Jacob and Samuel disappeared into their hut for the night.

There was a spear in the ground next to the hut. Could she get it and demand that Jacob take her back to Nairobi?

That thought seemed as crazy as her next one. *Should I take it with me and escape across the wilderness?*

Just then, she heard what sounded like a deep growl. A lion?

Maybe one night won't be so bad.

She swatted at a mosquito. *Great. My malaria prophylaxis is back in my bag in Nairobi.*

My team must be going crazy.

She found herself feeling as if she should pray — and therefore feeling like a hypocrite. Despite her family's regular appearance in church on Sundays during her growing-up years, religion hadn't played a big part in Becca's adult life.

Now, on the African plains beneath a billion stars, she felt insignificant. She'd heard the stories in church, but they all sounded

27

too nice to be true. *If God made all this, how could He care about me?*

She didn't undress. Instead, she slipped into the sleeping bag fully clothed and pulled the flap up over her face as a defense against the mosquitoes.

The ground was hard. She didn't have a pillow. She was hot but dared not expose herself to the risk of malaria by opening the bag. Cicadas serenaded her, pushing away sleep. Over and over, she reviewed her options: escape, or submit to whatever lesson Jacob seemed determined that she learn.

Will they really spare my life?

Beneath the expanse of the African night canopy, she took inventory. She lay listening to a chorus of cicadas and wondered if she would ever have a chance to live out her life. Her thoughts naturally turned to her biggest regret. *I had a chance at love once. But I let him down.* She brushed a tear from the corner of her eye and waited for the dark emotions that always followed a remembrance of *him.* Guilt. Shame. She closed her hand into a clenched fist. *All because I was unwilling to tell the truth.*

There, in silence and without confidence that she was being heard, she cried to God for rescue. *I'll do better. I'll attend church. I'll think more about the patients who need the medicines than I do my stock-market portfolio.*

Will I ever again have a chance at love?

She sighed, wishing for sleep. Escape really wasn't an option. She wouldn't survive a night in the wild. So she lay wide-eyed at every night noise and stared at the stars.

Long into the night, the respite of sleep finally dropped in like a welcome friend.

3

On Friday just before 5:00 p.m., the CEO of Bradshaw Pharmaceuticals came into Noah Linebrink's office without knocking. Noah looked up and tried to hide his disappointment. Whenever Gregory Thatcher opened his door, it meant work, the kind where Noah spent hours chasing after another of the big boss's grandiose ideas.

Noah stood and extended his hand. It was an unnecessary courtesy but something Noah's father had instilled in him. "Hey, Greg, what's up?"

Greg dropped an inch-thick stack of bound paper onto the desk between them. "A little weekend reading."

The author of the paper caught Noah's eye. *Rebecca Jackson, PhD.*

Greg touched the tip of his graying goatee and spoke before Noah sat down. "I'm sure you've read her memoir."

Noah nodded. He had. And it wasn't such

a pleasant trip down memory lane.

"Well?"

Noah cleared his throat and tried to swallow the sudden tightness. "I read it."

Greg Thatcher stood six feet, two inches tall and had the slim build of a runner. He dressed the part of the successful CEO; business casual on Fridays meant he left his vest at home. He adjusted the knot on his designer silk tie and smirked. "So I take it you're the quarterback boyfriend."

It didn't surprise Noah that Greg had figured it out. His past had been open and on the table after the background check they performed before they hired him. Noah sighed and stepped away from his desk. "At least she didn't name me."

"Makes quite a heart-wrenching story, don't you think? She's involved in an accident, and a young boy is injured. The boy receives a tainted blood transfusion and develops HIV. School board won't let him attend school. Eventually, the kid dies of AIDS and the girl goes off to college and grad school and becomes a pharmaceutical researcher with a passion to develop a safe artificial blood."

"Yeah, Greg, I read the story."

"Sounds like she stole *your story.*"

Noah nodded. "Doesn't matter. She didn't

31

admit to anything that didn't come out in court." He stared at his immaculate boss. "You've got a point to make?"

"I was fascinated enough to look at her doctoral work in blood substitutes and artificial hemoglobin," he said, tapping the stack of papers on the desk. "Sounds like her work may be a perfect complement to yours."

"It's not like I'm completely unfamiliar with her work," Noah said. "But Jackson Pharmaceuticals is our biggest competitor. And she's a Jackson."

"That's never stopped us before."

"Stopped us? What are you suggesting?"

"Read her research and see if you agree with me. If you do, I want you to hire her away from JP."

Noah coughed into his hand. "You're kidding me, right? You read her story. We're not exactly chummy anymore."

"That was a long time ago."

"Yeah, and I seem to remember being the one who went to jail."

Greg's blue eyes softened. "Look, Noah. I know there may be some issues between you, but if I understand what I'm reading, Rebecca Jackson may be one of only a few people with the expertise we need to succeed." He paused. "And I mean one of a few people *in the whole world.*"

Noah shook his head. "Anyone but her." He paused, eyeing the stack of papers pensively. "Besides, you can't offer the woman enough money to leave her family's company."

"I'm willing to offer a sign-on of seven figures and a percentage of future sales if we can bring a blood substitute to the market."

Noah sighed.

"I'm not asking you," Greg said, turning and pausing at the door. "Why don't you give it a look-see and call me Sunday, say around ten?"

"I'll be in church." *You know that.*

His boss offered a thin smile. "Oh yes, some people still go to church. Well, call me later. I'm having brunch at Middleton's."

Noah watched the CEO disappear from his doorway. He picked up the bound volume of Becca Jackson's work, shook his head, and whispered, "Why does it have to be you?"

Becca Jackson startled awake to face the wet muzzle of a Maasai cow. Screaming, she sat up and shooed the animal away.

She wiped her mouth with the back of her hand and spat.

33

Across the small campfire, Jacob and Samuel were sipping chai and laughing loudly at her.

She extracted herself from the sleeping bag, feeling sticky. Her clothes were hopelessly wrinkled, her hair fell limp around her face, and her bladder screamed for attention. She looked around.

Evidently, Jacob understood her need. "There," he said, pointing. "You may relieve yourself behind the house. Then come for tea."

She walked behind the mud structure and squatted. There was no way she could do anything but urinate. Anything else would have to wait.

She combed her fingers through her tangled weave of blonde hair and wished for lipstick. She touched her upper lip. She'd not been out in public with her scar uncovered since she was seventeen.

Walking back to the small circle around the fire, she joined Jacob, Samuel, and Daniel Ole. Daniel handed her a tin cup with warm sweet chai.

Jacob nodded. "Breakfast," he said. "Enjoy it."

She worried about parasites. She knew the milk wasn't pasteurized. Who knew if they'd heated it long enough? But she was hungry and took the cup without complaint.

"Who are you?" she asked Jacob. "Why would a doctor kidnap a pharmaceutical company vice president?" Before he could answer, she gave her own answer. "You want drugs for your people, don't you? A handout. You brought me out here to show me pitiful people dying of AIDS, I bet."

"No."

"It's the same in every developing country I've been in," she said, not caring if her words offended him. "Everyone thinks that the color of my skin is a license to demand money."

Jacob stayed quiet, so she continued her rant. "Do you have any idea how much money it costs just to bring a new drug to market? Take a wild guess."

Jacob shrugged.

"Over eight hundred million US. Most of that goes into drug testing to get the FDA's approval."

Jacob sipped his chai. "And a blockbuster drug can bring in a billion in revenue a year."

Becca straightened. He'd clearly done his research. "JP invested thirty million last year just in measures to assure it wouldn't be the victim of corporate espionage. Can you imagine? Just to keep others from seeing my business."

Her audience seemed nonplussed. Her Maasai host smiled silently at her words, understanding nothing but her passion.

Jacob gestured toward her cup. "Drink your tea. We need to go."

"I'm not going anywhere until I know what you want."

"You're not in a position to bargain."

"At least tell me where we are going."

"Loita Hills." Jacob paused, searching her face.

It sounded vaguely familiar. Perhaps she'd read about it in a memo. "Loita Hills."

Jacob looked exasperated. "Tell me you've heard of it."

She stayed quiet.

"It was the location of the phase III trials for Mopivadine," he said.

She offered a nervous laugh. "Then I'll get to see my grateful public."

Jacob mumbled something about her needing to get out of her ivory tower. She tried to ignore him.

She drained the last of her chai. The sugar would give her some energy, but her stomach still felt empty.

He pointed. "Get in the van."

"I can't ride in the back."

Samuel looked at Jacob and raised his

eyebrows in question.

Jacob waved his hand. "It's okay. She will know where she is soon enough. Let her see the wildlife."

He stepped over to a small scrubby tree and cut off a small branch with a knife he removed from a holster on his belt. He fashioned an eight-inch segment and frayed the end by making multiple cuts. He handed it to Becca. "It's a Maasai toothbrush," he said.

She ran her tongue over her teeth and walked to the side mirror on the van. There, she studied her image for a moment. Disgusted, she pulled back her lips to expose her teeth. She touched the edge of her upper lip and then lifted her limp hair. She let it fall onto her forehead again. "Ugh."

She began rubbing her teeth with the end of the stick. It worked. Remarkably well.

A few minutes later, they waved to Daniel, who had gathered with his three wives and at least six small children, before bouncing off across the plain, following a road of packed rock and dirt. It was only the trio: Samuel the driver, Jacob Opondo, and Becca. She gripped a handle attached to the roof next to the window to prevent being thrown into Jacob's lap. Soon she was seeing antelope, gazelle, zebra, baboons, wildebeest, giraffe, and the funny little wart-hogs whose tails looked like remote-control antennae as they ran.

After two hours, they pulled to a stop in what appeared to be a small African version of a strip mall — carts with fruits and vegetables, small shops splashed with bright orange paint advertising some sort of cell-phone network, and what appeared to be a bicycle repair shop set up under an acacia tree. She looked at the side of a wooden building bearing the familiar symbol for Coke. She read the words of the slogan. *"Burudika na Coke baridi."*

Jacob raised an eyebrow. "Do you understand?"

"No."

" 'Enjoy a cold Coke,' " he said. "You see? We are civilized here, even in the bush. We have Coca-Cola."

Becca watched the thin men milling around the dusty streets. A few women sat behind large baskets of wares. A long, low building with a tin roof was emblazoned with a sign: Uhuru Primary School.

A tire swing hung from the branches of a tree. Noticeably absent were any children.

She looked around. "Are the children in school?"

Jacob smiled. "You are very observant,"

he said. "But it is Saturday. School is out."

"But the children —"

"Gone."

Before she could question, he continued. "Dead. The results of your drug. Or taken by fearful parents into the mountains to escape the curse."

Noah Linebrink loved Saturday mornings. And routines.

So this Saturday started like the rest: a five-mile jog followed by a shower and a jaunt down to Mabel's Trailer for breakfast. Mabel's place had been a Richmond local hangout for over thirty years and had earned a reputation for the finest cholesterol-laden breakfast on the Southside of Richmond. But since a scare with chest pain six months before (turned out to be his esophagus spasming, but he was staring down his fortieth birthday and it couldn't hurt to be safe) he'd laid off most meat, taken to reading a blog dedicated to hummus and avocado lovers, and started jogging again. His one concession was his weekly visit to Mabel's, but even then, he ordered the oatmeal.

He sat at the counter, third from the end, just like every Saturday morning. Joe Rothfus sat on his right, eating pancakes and chuckling as he read the *Times Dispatch* comic page. Just like every Saturday.

Noah lifted his head in acknowledgment to the Saturday morning breakfast club in the corner booth. It included Medical College of Virginia's finest: the chief of cardiology, the chief of medical oncology, and two cutters — a trauma surgeon everyone called "Buck" and Matt Dennis, plastic surgeon to Virginia's elite. From the looks of the breakfast dishes in front of them, they'd missed the memo that heart disease and cancer are associated with high intake of animal protein.

Noah poked at a brown clump in his oatmeal and lifted it on his spoon up to his nose.

Mabel's wrinkled face cracked into a smile. "You gonna examine that or eat it?"

"What is it? I ordered what I always order. Oatmeal with apple and cinnamon."

She wiped her hands on a stained white apron gathered around her generous waist. "Live a little. Try it. It's good."

Noah obeyed. It *was* good. Very good, in fact. A sweet taste and a crunchy texture complemented the smooth steaming oats and was offset by the tangy green apple. When it dawned on him just what he was eating, he shook his head. "Seriously?"

Mabel refilled his coffee mug. "Everything is better with bacon," she said.

"But this is . . ." Noah struggled to define it.

"Caramelized," she said.

He tried to silence his conscience. *Not just bacon. Not just fried. But fried in sugar! But there are small chunks of apple in here too. That should count for something.* He resolved to run an extra mile the next morning.

Just then, the image of a familiar face on the flat-screen TV mounted behind the counter caught his eye. "Hey, Mabel, could you turn that up?"

Noah listened as the morning news anchor spoke. "The pharmaceutical doctor, and niece of Jackson Pharmaceuticals's CEO, has vanished from a Nairobi slum where she was filming an advertisement to promote her biography and the latest HIV drug manufactured by Jackson Pharmaceuticals. A kidnapping is suspected, but so far, no one has claimed responsibility. Speculation includes abduction by Somali pirates, something that has been happening with increasing frequency in recent months, even inside the borders of Kenya."

Becca Jackson's face appeared with the subtitle "Author of *Pusher: Confessions of an American Pharmaceutical Giant.*"

41

The news anchor continued. "Jackson made quite a stir earlier this year when her book, *Pusher,* hit the stands, revealing some of the cutthroat tactics that govern the development and marketing of the American pharmaceutical industry." He paused. The picture of a swirling weather pattern replaced Becca's face. "In other news, hurricane trackers postulate landfall of this season's first big storm . . ."

Mabel looked over the counter, her face appearing even older than usual. "You okay, Noah?"

He cleared his throat and tried to swallow away the cotton that had suddenly appeared there. He told himself it was the caramelized bacon. *The news about Becca is a strange coincidence, that's all.*

But he knew better.

He looked down at his oatmeal and avoided Mabel's question. "Looks like we might be getting some rain from that storm," he said.

Only when she walked away did he risk a glance in her direction. She was still staring.

He looked out the front windows toward the James River beyond the little parking lot. *Why should I care if Becca's in trouble?*

She made her choice a long time ago.

And I went to jail to cover for her.

■ ■ ■

Becca Jackson wiped the sweat from the back of her neck and lifted the hair from her collar. She stared wishfully at an immobile ceiling fan in the front room of the Uhuru Primary School and resumed listening to the sixth sad story of the afternoon.

A young Maasai woman bearing the name Namunyak, which meant "the lucky one," was anything but lucky. She'd contracted the AIDS virus from her husband, a man with six wives. She cried as she told of the joy she'd experienced when a Jackson Pharmaceuticals researcher promised her free medicine that would protect her then-unborn son from contracting the virus.

But then she discovered that in order to get the free medicine, she would not be allowed to breast-feed her child. Her husband enforced the rule and tightly bound her breasts with strips of cloth to dry up the flow, telling her that if his son developed HIV, he would blame her and take another wife.

But infant formula wasn't available. The child became irritable on the unpasteurized cow's milk, soon fell ill with typhoid fever, and passed away at only two months of age.

Jacob Opondo pointed at a data sheet shoved in front of Becca. "See? Here is the baby's listing."

Becca's voice revealed her incredulity. "A success?"

"According to Jackson Pharmaceuticals, yes. The baby died without HIV, so the positive outcome goal of AIDS virus prevention was met."

Becca shook her head as the Maasai woman in front of her wiped the tears from her face. "But the baby died."

Jacob Opondo offered a saccharine smile. "But without HIV, and so the case was recorded as a success and reported in your landmark study on HIV prevention."

A throbbing sensation gathered behind Becca's eyes. "I'm not feeling well," she said.

"You find the truth upsetting?"

"I didn't know about the problem with breast-feeding."

"There is no other option for these women. They can't afford formula. So the children don't get the nutrition they need and succumb to parasites, malaria, typhoid, or a dozen other infections lurking in the tropics."

"I get it," she said, rubbing her eyes.

"No, you don't. I've got dozens of women ready to tell you their stories. And each of them has dead children, children who didn't have HIV but died because their mothers were kept from breast-feeding them." He tapped a notebook. "And your researchers counted each one of them as a success. Score one for Mopivadine. Zero for the children of Loita Hills."

Becca wasn't sure she could keep this up. A vague nausea scratched at her gut, and she tried to remember the last thing she'd eaten. *Maybe it was the unpasteurized milk I had in the breakfast chai.*

A tall, slender woman named Sankau was next. She wept as she talked through the translator, explaining how her father had taken the rest of her children away after the death of her infant due to some unnamed diarrheal illness. He said there was a curse on the village, brought on by the drug company. The American company was trying to control the Africans by killing their children.

Becca shook her head. "Tell her it isn't true. Tell her we wanted to help. Tell her there isn't a curse." She felt her throat thicken. "I wanted to help her."

Jacob Opondo said nothing.

"Tell her," Becca pleaded.

"It will not make a difference. The Maasai women trust the elders in the tribe. What they say is what they believe."

Pain escalated in her right temple. "I need something for a headache," she said, trying hard to make eye contact with the Kenyan physician.

His plastic smile greeted her. "After you've heard the stories."

4

Noah spent most of the afternoon reading Dr. Rebecca Jackson's doctoral thesis on development of a blood substitute. She outlined the problem well, citing three or four significant hurdles in bringing a successful product into clinical usefulness.

Noah had spent his professional life working on one of them, an artificial red cell to house the oxygen delivery molecule, hemoglobin. Most of Becca's work focused on the micromanipulation of an artificial hemoglobin molecule, knowing just where to form and break molecular bonds in order to make the hemoglobin molecule fold in a way that allowed oxygen to be taken up by hemoglobin in the lungs and released again when it was circulated out to the body in need. As problems went, this one was a monster. Part of the molecule loved water; part repelled it. Thus, when a single bond holding two elements together was snipped, the molecule reacted by moving into a different shape. Becca reported that she'd seen the molecule clump, curl, tighten, straighten, and assume just about every position possible *except* the four-compartment complicated fold that would mimic real human hemoglobin. The problem was, there were thousands of possible bonds to dissolve, and she hadn't been able to predict which way the molecule would fold to create the necessary shape.

As Noah read, he realized that the problems he was encountering were small compared to the ones Becca and her team were facing. *Finding the right bond to destroy is like finding the proverbial needle in a haystack,* he thought, pushing the stack of papers away and switching on a news channel, hoping for an update on Becca's abduction.

He was rewarded a few minutes later when CNN carried an interview with James Jackson, founder and CEO of Jackson Pharmaceuticals. "We have not yet received any more information, and no ransom demand," the distinguished man in a black suit intoned. "I fear the worst, that her disappearance was a deliberate ploy by one of our competitors who wants to be the first to bring an artificial blood to the market."

A male interviewer's voice was heard as

48

the camera stayed focused on the CEO. "That's a pretty strong accusation. Do you have any proof?"

"Rebecca's recent memoir didn't win her any friends in the industry. In a world where a successful new pharmaceutical could mean billions in income, the development of a blood substitute would outstrip every previous record."

"Is Dr. Rebecca Jackson critical to the product's development?"

"She is the project. Without her, the project falls. With her, we are very" — he paused dramatically — "very close to success, a success that will have a worldwide impact. A huge impact."

A man-on-the-street interview followed. A fiftysomething man with a gray goatee shrugged. "I'll bet it's all a ploy by her publisher to sell books."

Noah's cell phone sounded. The theme from *Chariots of Fire*. He looked at the display. *Kristen.* His not-so-baby sister.

"Hey."

"You looking at the news?"

"Hi to you, too," he said. "Yeah, I'm watching. Hurricane Heidi may hit Virginia Beach by tomorrow morning."

"You know what I'm talking about."

"You worry too much."

"I just know what kind of dent that woman put in your life. All you need is to have everyone talking about her again."

He sighed. "It's the craziest coincidence, you know? Thatcher just asked me to review Becca's blood-substitute research. If I think it has the merit he believes, he asked me to hire her away from JP."

"No way. She'd never leave."

"She hates her uncle."

"You have a good memory."

"Sometimes too good."

"What are you going to do?"

"I don't know. My boss wants me to go talk to her, but I'm not sure I'm up to going back home."

"Maybe it's time."

"Why stir up all those bad feelings?"

"Because behind the pain, there's healing. Because they need to see you. Show 'em you've made good."

"Yeah, well, it may have to wait. Maybe Becca's disappeared for good."

"Sad to say" — Kristen sighed — "but that would be best for you."

He listened to silence on the phone for a moment, not sure how to respond.

Kristen cleared her throat. "Seen Mom lately?"

"A while ago."

"Noah, you need to see her."

"She doesn't remember five minutes after I visit."

"She's your mom."

He wanted to get her off the phone. He loved Kristen and her three girls. But two things he didn't like: she bugged him to see their mom, and she set him up on too many failed blind dates. *At least this time you didn't tell me you had someone for me to meet.* "I'll go," he said.

He heard the message in her sigh. *When?*

He held up his hands. "After church on Sunday, all right?"

He listened as she said something muffled to a child. It sounded like, "Where'd you get my lipstick? Not until you're fourteen, young lady."

He smiled. Kristen's oldest was just like her mom.

"I met a nice gal at the fitness center," she said.

Two for two on my what-I-love-about-you list! "Look, Kristen, I'll take care of myself, okay?"

"You've spent twenty years trying to get over Becca Jackson. Don't think I don't know you."

"Look, I've got to run," he said. "I've got a ton of work on my desk." He held the

51

phone away from his ear and added, "Love you, bye," as he pressed a button to disconnect the line. Then he set the phone on the table beside the brilliant work of Dr. Rebecca Jackson.

He felt a knot tighten in his stomach. *God, I hope she's all right.*

An ocean away and a two-day drive into the bush, Becca Jackson listened to Maasai mothers tell heart-wrenching stories of watching their babies die.

When the last one was ushered out, she pleaded with Dr. Opondo. "Please," she said. "My head."

He tossed her a small pill bottle.

She swallowed three ibuprofen tablets without water and pleaded with her captor, "Can you take me back to Nairobi now?"

"What have you decided about the children?"

"I'll have Jackson Pharmaceuticals suspend the Mopividine trial."

"For these mothers, it is too late. The community needs a new HIV clinic, a new well, and a supply of infant formula for those women who decide not to breast-feed. The fields need an irrigation system. The district hospital needs new operating theaters." He paused dramatically. "And these women, all HIV positive, need a lifetime supply of antiretrovirals and financial compensation for the loss of their children."

"You brought me out here to bribe me into making a contribution to the village?"

"Not a bribe. Just a goodwill gesture from a very wealthy American company. Five or six million from you wouldn't even affect your company. But it would change our village forever."

She shrugged. "My uncle controls the finances. He'll never agree."

"What is your life worth to him?"

"You said you weren't a violent man."

"Not normally. You need to convince him of the proper way forward."

"Or else?"

"We will see what he is willing to pay to protect you."

Becca rubbed a spot on her right temple, trying in vain to massage away the throbbing pain.

"Well?" Opondo asked.

She looked up. His image had started to blur. "There may be another way."

5

Noah Linebrink pushed the stack of papers to the side. He'd spent the last two hours reading and rereading some of Becca Jackson's ideas on chemical synthesis of artificial hemoglobin. The task was monumental, and she had outlined the obstacles well.

He sighed. *If anyone can pull this off, it's Becca. I could help her, but would she even want to work with me?*

Could I face working with her?

He stood and paused at the shelf behind the desk in his study. He took out a linen handkerchief and dusted the trophy sitting there. High school football state champions. He'd been the star quarterback, the talk of the town. Always the driven leader, Noah would compulsively go over the films of his performances. Even now, Noah could remember significant plays gone right.

And significant plays gone bad.

Yes, once he had been the talk of Dayton.

But that was before he'd been sidelined. Humiliated. *It was a choice. I can't blame anyone but myself for the choices I made.*

He shook his head. *I did it because I was in love.*

So why didn't she wait for me?

Instead, she let me take the blame.

Is that what I was to her? A tool? A bridge so she could pass over the troubled water and not get wet?

He adjusted the trophy and sighed. A small-town hero, now forgotten.

He walked to the kitchen, pausing to look at himself in the hallway mirror, pleased at the results of his new diet and exercise routine. *I can be a hero again,* he thought.

He patted his flat abs, grabbed his car keys, and headed for Food Lion — because despite his better overall health routine, he remained a stress eater, nibbling his anxiety away and starting a crazy cycle. Eat more and then run more to compensate.

He frowned as he exited his garage into a light rain. He should have known better than to wash his brand-new Lexus ES 350. He paused at the end of the driveway to adjust the Bose sound system before powering into the night. By the end of the block, Noah was singing loudly with Billy Currington on the radio. It was a song about

God's greatness, beer's goodness, and people's craziness.

Praising God and drinking beer were two things his late father had loved. And the memory made Noah smile. The hard-working janitor had been an angel with a tilted halo, a deacon in the Baptist church with a penchant for Newcastle brown ale. He'd sacrificed everything for Noah to attend a community college after Noah's football scholarship to the University of Virginia had evaporated.

Jail time wasn't exactly good for an athletic career.

When Noah pulled back up to his house fifteen minutes later, he spied his sullen niece on his front steps, slouching beneath an umbrella. He tapped his horn in a greeting, and she ran into the garage in front of his car.

He turned down the music and exited the consoling arms of his Lexus. "Hi, baby," he said, wrapping his arms around Amy Rivers, the oldest of his sister Kristen's three daughters.

"Hi, Unc."

He pushed her to arm's length. "You walked through the rain?"

"It's only half a mile."

"And Kristen —"

"Mom knows I'm here."

"Text her," he said, walking into the house in front of her. "Tell her you're with me and okay."

The thirteen-year-old going on eighteen sighed heavily.

He glared at her.

"Okay," she said. Her fingers danced across a series of buttons on her cell phone. "Done."

He dropped a plastic bag on the counter — the trophies of his jaunt to Food Lion.

He looked at Amy — really looked at her since coming out of the garage's dim light. She had put on her mother's makeup — a bit too much eyeshadow for his taste, but the overall effect of the lipstick, eyeliner, and shadow were striking. He shook his head. "Wow. You look . . . well, old!"

She pranced over to a bar stool, set her backpack on the counter, and plopped down to inspect the contents of the plastic bag. "Yeah, Mom freaked."

He looked at the backpack. "You moving in?"

"Of course not. But I know your rules. Saturday night with Noah means church on Sunday."

"Your mom must have sent you."

"It was my idea," she said, pulling a box

of vanilla ice cream out of the bag, eyes widening. "A hurricane is coming. I didn't want to be trapped in the house with Mom and Thing One and Thing Two."

"Your sisters adore you."

"They're annoying." She pulled a pound of bacon out of the bag. "What the —" She stopped and covered her mouth. "What happened to Mr. Broccoli Sprouts?"

He shrugged. "It's been a rough day."

"Mom said that the love of your life had been kidnapped."

"She said that? In those exact words?"

"Pretty much." She looked down and twisted a silver ring around her index finger. "Is that true? Do you have a secret love?"

"No and no." He started opening the bacon. "Come on, I want to try something. Grab a frying pan from under the stove and start that bacon."

"Noah, it's ten o'clock."

"Amy," he said, drawing out her name, "you heard the weatherman. A hurricane is coming. We'd better celebrate, for tomorrow may be the end of life as we know it."

"We don't live near the ocean."

"You can't be too careful. Now start frying."

"Can I spend the night?"

"Ask your mom."

"She already said it was okay."

"Depends. Can I pick the movie?"

"Just not *Dumb and Dumber*. We watched it last time I let you pick."

"We'll watch *The Shawshank Redemption*."

"A religious movie?"

"Not like you're thinking. You'll like it. I promise."

They fried the bacon crisp, and then crumbled it, added sugar, and returned it to the burner. Noah stirred furiously. After a minute, he smiled. "Now for the ice cream."

"You're kidding, right?"

She giggled as he stirred the caramelized bacon bits into the softened vanilla ice cream still in the box.

She took a small spoonful. "Wow. How'd you ever think of this?"

"I had a revelation over my oatmeal this morning." He pushed away her hand. "Hey, no double dipping." He scooped out two large helpings.

Then, with bowls of comfort food in hand, they plodded to the den for a late movie.

The next morning, Noah tiptoed past Amy, who was asleep on the couch, and headed straight to the coffeepot. Despite his overall commitment to a healthy lifestyle, he stubbornly rebelled at the thought of giving up his morning coffee. He liked it black. Kenyan AA, the best in the world. The way he figured it, coffee was full of antioxidants, and that was supposed to be good, right?

He ground the beans and looked at the evidence of last night's caramelized bacon indiscretion.

Ugh. I'm going to have to run more than just an extra mile today.

Amy pushed past him when the coffeepot was half full and poured the black juice into a mug emblazoned with a Bradshaw Pharmaceuticals logo. "Don't look at me like that," she said. "I drink coffee."

"You're stealing the strongest stuff. It wasn't finished dripping."

"I need the strongest stuff. I stayed up watching" — she held up her fingers to make quotation marks in the air — "the best movie of all time."

He rolled his eyes, mimicking her expression. He poured himself a mug, then used his remote to turn on a small TV mounted under a kitchen cabinet. He watched the Weather Channel update on Hurricane Heidi. Virginia Beach had taken a direct hit, and there was footage of people canoeing down city streets. The local outlook for Richmond was rain, rain, and more rain.

He switched to CNN and let the talking heads drone as he listened to Amy complain about her mother's tight restrictions on her life. "Danny Southerland wanted to take me to the movies, and Mom wouldn't let me go."

"Was it just you two?"

She gazed at him through the steam rising from her coffee. "Of course."

"Well, then, I'm siding with your mom on this one. Go out in groups for a while. Learn how to treat boys in groups before you start spending time alone."

She grunted and stared at her coffee. She stayed quiet for a few moments while Noah leaned against the kitchen sink and looked out at the downpour.

"Are you worried about that girl?"

Noah looked back at Amy. "How old are you?"

"Old enough. I know stuff. Mom told me you would be thinking about her. Worried and stuff."

He rubbed the stubble on his cheek with the back of his hand and sighed. "I knew her a long time ago."

"Mom told me she was your prom date. That's romantic."

"Like I said, it was a long time ago."

"Mom says you should stay away from her."

He raised his eyebrows.

She shrugged. "That's my mom's advice."

"Oh, and I guess your mom is the one who should be passing out relationship advice, huh?"

The hurt on Amy's face stabbed his gut.

"Look, Amy, I'm sorry. I didn't mean that."

She looked away. "Mom doesn't like us talking about her relationship with Dad."

"I know, honey. I'm sorry."

He pulled a Tupperware container off the shelf. "Here," he said, placing a bowl in front of her. "It's homemade granola."

She started dissecting the concoction. "What's this?"

"Pumpkin seeds."

"And this?"

"It's a hazelnut."

"And this?"

"Flaxseed. Would you just try it? It's good. And good for you."

She ate silently for a minute. "Noah?"

He made eye contact with her.

"Mom isn't right about everything."

Noah nodded, not really convinced.

When he heard the word *Kenya* on TV, he looked up at the screen.

A Kenyan man in a white coat stood in front of a bank of microphones. A tagline at the bottom of the screen read, "Dr. Jacob Opondo, Kenyatta National Hospital."

He laid a script on the podium. "Thank you for coming. We felt it was necessary to clarify a story that has gained international attention. For the sake of the privacy of our patient, we have delayed making an announcement, but we now have the patient's permission to make a brief statement."

"Noah?" The voice was Amy's.

Noah shook his head. "I want to hear this," he said, grabbing the remote to turn up the volume.

Dr. Opondo paused, looking soberly at the cameras. "Two days ago, I admitted an unknown white female. She was confused and initially unable to give her name. She was brought to us by a good Samaritan who found her wandering in a dangerous section of Kibera slums. As it turned out, she was suffering from complex migraines, which we have successfully treated with complete restoration of her memory. The patient is no other than Dr. Rebecca Jackson, the pharmaceutical chemist who was reportedly abducted."

Amy squealed.

Noah gasped and shushed Amy with a

touch of his hand. *She's okay?*

The doctor on TV continued. "This misinformation has cast Kenya in a poor light as a favored safari destination, but of course, that is not our main concern. Our concern is for the welfare of Ms. Jackson. When she became aware of the confusion and attention surrounding her disappearance, she asked us to make a statement. Dr. Jackson was released into the custody of the other members of the Jackson Pharmaceuticals team just a few hours ago."

A couple of reporters shouted questions, but Dr. Opondo waved them off and exited without further announcement.

The scene in Kenya disappeared, and the screen transitioned to the image of flooded streets in Virginia Beach. "In other news, Hurricane Heidi has left three hundred thousand Virginia residents without power . . ."

Noah's hand trembled as he used the remote to switch off the screen. He closed his fist to hide the tremor, but it was too late. He looked up to see Amy staring at his hand, and then her gaze moved up to his face. He quickly brushed away a tear and diverted his attention to his granola.

But his heart couldn't be diverted. Relief flooded him. He uncurled his blanching fingers from around the remote. *Why this reaction?* he thought. *I'm over her.*

Oh God, he thought, his heart swelling. *Becca's alive!*

6

Becca Jackson was thankful for the reclining seat in business class, but the comfort did little to calm her anxiety. She signaled for the flight attendant, ordered another glass of white wine, and moved down the aisle to the bathroom. Her third trip in as many hours.

She stared at herself in the mirror and couldn't keep back the tears. *What is happening to me?*

She took a deep breath and blotted her eyes. She leaned toward the mirror and concentrated on the little she could control: covering the tiny flaw on the edge of her top lip. This time her lipstick choice was Guerlain Rouge G. It was expensive but worth every penny. After a few minutes, she slipped the small tube into the front pocket of her designer jeans and slid the door release to the side.

Back in her seat, she nursed the wine and

tried to find something of interest in the airline magazine. Next to her, a teenage boy struggled with a Rubik's Cube. He seemed frustrated, having failed at getting each side to twist into a single solid color. *Really? They still make those things?*

It was then that Becca noticed a vague sensation just inside her left temple. It wasn't entirely unpleasant, almost a buzzing sensation, but not the kind that came from drinking too much chardonnay. She looked toward the window, noticing that when she turned her head to the left, she could hear a distinct swishing sound in her left ear. *My heart.*

She closed her eyes. She could see the Rubik's Cube in her mind, solid color on one side except for two corner squares that were out of place.

That's strange. I can see how to solve it. I can think ahead five or six moves and see how the colored squares will change.

Inside her mind, she turned the small cube. Bottom twist two times to the left. Right side down one. Bottom twist back to the right. Left side up. Top to the right. Then left side down.

She looked at the boy in the next seat. "Mind if I try?"

He shook his head. "Go ahead. I'm stuck."

She turned it around in her hands, inspecting each side. "The goal is to have only one color per side?"

The boy laughed. "I thought you meant you knew how to solve it," he said, holding out his hand. "My friend back home can show me."

Instead of putting the cube back into his outstretched hand, she used a series of moves to twist the sides of the cube up, down, clockwise, and counterclockwise until the puzzle was solved. Thirty seconds, max.

The boy's jaw dropped, and he uttered a curse word. When his eyes met Becca's, he winced. "Sorry. But wow, I've never seen anyone solve it so fast."

He took it back from her and turned to shield her from seeing. In a few moments, he handed it back, completely messed up. "Now solve it."

Becca noted that the strange sensation in the left side of her head seemed stronger. *That's weird. Not really pain, but my head feels full.*

Maybe it's just the altitude.

She twisted the little cube, the colors vivid in her mind. She could see the consequences of a series of choices four, five, or even six moves out. In thirty seconds, the top layer was complete. Another minute, and two other sides were done. At one minute forty-five seconds, she handed the cube back to the boy.

He smiled. "You had me fooled. You sounded like you'd never seen one of these before."

She smiled back and tapped the edge of her wineglass against the cube in a toast. *Oh, I've seen one before. On the shelf in a store. I've just never tried to solve one.*

After church, Noah took Amy to Middleton's, a quaint Americana restaurant with a killer Sunday brunch.

As they were being led to their table, he stopped at the corner booth, where Greg Thatcher, his boss at Bradshaw Pharmaceuticals, was reading the *Richmond Times-Dispatch*. Noah introduced his niece.

Greg smiled pleasantly but otherwise didn't acknowledge Amy. Instead, he looked at Noah. "Did you look at Dr. Jackson's research?"

Noah nodded. "It's brilliant."

The CEO laid down the paper. "Noah, if we could combine your work with PRINT and her work on the synthetic hemoglobin, we'd be looking at a breakthrough unparalleled in modern medicine. You'd be looking at a Nobel Prize. I'm not kidding. A Jackson and Linebrink team would be a match made in heaven." He paused, reaching for his glass. "Just think, an artificial hemoglobin at last."

"Yeah, well, you seem to forget that I've got a history with Dr. Jackson. I wouldn't exactly call us a match made —"

"You need to get over that," Greg said, interrupting. "Now that we know Dr. Jackson is safe and sound again, it's game on." He paused, sipping from a glass of champagne. "I want you to give her a few days to get settled back in the US and then make contact."

But there is so much unsaid between us. Noah stood still, willing his heart not to race away.

Greg's voice brought him back to attention. "Noah? I think your date is waiting."

Noah blushed and cleared his throat. "Oh, uh, sure."

As he turned to follow the hostess to their table, his boss repeated his order again. "Give her a few days to get her head straight, then I want you to make your best pitch."

Noah just walked away.

He sat opposite Amy, who had obviously absorbed the entire conversation. "Why does Mr. Thatcher think you two are a match made in heaven? Does he know you took her to the prom?"

"Of course not. And I didn't exactly take her to the prom. I *asked* her to the prom."

"What, she said no?"

"It's a long story." He hesitated. "Mr. Thatcher wasn't talking about *us* as a couple. He was talking about the ways her research complements mine."

"That's not what I heard," she said, eyeing the buffet breakfast.

"Well, that's what he meant."

"Oh, I think I got what he meant," she said. "But what did he mean about your printing? I thought you made drugs or something."

"PRINT," he said, "not printing. P-R-I-N-T stands for Particle Replication in Non-wetting Templates."

She yawned. "Sounds wonderful."

"It is. I make soft microscopic particles that look just like little red blood cells. Dr. Jackson is working on making artificial hemoglobin molecules. If we put them together —"

"You get fake blood. I get it. Now can we go get brunch?"

"I don't think you do get it, Amy. This could change everything. No one would have to get real blood and all the risks associated with it anymore."

He shook his head. *Why am I explaining this to a thirteen-year-old?*

Amy offered a sly smile. "So then you won't have to feel guilty."

"What are you talking about?"

"Mom says you feel responsible for giving that little boy AIDS." She folded her arms across her chest. "But you didn't donate the blood that infected him."

"Your mom says too much."

"I ask a lot of questions."

"So I've noticed."

"Can we eat now?"

Noah sighed. "Sure," he said. "Let's eat."

He followed her to a brunch bar laden with foods he'd sworn off. But not today.

Besides, maybe if she had her mouth full of food, Amy wouldn't ask so many painful questions.

An hour later, Noah drove west on Midlothian Turnpike, playing country music as Amy blocked it out with her iPod. "Where are we going?" she asked.

"To see your grandmother."

"I saw her last week."

"Well, I didn't, and I promised your mom I would go."

"Can't you take me home first?"

"It's on the other side of town. Besides, if we're both there, it will be easier to talk."

"She doesn't remember what she ate for breakfast anymore."

"Yeah, but she remembers the old stuff. Ask her about the remote past and she'll talk."

They pulled into James River Presbyterian Home and parked beneath a huge magnolia tree. Inside, they found Elizabeth Linebrink sitting alone in her room.

"Hi, Mom," Noah said, greeting his mother with a kiss on her wrinkled cheek. "Look who I brought to see you."

Elizabeth brightened.

"Hi, Grandma." Amy went over and pulled up the shade on the room's single window. "Let's let a little light in this place."

Elizabeth folded her hands in her lap. "How's your work?"

Noah sighed. He wasn't sure she knew just what he did. "It's fine, Mom."

Amy leaned forward. "Guess what, Grandma. Noah's old girlfriend was in Africa. She's famous, you know. She wrote a bestselling book about the drug industry called *Pusher*. My mom said I could read it."

Noah frowned.

It didn't stop Amy from plunging ahead.

73

"Do you remember Noah's prom date?"

"Of course, dear, it was Becca Jackson. But he didn't actually take her, child."

"Why not?"

Noah cleared his throat. "Why don't we talk about something else?"

"Because he was in jail, dear."

Amy looked away from Noah's gaze. "Oh."

Elizabeth smoothed the edges of a small quilt on her lap, looked at her son, and shook her head. "You've been on a quest to prove you're good enough for her all these years. Is that why you work so hard?"

Noah coughed. His oft-forgetful mother had turned psychologist, and her arrows of analysis were dangerously on target. "I'm not trying to prove myself to anyone."

"Know what I think?" Elizabeth said.

Noah sighed. "Afraid I couldn't stop you from telling me even if I tried."

"You're enough. Just by yourself. God loves you, so you're enough."

He was pierced. *How does she do this?* He wiped a tear from the corner of his eye and hopped up to look out the window. After a moment, he cast a stern glance at Amy. "You just had to bring her up, didn't you?"

Amy shrugged. "You were the one who told me to talk about old times. I was just following orders."

■ ■ ■ ■

Evans Kilongo, personal assistant to Kenya's Health Minister, pushed back a stack of papers and looked across his desk at Jacob Opondo. "I hope you know what you're doing." He sighed and pointed a meaty finger at the doctor. "You think this American woman can be trusted?"

"I think so. I watched her cry as she heard the Maasai stories."

"She may have said those things only so you would release her. We will see how real her tears were when she gets back to her cushy American life." He began to pace his small office. "What if she contradicts our story? We will look like fools." He turned back to face the doctor. "You shouldn't have let her go."

"And what was I to do? It's not like I could keep her forever."

"Only until we got our compensation."

"She'll come through. I think we really got to her."

"You're sure?" Evans's words were edged with sarcasm.

The doctor nodded. "Sure enough."

Evans huffed. "I think you are naive. Wealthy executives like Dr. Jackson have learned the value of saying what people want to hear."

Jacob stood to face the larger man. "Like Kenyan politicians?"

"You should have let me clear the plan with the Health Minister."

"It wasn't his call."

"For your sake, you'd better be right."

The door opened following a soft knock. Evans's secretary's dress was too tight and low cut for business attire. She held a silver tray with a tea set. "Chai, Mr. Kilongo?"

He nodded. "Set it on the desk."

When the doctor reached for a cup, Evans said, "Dr. Opondo was just leaving, Mary, so why don't you join me?"

Jacob met the man's icy stare and then exited the office without another word.

During hour four of Becca's flight to Heathrow Airport in London, the slight buzzing in her left temple changed. Throbbing pain pushed aside the dull feeling of fullness. Again, she slipped from her seat to the aircraft restroom, where she took out a small preloaded syringe of Imitrex, a powerful medication intended to relieve migraine headaches. She pulled up her blouse and prepped the skin of her abdomen with an alcohol swab, jabbed the needle in, and injected the full six-milligram dose.

She checked her reflection and contemplated refreshing her lipstick, but the light in the restroom was too uncomfortably bright. Besides, she could freshen up just before landing. She still had a few hours.

Back in her seat, she glanced over to see her neighbor struggling with the puzzle cube again.

He shook his head. "Help me out here. I'm stuck with the corners reversed again."

She held out her hand. She turned the puzzle around in her hand, waiting for an understanding of how to exchange the corner blocks. She twisted the layers, rolling the levels both right and left. After a few minutes, she'd only messed it up. She looked up. "I'm sorry. I have a headache. I can't seem to figure it out." She handed it back.

That's strange. I wonder how I ever did it before. That thing's impossible.

Maybe it's just the headache.

But something told her it was more.

7

After clearing customs at Dulles International Airport, Becca walked through the double doors leading to freedom only to be greeted by a half-dozen paparazzi and reporters shouting questions as she walked.

"Is it true that you're close to completing a project on an artificial blood?"

"What role did Putnam Books play in making it appear that you had been abducted?"

"Is Noah Linebrink the mystery boyfriend mentioned in *Pusher*?"

She halted, looked at the cameras, and smiled, thankful that she'd freshened her lipstick in an airport restroom on the other side of customs only moments before greeting her public. "Africa has a way of changing you," she said slowly. "And making your questions seem a bit unimportant." She paused while someone shouted another question about the sales of *Pusher*. "I'm not answering any questions that may compromise the privacy of old friends." She held up a hand toward the small group of reporters. "And thanks for your concern about my health."

She walked away, ignoring the questions. She spied her parents standing next to a book rack in front of a small airport kiosk. Barry Jackson enveloped her with a hug as the paparazzi snapped away. "Please," he said, smiling toward the photographers, "respect my daughter's health."

She pulled away to hug her mother and whispered in her ear, "Hi, Mom. When did Daddy dye his hair?"

Her mother, Rachel, giggled quietly. "Oh, you wouldn't believe what people do in a campaign."

Becca squeezed her mother tightly and turned away from the photographers as her father grabbed her suitcase with one hand and guided her toward the exit with the other.

Barry Jackson was police chief in Dayton, Virginia; a small-town cop turned politician wannabe, he was now running for his district's seat in Congress. At the curb, a Crown Victoria police cruiser waited. Barry lifted his daughter's suitcase into the trunk as his wife got into the backseat. Becca slipped into the front passenger seat and immediately lowered the sun visor to use the mirror.

She pursed her lips toward the image of her face. *Lipstick. Check.*

As they drove away, Becca sighed. "Are you sure you want to trade small-town life for all this traffic?"

Barry said, "We're going to keep our home place, honey. I'll get an apartment close to the capitol so I can walk and avoid this traffic. I'll be home every weekend so I can stay close to my constituents."

"Whatever," she said. "When I get to your stage in life, I'm going to want to slow down."

"I've been a cop all my life, baby. It's time for a change. But it may never happen. I was a shoo-in when everyone thought my daughter had been abducted."

"Oh, so I ruined the sympathy vote? That's real nice, Daddy."

Rachel touched her shoulder. "He didn't mean it like that, dear. Of course, we're glad you're safe. I want you to see our doctor to be sure you're all right. I'm sure Dr. Albright can fit you in."

Becca lifted her hand to massage her left temple. "I'm fine, Mom. Really. The doctors in Nairobi were very thorough."

"Yeah," her father said with a chuckle. "What'd they use for a CAT scan in Africa, a lion?"

"Very funny. Dr. Opondo wore a tie, Daddy, not an animal skin."

Her head felt full, as if she needed her ears to pop. She looked out the window at the passing collage of city life: shopping malls, concrete, and a snarl of cars fighting for position.

Africa seemed a world away, a fleeting reality that floated in a haze of jet lag. She closed her eyes and tried to recapture images of giraffes eating from the tops of acacia trees, the grassy savanna dotted with grazing wildebeest, and the color of the Kenyan sky at sunset.

But all she could see were the colorfully beaded Maasai women mourning the loss of their children.

Two days later, Becca Jackson exited the comfort of her blue BMW sedan and touched the edge of her hair as she stepped across the parking lot outside the opulent headquarters of Jackson Pharmaceuticals. She'd already passed two security checks and would encounter three more: a metal detector in the front lobby, fingerprint-protected access to the research facility, and finally a retinal scanner allowing access to management.

In the corporate world of high stakes and high reward, Jackson Pharmaceuticals sat prominently in an elite position. For most of her life, Becca had taken it for granted. But today, she found herself unimpressed and pushed down a sense of guilt as she passed the massive sign with the JP logo in the large circle drive leading to the front entrance. Inside the circle of marble street-paving blocks stood a twenty-foot-high cascading fountain that served as the base of the company logo. It was even more spectacular at night, when the logo and the fountain were brightly lit with floodlights. The large *J* and *P* letters were outlined with an invisible electric strip that allowed a glowing blue light to dance around the perimeter, tracing the initials into the night sky.

In the lobby, Becca passed through the security check, placing her phone and bag in a plastic tray to be X-rayed. A jovial African-American male with a wide smile nodded. "Welcome home, Dr. Jackson. You had us all a little worried."

"Well, I'm back, so look out," she said, bantering as she often did with security.

Behind the scanner, the lobby led into a

massive six-story atrium. A sixty-foot rotating metal mobile sculpture hung in the center of the atrium, and hallways from each floor bordered the opening to allow the workers a view of the modern art. The sculpture always reminded Becca of an elementary-school solar-system model with large orange, purple, and red spheres languidly circling over everyone who entered.

Stepping behind a welcome desk, she pressed her right thumb against a small pad beside a large door. A green light indicated that she'd been allowed access. Twenty feet into the hallway, she activated an elevator with a swipe of her badge and pushed the button for the top floor. A small panel opened at eye level. She pressed her forehead against the detector and stared into a dim red light. A digital readout indicated her identity and allowed the elevator to proceed to the top floor.

Exiting the elevator, she sighed. Two life-size brass tigers stood guard before the executive hallway, art trophies from a trip her uncle had taken to one of their pharmaceutical plants in China. The ceiling was twelve feet high. But instead of being impressed, Becca felt shame at the decadence.

What's happening to me? I never cared how

rich this all looked before.

She smiled at her uncle's receptionist and walked straight to his door, knocking as she pushed it open. *He might be king of his domain to everyone else, but to me, he's still Uncle Jim.*

He looked up from behind his mahogany desk. "Ah, Rebecca. I was wondering when you'd find your way back to work."

"Good morning to you, too, Uncle Jimmy."

"You gave us quite the scare over there, you know. I could almost see our progress flying out the window."

She tried to hide her reaction. *Glad to know you were worried about me and not just your precious research.*

She sat opposite the imposing desk. Her chair sat lower than her uncle's, intentionally designed for intimidation. She called it the "little girl chair," because she felt like she was sitting at the children's table at Thanksgiving.

She cleared her throat.

"Something on your mind, Becca?"

"I'd like to tell you a few stories," she said.

"Stories? Really, Becca, I've got so much work to finish here," he said, gesturing toward the stack of paper in front of him. "I'm sure you can tell me the next time our families get together." He lowered his gaze to his desk again.

"Do you know what the name *Namunyak* means?"

He looked up. She didn't wait for him to protest.

"It means 'lucky' in the Maasai language. I met a woman by that name. She was one of six wives and contracted HIV from her husband. Her joy over learning that she could prevent her child from contracting HIV by taking our drug was short-lived. When her husband heard that she was not allowed to breast-feed while on the trial, he bound up her breasts with strips of cloth and warned her that if his baby developed HIV he would take another wife."

"You realize it's their lifestyle that led to contracting the virus in the first place —"

"She complied with our study requirements, but her son developed typhoid fever after drinking unpasteurized cow milk and died."

"Are you finished?"

"No! That baby was listed as a success in our trial because he didn't contract HIV." She stood and started to pace with nervous fervor. "I met a beautiful, slender woman named Sankau. Her father took her other children away after her infant died while taking Mopividine. He claimed that the whole village was cursed because of our drug and he didn't think it was safe to leave the children in her hands."

James sighed. "Backward thinking of a backward tribe," he said.

"Didn't you hear me? They didn't think Mopividine was a blessing, but rather a curse!"

"Again. Are you finished?"

"I have many more."

He leaned back in his chair. "Rebecca, Rebecca," he said in a lofty tone. "There are negative consequences to research. We knew that going in. But we proved what we set out to prove. Our drug is effective at preventing maternal-child transfer of HIV."

"Yes, but —"

"And after our little public relations snafu with Camplex, Mopividine is going to help restore JP's reputation."

"Perhaps compensating the village people for their loss, financing their drugs and a new clinic, and providing a new well would help."

"Is that what these sob stories are supposed to do? Motivate me to make a donation?"

"I'd like JP to set up a foundation to compensate the village." She tried a different approach. "Think of it as an investment in bolstering JP's public image."

"How much?"

She tried to sound casual. "Five or six million."

He chuckled. "Have you seen the footage from your video shoot? The director was so excited that he called me himself. The ad campaign will erase any problems JP has with public image." He paused. "An ad campaign that is costing JP fifteen million in prime-time ad space." He picked up his cup of coffee. "Bottom line: we won't need to spend any more after the public sees your ads."

"But the people of Loita Hills —"

"Will carry on just like they have for centuries, living in their mud huts and taking care of their goats. Money would just spoil them."

"JP could build a clinic."

"Why don't you put your anxieties to work solving our hemoglobin problem? Now there's something that can have a worldwide impact."

"A worldwide impact begins with one life."

He smiled. "A nice slogan. Maybe I'll suggest using it in our next ad campaign." He punched a button on his intercom. "Arlene?

Could you see if Drs. Davis and Bird can meet me for lunch at the club?"

Becca stood. Evidently her audience with the almighty had ended.

8

Noah peered out from around the long rows of bookshelves, careful to stay out of sight of the woman signing books at the front of the Barnes and Noble store. He'd traveled west from Richmond that morning to the Shenandoah Valley. Jackson Pharmaceuticals had its headquarters and one of its largest research facilities tucked in between the Blue Ridge and Allegany ranges in unpopulated countryside, away from urban areas where residents might complain of chemical odors.

He'd arrived unannounced so as not to give Becca a chance to reject the idea of meeting him. Her secretary had been pleasant and punctuated the end of most of her sentences with a forced little laugh. She'd said Dr. Jackson was in town for a book signing. He entered "bookstore" on his GPS and followed the voice into Harrisonburg.

Now, as Noah sneaked another look at the

back of Becca Jackson, who was seated with perfect posture, greeting her adoring public, he was transported back to high school.

They'd been juniors, an unlikely pair: he the star quarterback flirting with an offer from the University of Virginia Cavaliers to play football, and she the quiet nerd with hair that threatened a frizz rebellion at the first hint of summer moisture. Socially, too, they were mismatched. Her uncle ran a multimillion-dollar pharmaceutical company; Noah's father was the school janitor.

But because he was so focused on football, he needed help with physics and math — and poor grades could cause him to miss out on a scholarship. He watched as she worked in study hall. Observing her lack of makeup and the glasses that nearly hid her dark eyes, Noah saw an independent girl unlike his other female classmates, who were so enamored of his status and appearance. It took him ten minutes to work up the nerve to ask her for help. And when he stood in front of her, she didn't even look up from her calculus homework.

Noah cleared his throat. "I was wondering if you could help me with a physics problem."

She held out her hand, still concentrating on her own assignment. He placed the book

90

in her hand and pointed to the second problem. "This one," he said.

She read it silently and tore a sheet of paper from her notebook. "It's about force vectors," she said. "Draw them so you can visualize the resultant force when they're added together." She demonstrated, then circled the final arrow. "See? Easy if you draw it."

He looked at the notepaper. At the bottom, she had written a phone number.

His finger pointed to the number. "This is your —"

"The problems get harder in the next section. You're going to need to use that."

Noah smiled at the memory. Now, it was amazing how much he felt like that high school student, admiring the girl from a distance.

Now or never. Noah picked up a copy of *Pusher* off the shelf and walked over to join the line.

It wasn't exactly the appropriate time to have a significant breakthrough on her research, but the buzzing fullness in Becca's head had come back and brought with it a flash of inspiration. She asked the clerk for a piece of paper, which she quickly folded, mimicking the quaternary structure of hemoglobin. She then smoothed it out and began to write, pausing to sign books as people handed them to her. Inscribe a book, scribble another note, sign another book, and then concentrate on her problem again. Carefully, she sketched out the molecular form she needed to create. *I can see how it will fold! If this bond is severed, because this area fears water the outer rim will fold toward the center, just like a real hemoglobin molecule.*

She held out her hand, barely looking up to see a girl probably still in high school.

"Could you put my name in the front? I want to be a researcher someday, just like you."

Believe me, young sister, you don't want to be "just like" me. Becca forced a smile. "Your name?"

"Connie."

Becca wrote the inscription. "For Connie. Never stop believing in the power of you." She signed her name. The only legible part of her signature was the big "Dr." in front of Jackson. Becca almost winced as she wrote. *That was just the lame feel-good psychology crap we feed our children. Is this what Maasai women tell their daughters too?*

She looked back at the sheet of paper and scratched a line through a bond holding a carbon atom adjacent to an oxygen atom. While she worked, she massaged a dull pain coming from deep below her left temple. *Someone is waiting.*

She held up her hand but kept staring at her sketch. "Name?"

The voice carried an unforgettable familiarity. "Could you just make it out to Noey?"

A voice she'd never forget. A voice with the gentle awkwardness that she'd noticed the first time he'd asked for her help. *Noey? I'm the only one who called him that.*

It felt as if she were paging through an emotional playbook in mere seconds, each page a different feeling, flipping through her mind in fast-forward. She began with guilt and passed through anger, love, delight, hatred, sorrow, joy — and ended on self-loathing. The buzzing in her brain intensified and sped the processing of each one. His voice had been so gentle, yet the memories slammed her as a powerful punch in the gut. She moved the pen toward the book, not looking up and hoping he wouldn't notice the tremor. She attempted to hide her recognition, but her voice betrayed her. "No —" The name caught in her throat. "Noey." She wrote it without asking for the spelling.

"Nice to know you remembered," he said.

"We should talk."

She met his gaze and looked away. "Not here. Not now."

"I'm staying in town a few days. Business," he said.

She looked beyond him at the line of people. She didn't want to — *couldn't* — talk to him right now. She couldn't make herself look at the hurt in his eyes again. Instead of signing "Dr. Jackson," she simply signed "Becca."

She waited for him to move away and then chanced a glance in his direction, watched him place his finger against the phone number she had written at the bottom of the page.

By the time the book signing was over, a throbbing headache had elbowed the vague feeling of fullness aside, and Becca excused herself to the bookstore's employee restroom. There, in the privacy of the stall, she injected Imitrex into her thigh and waited for the migraine to lessen. After ten minutes, she was sure the store manager would be worried, so she washed her face, reapplied her lipstick, and exited the bathroom, feeling a bit better.

She thanked the employees, gave them all

copies of *Pusher,* and walked to her blue BMW.

She'd wanted the convertible, but summer moisture in Virginia did not agree with Becca's hair, so she'd settled for the sedan so she could control the temperature with the AC. Instead of returning home, she headed back to her lab. She paused to chat with the security guys, passed through the metal detector, swiped her ID card to allow access to the restricted area, and finally placed her eye against the retinal scanner to unlock the inner sanctum of her artificial blood lab.

She unfolded on a lab table the sheet of paper she'd been using at the bookstore and stared at it.

I know I understood this an hour ago. But how did I predict that severing chemical bond thirty-one would cause the molecule to fold in the right way?

Try as she might, she couldn't seem to recapture the revelation.

Nonetheless, she changed the protocol and wrote a note to one of her research assistants to change the lysis reagents to act at step seventeen instead of fifteen. She wasn't sure how she knew it would work; it had just been so plain to her back at the store.

Her office could be entered only through

the lab — a security measure she'd demanded. She walked to her desk, pausing to look at the ornate Maasai beaded necklace that now hung on the wall directly behind her chair. She smiled and placed the sheet of paper from the bookstore in a locked file.

She thumbed through the items in her in-box and then accessed a wall safe hidden behind a framed copy of her diploma for her PhD in pharmaceutical chemistry from Stanford University. From the bottom of the safe, she pulled out a brown manila envelope, dropped it into her leather satchel, and headed back out through security.

For Noah, the trip back to the Shenandoah Valley hadn't been just about obeying his boss and trying to recruit Dr. Rebecca Jackson. It was about going home, something he'd been avoiding for a long, long time. Going home meant facing his past, and he wasn't confident he was up to it.

He waited until he thought most of the regulars would be gone, then sauntered in and sat at the counter at Melissa's BBQ on Main Street in Dayton. Melissa had been a classmate of Noah's in high school. She was the yearbook photographer, and the framed photographs on the wall of her restaurant reflected her ongoing love affair with the camera lens. The black and whites were mostly poignant images of small-town life: a young boy in a barber chair; a girl standing next to a cow, holding a 4-H blue ribbon; an Old Order Mennonite man driving a tractor through town; a ten-point buck standing in a plowed field on a misty morning.

Melissa wore her years well. There wasn't a speck of gray in her auburn hair. It was pulled back and braided. She filled a water glass and set it in front of Noah, paused to stare — and gasped. "It couldn't be."

He looked up, offering a half smile. "Hi, Mel," he said. "Been too long."

She looked around at the patrons, perhaps to see if trouble would be brewing because of his presence. She kept her voice low, just above a whisper. "Noah. What brings you back?"

"Business."

"Oh my, you've hardly aged. You look great."

He felt heat in his cheeks. "You too." He paused. "So catch me up. How's life? Ever leave Dayton? Married? Kids?"

She wiped the counter with a damp rag. "Slow down." She placed her hands on her trim hips. "Life sucks. Never left. Married once, Dale Evers, remember him?"

97

"You married *Dale*?"

"Shut up. He loved me. Well, until he loved another girl up in Broadway and another up in Luray. You get the picture. I sent him packing." She took a deep breath. "But not before he gave me a real gift. Her name is Tiffany, and she's a senior in high school. Wants to be a doctor. How about that?"

"That's wonderful, Mel."

"You?" she asked, leaning against the counter. "You were the town hero once."

He shrugged. "Fallen from grace. Couldn't face coming back after — well, everything that went down our senior year." He shook his head. "I just couldn't." His voice thickened, and he couldn't seem to swallow the rock in his throat.

"I get it," she said. She smiled. "So what'll it be?"

He shrugged. "Got a special?"

She nodded. "Beef brisket with my home-made barbecue sauce, mac and cheese on the side. Served with salad."

"Sounds great."

She disappeared, and he heard her raise her voice to the kitchen staff, placing his order. A minute later, a shadow appeared to his left. He turned to look. The Dayton police chief, Barry Jackson. *Becca's father.*

"You got business here, Noah?"

He nodded. "Something like that."

"Didn't expect we'd see you since your mom moved away."

"I'm not looking for trouble."

"Maybe you should think about how your presence affects Mr. Peters over there."

Noah jerked his head to the right. *Mr. Peters!* "Look, I didn't see him there."

"I thought we had an agreement."

"Come on, that was a long time ago."

"Small towns have a long memory, son."

Melissa reappeared and placed a salad on the counter. "I hope you're not interfering with my customer, Chief. He's got as much a right to sit at my counter as you do."

"Tell that to a man who lost his son because of a drunk driver." The chief turned, gave one more somber look at Noah, and walked away.

Noah watched him leave, then looked at Melissa. "Thanks."

She shook her head. "When are you going to tell somebody the truth?"

He looked at her, trying to judge whether she meant it.

Her stare bore in on his. She whispered, "I was there too, Noah, but you wouldn't have remembered me, would you? You could see only one girl. The rest of us were background noise."

"That's not fair," he said, but inside he knew she was right. He *had* seen only one girl.

He looked down at his salad, unsure what to say.

Melissa left and returned a few minutes later with his brisket, setting it in front of him without further comment.

He ate in silence, paid his bill, and left a ten-dollar tip. As he left, he glanced at his receipt. Melissa's phone number.

He shook his head. *What a strange day. I'm two for two.*

He glanced at the man slumped in the corner booth. Defeated. Angry? Noah was glad Mr. Peters hadn't seen him.

He'd had enough trouble for one night, and tomorrow already bulged with opportunities for misery.

That night Melissa Mitchell placed her Coke Zero on the top of the filing cabinet in her office and pulled open the second drawer.

It's in here somewhere.

Her fingers tiptoed across the top of a dozen folders before pausing and lifting out a thick one near the back. She laid it on the desk, and the bulging contents threatened to spill like memories brought up by siblings at family reunions.

She lifted the photos one by one and smiled. *He sure was handsome.* She lined up the photographs of Noah Linebrink and studied the first: after practice, holding his football helmet, sweat glistening on his face. She'd caught him laughing. Of course, that wasn't hard. In those days, he was always laughing.

She lifted another. Noah back to pass, his arm cocked, his eyes focused on a target downfield. Another: Noah sitting in study hall, face serious as he worked a calculus problem, unaware of his admirer behind the lens.

She sighed as she looked at the last one. *The Halloween party. The night of the crash.* Noah sitting on a couch in that silly Superman costume.

Melissa smiled. *He was always wearing that goofy grin. He had no idea how hot he was . . . and that made him all the more attractive.*

She studied the photograph a moment longer. She'd cropped out the girl holding his elbow long ago, but she could still see a hand gripping him.

You still have a grip on his heart, don't you, Becca?

Or do you?

Melissa covered the hand with her thumb. *Yes,* she thought. *Much better.*

9

Becca retreated to her secluded backyard with a bottle of sweet red wine from South Africa. The only light came from the blue glow of her pool, and soon she turned even that off so she could stare into the night sky without interference.

She lay on a padded wicker lounge chair and wondered whether Noah Linebrink would call.

With her gaze on the white smudge of the Milky Way, her thoughts turned toward the night she'd spent on the hard ground in a Maasai boma.

It was only a few nights ago.

But a world away.

I can see the same stars.

And I feel the same insignificance.

She sipped wine and massaged her left temple, where a buzzing fullness had returned.

She blamed stress for the frequency of her

migraines. By now, she understood that the vague feeling in her head was just a prelude to the pain that would follow, so she interrupted her stargazing to seek medication. In the kitchen, she took four small orange tablets of ibuprofen and two Tylenol, knowing that she was only to use her Imitrex once a migraine was in full swing.

Back by the pool, she wondered if the red wine had triggered her misery, but she longed for a brief respite from her anxiety over seeing Noah again, so she yielded to the temptation to continue wrapping her problems in a blanket of fermented grapes.

Sometime beyond midnight, her musings about dying African children, an old boyfriend, the possibilities of a groundbreaking medical discovery, and a night so long ago when her life changed in a moment all swirled together with the South African wine until she fell into a fitful slumber.

She awoke, or thought she awoke, in the early hours with her head splitting and her stomach in rebellion. Perhaps it was seeing Noah that prodded long-buried pain to the surface again. Regardless, she remembered a time twenty years before when she'd awakened in a hospital with her head pounding.

At first, she knew only that she was in a

strange place with fluorescent lighting. Her mother grasped her hand. "Oh baby, you're awake."

Everything blurred. "W-wh-what happened?" She vaguely remembered getting in a car after fighting with Noah.

Her mother touched her cheek. "Oh, Becca, your face, your beautiful face."

Becca reached up to touch her lips, but her mother caught and restrained her hand. Her lips felt like Georgia peaches. *What is going on? I can hardly push the words past my face.*

Her mother wore an expression of horror. *My face! I must be a monster!* She ripped her hand away from her mother's grip and gingerly touched her lips. Her fingers met prickly stitches protruding from a swollen fleshy mound wet with slime. *My lips! What happened to me?*

She pulled her hand away and shook off what appeared to be bloody snot. "Mommy!"

"Don't worry, dear. Your father's taking care of everything. They already have Noah in custody."

"What? He didn't —"

"That horrible janitor's son!"

Becca shook her head. "I need to see my face!" She looked around. A door exited off the hospital room. *A bathroom. I can look at a mirror.*

She started to pull away the covers, but her IV line tangled around a pole where a bag of clear fluid hung.

Her mother reached out to stop her. "Calm down, honey! You can't get up."

She pushed her legs over the side of the bed, but something else was tugging for attention. She looked down and saw a clear tube with yellow fluid exiting over the side of the bed. *My pee? What have they done to me?*

She screamed, "I. Need. To. See. My. Face!"

Her mother grabbed her shoulders. "No!"

"I want to see Noah!"

"He's the last person you'll see. He's in jail for what he's done. Your father has seen to that."

She tried to push her mother away. "My face! What happened to my face?"

Her mother screamed for help, repeatedly pushing a button on a cord. "Nurse!"

A large man in a white lab coat appeared. "Okay, just calm down." He seized her wrist. "You'll pull out your IV!"

Vise grips around my wrist. You're hurting me!

A syringe filled with clear fluid.

106

"Hey, stop! What are you doing? I want to see my face!" Her words were clear in her head, but when she screamed them, it was as if she spoke through a mouthful of food. "No!"

The man emptied the syringe into her IV. Everything faded.

The memory terrified Becca, so she tried to push it away and pulled a beach towel over her on the chaise lounge. There, next to her pool, she concentrated on the trickling sounds of her man-made waterfall. She lazily stood and wrapped the towel around her to ward off the morning chill. She walked over to turn off the pump cycling the pool water over the stone waterfall. It was her favorite part of her outdoor decorations. She'd collected the stones from the Dry River behind Dayton, and the cascading water design was something her architect had dreamed up. It didn't matter how stressful the day, listening to the flowing water late at night never ceased to soothe her soul.

Until last night, evidently. She massaged the back of her neck and groaned, talking to herself. "Need coffee."

She ground and dripped Kenyan AA coffee straight into a mug that said "I'll have a double mocha Xanax vodka latte to go."

Sipping her coffee over happy taste buds, she looked at her phone. *Two missed calls. Must have been last night.*

She didn't recognize the number, but wondered . . .

She hit a button to dial. A man's voice answered. *His voice.* "Hello."

"Noah." She hesitated. "It's Becca."

She wasn't sure what to say. She had no idea why he'd reappeared and why she even cared.

But she did.

Being abducted in the African wilderness could do that to a gal.

Noah didn't waste any time. "Listen, I was hoping we could get together and talk. You know, business. I'm working for Bradshaw Pharmaceuticals, and I'm hoping you'll be open to a little proposition."

"I'm listening," she said, her heart sinking.

"Not over the phone. Is there a place we can meet? Maybe for lunch?"

She thought for a moment. "We can meet in Harrisonburg."

"That's good." He chuckled. "Not sure if being seen in Dayton in broad daylight would be in my best interest just now."

"Noah, you didn't —"

"Hey, I was driving through town and

thought I'd stop and see Mel."

"An old crush."

"What? I never had —"

"No, silly, she had it for you."

"Never noticed," he said.

"My dad loves her place."

"So I discovered."

"You saw Daddy?"

"Let's just say he reminded me of why I hate small towns, and it has to do with no one ever forgetting anyone else's business." He sighed. "Anyway, Harrisonburg's great."

"I'll meet you at Jack Brown's at one o'clock. Beer and burgers okay?"

"Sure."

"It's a little dive on Main Street opposite the big bank. We can sit outside."

"See you then."

She ended the call with the push of a button and stared at her coffee.

Business?

The whole conversation had been so Noah. He was king of avoiding the elephant in the room. There was pain between them, and although she'd never taken steps to reconcile, she blamed him for staying away and avoiding confrontation. So why should she expect he would want to pick the scab of their past if he didn't need to?

Why would I ever want to do business with

Noah Linebrink?

She sighed. *Every time I think of him, I feel so guilty.*

Amy Rivers plodded to the breakfast table, carrying her mother's copy of *Pusher.*

Her mother set a glass of orange juice in front of her. "You were up late."

She shrugged. "Reading. I just got to the good part." She poured herself a bowl of Life cereal. "Something I don't get, though. Why did Uncle Noah have to go to prison if it was all an accident?"

"He was underaged, honey. He'd been drinking at a party and struck that little boy."

Amy stayed quiet for a while. She couldn't imagine her uncle drinking at a party. "Oh," she said softly.

A minute later, she asked, "And why did the school board tell that Peters kid he couldn't go to school? That was stupid."

"He got AIDS from a blood transfusion."

"After Uncle Noah hit him."

"Yes," her mother said, sighing. "But nobody understood AIDS back then. No one knew you couldn't get it just sitting in school beside someone with the virus. So they kept him at home. Eventually, the kid got so sick, he couldn't go to school anyway.

But that didn't stop Mr. Peters from appealing his son's case. When he finally got approval for his son to attend school, the boy was already in the grave."

"That's why he threatened Noah?"

"Yep. He was an easy target. Noah didn't exactly cause the AIDS, but Mr. Peters didn't see it that way. Noah didn't want to stir up problems, so he never stayed back home for long."

"He sounds stupid."

"He was just hurting." Her mom started washing breakfast dishes in the sink. "But don't think badly of Noah. The man's a saint. If one night hadn't changed his life, I think he'd be giving Mother Teresa a run for her money."

"Mother Teresa is dead, Mom." Amy pushed away her cereal bowl. "And she didn't *have* any money."

10

Noah arrived before Becca, remembering that she'd always been the one to arrive fashionably late for anything. He was given a table outside Jack Brown's and promptly started examining a menu that featured over a hundred beers and a rotating tap. He finally decided on something called Original Sin Hard Cider and sipped from a mug as he finalized his planned approach. If he couldn't appeal to her material side, maybe he'd go for old-fashioned Catholic guilt.

When Becca found him, he stood, his chest tightening. Her blonde hair was down, shoulder length, and she wore just enough makeup to highlight her eyes. But what struck him right away were her lips. He hadn't really thought much about his old attraction to her, but when he saw her this time, it was her absolutely perfect and pouty lips that made him want to touch —

"Noah?"

He realized he'd been staring. "O-oh," he stuttered. "Sit down. I ordered hard cider. Hard to decide. Over one hundred different brews listed here," he said, aware that his speech was flowing like an open faucet. *Shut up!*

Becca looked at the waitress. "I'll have a water with lemon."

She sat. "The burgers here are great," she said.

He ordered the day's burger special, something called a Greg Brady: a grilled burger topped with a scoop of mac and cheese and covered with crushed barbecue potato chips. He made a mental note to run an extra mile in the morning.

When he saw the burger, he added a mental addendum: *Make that two miles.* He lifted the bun and examined his prize. *And some abdominal crunches.*

"It's no secret that you've been working on an artificial hemoglobin," he said.

She offered a thin smile. As thin as those perfect lips would allow. "That part is no secret."

"What you may not know is that my career goals have been remarkably similar, but I have been approaching a different aspect of the problem."

She stayed quiet and closed her red lips

113

around a straw.

"I've read your doctoral thesis." He took a breath. "It's brilliant. I think the combination of our projects could push a viable artificial blood onto the market several years ahead of when it would hit if we continue to work on our own."

"You're my competition. Why would I work with you?"

"My CEO is willing to pay whatever it takes to bring you over to Bradshaw."

She laughed. "I'm working for the family business. Why do you think money would tempt me?"

"Because I seem to recall that you weren't like most emotionally laden females who would hang on to relationships even if scientific progress would be hampered."

"You have no idea how close JP is to completing this project. We don't even speak about it outside our soundproof board room." She paused. "There are sound oscillators in our air-conditioning vents to prevent anyone from trying to eavesdrop on our conversations. We've spent more on measures to counter corporate espionage than some small countries spend on intelligence. I'm probably in violation of some company policy just meeting with you."

He shrugged. "But here you are."

"Here I am." She took a bite of her burger and patted her lower lip with a napkin. She then extracted a small mirror from her purse and puckered her lips toward the glass. Evidently satisfied, she returned it to her bag.

He was mesmerized. After a moment, he added, "Seven figures and stock options. A percentage of future sales if we bring a successful blood substitute to market."

She pushed her plate back and glanced around. Although they were outside, they weren't alone. Another couple sat a table away. Becca kept her voice quiet. "Just what are you doing here?"

"Trying to hire you."

"Seriously? You think you can waltz right back into town, sit down, and just talk *business*?"

He opened his mouth, but nothing came out.

"I haven't seen you in what, twenty years, and you just show up in my life to talk *business*?"

"Becca," he said, finding it hard to think, "I'm sure I have — no, *we* have — things to say, but I wasn't sure you wanted to start that way." He hesitated, trying to read her silence. "Maybe I couldn't face starting that way."

She shook her head and muttered, "Twenty years."

"Nineteen years, eight and a half months and" — he looked at his watch — "three days."

"You didn't write."

"I did write. Just about every day. There's not a lot to do in jail, but I do remember writing. You didn't answer."

"I never got them." She pointed across the table.

He winced. This wasn't going like he'd planned.

She stared at him, piercing his soul. "You never came back."

"Your father warned me to stay away. He said you didn't want to see me."

She shook her head. "That's crazy."

They fell into an awkward silence. Finally, he asked, "Why didn't *you* write?"

Her eyes moistened. "Because I felt" — she hesitated — "so, so guilty."

He could tell she was on the edge of losing it. She dabbed at her eyes and stood. "This was a bad idea."

He slid back his chair. "Becca. Don't leave. Not like this."

She rolled the flesh of her lower lip into her perfect mouth and bit down, shaking her head. She didn't say anything, only making a small squeak as her next breath suckcd in with a rush.

He watched her walk away and disappear around the corner.

He sighed and drained the last of his cider.

That went well.

His waitress, a twentysomething co-ed wearing a purple James Madison University T-shirt, smiled pleasantly as she looked at the half-eaten burger at the empty place across from Noah. "Will your date be returning?"

Apparently not in this life.

Noah couldn't talk. He just shook his head and pushed away his empty glass.

Becca drove away. Fast. South on I-81, racing back toward her research lab and the things that made sense.

Could it be?

He wrote to me? Then where are the letters? I'll have to ask my parents about that!

My father warned him to stay away?

My guilt blinded me to what was really going on.

She couldn't make sense of it. Had her parents lied to her to keep him away? They'd never been crazy about her dating Noah; they'd made that much clear. Her parents, as middle class as they were, seemed to look down on the Linebrink family, often remarking about Noah's father's work as a janitor or his mother's work as a waitress.

But lie?

That didn't seem like her parents.

Is Noah lying? Is he just bitter about his jail sentence after all these years?

But Noah didn't seem to be lying. She prided herself on being able to read people, and he'd seemed genuinely surprised that she would ask him why he never wrote.

That means he still cared about me.

At least he did twenty years ago.

Tears threatened her mascara, but she didn't care. She could freshen up in the car before going into the lab.

She thought about their unlikely pairing — the nerd intellectual and the jock. She remembered how shocked she'd been when he first asked her out and how scared she'd been that he would find a reason not to follow through.

In the beginning, she helped him with physics and math. Later, when she wanted to tell him how much she cared, she turned it into a joke. "I love you for your brains," she said. He'd protested, but she explained that he was really smart.

And she believed he was. Noah wasn't just

a dumb jock. He was smart and needed her to help him see it.

He smiled, shrugged, and replied, "And I love you for your looks."

When she protested, he turned the tables on her. He wanted her to understand that he really saw beauty where she saw only her awkwardness and rebellious hair.

It became their favorite playful banter, with both of them reassuring the other in the areas they felt most insecure: Becca in her looks, lacking fashion sense and constantly battling a tangle of frizzing hair, and Noah, having relied upon his physical attributes as an athlete and to attract girls but lacking confidence that he could cut it academically. Anyone who overheard would think they were joking, but Becca took it to heart. *Noah Linebrink loved her.*

They used the words to close every phone conversation.

"Love you for your brains," she'd say.

"Love you for your looks," he'd say.

In the end, what they built in each other provided the foundation for Becca to move forward in social situations with confidence and for Noah to believe enough in his scholastic abilities to face the academic rigors of a university.

Now Becca was unsure what to think.

She'd successfully paved over her past life with a series of layers she wasn't sure were true.

She took a deep breath and tried to focus, even as she felt a tingling sensation just below her scalp on the left side. *All of this is a distraction from the important work I have to do.*

My research could impact millions, she thought, aware that her musing could be interpreted as grandiose but confident of the truth. *Just think. Transfusion without risk of virus transmission.*

Transfusion without the hassle of finding donors. That alone will save billions of health-care dollars.

Transfusion without risk of transfusion re-action, since the artificial blood won't have A or B antigens. Everyone can get the same product without blood typing. Again, just eliminating blood typing will save billions!

She thought, as she often did, about little Jimmy Peters, who contracted HIV through a blood transfusion given because of a ruptured spleen. *He would still be alive if a safe alternative to blood had been available then.*

After she parked in the secure lot at Jackson Pharmaceuticals, Becca adjusted the rearview mirror and freshened her makeup.

As she did, she tried to quiet an inner voice of accusation that she heard every time she applied her lipstick. *Because of what you did, you deserve to be disfigured.*

She pushed back against the guilt and lifted a leather satchel from the passenger seat. She pushed aside thoughts of Noah. *I don't have time for relationship drama. I'm on the edge of a phenomenal discovery.*

She passed through the necessary security checks, but instead of heading straight to her lab to check on the day's progress, she pressed the elevator button for the top floor, where her uncle Jimmy had his office.

She walked past his secretary without acknowledging her and pushed open the CEO's door. She sat in the "little girl" chair and folded her arms across her lap. "Interesting development," she said. "Noah Linebrink came to visit me today."

11

James Jackson folded his hands behind his head and looked across his massive desk at Becca. "It's pretty obvious, isn't it? He hears about your research on the news while you're in Africa, has been working on a similar project, and they want to steal our research."

"But he didn't really ask me about our research. He just offered me a job." She smiled. "He wants me to work for Bradshaw."

James shook his head. "He's a spy, pure and simple. He'll get you talking about a new position in their company, then as you get closer to signing on, they'll ask for more information about your project to be sure you are a fit, and then when your guard is down, they've got our secrets."

"He says our research is complementary and that we could move ahead at a significantly faster pace if we worked together."

"What did you find out about *his* research?"

Becca paused. It was the first time she realized that she had found out exactly nothing about what Noah was doing, other than that he was working on an artificial blood. "I — uh, he really didn't give me any specifics."

James tapped his fingers on the desk.

"By the way, I stopped by your lab today. A few of your techs were pretty pumped by your last suggestion. They said they weren't sure how you knew what change to make in the protocol, but whatever you suggested worked." He paused. "So how did you know?"

She tried not to smile. *It worked!* She feigned nonchalance. "Intuition."

"Well, whatever you're doing, keep it up. The techs seem to think we're finally on the right track to getting that molecule to fold in the right way."

Excellent. Two folds down, two to go.

The CEO took a deep breath. "About this situation with Noah. I want you to find out what he's doing."

"I'm not sure that I'm the one to do that. We have kind of a crazy past, and I didn't leave him on the best terms today."

"Your crazy past is exactly why I want you

to do it. His guard will be down with you."

"What do you propose?"

"Use this situation to our advantage. Lead him on. Let him believe you're interested in his offer, and then when he lets down his guard, find out just what Bradshaw Pharmaceuticals is doing."

"I'm not sure that will work."

"Sure it will. Tell him you need to see what he's doing to establish whether it will be worth your while to jump ship."

"And why should he cooperate?"

"Because I seem to remember two teenagers who were in an accident and ran over a little boy."

Becca pinched her eyes shut and rubbed the back of her head. "What's that got to do with this?"

"Because, Becca, Noah's motivation to establish a safe, effective blood substitute is as complex and twisted as yours." He offered a thin smile. "Guilt is an emotional crutch, but it can prod some people to greatness."

"I think you're wrong. That was a long time ago."

Her uncle just kept staring across the desk, his slate-blue eyes fixed on hers.

"I know you better than you think."

■ ■ ■ ■

That evening, Becca stopped in unannounced at her parents' Dayton home. Pausing only briefly after knocking, she entered the living room. "Mom?"

"In the kitchen, honey."

She walked in to find her mother putting the finishing touches on a pair of peach pies. "Wow, smells great."

Her mom wiped her hands on the front of her apron. "So how has it been getting back to work?"

Becca shrugged, already annoyed at the superficiality that guided most of her conversations with her mother. Today needed to be different.

But instead of launching straight into the deep end of the pool, she continued to wade in the shallow end. "Oh, you know, making progress."

Becca stayed quiet for a minute, watching her mother work. When the pies had gone into the oven, Becca said, "Did Daddy really tell Noah Linebrink to stay away from me?"

"Oh, he mentioned he saw him yesterday at Melissa's place." Her mother paused, looking at her daughter with a frown. "But no, I'm sure he didn't mention *that*."

"I don't mean yesterday. I mean back when we were in high school, when we had the accident."

"You mean when that boy nearly ruined your life."

"He didn't ruin my life, Mama. He saved it."

Her mother waved her hand in the air. "We see things differently, that's all."

"Mom, you can't do that with me. I'm not your teenaged daughter anymore. You can't just wave this off as a difference of opinion."

Her mom looked away, but not before Becca saw her mother's lips tremble.

Mom pressed a hand to her mouth and gently released it before speaking. "Your father hasn't always been easy to deal with." Her voice was small, a little-girl voice.

Becca was startled by the change but persisted anyway. "Did Daddy tell him to stay away?"

"Barry loved you —" She halted. "No — *loves* you very much. The things he did, he did because he thought it would be better for you."

"Love tells the truth, Mom. Love doesn't keep secrets."

"Sometimes you do the wrong things for the right reasons."

"What, you're saying he did tell Noah to

stay away?" She stared at her mother.

"He felt it was best. I'm sure he advised him to move on. You had. You were off in college. He was in jail for what, two years? He would have only dragged you down, honey."

"So you just went along with it because Daddy thought it was best?"

"I felt bad, honey, but I guess I let your father convince me that Noah wasn't the kind of boy you needed to keep in your life forever. He was a high school crush, but I didn't think Noah would amount to anything — and I knew you had such potential."

Yeah, well, he's done okay for himself lately. "Did he write to me? You never showed me any letters."

Her mother sighed. "It was a long time ago, Becca. Why bring this up now?"

"Because maybe I've been living my life based on a few well-kept secrets — which happen to be lies my parents kept telling me."

"We didn't lie to you, dear. We just didn't want you to be hurt by that boy anymore. We felt it was best if he not —"

"That should have been my choice!"

"Becca, we did this out of love for you!"

"But you didn't have the right to make

decisions like that for me!" Becca turned away.

"Becca, please. I didn't mean to hurt you."

Becca walked into the front room. She looked out at the front lawn that bore not three but four campaign signs for her father's run for Congress.

Her mother followed her. "Becca, I didn't think you'd understand —"

"No!" she said, whirling around and pointing at her mother. "*You* are the ones who don't get it. What Noah did — going to jail — he did to protect me and my chief of police father."

"What do you mean?"

"He wouldn't have been in that car if it hadn't been for me."

"It's just like you to twist things so you can feel guilty and responsible."

"Oh, I think you've heaped enough guilt around this house for a lifetime!"

Her mother put her hand to her mouth.

Just then her father entered, saw the two of them, and exclaimed, "Guess who just nabbed the state police endorsement for Congress?"

Becca couldn't respond. She pushed past her father and ran out the front door.

After his lunch appointment with Becca,

Noah wanted to get out of town and back to Richmond fast, but something held him back.

It was something Melissa Mitchell had said. At the time, he hadn't responded, too upset by the heavy-handed treatment he'd gotten from the town's chief of police.

But later, her comments started gnawing an anxious hole in his gut. What did she really know about the night of the accident?

He thought about the consequences of news like that getting out just as he was reaching out to Becca again. It would destroy her.

Back in his hotel, he thought about checking out and heading home, but instead, he fished a receipt out of his wallet and dialed the number scribbled on the bottom.

Her voice reminded him of a country song. Soft. Southern and just feminine enough to hint at danger. "Hello."

"Melissa. It's Noah."

"I'm surprised you called," she said before adding, "I'm glad."

"Well, I'm kind of surprised too." He hesitated. "Any chance you can get away from that place of yours to see an old friend?"

"For you? I think I might. What do you have in mind?"

"Nothing fancy. Drinks and dinner."

"Sounds perfect. I can get Mary to close up."

"After yesterday, I'd rather not show my face in Dayton."

"Chicken."

"I'm staying out behind the mall. A place called the Jameson Inn. Texas Roadhouse is across the street."

"I know it. I can meet you there. Say an hour?"

"Sure."

"My kind of place. I'll meet you at the restaurant."

An hour and fifteen minutes later, Noah was sipping sweet tea and eating the peanuts out of a small bucket on a table at Texas Roadhouse.

When Melissa showed up, she wore a black-and-white dress that stopped at the knee. Classy. She had on what Noah's mother always called "the bare minimum": eyeliner and lip gloss. When she smiled, dimples broke out beneath her green eyes. She wore a simple necklace with a single pearl that fell right into that notch above her sternum. Noah wasn't sure what that area was called, but he knew it was nice.

This wasn't the same girl he'd known in

high school.

She sat and ordered a strawberry margarita.

He stuck to tea.

He cleared his throat. "You look great."

She shrugged. "Clean living, I guess."

He raised his eyebrows in question. "Seriously?"

She nodded. "I still attend the same church we did as kids. I went through a rough patch where I didn't go for a while after Dale and I split. Didn't feel worthy, you know? But then I finally figured out that Jesus didn't need me to be perfect before I came home. He did a better job at cleaning me up than I ever could."

"Sounds like you've had a dose of grace," he said. "Me, too."

"Want to know the truth?" She offered a mischievous smile. "I'm so busy with the restaurant, Tiffany, and her college applications that I don't have time to sin."

He laughed. She did too.

They ordered steaks. Noah decided to write off the whole trip in terms of his diet. And for today, he stopped promising himself he'd run more. He'd have had to do a marathon or something to make up for all the calories he was taking in.

Melissa brought him up to speed on their

old classmates, all of whom Noah had lost touch with when he'd moved away.

He lowered his head. "When I was a senior, half the houses put signs in their yards with my number on them on game day." He looked up. "When I got out of jail, I walked down Main Street and no one even seemed to recognize me. I was invisible." He sipped his tea. "I think I've spent a lot of time since then just trying to prove I could be a hero like I was before."

"Tell me what you do." She touched his hand, gave it a squeeze, and then reached for her glass.

"I'm a pharmaceutical chemist," he said quietly. "I've been working for years on a project to produce an artificial blood."

She twisted her nose at the word *blood.*

Cute. He smiled. "It's not really gross. Basically, we want to make a fluid that can be given in emergencies and doesn't require a human donor pool or blood bank. What about you? How long have you had the restaurant?"

"Since I couldn't make a living taking photographs," she said. "I needed something dependable after my marriage crashed." She looked down at the table as if counting the years. "Twelve years. Hard to believe it."

"But the place looked great."

"We get by."

After they ate, Noah leaned forward, his voice low. "You know what I did on the night of the accident?"

She nodded without speaking.

"Have you told anyone?"

"Why should I?"

"You shouldn't," he responded a bit too quickly. He softened. "I mean, it was a long time ago, and people could get hurt."

When Melissa spoke her name, he could hear the disappointment in her voice.

"Becca."

"Maybe others."

"Certainly you don't care about her father's silly campaign? I saw how he treated you."

"He was also responsible for me making parole early. He spoke at my parole hearing."

Melissa drained her frozen drink and set the glass on the table. "Is that what this was all about? I thought maybe you actually wanted to see *me,* but what you really wanted was for me not to tell your old secrets."

"It's not like that." He paused. *Well, maybe it's a little like that.* "I've had fun. You're great."

"You're great," she imitated before adding, "but Becca . . ." Her voice trailed off.

"I haven't talked to her — I mean until the last few days — since the night of the accident." He reached for Melissa's hand, but she pulled her hands into her lap, where she knotted her paper napkin. "I had a discussion with her today about the pharmaceutical business. That's why I came up here."

He could see that Melissa was conflicted. A little angry and maybe a little embarrassed by her own honesty. After a moment of silence, she took a deep breath and sighed. "To tell you the truth, I always thought you and Becca were perfect for each other. So maybe it is time for rekindling old flames." She paused. "But just not ours." She slipped out of the bench.

Noah stood, sensing she was just going to flee. Instead, she kissed him. Not full on the mouth or anything, but darn close. He was so startled that he didn't have time to adjust his position before her lips landed — a bit off center, but lips against lips nonetheless.

Her lips were soft, and she was so gentle.

He stood there, too shocked to respond.

"Bye," she whispered, wiping away a tear. "Thanks for the dinner." She shrugged. "I've been wanting to do that since high school."

With that, she turned and walked out, stepping around the waitress, who stood there confused.

Noah stared after her, thinking about Becca walking out on him at lunch.

Two for two!

12

The next day, in a locked conference room adjacent to her lab, Becca stood next to a whiteboard with a marker in her hand.

"Where do we stand?" she asked the members of her research team.

David Letchford looked up from his laptop. "We've basically reproduced the heme group and incorporated the iron, but so far, we've only been able to get it into a binary structure."

Jessica Choy smiled. "Yesterday's advance was huge. But even with that, the design program can't seem to predict the consequences of the hydrophobic interactions that create the proper folding into the quaternary structure that we need."

Becca began sketching the molecule on the board. "Okay, we've got four types of forces that cause the molecule to fold correctly." She held up a finger for each one. "Hydrophobic interactions, Van der Waals forces, hydrogen bonds, and ionic bonds." She pointed at the center of the molecule. "We've come a long way, but we still need to protect the interior of the protein from water. For that to happen, it has to be folded correctly. Where do we stand on the supply of hemoglobin from our E. coli strain?"

David looked at his cell phone. "I went by the bac-T lab this morning. They'll have a new batch ready for harvest by this weekend."

It was a grueling process. The E. coli had been taught to make a type of modified hemoglobin molecule close to what could be used in humans. This work alone had taken the team years. The preliminary hemoglobin molecules synthesized by the bacteria were then put through a series of further modifications so that they would fold into the quaternary structure needed by humans, capable of carrying and delivering both oxygen and carbon dioxide. Becca's team, the company's best, had been working on the folding problem for the past eighteen months without success.

Becca looked at Jessica. "Enter the new shape of our molecule and run the predictor program again. See if you make any progress."

"And what of the artificial red cell structure itself?" David asked.

"Some guys have been working down in sector D, using the PRINT technology some of our competitors are using. They're making progress but are having difficulty with membrane pore size. If the openings are big enough to let the hemoglobin in, it doesn't seem to want to stay there."

Jessica raised her perfectly plucked eyebrows. "And free hemoglobin in the blood will kill the kidneys."

Becca nodded. "I'm going down to Richmond tomorrow to see someone who may be able to help us with that problem." She paused and snapped shut the marker in her hand, signaling the end of their little gathering. "I'll keep you posted."

Her team exited, but Becca kept staring at the whiteboard. Soon, she was furiously drawing symbols for the various amino acids involved in the formation of human hemoglobin, vaguely aware of the buzzing sensation that had returned to the left side of her head. She grabbed four different color markers to represent the different forces present that kept the molecule in its unique shape.

She shaded an area that loved water one color; another area that hated water a second. With a red marker she circled the ionic bonds, and with a blue marker she circled the hydrogen bonds.

Forty-five minutes later, she wiped the perspiration away from her brow and looked at her creation. She whispered, "We need to create bonds here" — she drew a circle between two atoms — "and here" — another circle — "and here."

Before leaving the conference room, she opened a small compact mirror and adjusted her lipstick. After that, she searched her purse for her injectable Imitrex.

The headache had sneaked in while her attention was on the whiteboard. She should have paid more attention to the signals that pain was coming, and coming strong.

For the next hour after injecting the medicine, she lay on the floor behind her desk, looking up at the Maasai necklace and planning her next move.

That evening, Becca scrolled back through her phone log until she found Noah's number. Then she paced her kitchen, working up the nerve to call. She poured wine. She sat down and worked on a sudoku puzzle, which took her all of three minutes. *What is it with my brain lately? It's like half of it just woke up from a long sleep.*

She glanced at a stack of mail and ignored it.

She ordered pizza delivery from Papa John's.

She checked email and Facebook.

Finally, she picked up her iPhone again and called.

He answered on the first ring. "Becca? I didn't expect to hear from you."

"I want to know if you're serious."

"Serious?"

"If you really didn't come back to see me, then maybe you're genuinely interested in our common research for a larger good. If that's true, I want to know more."

"Okay," he said slowly. "Truth be told, my boss made me come and see you. I can say that I am genuinely interested in our research, but . . ."

"But?"

"I'd be lying if I said that after seeing you after all these years, I'm not pretty conflicted about everything."

"Conflicted?"

"Well, there are a lot of old and new feelings coming up." He took a deep breath and exhaled into the phone. "It sounds to me like your parents had a lot to do with keeping us apart. I thought you must have wanted it that way. I believed that for a long time, but maybe it wasn't true?"

"Do you want it to be true?"

"Maybe you should tell me what you're thinking."

"I talked to my mother. She basically admitted not showing me your letters."

He stayed quiet.

"I thought you hated me for what I did," she said.

"No!" He raised his voice. "Never. I did what I did for exactly the opposite reason. I thought I loved you."

"I wouldn't blame you if you didn't want to work with me. What my parents did to you was horrible."

"Your dad was trying to protect you."

"He was protecting his own reputation."

They were silent for a moment before Noah asked, "So you really want to know more about our research?"

"If you think you can work with me, yes." She began pacing around the kitchen again. "But I'll come to Richmond. That's where Bradshaw Pharmaceuticals has its R and D, isn't it?"

"Yes, but we should meet outside head-quarters until we've talked a bit more."

"But I want to see what you're working on. How will I ever know if I could work at Bradshaw if I can't see the facility?"

"Oh, you'll see it soon enough."

"Can I come tomorrow?"

"Shall we try lunch again?"

"Let's try coffee instead."

"Good idea. There's a Starbucks in the fan district on north Robinson, not far from my place. I'll meet you there. Say ten o'clock?"

"I'll see you then." She ended the call and looked at the stack of mail.

She tossed two unopened offers for credit cards, laid aside the discount coupons from Kohl's, and fingered a manila envelope that had no return address.

She used a letter opener to slide open the end of the envelope. Inside was a brief handwritten letter and a photograph. The printing was very stiff and straight, almost block letters, all capitals. "I KNOW THE TRUTH."

She turned over the paper. Another message. "YOU WILL PAY."

She slid the photograph out onto the kitchen counter. A black-and-white photograph of the '72 Camaro she drove in high school, smashed against a tree.

She sighed. *The night that changed everything.*

So it begins.

13

The next day Noah nodded at the barista behind the counter at his neighborhood Starbucks. It was all the communication needed for the young woman to complete his normal order.

She pulled an espresso shot, poured it into the bottom of a grande cup, and filled the rest of it with freshly brewed black coffee.

"Thanks," he said before finding a seat at a high table where he could watch Robinson Street for Becca's arrival. For this meeting, Noah wore business casual: a black shirt with an open collar and a sport coat made up of a tight weave of brown, black, and tan.

Becca, when she arrived, could have been mistaken for any one of a dozen artsy-type Virginia Commonwealth University grads; she wore designer jeans and a loose flower-patterned blouse with a wide asymmetric neckline that allowed Noah to see a black bra strap heading over her left shoulder. She slid a pair of amber sunglasses to the top of her head. "Hi, Noah," she said, placing her satchel on the table. Despite her casual, eclectic dress, her makeup, especially her lipstick, was perfect.

She stood in a short line for coffee, giving Noah another chance to observe his old friend. She was a complex mix of nerd scientist and Hollywood reality show — a carefree exterior hiding a tiger beneath the surface. When she turned around and offered him a slight smile, Noah had a hard time not staring. *Those lips!* He forced himself to look away, not wanting to be over-the-top enraptured, but that was exactly what he felt. *What is it? Has she had some collagen work done or something? Or is it just the perfect way she applies her lipstick?*

When she sat down, she said, "I've been working on this project for fifteen years, but never before have I felt within striking distance of completion." She sipped her coffee and checked her perfect lipstick with a small mirror. "When you expressed the idea that we could move ahead at a faster pace working together, honestly, my first reaction was, *Get real!* You have no idea how close JP is to the finish line. But perhaps I judged you too soon. Maybe I need to see exactly what you're doing."

"Fair enough." Noah watched a mother pushing a double stroller. *How can I reveal enough to make her interested, but not enough to give away trade secrets?* "I'm working on the shell that will house the hemoglobin."

"The artificial red cell."

Noah nodded. "Exactly." She seemed to be staring right through him. "We've been using PRINT technology to create small hydrogel spheres that will be pliable enough and small enough to fit through capillaries."

She nodded. "I know."

He leaned forward. "And you know this how?"

"I read Bradshaw's annual report to stockholders." She paused and offered him that perfect smile again. "Among other ways."

While he was processing that admission, she continued. "We've been using PRINT for some time as well, but we're having problems with micropore size. We need to figure out a way to get the hemoglobin into the gel spheres and make it stay put. When the pores are big enough to let the hemoglobin molecules in, they are big enough to let the hemoglobin molecules out. For a while, we tried keeping the pore size so small that oxygen would get in, but the hemoglobin would be trapped. But then we had to consider how impossibly labor intensive micro-injecting each sphere would be."

"Yeah," he said, "that's pretty much impossible."

"And how are you dealing with the problem?"

"We've created a way to widen and shrink the pores."

He watched as her jaw slackened ever so slightly. Her mouth hung open for a few seconds before she regained her composure. "Interesting." She sipped again at the top of her latte, and Noah observed how careful she was not to immerse her lips into the foam. "Are you working on a synthetic hemoglobin?" she asked.

"Not me personally." He shrugged. "But of course any company committed to successful development of an artificial blood will need to tackle that as well."

"Methodology?"

"Recombinant DNA. We're trying to teach E. coli to make human hemoglobin." He looked across at her, studying the intensity with which she seemed to be taking it all in. "Let me ask you something. Why does it all matter so much to you?"

"I think you know the answer."

"Enlighten me."

She took a deep breath. "When I was in high school, I used to babysit little Jimmy Peters," she said. "You know, before the accident."

Noah nodded. *Guilt.*

"He was such a fun kid. And innocent. He didn't deserve the treatment he received."

"Nobody understood AIDS back then. Every school board in the country was trying to decide what to do with kids with HIV."

"It's not just that. He deserved to live."

"You didn't give him HIV."

"Don't give me self-righteous crap. I have a pretty good idea what has been motivating you, too."

"I'm not sure you know me at all anymore."

"So help me out. Who is Noah Linebrink?"

He felt his throat tighten. "I'm still figuring that out." He halted, then lowered his voice. "Every night as I was heading off to bed, my father used to say the same thing. 'Remember, son, you were made for more. You were designed to *enjoy God.*'"

"Yeah, well, excuse me if I don't share your enthusiasm. God hasn't exactly given me an enjoyable life."

"And maybe we don't see the message behind the pain. Maybe God is simply trying to redirect our attention toward Him."

She looked away, out across the street, her eyes unfocused. "It's funny, Noah. It's like you picked up right where we left off." She straightened in her chair and touched the edge of her hair. Noah could see that she was studying her faint reflection in the wall of windows in the front of the shop. "Do you remember our fight?" she asked.

"I've only had twenty years to replay it."

"And you're stuck on the same theme."

"Maybe it's taken me a long time to believe it."

"You seemed sure of it that night."

"I was an arrogant high school senior, Becca. There's a difference in knowing something here," he said, touching his forehead, "and here." He touched his heart.

They stayed quiet for a few minutes as if the need to talk had been pushed aside while they lost themselves in memories of high school pain and struggle.

When Becca finally spoke, she had tears in her eyes. "So you really wrote to me?"

Noah nodded and was about to reply when her eyes suddenly glazed over. They deviated left and up as if she were trying to see into her own forehead. Her latte slipped from her right hand. He caught it just as her arm began to twitch.

For Noah, everything slowed. He watched as she began weaving on her stool, with first her right arm and then her right leg beginning to jerk. "Becca!" He reached for her just as she careened off the stool toward the floor. He managed to cushion her fall, then watched in desperation as her arms and legs began a rhythmic jerking.

Other patrons quickly gathered. A young man knelt by her side. "She's having a seizure," he said as if he'd seen it a hundred times. "We need to keep her from biting her tongue."

Noah tried to turn her onto her side. Her pants were wet. *Urine?*

He looked at the barista. "Call 911!"

When Becca awoke, the first thing she was aware of was how cold she was. She opened her eyes and gazed into bright lights. She moved her arm to the side and discovered that she was on some sort of stretcher with the rails up. *Where am I?* An IV bag hung above her. It seemed like some weird nightmare from her past. Instinctively, she put her hand to her mouth. *No, my lips are okay.* She looked down; she wore only a thin patient gown.

"Rebecca?" The face of a woman in blue scrubs appeared over hers. "Don't be alarmed, dear. You're in the hospital. Apparently you had some sort of seizure."

Hospital? I remember drinking coffee with Noah. She looked around. "Where are my things?"

"A man has been inquiring about you. I think he has your bag."

Becca covered her mouth with her hand. "Could you ask him to bring me my things?"

"The doctor will be seeing you first. When he's checked you out, we'll allow your husband to come in."

"He's not my husband. He's just . . . a friend."

"Just relax for now. The doctor will be in shortly."

"What hospital am I in?"

"St. Mary's."

For the next hour, Becca endured seemingly endless questions from an ER physician and a neurologist.

Five times, she denied taking illegal drugs.

She denied taking prescription drugs except for Imitrex.

She admitted she liked rosé wine.

She acknowledged a recent uptick in her

migraine headaches, but she didn't mention her increase in ability to predict three-dimensional consequences of breaking and forming molecular bonds. That just seemed too crazy to admit.

She underwent a complete, fingers-in-every-orifice exam followed by a urine drug screen (which prompted her to deny taking illegal drugs a sixth time), a venipuncture for lab work, and an MRI of the brain.

When a patient-care technician, a boy still fighting an acne problem, wheeled her back into her emergency-room cubicle, Noah was waiting. "Hi," he said, reaching for her hand.

"Hey, you," she said, covering her mouth with her hand. "Could you hand me my satchel?"

He placed it on the stretcher beside her.

"Now turn around."

He obeyed.

"No peeking." She extracted her small mirror and a tube of YSL Rouge Volupté Perle in Coral Sun number 102. She rolled up the stick and glided it over her lips with the dexterity of a surgeon.

"Okay," she said.

He turned around as she deposited the lipstick tube into her satchel. "Becca, you don't need to do that for me. I think you look great —"

"I've been doing that every day since the last time I was in an emergency room," she replied, knowing that her sharp tone would keep back any further comments about her makeup needs.

He let her comment fall. "How do you feel?"

"Like I've been poked and prodded. I just need my clothes so I can get back out of here."

"Not so fast, Ms. Jackson."

She looked over to see a man in a white coat. He held out his hand to Noah. "Mr. Jackson? I'm Dr. Davis, the neurologist on call today."

Noah shook his hand.

"Why does everyone think he's my husband?" Becca said. "He's my friend."

The doctor looked concerned. "We need to talk."

Becca touched Noah's hand. "Can you leave me alone for a bit?"

Noah nodded. "I'll be in the lobby."

"I'll just be a minute," she called after him. Then, looking at the doctor's sober face, she said, "I'll bet you're no good at poker."

"Ms. Jackson," he began, "you've got a serious problem."

14

An hour passed before Becca came strolling into the waiting room with her satchel over her shoulder and a small CD in a plastic case in her hand. "Ready to go?"

"Wow, that must have been some talk. Are you okay?"

"I'm fine. Just need to get my migraines under control."

Noah pointed to the disk. "What's that?"

"A digital copy of my MRI scan in case I want to seek another opinion." She frowned. "There is one problem. Since apparently I had a seizure, the doctor says I can't drive."

Noah scratched his head. "I can give you a ride."

"Noah, I need to get all the way back to Dayton. I can call my dad. He can probably even get some state patrolman to give me a lift."

"Forget that. I'm not leaving you. We can even take your car. I can catch a bus back or something."

"Not on your life. If you insist on taking me, we'll go in your car and I'll arrange for someone to pick up my car." She started for the door. "I need to stop at a pharmacy before we get out of town."

Once they were in his car, Noah said, "Are they sure it's just migraines? I've never heard of seizures going with migraines."

"*Complex* migraines," she corrected and didn't elaborate.

He watched as Becca tugged at her sleeve, but she wasn't fast enough to keep him from seeing the IV port still in her arm. "What's that? They forgot to take out your IV?"

"No, silly, just a precaution in case I have another seizure in the next twenty-four hours. I'll take it out after I'm at home."

He shook his head. "Are you sure you shouldn't stay in the hospital? Didn't they want to observe you or something?"

"Oh, you know doctors. They're always worrying about getting sued, so they'll advise you to do whatever the absolute safest thing is, even if there's one chance in a thousand you'll have a problem."

"So they wanted you to stay?"

"You worry too much. I'm a big girl now."

They stopped at a pharmacy, and Becca handed the pharmacist four different pieces of paper. "We'll wait for these."

As they drove toward the Shenandoah Valley, anxiety grew in the pit of Noah's stomach. Something just didn't seem right.

Halfway to Dayton, Becca pulled out a piece of paper from her satchel and started scribbling. Noah glanced over often enough to realize that, in her search to fold the artificial hemoglobin molecule properly, she was writing out a chemical reaction that would dissolve certain molecular bonds.

"Ideas flowing, are they?" he asked.

She pulled her paper to her chest to hide what she'd been writing. "Don't know what it is with me lately. It's like I can suddenly see the consequences of breaking certain bonds in a three-dimensional molecular structure." She shook her head. "I've been working on this problem for years, but only in the last few weeks have I really begun to predict the outcomes four or five steps ahead of where we are."

"Wow," he said slowly. "So all of a sudden, you're a genius?"

He glanced over to see her lipsticked smile. "I've been a genius all along. But it's like I've been approaching the problem with half my brain tied behind my back." She laughed.

He joined in. Nervously. *What is with her?*

After passing the Charlottesville exits, the road began to climb toward the overpass at Afton Mountain. Becca continued to work, and Noah quietly watched.

He raised his eyebrows. "So have you heard enough? Can I convince you to join Bradshaw Pharmaceuticals?"

"I need to see your lab."

"That might be tough."

"Well, if BP really wants my research, you'd better make it happen." She shoved the piece of paper she'd been writing on into her bag. "Whether you're with me or we continue separate paths, I have a feeling we're on the edge of a huge breakthrough. I just need to press on toward the finish."

"Do you have any idea what this could mean?"

She nodded. "The impact on medicine will be unbelievable."

"The positive impact on people needing blood will be like nothing else we've seen in the last century." He paused, reached over, and lightly touched her hand with his. She turned hers over, and he gave it a squeeze. "What's with all the urgency I'm sensing? It's like you need to get this done yesterday."

She stayed quiet for a moment before answering. "Maybe I'm starting to believe that stuff you preached to me back in high school, the stuff about never being sure if we'd have tomorrow."

He glanced at her again. *This is Becca?*

When they finally reached her country home, Noah grabbed the pharmacy bag off the backseat and glanced to see that Becca was walking toward the door in front of him. He peeked inside the bag as he walked toward the front door. *Syringes?* He moved aside a small box labeled "dexamethasone" to see a bottles of Dilantin and hydrocodone/acetaminophen. He closed the bag and looked up to see the back of Becca's head. She hadn't seen him checking the bag's contents.

Inside, Noah sat on a leather couch in front of a stone fireplace. "Your place is beautiful," he said. "Are you sure you'll be okay alone?"

"I'll be fine. Are you hungry? I'm not much of a cook." She paused. "I think I have some things we could make a salad with, and some leftover pizza we can heat."

"You rest. I'll take care of dinner."

"I'm going to shower and change. I desperately need to get out of these jeans!"

She disappeared down a hallway, and Noah began poking around the inside of her refrigerator. A few sad tomatoes sat next to a partially wilted head of lettuce and a wrinkled cucumber. He cautiously lifted the top of a Tupperware container to see something that looked like spaghetti sauce. *Is that mold?*

Listening for evidence of a shower running, he took out the salad items and a second container with leftover pizza and set them on the counter next to Becca's partially opened satchel. He saw a paper with the St. Mary's Hospital emblem on the top. After glancing back down the hall, he lifted the paper and read. At the top, it said, in bold red letters, "Against Medical Advice."

The small print detailed how the attending physician had determined Becca had a condition that had not been stabilized, and to leave the hospital was to do so with the understanding that there may be negative health consequences, including death, and that by signing the form, the patient acknowledged full understanding of the situation and took full responsibility for their actions to leave *against medical advice.*

She had signed the form: Rebecca Jackson, PhD.

Noah felt his breath quicken.

Becca, what's going on?

Becca stripped out of her clothes, including her urine-dampened jeans, gave them a disgusted sniff, and dropped them into a laundry hamper just as a now-familiar buzzing feeling began in her left temple.

I should look at my sketches now. My ability to successfully predict how hemoglobin will fold seems to be enhanced when I feel this way.

But I can't risk having another seizure in front of Noah.

She slipped into her bathroom, prepared a syringe of dexamethasone, and jabbed the needle into the IV port in her arm. She emptied the contents into her vein and then took out her Imitrex and stabbed her right thigh. In moments, the weird feeling in her head disappeared. Then she removed the IV port and held pressure on her arm as she stepped into the shower. There, she allowed the hot water to soothe her soul and wash away the stains of the day. As she washed, she thought about how Noah had so suddenly reentered her life just as so many other circumstances had started to gel.

And she invariably thought back to the days *before.* That's how she divided her life. *Before* and *after.*

Before the accident, she used to sneak out of the house to meet Noah for midnight swims in the Union Springs reservoir. On hot summer nights they would swim out to the concrete tower, climb the forty-foot structure, and lie there in the moonlight.

One night, although she was afraid to jump, he held her hand and jumped with her. Exhausted but exhilarated, they climbed back to the top, where they talked of their future at the University of Virginia.

She touched the side of his wet hair. "I can just see you being mobbed by the cheerleaders. Why would the quarterback of the football team want to hold on to his nerdy girlfriend?"

He kissed her and laughed. "Because I love you for your looks."

"Shut up!" She kissed him back, stood up, and jumped off the tower by herself. When she broke the surface of the water, she yelled at him, "See, I can get along fine without you."

He had called into the darkness. "I'm not going anywhere. We are going to school together!"

That was *before.*

Now, she stepped out of the shower and dried her hair in front of the mirror. She traced the outline of her upper lip with her index finger and selected a nice lipstick for the late evening: one of her favorites, Guerlain KissKiss Strass. She loved it for more casual occasions. It had just the right scent, consistency, and finish.

When she came out, Noah had performed his own small version of the loaves and fishes. On the table sat a green salad next to a plate of hors d'oeuvres. She looked at an arrangement of Wheat Thins crackers, each topped with a piece of cucumber, a small slice of cheddar cheese, and a green olive. Noah smiled. "Pizza is almost heated."

"Wow. I'm impressed. I had olives?"

"I found them below a container of what I think was mac and cheese. It had an interesting color that matched the olives, so I pitched it."

"Scaredy-cat!"

He looked at her face and seemed to freeze. "Uh, wow," he said, "you look great."

They sat across from each other, and their conversation fell comfortably to life *before.*

Noah smiled. "Remember when you pulled me over on Christmas Eve?"

She laughed. "My dad almost killed me."

Her mother had insisted she make a last-minute run to pick up cranberry jelly. Because her Camaro was in the shop, she took her father's unmarked Gran Fury. When she saw Noah heading out of the Food Lion parking lot, she pulled out behind him, flipped on the lights under the grill, and tapped the siren. Everything was

161

laughs until the on-duty Dayton police officer stopped to see what the problem was
and found Noah and Becca in the front seat
of Noah's VW, lip-to-lip without any mistle-
toe.

While they were washing dishes, Noah
said, "Don't you think you should tell your
parents about your seizure?"

She shook her head. "They'll just worry.
Besides, I always have coffee with Daddy
on Wednesday mornings. I'll fill him in
then."

"Then I'm not going home. You shouldn't
be alone."

She raised her eyebrows to tease him.
"Noah!"

"I read the paper they made you sign," he
said, pointing to her open satchel. "It was
practically falling out of your bag there."

"You read my private medical information?"

"Becca, it says you could die because you
left. You're not staying alone."

"Noah, you know how medicine is practiced these days. The doctors make you sign
stuff like that to cover their backsides.
They'd have made me sign that if I had an
infected hangnail."

"Funny. I didn't know you could die from
a hangnail." He touched her hand that was

soapy from the dishwater. "Now, would you tell me the truth?"

She pulled her hand away. "I'm telling the truth. The doctor said that my migraines and the seizure are related." *That is true. He said that.*

"So he just sent you home with an IV and medications? When are you supposed to follow up?"

"He gave me the name of a neurologist at UVa. I'm supposed to call for an appointment." She let her eyes bore in on him and tried to stay annoyed, but she found his concern endearing. "Okay?"

He shrugged and looked away and appeared to wipe something from the corner of his eye. *A tear?* "I'm still not leaving."

"Suit yourself. I have a spare room." She smiled. "But don't let my father find out you stayed here."

He walked away from her and stared out at the pool off the back deck. "You know what I kept thinking of when I was in the waiting room today?"

She studied him. It was as if he were a high school senior again; his face reflected his anguish. "What is it, Noah?"

"I just remember how frustrated I was the night of our accident. You were in the ER, and I couldn't be with you. I kept asking about you, and they wouldn't tell me anything."

"I knew you would have been there if you
could." She hesitated. "And I kept asking
about Jimmy Peters, and the nurses
wouldn't tell me anything either."

They walked outside, and Becca flipped
on the switch to her little waterfall. They sat
on wicker chairs, listening to a symphony of
cicadas and the sound of the tumbling
water. "Did you know your father came to
my parole hearing?" Noah asked.

She shook her head.

"He told them how I'd never been in
trouble, how everything was an accident,
my first offense and all that. They let me
out early because of him."

"I didn't know."

"He acted like I was a saint. But when I
walked out of the jailhouse a free man, he
was leaning against his car at the curb. He
told me to leave Dayton and never contact
you. He said he had friends who could pick
me up for violating my parole if I acted up.
He didn't exactly say what 'acting up' was,
but I understood. I'd be going back to jail if
I tried to see you."

"So you didn't try."

"He said you'd moved on. That you didn't
want to see me. I called your dorm a few

times. A guy always answered, and I hung up."

"I lived in a co-ed dorm, stupid."

"At first I tried to live at home, but it seemed the whole town had gone on without me. I'd been such a celebrated kid, but now nobody seemed to notice. I ran into Mr. Peters one morning, and he spit on the sidewalk at my feet." Noah seemed to be staring off into the night sky. "I knew it was time to leave."

"I'm so sorry, Noah."

"I was so down." He paused. "I think I waited until I made something of myself before I returned just because I wanted the town's respect again."

"Did you ever marry?"

His voice was a whisper. "No."

"You?"

"To my job."

"Wow, aren't we a pair?" He forced a chuckle. "Okay, so that's my darkest moment. What about you?"

"Oh no, I can't go there."

"Hey, I showed you my pain. It's only fair."

She took a deep breath. *Can I trust him?*

They sat quietly for a moment. She slipped off her sandals, picked up a beach towel from a small table, and draped it over her shoulders. She walked to the side of the pool and sat so that her feet could dangle in the water. Noah rolled up his pants and took off his socks and shoes to join her.

"My darkest moment came on prom night. I was alone. You were in jail. I locked myself in the bathroom when all the other girls had dates. I had gone from dating the star quarterback to my nerd study hall. No one else would look at me the way you had. No one wanted to date the freak with the notched lip. I stared at myself in the mirror, and all I could see was how screwed up my appearance was. The scar on my lip doesn't match up, so I swore to myself that night that no one would ever see me that way again. I stole some lipstick from my mother, and I've never been without it since."

She looked at Noah. He had tears in his eyes.

For a moment he gazed at her and then reached up and so tenderly touched her top lip where a faint scar extended up toward her nose. Then, he lifted the towel from her shoulders and held it in his hand. He moved it toward her face and paused as if to ask for permission to continue.

She offered a slight nod, then felt the towel press against her lips. She began to cry softly as he gently wiped off her lipstick.

When he finished, he just gazed into her eyes. She couldn't have felt more exposed and vulnerable if she'd been completely undressed. *He can't love me like this.*

But instead of showing revulsion, he touched her lips again, tracing the outline with his index finger. He slid his fingers beneath her chin and encouraged her forward.

15

Noah rose early, showered, and put on the same clothes. When he padded quietly down to the kitchen, he found Becca already awake, making notes on her laptop and sipping her morning coffee.

She was already made up; her lipstick was impeccable.

Noah poured himself coffee and inhaled the aroma deeply. After one sip, he smiled. "Now this is coffee."

"Java House, Kenya AA. I bought it at the airport in Nairobi on my way out."

"What's your schedule this morning? I can give you a lift to work before I head back to Richmond if you want."

"Won't be necessary," she said, all business. "I already arranged for a company driver to pick me up. Should be here in fifteen."

Noah stared at her for a moment. It was as if they hadn't even shared a tender moment the night before. *So much for romantic morning afters, even if it was just a kiss.*

He smiled at the memory. *But what a kiss.* "So when do you want to come down? I'll see if I can arrange a tour of the Bradshaw research facility."

"It will have to wait," she said. "I've made a couple of modifications to our protocol, and I'm anxious to see the result. We're closing in on our goal, and I can't risk losing momentum."

"What can I tell Mr. Thatcher?"

"Tell him I'm intrigued. And motivated. If BP can help me move an artificial blood product to market sooner than JP, I'm interested in the specifics of an offer."

"Do you have any idea what a successful artificial blood product would mean in terms of sales in the US alone?"

"We estimate ten billion annually, US sales alone, but that's far from the financial impact it will make worldwide." She paused. "Can you imagine eliminating the blood-banking costs of typing and storing blood?"

He sat quietly, watching her type away.

A few minutes later, her phone made an electronic chirp. "My ride's here." She stood and gathered her things. "Stay as long as you like. Just lock the door behind you."

He took her hand and stepped in her way.

"Not so fast," he said. "I wanted you to know how special last night was for me. I'll call you, okay?" He leaned forward, hoping to touch those perfect lips again, but she turned her head quickly, offering him only a cheek.

"My lipstick," she said. "Careful!" She pulled away and studied her reflection in a gold-framed full-length mirror in the foyer.

"Becca, you're perfect even without that —"

She interrupted. "Bye, Noah." She stepped out the front door.

He watched her get into a limousine with tinted windows. He shook his head. Talk about flipping a switch. Becca had gone from warm-vulnerable to cold-business overnight.

He walked back into the kitchen and looked at the small collection of pharmaceuticals on the counter. Sipping his coffee, he opened his laptop and googled "dexamethasone."

It was a powerful steroid with a variety of uses, but one caught his eye: "Can be used to treat brain edema associated with brain tumors."

She wouldn't have been that stupid. After she signed out AMA from the emergency room, she had promised him it was migraines, but he found it hard to completely suppress his doubts. *Is she hiding something from me?*

Why?

He finished his coffee and texted his boss. Jackson intrigued and interested in details of job offer.

He searched the kitchen cabinets and borrowed a large travel mug into which he emptied the remainder of the coffee. *Nice excuse to see her again.*

Five minutes later, he was in his car and heading back toward the interstate. He slowed at the top of a hill, the location of an Old Order Mennonite church, and puzzled over seeing a car on the side of the road. He knew that the Mennonites who attended the congregation still drove only horse and buggies, much like their Amish cousins.

Once he was a bit closer, he saw a woman with a camera standing in front of the church. Melissa! He pulled over and lowered the window, watching as she captured the way the morning sun filtered through a grove of pecan trees onto the steeple of the white clapboard building.

He got out and approached her. "Morning, stranger."

She turned. "Noah." She pushed a rebellious strand of auburn hair behind her ear

171

and squinted at him suspiciously. "You're out in these parts pretty early."

"I could say the same about you."

"The light is perfect at this hour." She paused. "What *are* you doing here?" She shook her head. "You spent the night with her, didn't you?"

"Not like you think." He didn't know why it was so important for him to justify his actions to her. It probably had something to do with being raised side by side on the same pew at the Presbyterian church. "I stayed out at Becca's place, but I slept in the guest room. She's sick, Mel. She came to Richmond yesterday on business and had a seizure right in front of me. She was evaluated at a hospital, but they didn't admit her. I drove her back and just played nurse, making sure she was okay until this morning."

Melissa raised her eyebrows as if to say, *Yeah, right!* She glanced over her shoulder and then turned to face the church. "This is the moment I've been waiting for," she said, raising her camera. "See how the light passes straight through the windows from one end to the other and then onto the hitching posts on the front lot?" Her camera emitted a steady rhythm of shutter noises, something he was pretty sure was generated electronically. "It's perfect," she whispered, as if speaking loudly would break the magic of the moment. She took another twenty or so shots, walking closer to the building until she was shooting almost straight through it with the morning rays of the sun.

After a minute, the magic had waned; she walked back toward him, looking at peace. She wore absolutely no makeup, an old pair of jeans, and a sweatshirt with a Virginia Tech logo. But what really stood out to him was that she seemed comfortable with herself. There was nothing put on; with Mel, it was — and always had been — what you see is what you get.

"Sit with me," she said, gesturing toward a patch of moss beneath a maple tree.

He sat, and she lifted her camera again, snapping a few photos of her old friend. He offered a goofy grin.

She said, "Becca."

He felt heat rise in his cheeks. "Be quiet. Put that camera down."

She sat next to him and touched the back of his hand. "I'm sorry for bailing on you the other night."

"It's okay, Mel."

She was quiet for a moment before speaking. "You know, I kept up with you by talking to your mom until she moved away."

"I'm sure she has her opinions about my life."

"She said you never married, that you were too busy trying to prove to Becca and the town that you were a worthy hero again."

Maybe Mom knows me better than I thought. "Why would I care what Becca thinks? We dated in high school. A long time ago."

"But you still blush when I say her name."

He didn't like Melissa's tone. He could tell she didn't approve. It was like high school all over again. Melissa had been his friend first, his church buddy. When Becca came along, Melissa seemed to be constantly playing the role of the elder sister (though she wasn't older) and warning him about Becca.

"She's not a Christian, Noah. Why is she so driven? She has to be so perfect!"

Noah fidgeted, trying to ease his backside off a root. He wasn't sure what to say, so he just looked at her and sighed.

"I just want you to be careful, Noah. Becca has issues, not the least of which is her inability to understand grace."

"And you know this how?"

"I'm her friend, remember? We used to all be friends, the three of us, and just because you exited the scene didn't mean that Becca and I stopped talking."

"I think she's changing. Something happened to her in Africa. She's softer, more contemplative."

"I know how it was between you two. You only saw what you wanted to see."

"I've grown up, Mel."

"So have I."

"This sounds a lot like our old conversations."

"That's because it is. Nothing has changed, Noah, except that Becca went from being smart, driven, and insecure to smart, broken, even more driven, and even more insecure."

"She's one of the most successful women I know."

"That's because she has to be."

Melissa hesitated and then gently laid her camera on a patch of moss beside her. "That was always the difference between you two. You were the star football athlete, but you always carried yourself like it was a present, like it was a privilege that you got to be great. With Becca, it was different. She was smart, but it was never enough. She always had to be more." She shook her head. "I'd like to believe it's because of your faith. You understood grace. Becca didn't — *doesn't* — get it."

"And this all means that you don't think Becca and I should get together?"

"She's broken, Noah. And you can't fix what's wrong. She may try to use you as a Band-Aid for a while, but eventually it won't work. The only thing that can fix her is grace." Mel softened. "Look, I'm the last person to think that someone is out of reach. Maybe she can change. Maybe you guys can have a great life together." She looked away. "Really," she said slowly, "I want you to be happy, even if it is with Becca."

He stayed quiet and gave her hand a little squeeze.

"You remember your fight before the accident?"

Noah nodded. "Of course. She drank too much, but that was kind of my fault too."

"Your fault? I seem to remember you telling her to quit."

"I did, but the whole reason she was hanging out with that football team crowd was because of me. She'd have never joined in if I hadn't been after her." He paused. "She wasn't herself. I told her the same message my dad always told me: 'You were made for so much more.' "

"She got so mad."

He nodded. "Called me a self-righteous

176

pig." Noah chuckled nervously. "I was, kinda, wasn't I?"

Mel took his hand and held it. "You were. But you were a caring pig."

Noah laughed. "You haven't changed."

She looked away toward the parking lot filled with hitching posts. "You know, I've been telling her the same thing for twenty years, but she just doesn't seem to get that God could love her after everything she did. She's pretty tied up with guilt over how she treated you."

"I don't hold it against her. It would have been worse any other way."

She stood up. "I've got to get over to the diner. Want some breakfast?"

"I really need to get back to Richmond, but thanks."

She reached out her hand and pulled him to his feet. "Some other time, promise?"

He nodded and smiled. "I promise."

When Becca arrived at JP, she handed a flash drive to David Letchford. "Here's the new protocol. I want you to oversee a new run."

"But we haven't even analyzed all the data from the last run, so how will I know which changes to incorporate?"

"Just do it this way," she said. "It will

work. I want it done today."

"But setting up the reagents alone will take us six hours."

She offered him a perfect lipsticked smile, this one courtesy of a true red by Urban Decay, the one she reserved for work-related meetings with the CEO. "Looks like you're in for a late night."

She walked to her office, where she saw that the mail had been dropped onto the center of her desk. Seeing a plain manila envelope, she turned and closed the door. She took a deep breath. *Just what I expected.*

She opened it and slid out another black-and-white photo, this one of a teenaged Noah helping Becca out of the passenger seat of her wrecked Camaro. *Or was he helping me in?*

She studied the photograph, which clearly documented the blood pouring from Becca's mouth down the front of her Princess Leia costume. Noah was wearing a Superman costume complete with a red cape and appeared uninjured.

Again, a note fell out onto the desk as she shook out the contents. Same block letters. This time, a demand. I WANT 15 MILLION TO KEEP QUIET.

She looked at the envelope. Unmarked except for her address at JP. Postmarked in

178

Richmond.

Doesn't reveal much. Most Virginia mail gets sent to Richmond for distribution.

She put the contents back into the envelope, tucked it under her arm, and walked the hallway to the elevator bank that would take her to the executive floor of JP. Once there, she paused at the desk of Arlene, the receptionist. "I need to speak to the big boss." Becca smiled. "It's urgent."

Arlene picked up the phone. She was young thirties, separated from her husband, and rumor had it that she was scoring more than a paycheck from the boss. "Mr. Jackson, Dr. Rebecca Jackson for you." A moment later, Arlene made eye contact. "You can go in."

Becca slipped past her desk and gently knocked as she pushed open the solid oak door. She skipped the salutations and dropped the two manila envelopes onto his desk. "We've got trouble."

"We?" he said after he'd dumped the photos onto his desk and scanned them briefly. He shoved them across his desk. "You maybe, but how am I connected?"

"Whoever is doing this knows you're my only source for this kind of money."

"And why would I bend to this kind of extortion?"

"To protect me." She paused. "To protect your brother."

"He's made his own bed."

"Well, like it or not, you hired me knowing just what we'd covered up." She sat in the low chair across the desk from him. "And JP is about to become very, very wealthy because of me. Think of it as the price you need to pay to keep me from going over to Bradshaw."

He scoffed. "You wouldn't."

"If you hang me out to dry —"

"Don't bluff with me, Becca. What did you find out about their research?"

"That they've made serious headway on a few problems that we've been stuck on for a long, long time. I think Noah Linebrink is right. If we joined with them, we could have a product in place for testing within the year."

James Jackson's eyes lit up. "I need to see details."

"Details I can get." She touched the manila envelope. "For a price."

"I'm calling your father. He stands to be the biggest loser here. He'll be disgraced and lose his bid for Congress."

"I know. But no formal police investigation. I don't want this to get out."

■ ■ ■ ■

That evening, after being dropped back off at her home by the executive limousine, Becca had just given herself an intravenous dose of dexamethasone when she heard the front door open.

"Daddy?"

Only her father entered her house without knocking.

She walked into the kitchen, where he stood glaring at her from the other side of her granite-topped island. "I need to see the photographs."

"Hello to you, too."

He didn't reply. She lifted the two manila envelopes from her satchel and watched as he studied them.

Her father said, "I need to talk to Noah Linebrink."

"He didn't do this."

"Don't be so sure. Am I to believe it's just a coincidence that he comes nosing around here after all these years, trying to find out what you've been up to, and now, at the same time, you get threatened like this?" He grunted. "He just wants to clear his name."

"So why not just tell the truth?"

181

"Because he's trailer-trash born, Becca. It's greed pure and simple. The boy wants revenge."

"Daddy, I think he came around for another reason." She hesitated. "I think he's been holding me in his heart all these years, and he's finally been given an excuse to act on it."

Barry Jackson shook his head. "I can't take any chances." He touched the edge of a photograph. "You know who took these, don't you?"

She nodded. "It's got to be Mel." She touched her father's arm. "But she wouldn't do this either. She's one of the few friends I've got."

"Yeah, well, she's stuck in a small town, a single mother with a dead-end life. Maybe she thinks she deserves better."

"Then everyone's a suspect, because, inside, we all feel that way."

"The suspect list is short." He hooked his thumb into the belt that hung around his generous waist. "I need this to stop now."

"Don't do anything stupid, Daddy. The last op-ed I read said you have a legitimate chance at winning."

"I won't be going anywhere if this gets out."

"So talk Uncle Jimmy into paying the

money. He could do it without flinching."

"Fat chance."

"I basically told him I'd leave the company if he doesn't. I don't think he believed me, but I know he can't afford to lose me."

Her father nodded and offered a thin smile. "That's why he asked me to take care of it."

He walked away, holding the photographs. "I'm keeping these," he said. He paused at the door. "I don't think you need to worry about this anymore."

He exited, shutting the door loudly behind him.

Becca pulled back the curtain and watched him slide into his car. She shook her head slowly. *You saying that is exactly why I'm worried.*

16

The next day after work, Noah hit the pavement for a run. What with all the extra calories he'd consumed lately, and the new prospect of Becca being back in his life, he needed the rhythm of shoes against pavement for a few miles to bring a little balance into his confusion.

He was three miles into his run, in a quiet suburb on the Southside of Richmond, heading down a tree-lined street toward the James River, when he became aware of a white van slowing beside him. The driver's window was rolled down, and a thirtysomething man with long hair looked out from beneath a New York Yankees cap. "Say, buddy, can you help me get to Broad Street?"

Noah slowed but didn't stop jogging forward. "Just go west a few blocks. You can pick up Westover Hills Boulevard. Take a right and go over the river. The road turns into North Boulevard. It will take you to Broad Street."

The guy shook his head and looked at his friend, "You gettin' this?"

"How far is it?" the passenger called out.

The driver stuck a map out the window. "Can you show me?"

Noah stopped running, and the van pulled over. The two men came out of the van and held up the map. Noah reached to point to their current location when a strong hand gripped the back of his neck and shoved him forward. His face slammed into the side of the van.

"I don't have any money on me." Noah grunted. Immediately, he felt sharp pains as the driver punched Noah in the flank.

"We don't want money. We want your co-operation."

Noah twisted his head around to look for help. The street was empty. The closest house was a good one hundred yards away and set back from the road across a large green yard. He tried to memorize features of the faces of the men. Thirties. Sandy hair. Unibrow.

They shoved a picture in front of him. *Amy!* It was a recent photograph. Taken today? She wore makeup, something Kristen would have been unhappy to see. She was carrying a textbook, probably for one of the classes she was taking in summer school to get ahead. The picture appeared to have been taken across from the school as she was about to board a bus.

The man with the hat spoke. "Lay off your demands of Dr. Jackson, or I'm going to have some fun with this one."

Noah shook his head. "I don't know what you're talking about."

"And no police! I know where the girl lives." The man struck him again, this time in the stomach. As Noah was pitching forward from the blow, the man's knee came up to impact his nose. The pain nearly blinded and immobilized him.

He stumbled forward, his hands now lifted to his face. Blood! He looked at his hands. "Really, I have no idea what —"

Noah stopped when he saw the man's raised fist. Then he pretended to stumble again, wobbling forward until he'd stepped away from the duo a few yards, as if about to pass out on the road. Then, with more adrenaline than he'd felt in a long time, he sprinted. Down the road, back the opposite direction. Just then, a car, an SUV, turned a corner and came toward him. Behind him, Noah heard the slamming of the van's doors and the vehicle speeding away.

He must have looked pretty scary, waving his hands like a maniac toward the driver of the minivan, the blood staining the front of his white running shirt.

A young woman slowed, put her hand to her mouth, and sped on, obviously spooked.

With a quick glance over his shoulder to look for the van, Noah took the first right and kept sprinting. At the second house, a two-story brick colonial with white columns, he slowed and jogged up the driveway. When he heard a vehicle coming up the street, he ducked behind the front of a blue Chevy pickup, dropped to his stomach, and watched as the white van inched up the street. When they were just beyond the next house, Noah jumped to his feet and ran through the yard, crossing behind the brick colonial to the yard of a house on a parallel street. He ran past a wooden privacy fence and stopped at a gate. He tried the latch. *Unlocked.*

Quietly, he slipped inside the fence to find himself standing next to an in-ground pool. He saw and heard no one. He sank to his knees, then crawled to the edge of the fence to give his racing heart a chance to recover.

Only after he'd waited thirty minutes, hoping it was long enough for the men in the van to give up the chase, did he dare move again, this time gingerly walking to the edge of the pool, where he lowered his hands to the water to wash his face.

After that, Noah slipped out of the gate and cut across yards, moving from tree to tree and car to car, approaching his house from the rear. He observed the back of his property from the vantage point of his neighbor's tool shed until he was satisfied that he saw no movement.

He dashed into his house and locked all the doors. Then, with trembling fingers, he dialed 911.

Melissa spent the dinner hour serving BBQ ribs to hungry locals. In a corner booth, seated so he could see the front door, was chief of police and Congressional candidate Barry Jackson. It was unusual for him to have stayed so long, but he said he needed to stay in the public eye, and what better place than Mel's BBQ? He said this, of course, while eating his second slice of "homemade" lemon meringue pie.

Melissa rounded the counter, carrying a coffeepot, and filled his mug for the last time. "Denise is going to close up for me, Chief. What do you hear out of Becca? I haven't talked to her since her trip to Kenya."

"I hardly ever see her. She's into her research, you know? Out to save the world."

"I guess."

Melissa set the pot back on the warmer, looked at the slim crowd, and flipped the burner to off. She took off her apron, hung it on a hook on the wall behind the counter, and went to her office to get the lockbox for the cash register. At the door to her office, she paused. Someone had left the door ajar. No one was allowed to be in the office except for her, and she always kept the door shut tight. She pushed open the door and gasped. Her filing cabinet was overturned, with her files of photographs scattered everywhere.

The desktop items had been swept onto the floor. In the center of her desk was a single photograph of her daughter, Tiffany. Melissa had taken it on Tiffany's sixteenth birthday. A red magic marker had been used to draw a circle around Tiffany's face and slash a line through it. Across the bottom of the picture were the words *The girl is ours if you threaten Dr. Jackson again.*

Melissa backed out of her office with her hand over her mouth, then turned and ran back into the dining room and over to the corner booth where Barry Jackson was just standing up. "Chief Jackson," she said, feeling breathless, "I need you to come with me. Someone broke into my office!"

The small town's chief of police followed Melissa back to her office. He pulled the radio from his belt and radioed a deputy to contact a detective from the Rockingham County Sheriff's Department and request a unit that could process fingerprints. He didn't touch the photograph, only moved it slightly with the tip of a pencil. "Do you understand the meaning of this warning?"

Melissa shook her head. "I don't know anything about Dr. Jackson or threats. I presume they are talking about Becca?"

He took her by the elbow and guided her a few steps away from the employees who were trying to see around the partially open door. He looked at one of the waitresses. "Denise, see that no one goes into the office. We need to consider it a crime scene and seal it off for now." He lowered his voice. "Look, Melissa, someone has been sending some old photographs to Becca. I'm pretty sure they are photographs that you took way back in high school. Anyway, someone else must think so too."

"Photographs? Why would I send her photographs?"

"They were photos of her accident." He shrugged. "Not sure what they are trying to prove, but they come with cryptic warnings that the truth, whatever that means, is going to be revealed unless JP pays a huge fee. It's extortion."

"If you thought I took the pictures, why didn't you talk to me?"

"I thought it best if I stayed out of it. She's my daughter. If she decides to get the police involved, it would be best if it wasn't me."

"Well, now I got you involved. And I can tell you, I didn't send Becca any photographs."

"I'm sure the Sheriff's Department will want to ask you some questions." He paused. "Who had access to these photos?"

"Anyone who wanted to come into my office, I guess." She touched Barry's arm and gestured with her head for him to follow. They stepped out of the office and walked through the kitchen into a small alley beside the restaurant. "Okay, tell me what's going on. I know what the pictures of the accident show. I took them." She lowered her voice. "And I think you know what they show as well, and if anyone doesn't want the truth to come out, I suspect it would be you."

He jerked his shoulders back. "I don't know what you're talking about. Just what do these photographs show?"

She shook her head. "A police cover-up?

You tell me."

"I resent your tone, young lady."

"Your deputies let you handle your own daughter's accident investigation, didn't they? I photographed you, too."

"I had nothing to do with threatening your daughter, if that's what you're accusing. And that," he said sternly, "is slander."

"I hope for your sake you didn't. Why would I threaten to show old photographs after all these years?"

"Maybe you just wanted money — I don't know. For most people, greed is the motive."

"Becca is my friend. I wouldn't use her. I kept quiet about the photos because I knew she would be hurt. But sometimes I wish I'd had the guts to tell the truth."

"You've got guts, Melissa. But you're misguided about me. I have no idea what you think your photographs reveal, and my department certainly doesn't have anything to hide."

Melissa didn't want to completely alienate the town's chief of police, but she was pretty sure he was bluffing. He had to have known what really happened the night of the accident. It was just too convenient for him to overlook the evidence staring him in the face.

He hooked his thumb on the edge of his belt. "Who else knew about those pictures of yours?"

She thought for a moment. *Becca. Oh, and I sent them to Mr. Peters after he practically threw Noah out of his son's memorial service.* "Becca knew," she said. Fortunately, she didn't have to say more because Barry's deputy, a young kid by the name of Harvey Downs, stuck his head into the alley, looking for his boss.

"Hey, Chief Jackson, I think you need to see something. That's no magic marker on Tiffany's photograph. It's blood."

Noah spent the best part of an hour explaining everything he could about his assailants to a Richmond PD officer who looked like he spent long hours after his shifts working out in a local gym. The guy was massive and not at all soft. He said, "I think it would be best if your sister and nieces spent some time somewhere other than their home. If these guys are serious, you don't want to take any chances."

"Shouldn't you just watch my sister's house?"

"We can make a few passes through the neighborhood, but we really don't have the manpower for keeping someone outside on the street."

Noah nodded. "I'll make some arrangements."

The officer promised to look into it further, saying he would need to interview Dr. Jackson.

As he left, Noah grabbed his keys and headed for his sister's.

17

Late that evening, Becca reclined at the side of her pool, listening to the sounds of the waterfall and thinking about *the kiss*.

She hadn't shown anyone her face sans lipstick for close to twenty years. And the first time she did, Noah had kissed her.

And apparently enjoyed it. She smiled and raised her finger to her upper lip. As a professional, she'd always thrived on control, but with Noah, she'd allowed herself to be something different, something that made her very afraid. With Noah, she'd been *vulnerable.* The whole thing had been so unexpected, so scary, and yet so wonderful.

I really shouldn't lead him on. He would only get hurt when he learned the truth.

But I can't seem to manage my heart!

Her phone sounded, and she felt her heart quicken as she saw his name on the display. "Hi, Noah."

"Becca, we need to talk."

She was immediately uneasy. *Why do things always have to be so intense with you?* She willed her heart to slow down. "Okay."

"Why didn't you tell me that someone was threatening you?"

"What? Threatening me? What do you know?"

"Not enough. But why don't you tell me why two goons nearly beat me senseless and threatened to harm my niece?"

"Noah, what happened?"

"Exactly what I said. Except that they told me to lay off my demands of Dr. Jackson or they would take it out on Amy. Is that what JP thinks I'm doing by offering you a job? Making demands?"

"No, it's not that, Noah. It's —" Her words stuck in her throat as she began to put together what must have happened. "I think this may be my father's fault."

"What are you talking about?"

"Look, I know this has nothing to do with you. Especially after we . . . well, we . . . were getting along so nicely."

"That's not exactly the vibe you gave me yesterday morning."

She listened as he sighed into the phone. "Look," she said, "I'm not sure what is going on, but let me tell you what I know.

Someone has sent me two envelopes with pictures that Melissa took of our accident. The first one said, 'I know the truth. You will pay.' I wasn't sure what to think of it. A second one came yesterday and said, 'I want 15 million to keep quiet.' "

"I don't get it. Why would you pay —"

"Not me — my uncle. Whoever is threatening me knows my uncle could do this without blinking."

"Okay, so why would your uncle pay such a high fee just to keep someone from showing pictures of our accident?"

"Because he's my family. He won't want to see me or my father hurt. And of course, negative family publicity puts JP in an unfavorable light."

"And how is the truth going to hurt your father?"

She lowered her voice, even though she was alone. "Noah, you know. It's criminal what he did to you."

"Wow," he said. "I'm not sure I expected you to admit it."

"Well, I said it. It's not like he's making an apology."

"So how does your father play into me getting jumped by the goons who threatened my niece?"

"My uncle told him about the threat. I'm

sure it's because he doesn't want to pay, but also because any attention on this now would completely derail my father's run for Congress. My father came over last night and told me he suspected you."

"Me? Why would I threaten you, especially now since, as you say, we were getting along so nicely?"

She could hear the sarcasm in his voice. "Noah, I know you didn't do this."

"So why does your father believe I would?"

"To clear your name in the public eye. So you can walk tall in our community again."

"Little towns have a long memory. I don't think it matters to them what I do now."

"Anyway, my father said he wanted to talk to you. But apparently his definition of talking is a bit different from ours." She listened to what sounded like cicadas singing through the phone. "Where are you, anyway?"

"I convinced Kristen and her girls to come with me to Bradshaw's lake house for a few days. The police didn't think they should stay at home."

"Police?"

"Of course, police. I called the police to report the assault."

Becca cringed. "I had hoped my uncle

would see fit to just keep this under the media radar. If the police get involved, it could get very messy for JP and my father."

"Or are you worried about your own reputation?"

"As I recall, you were the one who made me promise to never tell."

He stayed quiet a moment. "Maybe your uncle is the one who sent the guys to scare me. Maybe it's his way of dealing with the extortion threat."

She thought for a moment. *Could be.*

"Who would be motivated and crazy enough to threaten you?"

"It would have to be someone pretty close to our home community. Not many people know what really happened. A deputy, perhaps?"

"Or maybe your uncle has made an enemy or two, and the information has gotten into their hands somehow. A jilted lover?"

Becca thought about her uncle's receptionist, Arlene. *Could Uncle Jimmy have confided in her and then pushed her away, prompting her to pull a crazy stunt for revenge? Not likely.* "Look, I'm not sure who all the suspects should be or could be. But I'll talk to my father and find out what I can about your situation." She hesitated. "I'm so sorry, Noah. I feel like it's my fault."

"You're pretty good at that, aren't you? Blaming yourself?"

"Shut up," she said playfully. "Your motivations are pretty complex too." *If only you knew.*

Noah had heard that fishing for catfish is most successful between midnight and 2:00 a.m. That's why he had his fishing pole in his hand at twelve-thirty when Melissa Mitchell called.

"Melissa? Is something wrong?" He looked at his watch. "Where are you?"

"I'm at a Hampton Inn in Staunton." Her breathing was heavy against the receiver. "I wasn't sure who to call. Something's happened, and it may involve you."

"Slow down. Tell me what's going on."

"Remember the pictures I took the night of your accident?"

"Of course."

"Someone has been sending them to Becca and asking for money."

"So I hear."

"You know about this?"

"Someone thinks I sent the pictures. Basically got the crap beaten out of me, and they also threatened my niece. I left town to keep Amy safe."

"Wait a minute! Someone is threatening

you? Someone threatened me! They accused me of extorting Becca and threatened my daughter," Mel said.

"So you left town too?"

"I was afraid. The town is small. Whoever it is knows where I live."

"We did the same thing. We're at Smith Mountain Lake. My company has a house here." He paused. "Mel, who could have had access to those pictures?"

"Only a few people knew about them. Becca, of course; you, Becca's dad, Mr. Peters —"

"Wait," he interrupted. "Mr. Peters?"

"Yeah, I sent them to him after the memorial service for Jimmy. I saw how he treated you, so I wanted him to know the truth."

Noah remembered the day well. He'd slipped into the back of the Dayton Methodist Church for the memorial, the first time he'd been back to Dayton in years. But when Mr. Peters saw him, he'd basically thrown him out. He'd asked Noah how he dared set foot in that memorial service when he'd caused all the trouble in the first place. "You didn't need to defend me, Mel."

"Well, you sure weren't!"

He was quiet for a moment. "Well, thanks, I guess. Look, I told Becca about the threat to my niece. She thinks her father might be involved."

"Wouldn't surprise me."

"Look, I feel terrible that you've been involved with all this. Why don't you come down to the lake and stay here for a few days? No one will know where you are, and you won't have to spend money on a motel."

"I could bring barbecue."

He gave her the address to enter into her GPS.

Noah felt a tug on his fishing line. "Bring your swimsuit. Might as well have some fun while you're here."

18

The following day, instead of heading straight to her father's for a face-to-face showdown, Becca kept an appointment with John Harrelson, MD, chief of neurology at the University of Virginia hospital.

Harrelson was probably fifty but looked forty and had the chiseled features of someone comfortable advertising after-shave. He touched the tip of his chin and leaned forward from his chair to talk. "I want to know about subtle changes," he said. "Have you noticed any personality changes? Different desires?"

"Desires?"

"Sex drive, appetite, that sort of thing?"

She thought for a moment. "Not really."

"New focus or concentration? Hallucinations?"

"No for hallucinations, but perhaps yes for new ability to concentrate. I've been working on a problem involving three-dimensional molecular structure for a few years. Predicting how the molecule will react and fold in response to structural bond changes always seemed nearly impossible . . . until recently. It's as if I have this crazy ability to see in three dimensions."

He began typing, looking at a computer screen on a small rolling cart, something she imagined that he wheeled from room to room to interview patients.

"I noticed it for the first time when I was coming home on a flight from Kenya. I was sitting next to a boy playing with one of those Rubik's Cubes. He was stuck, but he let me borrow it, and I could see and understand how twisting the layers would cause a certain square to change position. I solved it in under two minutes."

His eyes lit up. "And you'd never done it before?"

"Never. It was weird. I had a serious migraine attack, so I gave myself Imitrex, and after that I couldn't seem to regain the ability to do the puzzle."

"Any other similar events?"

"A similar pattern with my work. I'll get flashes of near-brilliant insight that will speed along our work significantly, followed by a migraine, and then my insight fades.

It's as if the migraine robs me of my creativity."

"But each time, you take treatment for your migraine?"

"If I didn't, I couldn't function."

He looked at her, slowly nodding, as if having his own flash of insight. Finally, he pulled up the images of her MRI that she had brought along. "Here," he said, pointing to the computer screen, "is an area of neovascularization around the tumor."

"Neo . . ."

"The term means new blood vessels. This tumor is literally bringing along its own new blood supply that is giving extra oxygen to the brain around it, bringing on the enhanced abilities you've been experiencing. And it's not the migraines that shut down your creativity."

"The migraine *always* shuts it down."

"No, the Imitrex does. The Imitrex causes the blood vessels to contract, slowing the blood flow to the areas around the tumor."

"You keep saying *tumor.* Do you mean it's cancer?"

"I can't say that." He leaned forward, assuming again the thoughtful posture with his finger touching his chin. "It is very suspicious. With a biopsy, we'll know what it is and how to treat it."

She sat up straight. "Biopsy? You mean stick some kind of needle probe into my head?"

"You'll be sedated. No worries." He paused. "The thing is, this may not be surgically resectable." He pointed at the MRI again. "It crosses the midline here in a very critical spot."

Translation: I'm hosed.

He nodded thoughtfully. "Yes, I believe a biopsy would be the way to go here."

It's not your brain. "Could you show me how it's done?"

He used a small notepad with a drug insignia that Becca recognized as a competitor. He drew her brain in cross section and then pointed. "I believe the least risky approach is to bring the needle straight in from this angle. It will avoid contact with the motor strip."

"Motor strip?" *Sounds like I have a racetrack in my head.*

"The area of the brain that has to do with movement."

She smiled at the drawing. "Oh, this is nice. Won't you sign your masterpiece for me?" She forced a laugh.

He chuckled back and signed his name under the picture.

"The reaction to the Imitrex is a very good

sign. It means the tumor will likely react to a new chemotherapy regimen that attacks new blood vessel growth."

"How long can I go if I decide not to get treated?"

The finger came off his chin, and his thoughtful expression changed to alarm. "That's not a real option here. This is likely a lethal brain cancer that without treatment could kill."

I'm familiar with the term lethal. "It's my body. It's my choice. Maybe I don't like the idea of someone poking a needle through my brain. Couldn't that cause all these blood vessels around my tumor to bleed?"

"That's certainly a risk." He seemed to hesitate. "But without a sample of tissue showing us the tumor type, the oncology consultants won't know how best to treat it." He stood up. "I'll have my nurse practitioner set up the biopsy," he said, reaching for the door. "Carrie will be in to see you in a minute."

Becca didn't wait. As soon as he left, she lifted a prescription pad from the top of the desk, folded the sketch the neurologist had drawn, and dropped them into her leather satchel.

Then she walked out, passing the receptionist without speaking.

■ ■ ■ ■

Becca spent that afternoon squirreled away in her research laboratory, writing and rewriting an algorithm for the formulation of her artificial hemoglobin. The buzz was on; her brain was tingling and alive and the migraine was certain to follow.

She interrupted her work only twice: once to use the restroom and give herself an injection of steroid, and a second time to call her father.

"Chief Jackson."

She rolled her eyes. *Why does he answer that way when he knows who's calling?* "Daddy, it's me."

"Of course."

"Daddy, what's going on? I've heard from Noah. He tells me that both he and Mel have been threatened because someone seems to think they're the ones behind the photographs."

"Interesting."

"Stop the games, Daddy. You told me you were taking care of this problem. I suppose that means you're the one torturing my friends."

"You said your friends wouldn't extort money from your company."

"So it is you."

"I don't know what you're talking about. Besides, your friends are the ones who should be explaining themselves, not me. They've got access to the photos and the greed to make a buck."

"Daddy, Noah and Melissa don't have anything to do with this!"

"How can you be so sure?"

Becca hesitated. "Call it women's intuition. Listen, you've got to stop harassing them."

"I can't believe you'd accuse me. Your uncle is the one on the string for fifteen million. Maybe he's calling the shots here. Ever think of that?"

"Uncle Jimmy isn't a get-your-hands-dirty kind of guy."

"That's why he'd get someone else to do it for him."

"Talk to him, then. Tell him to back off."

"James isn't likely to pay anyone anything if he has a way of stopping it."

Becca massaged the back of her neck. She needed to get back to work. "So you'll talk to him?"

"It won't do any good. Where is Melissa, anyway? I was by her restaurant, and she was nowhere to be found."

"She's safe."

"Hiding?"

"Afraid." *Afraid of you!*

"You need to tell me where she is. I need to ask her a few questions about the threats."

"And you need to call off the goons who are scaring her."

Becca ended the call and looked back at the papers scattered in front of her. She circled an area of the molecule and then drew an arrow in a counterclockwise circle. *As soon as it gets in the presence of water, it will recoil around this axis.*

Why couldn't I see that before?

The irony wasn't lost on her. The threat to her life was making her smarter.

Amy Rivers stood on the edge of the dock and admired Tiffany Mitchell's skimpy yellow bathing suit. "My mom would never let me wear something like that." She looked down at her own blue one-piece and sighed. "I'm not sure it would stay up on me anyway."

"You could totally pull it off." Tiffany sat down on the dock and let her feet dangle just above the water.

"Do you know what's going on? My mom won't tell me anything. All I know is my uncle Noah comes over, and just like that, we're going on a family vacation. I had to quit my English class and everything."

"You're taking summer school? What happened, did you fail?"

"No," Amy said, shrugging. "I just wanted to get ahead."

"You really don't know what's going on?"

Amy shook her head.

"Someone has been trying to demand a huge amount of money from Becca Jackson, that famous drug doctor, and somehow, they got the idea that it might be Noah or my mom."

"Why would they think that?"

"Because whoever is demanding the money sent photographs that my mom took way back when they were all in high school together. Only a few people knew about these pictures, including Noah and, of course, my mom."

"So why do we get a quick vacation at this lake house?"

"Because some weirdo who thought Noah or my mom did it sent them a warning to stop or else —" Tiffany halted.

"I don't think she needs to hear that just now," Noah said, his voice causing Amy to startle.

"Noah!" Amy screamed and whirled around.

He pointed at a pair of Jet Skis hanging on loading cradles just above the water. "You guys want to ride on a Jet Ski?"

The duo nodded. Noah handed them life jackets, and soon Amy and Tiffany were filling the air over the lake with squeals of excitement.

After twenty minutes, Noah parked the Jet Ski in its docking cradle and walked back up toward the beach house.

Amy watched him disappear into the house. "Okay, now you *have* to tell me what was in the warning to your mom."

Tiffany unzipped her life jacket. "My mother got a warning to stop, and my picture was pulled out of her filing cabinet with a big red circle drawn in blood over it."

"Blood!"

"The police did some tests. Turns out it was pig blood, but still, it was gross." She paused. "And someone sent a warning to Noah with your picture along with it."

"My picture?"

"Noah acts like it's not a real big deal. He told my mom it was just a good idea to stay away a few days."

"Oh wow, that's freaky. Why would anyone think Noah or your mom would do something like threaten that doctor?"

"Tell you the truth, I wouldn't be surprised if it *was* my mom. The way I see it, my mom's been crushing on your uncle, and she sees this Dr. Jackson as competition."

"My mom told me that Noah and the pharmacy doctor were boyfriend and girlfriend back in high school. My mom thinks she's trouble too. She said this girl basically ruined Noah's life and he should stay away from her."

"How'd she ruin his life?"

"Don't know. Mom kind of freaks if I ask too many questions about it."

Becca faced the mirror in her private bathroom just off her office. She was about to freshen her lipstick with Chanel Rouge Allure. She'd even rolled up the stick and brought the luscious color to within a breath of her upper lip when she froze. Then, instead of applying the lip color, she took a facial tissue and began to blot away the lipstick.

Finally, satisfied that she was completely natural, she pushed her lips into a kiss toward the glass. She sniffed, and a tear broke free from the corner of her eye and began a slow trickle toward her upper lip.

She stared at herself and tried to shove

away the companion she'd hidden for so many years: shame.

Why did he have to come back into my life now?

Would he ever believe me if I said I still loved him?

19

The next morning, Becca took out the prescription pad she'd lifted from Dr. Harrelson's office and carefully traced the signature he'd given her on the sketch he'd made to diagram her brain biopsy. She made out three prescriptions: one for Dilantin, an anticonvulsant; one for injectable dexamethasone; and one for syringes and needles.

She drove by the CVS pharmacy in Harrisonburg on her way to work. Handing the prescriptions to the pharmacist, she avoided eye contact until he called her by name.

"Hey, Dr. Jackson, how's the work going on the artificial blood?"

She studied him for a moment without answering.

Fortunately, he continued. "I read the interview they did on you in *Pharmacy Today*." He chuckled. "You know what I did? I went right out and bought Jackson Pharmaceuticals stock."

"Wow," she said, smiling. *You shouldn't have done that.*

He studied the prescriptions for a moment, frowning.

Uh-oh.

He shook his head and lowered his voice. "You okay, Dr. Jackson?"

She offered a plastic smile. "That's between me and my doctor, isn't it?"

He nodded, and a tinge of redness colored his neck. "Of course. I'll get right on this."

"I'll wait."

Melissa could tell by Noah's tone of voice that he was talking to Becca. His face had lit up when he saw who was calling, and he walked away from her in the kitchen, holding his cell up to his ear. "Hey, what's up?"

She listened, walking closer to the open living area where she could hear him — and watch him as he stood at the back of the house, where a massive wall of windows overlooked Smith Mountain Lake.

"Today?" He looked at his watch. "I could do that." He paused. "Look, this will take time. I'm not sure they'll let me take it out of the lab."

When he ended the call, she slipped back into the kitchen and picked up a spoon.

"Hey, Mel, I need to run into Richmond."

"I was planning a special dinner." She held up a dripping red spoon. "Ribs with my secret sauce."

He looked at his watch. "I'll come back. Save me some?"

She nodded. "Be careful."

He squinted at her.

"I know it was Becca." She touched his arm. "Hasn't she done enough damage to your life?"

"This is business, Mel. Nothing more."

But his voice on the phone had betrayed him. And so did his face as he looked away from her gaze.

Becca selected a tube of Estée Lauder Crystal Nude and applied it without thinking, guiding the color as she had a thousand times, a mechanical memory taking over when her thoughts were focused elsewhere. She smiled at the mirror. The color was the perfect blend of pink and beige to match the blouse she'd selected. Today was not a day for vulnerability and exposure. Today was about solidifying a chance to move forward toward a medical advance so significant that her place in history would never be forgotten.

My shame will be gone.

She'd chosen a blouse with sleeves that fell just below the elbow — important today, since the bruising inside her elbow might attract unwanted eyes or questions.

Becca lifted her sleeve but couldn't keep it up while managing the tourniquet, so she shed the blouse and sat on the commode in her underwear. She took a stretchy latex glove and pulled it tight around her left upper arm, fashioning a single throw of a knot. She swabbed her elbow with alcohol and jabbed the tip of a needle into the blue vein that ran just beneath the skin's surface. Slowly, she emptied the vial of steroid into her arm.

She was becoming somewhat of an expert; she'd upgraded to two to three times a day in an attempt to avoid the headache and press forward in her work without distraction. She slipped back into the blouse and pulled a brush through her hair. Today's humidity would threaten her hair with frizz, but thankfully, she planned to spend the day mostly inside. She looked down, sensing wetness on her arm. A small drop of blood was oozing from her latest venipuncture site. She chided herself for her carelessness. *I must hold pressure longer. I can't risk causing a bleed that will make me have to look for another vein.*

She gathered her things, carefully placing another vial and syringe into a ziplock bag and putting it into the front pocket of her satchel. Then, after a quick check in the full-length mirror in the foyer, she went to the garage, where she kept her BMW 328i xDrive Coupe. She'd selected the all-wheel-drive vehicle to handle the occasional snow in the Shenandoah Valley and had gone with the deep-sea-blue metallic upgrade for the paint.

She nestled into the driver's seat and inhaled the scent of leather. Beside her, on the passenger seat, was a bendable model of a hemoglobin molecule. Once she was on the interstate, she would lift the molecule momentarily in front of her, then lower it and practice visualizing it from all angles as she turned it in her mind. Before backing out of the garage, she lifted it, closed her eyes, smiled, and placed it beside her again.

Noah arrived at Bradshaw Pharmaceuticals and handed the security guard at the first gate a paper listing an approved visitor: Rebecca Jackson, PhD.

The guard nodded and waved Noah in.

Forty-five minutes later, Becca was ushered into his office. She looked fantastic and was back to her perfectly made-up self, every flaw corrected and every blemish covered.

He stood as she entered. "Hi," he said. "Have a seat."

"Thanks. It's good to finally be here. Let's hope it goes better than our last meeting."

"How are you?"

"I'm fine. Seems that stress may aggravate the migraines a bit, so my doctor has me on a special regimen to keep them at bay."

He nodded and joked, "So you're here to steal all my secrets."

"I need to see if coming over to Bradshaw is worth my time." She paused. "But there may be another way forward."

"Another way?"

"Perhaps JP and Bradshaw could join hands in a collaborative effort to solve this problem once and for all."

"Cooperate with the competition? That doesn't sound like James Jackson."

"He's aging. I think he'll warm to the idea."

"You haven't told him."

"I've worked with him long enough to know just how he operates. He's got to see it financially as a gain. If I can show him how much sooner we can bring a successful artificial blood to the market by working with you, he'll see it in terms of dollars."

"But will he want to share?"

She smiled. "Leave that to me." Her eyes seemed to dance around his office, taking everything in. "If he won't cooperate, I can always jump ship and work for you."

"You know," he said, staring at her perfect lips, "I can't get our kiss out of my mind."

She straightened. "I'm here to talk about a fluid that can deliver oxygen, not us."

"I know, but I need you to know how crazy this has been for me, seeing you again after all this time." He paused. "And the other night, by the pool . . . well, that was the first time you showed me that the old Becca was still alive."

"The old Becca?"

"The one I loved. Not this perfect version you show everyone now."

"I've grown up, Noah. Change happens."

"I'm just saying I liked what I saw. You. Uncovered."

She shifted in her seat. "Why don't you show me how you've managed to make a hydrogel sphere with an adjustable micropore size to allow hemoglobin to be trapped inside."

All business, is it? You let down for a moment, but what's it going to take to find my way back into your heart? He sighed, resigned to talk about research. He entered a

221

series of keystrokes to open a file called "PRINT Data." While looking at the screen and keeping it tilted away from Becca he said, "Basically, we've created the artificial red cell in an acid environment, and the micropores are sensitive to pH. When the pores are infused into serum with a pH of human blood, the pores close. The only things that pass easily at normal human pH are oxygen and carbon dioxide."

"And the hemoglobin is trapped."

"Exactly."

Becca nodded. "But we'll have to get the artificial hemoglobin into the microspheres while the pores are open, and thus the hemoglobin is going to be exposed to an acid environment. That might be another roadblock. My hemoglobin may not be acid stable."

"So we'll have to test it and change it if necessary." He tapped his thigh with a ballpoint pen. "But maybe, as soon as the hemoglobin molecule is back in normal pH again, it will revert to normal structure."

"Could be." She leaned forward. He edged the screen away from her. "I'd like to see the lab, if I may."

They stood and walked into the hall. When they were joined by an escort, Becca stopped. "Could I just use the restroom to freshen up?"

Noah pointed back to his office. "The oak door in the corner of the office. It's my private one."

Becca slipped back into the office, consciously pushing the door almost closed to block the view. Quickly, she inserted a flash drive into Noah's computer and dragged the "PRINT Data" file onto the stick. In twenty seconds, she was done and entering the bathroom.

There, she took a Dilantin tablet and four ibuprofen, freshened her Crystal Nude lipstick, and took a deep breath. *I can do this.*

Smiling, she exited the bathroom, carrying her satchel over her shoulder.

When Becca got back to Jackson Pharmaceuticals, she went straight to the executive offices. Arlene's chair was empty, so Becca went to the door of the CEO and pushed it open without knocking.

Arlene was sitting on the arm of a padded leather chair occupied by her uncle James. Apparently they were enjoying a drink.

James looked up. "Ah, my scout returns. We should have held off our celebration to hear of your conquests." He lifted his hand from Arlene's thigh and smiled. "Care for a Scotch?"

Becca shook her head.

"Are you sure? This is 1949 Macallan, a single single, the rarest of all."

Becca stared at the four-thousand-dollar bottle. Something had to be up for her uncle to break out his rare collection. "What are you celebrating?"

"Your father tells me that the little menace photographers have been sufficiently scared." He lifted his glass. "He may have just saved me fifteen million."

It was my father. Figures. She pulled a sheet of paper out of her satchel. "On the contrary," she said. "I picked up my mail from my desk on the way up."

The letter detailed the transfer of funds to an offshore account set up in Rebecca Jackson's name in the Bahamas.

James straightened and patted the backside of his receptionist to shoo her off of his chair.

"Let me see that." He read and cursed. "Why would they want your name on the account?"

"Perhaps they think I'm more likely to pay the bribe. It's only the first step in a series of transfers."

"I'm sure." He cursed again.

Arlene was reaching for the Scotch when James put his hand on the top of the bottle. "Celebration's over," he said.

Arlene frowned. Perfect pouty lips. Becca stared at her for a second, wondering what lipstick she was using. *I think it's Wet n Wild. I've seen it for $1.50 at Walmart.*

"So," James began, "the photo pushers weren't scared off as easily as we thought."

"Or maybe it's not the ones you think." She stepped forward. "It's not Noah. I know him. And it doesn't make sense that Melissa would be doing this. Why would she sit on this for twenty years and just spring it on us now?"

"Because of your memoir, silly. You told the story the way the media did nearly a generation ago, and picked an old scab, that's all."

"If Noah thinks you're behind this, he'll never agree to a collaborative research effort —"

"Who is talking collaboration? I want JP to bring this product to market by ourselves."

Becca shook her head and lifted her uncle's glass from the corner of his desk and sniffed. *Wow. That smells potent.* "I've seen what Bradshaw is doing. I know if we could come to an agreement, we could be a year faster in bringing our product into phase-three human trials." She set the glass down again. "A year quicker to market could easily mean an extra twenty billion is worldwide sales. Certainly that's enough to go around."

"Exactly my reason for not wanting to share. The larger the sum, the bigger the half we would be giving away."

"Think of the thousands of lives that could be helped if we did this a little sooner."

"Think of JP's stock price if we did this alone."

Arlene walked around behind the boss and began to gently massage his shoulders. James closed his eyes and let out a small moan.

You two certainly aren't making this subtle. Becca lifted the piece of paper and stepped toward the door. *Get a room.* "I'm going to open a bank account."

"You'll do nothing of the sort."

"It needs to look like I'm cooperating."

She glanced back at her uncle, who had pulled Arlene's hand to his chest, forcing her to lean against him even closer.

Becca shook her head, as if trying to dislodge the image. She shivered and visual-

ized the quaternary structure of hemoglobin.

Maybe I should invite Aunt Trish up to her husband's office to see what she thinks of his skanky secretary.

20

Barry Jackson stopped at the electronic gate in front of his brother's hilltop mansion south of Mount Crawford, Virginia, and stared at the security camera. He despised his brother's wealth and was more than a little irritated that he had to be screened like this to get in. "It's Barry," he said, leaning his head out of the police department's SUV. "Buzz me in."

The gate slid open, allowing him to drive through onto the winding lane bordered by Bloodgood Japanese maple trees. His brother had them brought in and planted nearly fully grown and had selected them because their name reminded him of his quest for pharmaceutical glory.

As Barry rounded the final curve, the house came into view, a stately home of stone, white siding, and more porch and deck space than Barry's entire house.

Trish, his sister-in-law, met him at the

door and handed him a cold imported beer. Barry's taste was uncomplicated, unlike his brother's, and Trish had rightly suspected that Barry might need something to take the edge off. He sat in the den, a room with a two-story-high stone fireplace, and waited.

A few minutes later James arrived, swirling a glass of some sort of golden liquid. He didn't say hello. "I thought we had our little problem taken care of."

"Perhaps we've misjudged our foe."

"Or maybe you haven't figured out just who is opposing us."

"I went after the likely suspects. Who else could it be?"

James lowered his voice and spoke over his single-malt Scotch. "I think Trish may have suspicions about my affectionate secretary."

"You think that Trish —"

"Keep your voice down," he whispered. "I don't know what I think."

Barry smiled at his rich brother's discomfort. "What've you been up to, Jimmy? Has Trish gotten wind of —"

"She should be grateful," he said, looking around his brother toward the kitchen. "Look at how well I've taken care of her all these years. Crazy woman has more shoes than a Kentucky flea market."

Barry chuckled. "You shouldn't worry about Trish. She's a good woman."

James didn't say anything. He just sat on a leather couch and stared into his drink.

Finally, when the glass was empty, he put it on a leather coaster. "Maybe I should just call their bluff. Why should I care if anyone shows those pictures to the media? What's that to me?"

"James, it would ruin me."

"You'd just look like you believed your deputies. A mistake, that's all. People can forgive."

"I'd look like I covered it up to protect my daughter." Barry pointed a meaty finger at his brother's face. "Try and put your family first for once. I'm finally on track to do something significant, and the rug could come out from under me at any time."

"Maybe I'm a little tired of keeping the family propped up."

"Becca will run away from JP if you do this."

"She signed contracts that forbid her from taking our information elsewhere."

"You know Becca. She's out to save the world, and you won't likely stop her. She'll take the information across the world to India or Africa if she has to. You'll be so tied up in international courts that you

won't see a dollar return on your investment for years."

"And you know this how?"

"Because she's always been that way. Guilt
makes her want this so badly that she won't
stop just because she's not working for you."

"So what do you propose?"

"Make this go away. Pay the stupid fee."

James coughed. "This is probably only the
beginning. I'd be a fool to pay it. It would
only be the start of something very bad."

"I'll need an infusion if I'm going to keep
digging."

James lifted his checkbook from his jacket
pocket. "I hope I don't regret this."

Barry laughed and set the beer bottle on
the table, intentionally avoiding the coaster.
"What's a few grand if you save fifteen mil?"

Tiffany heard the familiar ringtone of her
mother's phone when she was changing out
of her bathing suit. "Mom, your phone!"

But her mother didn't hear. Tiffany picked
up the phone as she squinted out over the
back deck to see her mother sunbathing on
the dock. Tiffany pressed a green button
and answered the call. "Hello."

"Melissa, 'bout time you answered me."

"This is Tiffany, her daughter."

"Oh, Tiffany, so glad to hear you. Are you

safe? This is Chief Jackson."

"Yeah, we're safe. We came down to Smith Mountain Lake to be with Mr. Linebrink and his sister's family."

"Smith Mountain Lake?"

"Yeah, it belongs to Bradshaw Pharmaceuticals. It's like a mansion. We all have separate bedrooms. It's amazing."

"Wow. Good to know you're safe. Say, I was just checking in, for security's sake. I've been handling investigative work here in Dayton, trying to figure out who might have messed up your mom's office. It's important for me to keep tabs on you guys. Do you happen to have an address there?"

"I think I saw one on some mail in the kitchen," she said, walking across the massive great room. "Yeah, here it is," she said, picking up an envelope. "1230 Huron Drive. I'm pretty sure we'll be here a few more days. Mom's starting to get the rhythm of this place."

"Okay, be sure to notify me if things change. I'll be in touch."

The phone call ended, and Tiffany went back to changing.

Amy was staring at herself in the hall mirror. "Can you show me how you did your mascara?"

■ ■ ■ ■

That evening, Becca loosened the tourniquet on her arm and held pressure on a gauze while staring at her computer screen.

A moment later, her doorbell sounded. She glanced out the front room window to see Noah's Lexus. She gasped and ran toward the kitchen. She grabbed the flash drive from the side port of her MacBook and shoved it into the front pocket of her jeans. Then she swept the evidence of her drug abuse into a kitchen drawer under the island, pulled down the sleeve of her blouse, and walked to the foyer. She checked her lipstick in the mirror before opening the door.

Noah stood there holding a Bob-A-Rea's pizza box and a bottle of wine. "I seem to remember you had a penchant for sausage and mushroom," he said. He raised the bottle. "And cheap wine."

She smiled. *Goofy Noah.* "Uh, that was like twenty years ago."

"Yes, but under all of your newly acquired sophistication, I'm sure we can find that girl again."

She shook her head. "You've made a long trip. Might as well come in."

"I was heading back to the lake house when I thought about how full of estrogen that place was going to be, and my Lexus just pointed me back to your place."

"And you thought this would be better. There's plenty of estrogen here."

"You refused to talk about us this morning. Dr. Jackson, pharmacology researcher extraordinaire, all business and no play." He held up the pizza box. "So I came to discover the Becca I once knew."

She felt her resistance weakening. Noah could be so persistent!

She set two plates on the island and handed him a corkscrew. "At least you didn't bring a screw-cap bottle."

"I almost did. But I couldn't find anything strawberry flavored."

"I was a lightweight. What can I say?"

They sat and ate. She found herself surprisingly hungry. *Maybe it's the steroids. I'm probably going to end up packing on a few pounds if I'm not careful.*

"I talked to my uncle. He pretty much confirmed my suspicions that he and my dad were responsible for scaring you and Mel." She sipped at her wine. "I think I convinced them that it wasn't you."

He smiled. "How can you be so sure? Maybe I'm here to convince you I'm a great guy so you won't think it's me. Then you'll give me your money, and I'll disappear."

"Just like you did the last twenty years?"

"Ouch."

"I'm kidding." She hesitated and looked in his eyes. "I know why you stayed away. I don't blame you."

He lifted another slice of pizza. "Just like I remembered it. Do you ever think about the Bridgewater Parade?"

"I remember you on that stupid farm wagon, wearing your football jersey and throwing candy to the kids like you were making touchdown passes."

"And you refused to put on a cheerleader uniform and stand up there with me."

"I wasn't a cheerleader." She sighed. "I wasn't even your type. I was a library geek."

"A very pretty one." He smiled. "Besides, what do you mean, my type? I wasn't a stupid jock. You convinced me of that."

"Why did you ever go after someone like me?"

He leaned across the island and took her hand. "I could see what everyone else was missing. You were hiding beneath your brains, intimidating everyone from getting close to you. But I could see who you really were."

She sniffed. "You're doing fine. Go on."

235

"You cared about me. You didn't care that my father was the school janitor or that your uncle was a kazillionaire. You didn't judge me the way the other girls did." He laughed. "They just wanted to hang onto my guns." He flexed his biceps in an exaggerated Atlas pose.

"Yeah, well, I'm afraid that girl is long gone."

"Maybe not. Maybe you've just been covering her up."

"Maybe I cover up what I don't want others to see." *I'm ashamed.* She brushed the corner of her eye with the back of her hand.

"But, Becca, you're beautiful. You always have been."

She sniffed again. "I'm not talking about all this," she said, gesturing her hands across her chest and face.

"Help me understand why you can't seem to see that I'm not talking about the outside package."

She followed his eyes to a small basket on the island where she kept a spare tube of lipstick. It was one of her favorites, the one she'd worn in Kenya for the filming of her advertisement: L'Absolu Rouge by Lancôme Paris. She always had a spare tube close by. He lifted it and shook his head slowly. "You don't need this to look good to me. Why can't you believe that?"

She stood up and took his face in her hands, then lowered her face to his and kissed him. Gently at first, and then with a growing passion. When she pulled away, she was aware of her need for breath. She blinked away a tear. "Because you don't really know me anymore, Noah." She carried her glass to the sink. "And maybe that's best for now."

By the time Noah slipped in the front door of the lake house, it was just after 1:00 a.m. The house was dark. As he tiptoed across the great room, he heard a voice. Mel.

"Hey, stranger. Who's coming in so late?"

"Hey, Mel, you didn't need to stay up."

"I figured you got caught up at work. I saved you some barbecue."

"It's late."

"Never too late for my secret sauce," she said. "I've got it on a warmer."

Noah felt bad. He wasn't hungry, but he wasn't about to fess up to having gone all the way back to Dayton to see Becca. He touched his lips in the dark room and hoped he didn't still have the evidence of her lipsticked kiss. As he walked behind Mel, he wiped his mouth with his hand.

She fixed him a plate of ribs with sauce

and placed a buttered biscuit beside it.

"Wow," he said, about to dig in.

"Hold on, cowboy. It's time to pray."

He bowed his head, his conscience stabbing him. *This is what I should have been doing ever since all this craziness with Becca started.*

Mel began with her voice just above a whisper. "Dear Father, thanks for the way You provide and care for us. Thanks for the opportunity You've given me to renew an old friendship. We commit this situation into Your hands and ask that Your perfect love would cast out our fear. Keep us from harm. We do not deserve Your grace, but we are grateful for it. Protect Noah. Guard his heart. Bless his research. Thanks now for this food. Amen."

He didn't realize he'd been gripping her hand until she asked him to let it go.

He winced. "Sorry." He hesitated. "Thanks, Mel. I think I've been missing that. I mean, I pray and all, but things have gotten crazy and I feel a little out of touch."

"Eat up, your ribs will get cold."

He ate despite not being hungry. The food was good — delicious, in fact. Mel's BBQ place in Dayton had been a landmark for a decade because she seemed to have found just the right balance between tangy and spicy. He looked up, and she was smiling. "This is awesome."

She yawned. "It was a good day. The girls are getting along. Tiffany treats Amy like a little sister."

"I hope better than Amy treats *her* little sisters."

"Her time will come. It usually starts when the younger ones want advice about boys. Then the bonding just happens."

He nodded and wiped his mouth with a paper napkin.

"How'd it go with Becca today?"

"I think okay," he said, unsure why he felt so guarded about talking about her to Mel. "She wants our companies to collaborate on a project. You know Becca, all business."

"I know she's been working on something for a long, long time."

"An artificial blood."

"Just like you?"

You remembered. He thought about the cute twist in her expression when he'd mentioned it at Texas Roadhouse. "Well, kind of like me. We've been working on different aspects of the project."

Melissa sighed and leaned her elbows on the table and set her chin in her hands. She didn't wear an ounce of makeup. She was the antithesis of Becca. Mel was comfort-

239

able just being Mel. The absence of lipstick didn't make her one bit less attractive to Noah.

He finished his ribs and rinsed his plate in the sink.

"Thanks, Mel. You really shouldn't have stayed up for me."

"I wanted to."

She put the rest of a saucepan's contents into a Tupperware and opened the refrigerator. "Hey," she said, offering him a slight smile, "do you think it's true?"

He walked forward to see what she was talking about. She held a little refrigerator magnet that said, "Kiss the cook. I kiss better than I cook."

"Oh wow," he said. "The ribs were past amazing, so I figure you'd have to be an exceptional kisser."

She stepped back playfully. "Well, Mr. I've-found-my-old-high-school-sweetheart, you may never know."

Noah laughed it off and turned. As he walked down the hall, he thought about the two women who'd returned to his life.

Becca is beautiful, smart, and just opening to grace.

But Melissa . . .

He stopped, shaking his head. *No, my life*

240

is too complicated with Becca to allow myself to consider another wonderful woman.

21

Noah lay down to sleep while his thoughts battled between two women. There was Becca, his first real love, now solidly at the center of his professional life and teasingly at the edge of his social one. And then there was Melissa, an old friend as well, solid as a counselor so many years ago and now revealing herself to be a woman of real depth and passion.

It was the unpredictable versus the reliable. Guarded versus open and comfortable. Door number one or door number two. A hint of excitement stood waiting behind either. Becca seemed uneasy letting down her guard, but when she allowed herself to be vulnerable, she was irresistible. Mel let everything show, and her innocence was charming. Becca was beauty beneath a veneer of guilt; Mel was incapable of veneer.

He tossed, his sleep fitful despite the late hour.

Becca. I know the girl I loved is still there.
Melissa. Who could have predicted that you would catch my eye . . . and heart?

Becca was up early, memorizing Noah's protocol, her mind almost numb with the speed of her understanding.

If this is deadly, why does it feel like such a gift?

She debated her drug schedule, then decided to take the extra time to give herself a fifty-milliliter infusion of Mannitol, a powerful diuretic that would reduce the edema in her brain. She started by inserting a small cannula, a clumsy maneuver since she had to do it one-handed into her other arm, and then plugged in the Mannitol drip.

She planned to go straight to work, but the Mannitol hit too quickly. She spent the next hour urinating every five minutes until the diuresis slowed.

So she waited until she could safely leave her bathroom, gave herself a dexamethasone injection, glided on a workday lipstick known as Meltdown, and headed to work in the BMW.

At work, she handed David Letchford a printout of a new PRINT protocol. "Give this to the guys working on the micro gel spheres."

"Don't tell me," he said, eyes rolling. "You had another stroke of genius."

"No, I stole it." She laughed.

He didn't laugh with her — just plodded down the hall toward their PRINT lab.

In her office, she drew two graphs. One predicted her likely life expectancy, the other the time until the artificial blood could be completed. The odds didn't look good.

Perhaps I could prescribe some chemotherapy that might slow the tumor. I could end up a winner.

But that might destroy my ability to complete the project.

Then everyone would end up a loser.

She leaned forward, noting for the first time that her head felt physically fuller when she leaned forward. *Weird. I'll have to elevate the head of my bed on some bricks. Gravity might help the swelling.*

Unbidden and unexpected, thoughts about Noah washed through her mind. *What a sweet guy.*

She made up a wish list. *Solve my research problem. Get treatment. Fall in love. Live happily ever after.*

Is that possible after all I've done?

Can I ever make it up to Noah?

■ ■ ■ ■

Noah rose early, taking his coffee and his Bible to the deck overlooking the lake.

At eight, he looked up as Mel stepped through the doorway. "You're up early," she said.

"Needed a little time alone." He lifted his Bible. "The way you prayed last night — well, it reminded me of priorities. I've been letting some things slip."

"Your father always had a verse for me. Every day at school. He'd come in, sit next to me in study hall, and quote me some encouragement."

"Sounds like my dad."

She sat down on a wicker chair and cradled a mug of coffee with both hands.

"I really need to go back to my lab today," he said.

She looked disappointed.

"I won't be so late."

"Pressing deadline?"

"It's this deal with Becca. It's like she wants everything wrapped up in a month."

"Is it possible?"

"We should be able to push the FDA into letting us do human trials sooner than we ever thought possible, if JP is as far along as they claim."

"You think Becca might be using you?"

He hesitated. "I don't think so." He looked out over the lake. "I sure hope not."

He stood and touched her shoulder as he passed, giving it a little squeeze. She put her hand on top of his. "See you for supper."

He smiled. "You know, I heard you were a great cook."

The corners of her mouth turned up ever so slightly. "Among other things."

He laughed as he went back inside to prepare for his day.

Around ten, Tiffany and Amy grew bored of lying out on the dock.

Amy looked over at Tiff. "I had to read a stupid play in school last year. It was called *The Matchmaker* by Thornton Wilder."

Tiffany gave her a look like she was being bored to tears.

"Anyway, there were these two goofy guys who had a code word they would say if they ever had an adventure."

"So? What was it?"

"Pudding."

"That's stupid. Why would you say *pudding* if you were having an adventure?"

"That's why it was funny. It was just their

code word so they would know that they were having a real adventure."

Tiffany poked her new young friend and whispered. "Let's take out a Jet Ski."

"You don't have a license."

"I know how to drive it. I watched Noah. It's not hard. We'll wear life vests, and no one will stop us." She hopped up.

Amy watched in disbelief. "But what if Mom —"

"They went to the store. We'll be careful."

Tiffany lifted a key from a hook inside a small supply shed at the dock's edge. "It's got, like, an attachment that I wear on my wrist. That way, if I fall off, it shuts off."

Amy shook her head. "Wonderful."

Tiffany positioned herself on the seat of the Jet Ski where it was still suspended on a cradle above the water. She pointed at a switch on a pole.

"Flip that," she said. "It will lower the cradle and allow the Jet Ski to float off."

Amy obeyed. In minutes, the craft was floating.

"Hand me a life jacket," Tiffany said.

The girls donned their jackets.

"Well," Tiffany said, "coming?"

Amy climbed on behind her as Tiffany started the Jet Ski. Tiffany shifted into reverse and backed out into the little cove.

"See? Easy."

They managed to turn around. Tiffany pressed the throttle with her thumb, and the duo sprinted out of the cove.

Amy yelled in Tiffany's ear. "This is crazy!"

"I know!" She laughed. "Awesome crazy!"

Amy screamed, "Pudding!"

After a few minutes, a ski boat with two very tan smiling young men pulled beside them.

Tiffany giggled and offered a little wave.

By the time Noah got to the office, he had two emails from Becca. In the first, she outlined the possibility of a collaborative effort between Jackson and Bradshaw to manufacture artificial blood.

Whoa. This is moving fast. I'll have to run this by the management team.

In the second email, Becca had produced a production chart for creation of artificial blood. It began by detailing the steps in the production of a modified hemoglobin by a special strain of E. coli bacteria engineered by JP and modified according to the protocol that Becca had personally overseen. As he read the steps, he shook his head, amazed.

She's telling me everything. She gives me

the entire process.

That's either really stupid or trusting.

He shrugged. *She trusts me.*

He read further. In the later stages of the protocol, she described the use of PRINT technology to create hydrogel microspheres that would act as the artificial red blood cells. Everything he read looked familiar.

This is my work! he thought with a shock.

He read further.

How did she get this?

And if she has it, why is she showing me that she has it?

The reality dawned hard and fast. *Jackson Pharmaceuticals can do this without Bradshaw.*

He picked up his smartphone and dialed Becca.

"Finally," she said. "It took you long enough to look at your emails."

"You took my work."

"Can I help it if I have a photographic memory?"

"I didn't show it to you."

"I saw your computer screen. Besides," she added playfully, "I'm suggesting we put our protocols together. I showed you my work too."

He sighed. She had done that. "I need to talk to my boss. He'll have to approve any collaboration." He drummed his fingers on the desktop. "Becca, your work looks amazing, but honestly, what's the rush?"

She laughed. "Eat, work, and be merry, Noah."

He frowned into the phone. *What — "for tomorrow we die"?* "Okay," he said, "I'll run the possibility of a deal by my CEO and our management team. Does this mean that your uncle is on board?"

"I'm taking care of James," she said. "No need to worry. Look, I'm giving the new hemoglobin synthesis program to my guys this afternoon. I need a few more steps to get it to fold just right."

"Okay, let me know how it goes."

"Okay," she said. "Love you for your brains."

The line went dead.

He stared at the phone. He hadn't heard her say that for twenty years, and he wasn't quite ready for his own reaction. He wiped away a tear. *Love you for your looks.*

Tiffany let the Jet Ski coast up to the dock of their two new friends, Dustin and Mark.

"Here," Mark said, reaching out to guide the Jet Ski to a stop. Tiffany and Amy got off and stood on the dock, watching as he covered their Jet Ski with a tarp. "No use letting it get too hot in the sun," he said. "Now, we'll show you what a real ski boat is like."

Amy followed Tiffany as they boarded the boys' boat. "Is this yours?"

"Belongs to my dad," Dustin said, shaking the water from his curly blond hair. "But my parents are working, so Mark and I just came down to crash for a few days. My dad doesn't mind if we use it."

Tiffany smiled. "This is so cool."

Amy watched as Dustin's eyes traveled over Tiffany's yellow bikini. She looked at her own one-piece suit and wished she had something that would make Mark look at her like that.

"Are you guys down here a lot?" Mark smiled at Amy.

"First time. We're staying at a place owned by a drug company or something."

"Hang on," Dustin yelled. In seconds, they were racing out in open water. Amy sat on a cushioned bench seat at the back of the boat. Dustin looked at Tiffany and motioned for her to come over to his lap. "Come on," he said. "I'll teach you to drive."

Mark sat next to Amy. "Cold?"

"Just the wind," she yelled.

In a moment, Mark had draped a large

251

beach towel *around them both.* She could feel his muscled arm pressing against her shoulder. She tried to swallow, but her mouth was dry. His legs were hairy and felt scratchy as they huddled together.

Mark leaned forward and opened a cooler. "Want a beer?" He looked at her and squinted. "Just how old are you?"

Amy took a deep breath and held out her hand. "How old do you think I am?"

He shrugged and smiled. A row of perfect teeth. "Old enough."

Melissa led Kristen and her two youngest daughters, Caroline and Lizzy, into the kitchen with the spoils from their grocery shopping. "Just put that stuff in the fridge," she said to the girls.

Kristen pulled a bottle of wine out of a bag. "When did you sneak this in?"

Mel smiled. "A good white will go well with the salmon." She squinted out the back toward the dock. Not seeing Tiffany, she called out, "Tiffany, we're back."

Kristen put a box of granola into the cupboard. "Amy has probably roped her into showing her makeup tips. I swear, that girl is thirteen going on twenty-one." She shook her head. "Last week, I caught her texting our paperboy. The guy's sixteen."

Melissa walked toward the bedrooms off the great room. "Tiffany?"

She checked four bedrooms and the bathroom and came back outside. "Maybe they're downstairs. Maybe they figured out how to operate that calf massager."

Kristen disappeared down the stairs. "Amy?"

A few moments later, Melissa heard her footsteps coming back up the wooden stairs. "Nothing. They must be down at the dock."

Melissa walked out the back onto the deck and called, "Tiffany!"

She walked down the sloped yard to the covered dock. No Tiffany.

One of the Jet Skis was gone.

She jogged back up to the house. "Kristen, a Jet Ski is missing."

"Does Tiffany even know how to drive one of those things?"

Melissa held up her hands. "Oh, this is just like her. Noah probably showed her yesterday morning, and now she thinks she can just take it out."

"What do we do now?"

"Nothing much we can do, unless the girls have their phones."

Kristen punched a number and the send button and held her phone up to her ear.

Melissa frowned. "I hear it in the bedroom. Let me try Tiff."

Fifteen seconds later, they heard another ringtone coming from the bedroom.

Melissa headed for her bedroom. "I'm going to put on my bathing suit and wait at the dock." She shook her head. *God, how can I love my daughter and want to kill her at the same time?*

Forty-five minutes later, Noah's cell phone sounded. He looked at the display. *Kristen.*

"Hi, sis."

"Noah, Amy and Tiffany took off on a Jet Ski."

"Uh-oh."

"You showed Tiffany how to drive, didn't you?"

"I was *with* her. I thought it'd be fun. I didn't tell her she could take it out without me."

"They've been gone an hour or more. Melissa and I were shopping, and when we got home, the girls were gone."

Noah rubbed the back of his neck. "They're probably out just beyond the cove. That was all I showed them yesterday. I'm sure they'll be back soon." He paused, moving a few papers from his desk into a briefcase and picking up his car keys. "Call me as soon as they get back, okay?"

"Sure."

Time to head back to Smith Mountain Lake.

Stupid girls.

22

Becca sat at her desk, staring at her laptop screen. David Letchford sat in a chair opposite the desk, yawning.

"Am I boring you, David?"

He stretched. "It's just our crazy schedule these past few weeks. I had the technicians here until midnight last night."

James Jackson appeared in her open doorway.

"Hi, boss," Becca said. "Weekly walkthrough?"

He nodded. "Got to keep my crew motivated. I need them to know I care."

Wow, what a load of . . . She interrupted her own thought, remembering something she wanted to tell him. "Hey, a new study just came out in the *Journal of the American Medical Association.* It claims that the costs of blood transfusion have been vastly underestimated."

"Really?" The CEO stepped into her office.

"The real figure is between six hundred and eleven hundred dollars per unit. It takes into account that every unit is screened for hepatitis B and C, as well as HIV-1 and HIV-2, syphilis, and Trypanosoma cruzi."

David leaned forward. "And how many people get transfusions every year?"

Becca pointed at her screen. "I was just checking that. About five million a year in the US alone." She paused, scrolling down the screen. "And another two million a year just in the UK."

Her uncle lifted his iPhone and began to tap the screen. "Let's see. Estimate an average savings of seven hundred and fifty dollars for every unit transfused in the UK and USA, times seven million, is five and a quarter billion dollars yearly."

David nodded his agreement. "That's a big chunk of money we could be saving each year with an artificial blood. And that doesn't take into account the personal cost to every donor. There's time, travel, and discomfort associated with donation."

Becca pointed at another statistic on her screen. "Five hundred people die from serious transfusion reactions in the US each year."

David nodded. "And I know that in spite of screening, some viruses are missed, particularly if the donor has just contracted the infection. And who knows how many people in the tropics get malaria from transfusion?"

James smiled. "Get those figures over to our marketing guys, would you? I want them to be working on press releases and a full market analysis. We may have underestimated the worth of our little project."

David's eyes lit up. "What are you thinking?"

The CEO turned to leave as if the subject was boring to him, but Becca knew he could hardly contain himself. She said, "Transfusions of a safe artificial blood would certainly outstrip transfusions of real blood because of its risks. I'd estimate that once the practice of medicine has changed, transfusions of artificial blood could bring in a revenue of fifty to seventy-five billion a year."

David took a deep breath and exhaled slowly. "Wow."

Becca looked at her colleague. "Wow is right. The stakes couldn't be higher."

The girls had been sunbathing on the front of the ski boat for a lazy hour, drinking beer and talking as if this was their everyday life. The weather was perfect. Amy's father would have called it a "chamber of commerce day," the kind of day every city advertised on their websites to attract tourists. Blue sky: check. Cool, glassy water: check. Two hot guys competing for attention: *double check*. Amy looked over at Tiffany and mouthed, *Pudding!*

Tiffany propped herself up on her elbows and watched as the boys cooled off by flipping off the side of the boat into the water. "Hey, Dustin," she said, "could you help me with some sunscreen?"

Amy couldn't believe her. Tiffany actually undid her bikini top to make it easier for Dustin to rub in the lotion. And he didn't stop with her back. Next, he striped the back of her thighs like he was applying ketchup to a hot dog.

Tiffany giggled.

Amy felt woozy from the beer and hoped she wouldn't need to throw up. She was pretty sure that barfing would be a real turnoff to an older guy.

After a minute, Mark was at her side. "And what about you? The sun's gonna fry that beautiful skin of yours," he said, applying the lotion to his hands.

Amy shrugged and hoped she wouldn't hurl.

Mark rubbed her shoulders and back, as far as her one-piece suit would allow, and then underneath the suit an inch further. Then, he caressed her legs. Her stomach tightened. No boy had ever touched her there before. And so gently, too!

He seemed to be lingering a bit longer than was needed to rub in the lotion. Fortunately, just as Amy was about to protest, Dustin said, "Who wants to ski?"

Mark stood up to put on a ski vest. "You can drive for me," he said to Dustin. "Amy can be my lookout."

Amy looked at the number of crushed beer cans on the floor of the boat. *I hope Dustin is sober enough to drive.*

Her next thought was how far away from the dock they were and how badly she had to pee.

At the lake house, Caroline and Lizzy Rivers were channel surfing on the big flat-screen TV.

They lingered on a news channel long enough for Caroline to notice an ad. "Hey, Mom, it's Noah's girlfriend."

Melissa felt heat rise in her cheeks as she looked to see a Jackson Pharmaceuticals ad featuring Becca standing in a little circle with some African children.

Kristen traded glances with Melissa.

A male voiceover said, "Jackson Pharmaceuticals is a worldwide leader in HIV prevention. Mopivadine prevents the maternal-to-child transmission of the AIDS virus."

Melissa stared at the screen. "She actually looks like she's enjoying the game."

"Perception is everything," Kristen replied.

A cover of *Pusher* and a photograph of Becca Jackson with a perfect smile replaced the scene of the playing children.

Melissa raised her eyebrows. "What, not a fan of the great pharmacy doctor?"

"Noah's had a long road back to a life he deserves." Kristen walked away from the TV. "I guess I just find it hard to believe that she won't hurt him again."

Kristen continued, "What's the deal with her, anyway? I mean, look at *us*. We're here, hiding out in fear of our lives, because of *her*! We were fine until a few weeks ago when Ms. Perfect Smile comes back into Noah's life, and then everything falls apart."

"Are you sure your analysis is correct?" Melissa asked.

"What do you mean?"

261

Melissa lifted her auburn hair off her neck, where she'd gotten too much sun. "Just think about what you said about timing. Our lives were fine until Noah decided to come back home for a visit. So maybe it wasn't Becca coming into Noah's life that screwed everything up. Maybe it was Noah coming back into ours."

"I'm not sure I like your spin. Noah coming back to Dayton and seeing you again seems like a good thing." Kristen paused. "Do you remember what Becca Jackson was like in high school?"

"We were friends. I remember."

"She couldn't stand being second."

"What are you saying?"

Caroline pointed at the TV screen as her sister flipped through the channels. "Disney channel?"

"Okay," Kristen said, "you can watch that one." She made eye contact with Melissa and walked toward the kitchen. Voice lowered, Kristen said, "All I'm saying is that Becca always had to be the best. She was never level, just enjoying her position. She always had her eyes on the next conquest. First it was grades, then Noah, then UVa, then Stanford."

"Noah was a conquest?"

"A stepping stone to getting where she

wanted to go. And when he'd served his purpose by elevating her status, how did she pay him back?"

"Okay," Melissa said, "I know what you want to say, but Noah made his own choices that night. Becca didn't make him do what he did."

"So you defend her?"

"Becca's insecure to a fault. More than anything else, she needs a good dose of grace."

"Grace?"

"Yeah, you know, 'Amazing grace, how sweet the sound'?" Melissa sat on a bar stool and leaned against the granite countertop. "Becca has to perform because it's the only way for her to accept herself. She's guilty, so she performs." Melissa sighed. "I can understand. For the longest time after my husband split, I treated myself like it was my fault. I kept thinking that if only I'd been a better wife, he wouldn't have run around." She looked at Kristen. "It took a wise pastor to show me I was relating to God in the same way, thinking I had to be better for Him to love me. That's when he made me read the book of Galatians about a thousand times until it finally sank in. I don't need to perform for Him to love me. It's called grace."

Kristen pressed the side of her index finger to her upper lip. "I felt the same way when Roger left me with three girls. If only I'd been a better wife."

"After all these years, Noah's heart is still tender toward her. I can see it when I mention her name." Melissa touched her own lips. "I could never compete with her perfect lips. How does she do it?"

"Easy," Kristen said. "High-end lipstick covers a multitude of sins."

Melissa pushed her lips up into a kiss. "Mine aren't full like hers."

"Honey, I've seen what your daughter can do with a little Revlon ultra gloss. Take a lesson from your daughter. You've got what it takes."

"If Tiff ever comes back, and I don't kill her first, maybe I'll ask her to show me."

Kristen laughed.

Melissa smiled. "Why weren't we ever friends in high school?"

"I was too young. Besides, whenever I was around, all you could see was my brother."

"That obvious, huh?"

"Sister, you were never hard to read."

Becca reviewed the analysis of their last protocol changes. The artificial hemoglobin molecule was perfect. Almost.

After introducing a new series of chemical reactions designed to make the molecule fold to imitate the real hemoglobin, the artificial one was actually clumping, joining adjacent strands with hydrogen bonds in long segments, destroying the quaternary structure. Two folds on the end were correct, but the other stood straight out.

It looks like a miniature mushroom. I wonder if it will still carry oxygen.

She shook her head.

What did I do wrong?

What am I missing?

Her head ached. She rubbed the back of her neck. More than anything else, she wanted to get this thing right.

She tried to concentrate, tried to will new insight, but she had exactly nothing new. She thought of praying but felt like a hypocrite. *I've been independent, leaning on myself, my brains, even my looks for so long. Is praying giving up?*

She almost laughed. *When was the last time I prayed?*

She knew the answer before she even asked: *The night of the crash, when I wanted to tell my father the truth but I was too afraid.*

With nothing to lose, and in a desperation she hadn't felt for a long time, she whispered to a God she wasn't sure even listened:

"Help me."

Maybe Noah is right. Maybe God uses pain to redirect our attention to Him.

Funny, but I've always thought of pain as a reason to run away from God.

Could my pain be a gift?

She repeated her earnest prayer. "Help me." She halted, then added, "I don't have much time."

She looked back at her analysis.

Wait a minute. What if I could introduce a hydrogen-rich environment that would reduce the ends of the molecule exposed to the acid?

She picked up a hemoglobin model on her desk. *Sure.*

Maybe foxhole prayers work after all.

She felt a stabbing pain in her left temple.

She picked up a pencil to draw her idea, but it flew from her hand as her hand began to jerk.

Oh, God.

Darkness.

David Letchford paused at the door to Dr. Jackson's office, upset not to see her at her desk. He was turning to leave when something caught his eye. It was a shoe sticking out from behind the desk.

He took a step into the office. The shoe was attached to a leg. He rushed to the edge of the desk.

Rebecca was sprawled awkwardly on the floor. Her skirt was hiked up, and there was slobber draining from her mouth.

He waved his hand in front of her face. Her eyes were open, unseeing. "Dr. Jackson?"

He saw a custodian pushing a rolling trash can through the lab. "Terrance!" he yelled. "Call 911!"

23

It was late afternoon by the time Noah pulled into the driveway of Bradshaw's Smith Mountain Lake retreat home. Kristen and Melissa were arm in arm on the front porch, waiting. Their numb looks said it without words: *They're still missing.*

He didn't waste any time. "Have you notified the lake police? Maybe the girls had some mechanical problem."

Kristen shook her head. "I should have called. I'll do it now."

Noah walked into the house. "I'm going to change and take out the other Jet Ski. Maybe they're just around the corner, out of gas or something."

Mel bit her bottom lip. "Mind if I come along? I feel worthless here."

He changed, and they hurried down to the dock and launched the second Jet Ski.

In seconds, they were skimming along quickly, eyes scanning the water for the girls.

As Noah accelerated, he felt his body push back against Mel's. She gripped his waist tightly. She yelled in his ear. "Think they could have gotten lost? There are so many coves, and they look so similar."

"That's what I'm thinking. They probably just got turned around." He squinted into the wind. "It happens."

They traveled a few miles in one direction, entering each cove and going slowly enough to inspect the docks. *Maybe the girls stopped somewhere to ask directions.*

Then they repeated the same examination in the opposite direction.

Nothing.

No sign of any girls on a Jet Ski.

"I don't get it," Noah said. "This doesn't feel right."

"Doesn't feel right how? You don't think . . ."

Noah slowed the Jet Ski so he could turn and talk to Mel. "I don't know what to think. How could anyone know where we are?"

Mel's tears were threatening to spill.

"I shouldn't have gone to work," he said. "I should have stayed here."

"It's not your fault."

Noah shifted so he could sit sideways on the now-idling Jet Ski. He pulled Mel into

269

his arms. "We'll get through this."

"She's all I've got."

He wasn't sure how to respond. He wanted to assure her that he'd be there for her, but he felt immediately conflicted. *If I'm hoping for a new start with Becca, that doesn't mean I can't comfort Mel. Mel's my friend. So why do I feel so conflicted with her in my arms?*

Instead of talking, he offered a gentle squeeze and slowly released her again.

When the group got back to the dock at Dustin's place, Amy jumped into the water to relieve herself. Whatever else the beer was doing, it was certainly running through her system quickly.

The boys jumped in with her, laughing and splashing.

Tiffany was sleeping on the front of the boat and hadn't budged.

Amy climbed a ladder to the dock and went over to the boat. She poked Tiffany's foot. "Come on, we should be getting back."

Dustin shook his head. "She's in no condition to drive anywhere. Let's get her up to the house."

Amy's stomach tightened with anxiety. Her mother was going to freak. "Got any coffee?" Her lips felt thick and uncooperative. "Maybe that will shober her up."

Dustin laughed as he and Mark lifted Tiffany out of the boat and draped her arms around their shoulders. "I hear a cold shower may help. We could do that."

Amy thought the ground felt uneven. Or was it the dull feeling in her forehead? She weaved her way after the boys and raised her voice. "Y-you're not allowed to give her a shower!"

Mark smiled back at Amy. "Don't be jealous. You can join us."

Dustin slipped his hand around Tiffany's side.

Amy shook her head. "Sh-she wouldn't want you to touch her like that."

Mark helped get Tiffany onto a leather couch in the great room inside. "We should see if she'll eat. She needs to dilute all that alcohol."

He looked at Amy. "I'm sorry, babe — looks like you'll be staying with us for a while. Your designated driver is down for the count."

Amy flopped clumsily onto a recliner. *Maybe a short nap would be a good idea. Then we'll be on our way.*

The last thing she remembered was Mark's beer breath against her lips. "How about a little good-night kiss?"

She was pretty sure all she did was open her mouth in shock. Mark did the rest.

Becca woke up in the back of an EMS vehicle. A young man leaned over her, adjusting an IV drip inserted into her left arm. Her first thought was that he must have discovered her needle tracks. She took inventory. *I'm wet. I remember holding the hemoglobin model. I must have had another seizure.*

The man spoke. "She's waking up." He looked at her. "Ma'am, can you tell me your name?"

She nodded. "Becca Jackson. Where are you taking me?"

"Rockingham Memorial Hospital."

She shook her head. "Take me to the University of Virginia. I'm a neurology patient of Dr. Harrelson."

The young man flexed his jaw. He didn't seem to like that idea. "I'll have to radio ahead to RMH for approval of location change."

She touched his arm. "Please. I've got a seizure disorder. He knows me."

The man lifted a radio to his lips. "Rescue two to RMH ER, requesting change of plans. Our patient is awake and requesting transfer directly to the University of Virginia, where she is under treatment for a seizure disorder."

"Vital signs?"

The man pressed a button on a monitor to Becca's left. She felt something squeezing her upper arm.

After a moment, the man replied. "Heart rate 104, respirations 20, BP 100/80."

"Okay, take her over the mountain. Thanks for the update."

When Noah got back to the Bradshaw lake house, he saw a police patrol boat already docked. Two officers stood on the deck, talking to a very animated Kristen.

"They're good swimmers," she said.

"They've been missing how long?"

"They've been gone for four hours."

One of the officers scratched the back of his head. "It's a big lake, ma'am. They could be anywhere by now. I'll send out a description of the girls, and we'll sweep the area completely."

Noah and Melissa joined the two officers and Kristen. Kristen nodded toward them. "This is my brother, Noah, and Melissa is the mother of Tiffany."

The officer nodded. "The presumed driver?"

"Yes," Melissa said.

The officers took down cell numbers for contact. "Listen, I know you're concerned, but it's only been a few hours and there are quite a few places to hang out and party around the lake. I'm sure they'll be back soon."

Melissa shook her head. "This isn't like Tiffany. She wouldn't just stay out like this."

Noah touched Kristen's arm. "Did you tell the officers about the threats?"

She shook her head.

Noah looked at the officers. "Look, this may have nothing to do with this, but the truth is, we're here at this lake house hiding out because both Amy and Tiffany were threatened."

The officers traded glances. "Threatened? How?"

"You've probably heard of Dr. Rebecca Jackson."

The officers shook their heads.

Noah briefed the officer duo on the threats and their reason for being at the lake house.

The taller officer squinted. "You're sure no one knows you're here?"

Noah exchanged looks with Kristen and Mel. "We haven't told anyone, and we told the girls to keep it quiet."

"Okay, thanks for that information. For now, we'll assume what would be much more likely — which is that the girls got lost or joined some party or are out of gas or have ventured way out across the lake and lost all track of time."

The older of the two officers, a man with a graying crew cut, looked ex-military. He seemed to be sizing Noah up. "Listen, if you get any more information that this might be more like an abduction, you need to let us know right away." He handed Noah a card. "That's my cell. Use it."

The officers left to begin their search.

Noah looked at the sky. *Night's coming. There's no way those girls could find their way back through all the fingers of this lake in the dark.*

He looked at the faces of the women. He knew they were thinking the same thing.

At the University of Virginia hospital, Dr. Harrelson insisted on a new MRI. After forty-five minutes in the claustrophobic scanner, Becca found herself back in an exam room in the ER, watching Dr. Harrelson's concerned expressions as he read the scan.

He made too many "ooh" noises while examining the pictures.

"Well, doc, what's the verdict?" Becca said at last.

He looked at her above his half-glasses. "Why didn't you schedule your biopsy?"

"I didn't think it would make any difference. Plus, I was afraid of the risks of bleeding."

"Rebecca, the tumor is growing. It's now starting to block off the fourth ventricle, causing your ventricles to expand. I still think the tumor is likely unresectable, but we need a tissue diagnosis in order to recommend any treatment. In addition, it looks like a shunt to drain the fluid off your brain is in order, perhaps as an emergency tonight. I'll have to talk to my neurosurgery colleague and see what she thinks."

"So we're back to recommending a biopsy?"

"Of course." He folded his arms in his lap and sighed. "Would you mind telling me just what is going through your mind?"

You'll question my sanity, then force me to stay against my will because I'm not thinking straight. Or at least you won't think I am. She thought through her options and decided to go with honesty.

For a change.

"Look, I told you the last time that I'm getting flashes of brilliance that are moving my research forward at an unprecedented pace."

He looked at his notes in her electronic medical record on his computer screen. "I remember."

"The thing is, I'm working on something important, and pretty life changing for millions of people. If I can solve this problem, millions of people around the world will benefit. But I'm afraid that if I allow you to treat the tumor, all of that good blood flow around the tumor that is bringing all the extra oxygen to the creative part of my brain may be destroyed."

"But if you die, you're not going to do anyone any good."

"But if I can live long enough to solve the problem, lots of people will win."

He sat up and seemed to stare right through her. "Noble," he said. "To be honest, I didn't see that coming. I thought you were just scared like everyone else."

"Oh, I'm scared all right. But I'm more scared of failing at my research."

"What are you working on?"

"Artificial blood. We're this close to finding real answers," she said, holding up her fingers about an inch apart.

"How much time do you need?"

"As much as you can give me."

"What if we started treatment and then stopped if your brilliance began to change?"

277

"What if we just did the shunt to buy some time and do a biopsy at the same time so you'll know what you're dealing with?"

He smiled. "I'll bet you're used to getting what you want, aren't you?"

"I have my ways." She hesitated and then added, "Some of them are a bit under-handed, but I think of myself as a Robin Hood of sorts."

"Rob from the rich to give to the poor?"

"Something like that."

He sighed again. "I'm calling Leslie Brighton. She's a neurosurgeon. I think she'll work with us. But I'm guessing by the looks of your scan, you don't have much time. We need to get the ventricles decompressed, or the chances of you making it through the weekend are looking pretty dismal."

"So I shouldn't buy green bananas, huh?"

He laughed and stood. "I'm calling Dr. Brighton." He lifted his cell phone and walked out.

Twenty minutes later, Becca watched as Dr. Brighton and Dr. Harrelson oohed and pointed their way through the slices of Becca's brain on the screen.

Dr. Brighton looked fit, a trim fifty, a run-ner from the looks of her, with gray-streaked hair that said she didn't mind showing off her natural highlights. When she spoke, she was all business. There was no "Hi, how are you?" It was straight to "Dr. Jackson, you need an emergency operation tonight if you want to live another week."

"Operation? You mean a shunt?"

"Yes."

For some reason, the straightforward neurosurgeon struck a nerve. Becca had held it together up until she heard the prognosis spill from the lips of her neurosurgeon. She choked back a sob.

Dr. Brighton nodded thoughtfully and lifted a strand of gray hair behind her ear. "There is a chaplain on call. I can give him a ring if you like."

Becca looked down. "No, thanks." *I don't deserve a deathbed conversion.*

Dr. Brighton nodded again and turned to leave. When she was a few feet away, Becca almost called out to tell her she'd changed her mind, but Dr. Brighton got away before Becca worked up the courage.

Everything moved fast. Becca was given an informed consent document by Dr. Brighton's PA, a young man in a white coat who told her at least three times that she could stroke, not wake up, bleed, die, be paralyzed, not be able to swallow or speak, and basically be a drooling vegetable for the rest of her short miserable life. The shunt could fail, become infected, clog up, need replacement — or, on the other hand, could work fabulously and relieve the pressure on Becca's brain. "Sign here."

She obeyed, but not without shedding a few tears.

A moment later, Becca found herself alone, waiting for a transporter to take her to the operating room.

She stared at the ceiling. She thought about her simple prayer. *It came right before my last good insight into my hemoglobin molecule.*

And right before the seizure that landed me back here.

So did my foxhole prayer work?

She felt so . . . alone. Becca brushed back her tears. She decided she shouldn't waste time. The surgeon had made it clear that she could die . . . today.

So she got straight to the point. This was not a time to beat around the bush. "I'm afraid to die," she whispered.

Her feeble attempt at a prayer.

She remembered conversations she'd had with Noah's father, the school janitor. Every time she saw him, she'd say, "How you doin', Mr. Linebrink?"

His response was always the same: "Better than I deserve."

When she'd finally asked him what he meant, he told her about grace and the cross. He wasn't preachy. For him, talking about the gospel was just . . . natural.

To Becca, it seemed strange that her conversations with the janitor came back to her as she faced possible death. But somehow, it comforted her.

I don't deserve Your love. I don't deserve answers. But maybe that's what Mr. Linebrink was always telling me. Is that the whole point of the cross?

She didn't try to stop the tears from rolling.

She closed her eyes and whispered the only verse she could remember — one Mr. Linebrink had written on the inside of his janitor closet. "For God so loved the world —"

She stopped when she felt her stretcher move. She opened her eyes to see a young man with long red hair. He wore a pair of blue scrubs and offered a smile. "Time for surgery, Ms. Jackson."

24

Becca lay on a stretcher in the pre-op holding area, trying to understand the frantic pace of activity around her. A nurse administered an antibiotic that was long off patent and available as a generic. The original had been successfully marketed by Jackson Pharmaceuticals Company and had netted the company thirty million in sales annually before going generic.

Dr. Brighton had accompanied her, walking along with her hand on the stretcher. She lifted a cell phone. "Is there anyone else you would like to call?"

"I called my parents. They should be here when I wake up."

Dr. Brighton lifted her eyebrows. "Anyone else special?"

"There is one person I wish would come. But I've sent him so many mixed messages, I'm not sure what he'd think, hearing from me."

The surgeon shook her head. "There's no time for regrets."

"You're right," she said. "I'll try him."

Amy awoke in a dim room. She squinted, sat up, and walked to a wall of glass overlooking Smith Mountain Lake. The last rays of the sun cast dark shadows across the sloped lawn leading down to the dock.

What happened?

It felt like someone was pounding a nail into her skull. She had to pee.

Now she remembered.

Where is Tiffany? Mark? Dustin?

She followed noises coming from another room. Tiffany sat at a round table across from Dustin and Mark. Cards were scattered in front of them, along with shot glasses and a half-full bottle of tequila. Tiffany leaned forward, her yellow bikini top sagging. She smiled at Amy. "Hi, Aims," she said. "Ever played poker?"

Amy glared at her. "Tiffany, we need to go. It's getting dark."

Tiffany waved her hand clumsily. "I'll call Mom later. She wouldn't want me driving like this." She wrinkled her nose toward Amy.

Dustin seemed to be enjoying the view of

Tiff's bikini top and what little it was covering.

Amy shook her head. "I'll drive. We need to go."

Mark reached for her. "Dustin's going to grill some steaks. There's no hurry, Amy."

Amy backed up so that Mark's hand grabbed only air.

"I need to pee."

Dustin pointed but didn't take his eyes off Tiffany. "Down the hall. First door on the left."

Amy wandered down the hall and stepped into the bathroom, locking the door. She wanted to find a phone to call her mom. She knew she'd be grounded for like a year for this, but she was afraid that Tiffany was too drunk to realize what the boys wanted.

She opened the medicine cabinet and found a bottle of ibuprofen. She swallowed three tablets with water sipped from her hand. Then she lowered herself to the commode to pee. And think.

After a few minutes, she eased into the hall and across into the first bedroom. She scanned the room for a phone. No luck.

The bed was unmade, clothes scattered about the room. On the nightstand, she saw a small foil packet. *A condom? How gross! Tiffany, we've got to get out of here!*

But something else caught her eye. Beneath the condom was a photocopy of a girl's photograph. She lifted it closer to inspect it and gasped. The top half of the paper was a picture of Tiffany smiling toward the camera. On the bottom half was a picture of Amy waiting for her school bus!

Amy's head hurt. *What? Does this mean that Dustin and Mark were actually looking for us?*

Were they the ones threatening Noah and Melissa?

She needed to find a phone, and they needed to escape — but how?

She didn't want to go back into the kitchen. Tiffany was in no condition to listen to reason. Amy would have to go back to their lake house by herself and tell her uncle Noah where to find Tiffany.

She walked to the doorway and peered down the hall. The three were laughing loudly and pouring another round of tequila. Amy shut the door and headed for a back entrance to the deck from the bedroom. On the deck, she crouched and ran as best she could to a set of stairs leading to a sidewalk. She ran to the boat dock and yanked the cover off their Jet Ski.

She tried to remember just what she had to do. She needed a key! She looked at the key slot.

Empty!

Time for plan B.

She ran for the front of the house and the street beyond. She'd just have to flag down a car and use someone's phone.

The street was deserted.

Right or left?

She chose right and ended up at a cul-de-sac after walking a half mile. She had no choice but to turn around.

She had passed Dustin's house and traveled about another ten minutes when she heard a car.

She waved frantically. The car slowed.

The window was down. Dustin leaned his head out the window, his expression one of smug amusement. "Hi, Amy, need a lift?"

Noah paced back and forth across the great room. "I should go back out there. Does the Jet Ski have headlights?"

Melissa shrugged. "Don't know." She was staring at her cell phone.

His phone rang.

"Hey, cowboy," Becca's voice said.

"Becca. I'm glad you called."

"You sound upset."

"Remember I told you I came down to Bradshaw's lake house with Kristen and her girls to be safe from whoever was threatening us?"

"Sure. Look, it may have been my father. I feel terrible getting you involved in all —"

"Becca, listen, Melissa was as scared as we were, so she brought her daughter Tiffany down here so no one could find us."

"Melissa's with you?" The sadness in her voice wasn't hard to hear.

"Just to be safe, okay?" He hesitated. *Why is it so hard to talk to Becca about Mel and to Mel about Becca?* "But listen, the girls have disappeared. They ran off on a Jet Ski. I have no idea how this could be related to the threats, because no one knew we were here, but just the same, the coincidence has us a bit spooked."

"I guess so. I'll talk to my dad again. Of course he denied everything, but when I talked to my uncle, it sounded like he knew more than he was saying."

Noah glanced at Melissa. Still staring at her phone, she had begun to shake, her hand covering her mouth. Something had scared her.

"Look, I have to run here," he said into the phone. "I need to look for the girls. Say, what'd you call me about?"

He heard Becca sigh. "Oh, nothing that can't wait. You look for the girls."

She sniffed, and her next words rushed out as if she was trying not to cry, but the words dropped out in a sob anyway. "Love you for your brains."

He didn't have a chance to reply. She'd ended the call. He wasn't sure what to think. He took a deep breath and turned to face Melissa again. "What's wrong?"

"I was looking through my phone logs. I have a bunch of missed calls from Barry Jackson. There was no way I was going to answer any of them. But even so, my incoming calls log registers that a call from his number *was* answered. It was yesterday morning. I must have been out on the dock sunbathing."

"Maybe Tiffany answered your phone."

"That's what has me scared. She wouldn't know enough to not tell him where we were if he claimed that he needed to know to keep us protected."

Noah frowned. "Okay, so it's possible Tiffany answered. And it's possible she told him where we are. But maybe it just means it went to voice mail?"

"I think it would register as a missed call, not an incoming one."

"It's still more probable that this is all a coincidence," he said, hoping to reassure Mel. "The girls probably ran out of gas or something."

"Noah, it's dark. They'll be afraid."

"So let's go out again. Grab some flashlights. It'll give us something to do."

Melissa walked to the kitchen to find a flashlight. "Are you coming?"

"I'm coming. But I think I'll call Barry Jackson first."

Barry Jackson knew his wife didn't like him speeding. He could practically feel her judgmental gaze. He glanced over to confirm her inspection of the speedometer.

Rachel cleared her throat. "Goodness, Barry, you might as well turn on the lights and siren if you're going to go that fast."

"It's the interstate, honey. Relax."

"How can I relax when our daughter just called to say she was having brain surgery?"

Barry took a deep breath. "I thought maybe something was going on. She hasn't really seemed herself since she got back from Africa. I just figured she was upset about all them AIDS orphans she saw."

"Why didn't she tell us before now?"

He shrugged. "She said she didn't want us to worry."

"That's our job. To worry about our daughter."

Barry's phone rang. He didn't recognize

the number. "Hello, Chief Jackson here."

"Hello, Mr. Jackson, Noah Linebrink here. I think you may know why I'm calling."

"Yes, I'm as shocked as you are. We just found out ourselves."

"Just found out?"

"So you knew about this?"

"I'm sorry," Noah said. "Knew about what?"

"Becca's condition."

"If you mean that someone is threatening her, yes, I know all about it. And I've got a hunch you know a whole lot more about some pictures that Melissa and I received."

"I don't know what you're talking about."

"Becca said you'd deny it."

"Deny what? Can you get to the point? I'm on my way to see my dying daughter, and you are talking in riddles."

"Dying daughter? What's wrong with Becca?"

"I thought you knew," Barry said. "She's got some sort of brain tumor. She's over at University Hospital in Charlottesville."

"Brain tumor? I should have known. She told me it was all about her migraines."

"Well, it seems she's been keeping all of us in the dark. She's in surgery now."

"Surgery? Oh man, I need to see her."

"Don't make trouble here, Noah."

"That would be the last thing I'd want."

"They won't let you see her tonight anyway, and her surgery probably won't end until sometime in the early morning hours." There was silence on the phone for a moment. "I guess you could come tomorrow. So listen — if it's not because of Becca, why are you calling me?"

"Because Amy and Tiffany are missing."

"Missing?"

"Yep, so if you don't mind skipping the bull, why don't you tell me where they are?"

"I have no idea what you are talking about, son."

"I'm talking about the people who have a huge interest in keeping the truth about Becca's and my accident quiet. I think you know exactly what I'm talking about. And I'm going to personally see to it that everyone knows you covered it up if you don't tell whoever has our girls to let them go."

"I don't think you want to do that. If someone doesn't want that news to get out bad enough to threaten you, don't you think it might endanger your niece if you did something that stupid?"

"Quit the crap. Just call off your goons."

"I don't know what you're talking about. And I'd appreciate you letting me deal with this crisis with my daughter instead of bugging me with your crazy theories."

Barry terminated the call.

Rachel's voice sounded tense. "You sound so mad at Noah. Maybe you should remember what he did for our family."

"Maybe you'd think differently if you knew what he's trying to do to Becca. He's taking advantage of her fame and the wealth of her company."

"What do you mean?"

Barry pushed the speedometer up past ninety. "Best you don't get involved."

Melissa touched Noah's shoulder. "What is it? What'd he say?"

"He denies knowing anything about our girls."

"You knew he'd say that." Melissa studied him for a moment. "What's wrong, Noah? What aren't you telling me?" She hesitated and then found her voice thickening as she tried to speak. "The girls?"

He shook his head.

Melissa didn't understand. "But you looked so shocked. What are you hiding?"

"Nothing." He rubbed the back of his neck. "But apparently Becca has been hiding something." He paused. "She's been lying to me."

"Lying? How?"

"Probably in some twisted way she figures it would be easier on me not to know."

Melissa found her voice and squeezed his shoulder gently. "Know what? I don't understand." She leaned toward him. "I heard you say that you needed to see her. What's going on?"

Noah cleared his throat. "Becca is in the University of Virginia hospital. He said she has a brain tumor."

Melissa gasped. "She's too young for that."

Noah paused before speaking at a whisper. "She's having surgery right now." His voice cracked. "Barry said she's dying."

Mel swallowed hard. She knew what she wanted, but she also knew what was right. "Look, you need to go to her."

Noah appeared conflicted. "I need to stay to look for the girls."

"She needs you," Mel said.

"For the time being, there's nothing I can do there." He sighed. "And Barry wants me to wait until tomorrow to come."

God, why is it so hard for me to push Noah away? "Then go tomorrow," Mel said, sniffing back tears. "You belong with her."

25

Amy's heart sank at the sight of Dustin's face in the car window.

"I want to go back to our lake house," she said. "My mom's gonna freak. She doesn't know where we are."

Tiffany leaned out of the car. "Just let me sober up a bit. Then we can go. The guys want to treat us to dinner. What's the harm in that? I'll tell your mom it was all my fault."

Amy thought about running. But where? Down the street with a car following her didn't seem like such a good idea. She needed to tell Tiffany about the photographs she'd seen. *Okay,* she thought. *Play along so they don't get too suspicious. I'll just tell them that I want to go home and won't let them know what I know.*

She climbed into the backseat with Tiffany and noticed immediately the stretchy band around her wrist — connected to the key to the Jet Ski!

"Okay, guys," she said with confidence she didn't feel, "what's for dinner?"

"That's my girl," Mark said.

Tiffany made a face at her and leaned closer. "Pudding," she said with boozy breath.

Yeah, this is an adventure all right. But you don't realize what kind.

Dustin laughed. "We're not making pudding. We're grilling. My dad left me his credit card, and I bought steak."

Back at the house a few minutes later, Dustin fired up the grill and Mark opened cold beers. He handed one to Amy and to Tiffany.

"None for her," Amy said. "She's driving."

When the guys took the meat out to the grill on the deck, Amy pulled Tiffany down the hall and into the bedroom. She showed her the photographs.

Tiffany's eyes widened. "Where did you find this?"

"Right here." She tightened her grip on Tiffany's arm. "Don't you get this? These were the guys threatening Noah and your mom!"

Tiffany paused as if her boozy brain needed a moment to process. She stuck her head out into the hall. "Okay," she said, "follow my lead. Let's get them to drink. Then we'll make our move for the Jet Ski."

Becca wasn't sure whether God listened to bargains. At least to bargains from spiritual ragamuffins, especially a baby one.

But as she was being wheeled into OR nine, she made God a promise. *Let me live a little longer, God. I promise to tell the truth.*

A masked face with a poofy blue cap appeared in front of her. "Hi, I'm Deb. I'm the circulating nurse in your room tonight. I'll be with you the entire time. Don't worry," she said. "Dr. Brighton is the best."

A man in a blue scrub suit patted the operating table as someone else lowered the railing on her stretcher. "Can you move over here for me?"

"Don't guess I have much of a choice."

She slid over to the OR table, trying desperately to keep her modesty with the crazy open-in-the-back gown she wore.

A man with kind blue eyes appeared above her, his face upside down. "I'm Dr. Kern. I'll be putting you to sleep." He placed a mask over her face. "This is just pure oxygen. Take some deep breaths."

She watched as they slipped a syringe onto

a port in her IV line and injected a clear fluid.

She knew there was a chance she would die.

But her memory of Noah's father had helped her find a peace in all of the craziness. So she lay there on the table with only a basic understanding of what might happen if she died — a theology built around a simple verse she'd first heard from the mouth of a janitor.

Weird. Everything in my life recently pushes me toward desperation. I want to live. I want to accomplish my goals. Is it possible to have peace?

Let me live so I can tell the truth.

In desperation, she began to quote the words she learned so many years ago, trying to wrap herself in the peace of John 3:16: "For God so loved the world, that he gave his only Son, that whoever believes in him will not perish but have eternal life."

She felt the mask lift off her face and realized that she must have been mouthing the words. Dr. Kern nodded. His eyes were smiling, but she couldn't see his mouth behind his mask. "So true," he whispered. "I wish everyone knew."

A female voice. "Knew what?"

"I was lip reading. She was quoting a verse

from the Bible."

Becca knew very little about theology, but one thing she understood: *I believe it now. It's true. The whole God thing that I've been running from all these years. Noah was right.*

She suddenly felt very woozy.

The room seemed to s l o w d o w n. *Whoa. That's —*

After an hour of slow searching in every cove, Noah and Mel docked the Jet Ski in its cradle and sat on the deck over the water.

Mel leaned against his shoulder and started crying.

"Know what I think?" he said.

She sniffed. "No."

"We need to pray. I mean I'm sure you've been praying most of the day, but right here, out loud, we should pray together."

"Okay," she whispered. Her voice was quiet and thickened by sorrow.

Noah wasn't as experienced as his father, but he'd heard enough to know how to lead. "Dear Father, thank You for the moonlight tonight. Our girls might need it to find their way. I know that right now, Your love for Amy and Tiffany is far greater than ours, and so I'm asking that You take care of them and put our hearts at peace. Bring them back to us safely. We don't know what's been happening with Becca, what with her getting threatened and the extortion and now hearing that she might have some sort of brain tumor, but we also commit her into Your hands. Show her Your grace and help her to accept Your love."

He didn't know what else to say. Mel had stayed quiet but had gripped his biceps with her arms and pulled close to him while they prayed.

"I guess that's it, God. In Jesus's name, amen."

Mel whispered, "Amen."

They sat quietly for a few minutes, staring out over the cove.

"You know what, Noah?"

"What?"

"You've turned out just like your dad."

Barry Jackson was on his third cup of vending-machine coffee when a doctor entered the surgery waiting room. She wore a pair of green scrubs, a white lab coat, and a cloth cap with a print of Scooby Doo. "Family of Rebecca Jackson?"

Barry grabbed his wife's hand and stood.

The doctor walked over and held out her hand. "I'm Dr. Brighton with the neuro-surgery department."

"I'm Barry, and this is Rachel. We're

Becca's parents."

"Everything went as well as could be expected," the neurosurgeon began. "There was quite a buildup of pressure in the brain. We will be watching her as she wakes up in the recovery room."

Barry shook his head. "We really know very little. Help us to understand. Does our daughter have a tumor? Or cancer? Or just what is going on?"

Rachel reached for the doctor's sleeve. "One minute we think our daughter is fine, and the next, we're getting a phone call saying she has a tumor on her brain and is about to have surgery. We're still in shock."

Dr. Brighton pointed to a row of chairs. "Why don't we sit?"

When they had, she began, "Rebecca's scan shows a tumor, most likely a cancer on the left side of her brain, but it has pushed across the midline and was starting to block off the flow of fluid that the brain creates. This buildup of fluid unable to drain is what causes the pressure problems. Without relieving the pressure, the brain will die."

Rachel gasped. "Oh no."

Barry took Rachel's hand. "But you were successful, weren't you, Doc? You took out the tumor, right?"

"No, no. This operation was merely to get

a small piece of the tumor by doing a biopsy and to put in a shunt to drain away the fluid from the brain. She now has a small tube that leads from her brain down into her abdomen." She traced her finger down from the top of her head toward her neck, across the chest and into the belly. "From here to here."

"It's permanent?"

"Most likely. We should know if the procedure worked pretty quickly. Her headaches will be easier to control and the biopsy should be able to guide our oncologists in a selection of chemotherapy drugs to fight it."

Barry shifted in his seat. "But why don't you just take it out?"

"It's surrounding too many vital things. I want to see if it is possible once the chemotherapy has a chance to shrink it."

Rachel leaned forward. "Why didn't she tell us?"

If Dr. Brighton knew the answer to that, she didn't flinch. "You'll have to ask her that." She stood. "Becca will be taken to the ICU to recover. If I were you, I'd check into a local motel for the night. She won't be awake for some time, and you'll need to be fresh for her tomorrow. There really isn't anything you can do for her tonight except let her sleep."

"Has she stabilized?"

"Right now, it's hour to hour. She hasn't come out of anesthesia yet, so I won't know about any complications for a while."

Barry nodded. "We'll be staying here tonight."

The surgeon nodded. "Okay. I'll bring another update when I can."

"When can we see her?"

"Not until she is settled into the neuro ICU."

Rachel squeezed the doctor's hand. "Will you at least tell her we came over?"

"Sure."

With that, the doctor disappeared, and Rachel looked up at her husband. "Oh, Barry — our baby has brain cancer?"

Tiffany carried the bottle of tequila out of the house, purposefully adding an extra sway to her walk, stumbling toward the boys at the grill. "It's five o'clock somewhere!" She took a swig from the bottle and held the burning liquid in her mouth and watched the surprised expressions of Dustin and Mark. She then covered her mouth, turned and forced out a laugh so hard that she spewed the liquid back out into the grass.

The guys each took hits straight from the bottle.

In the meantime, Amy watched from the kitchen and struggled with a corkscrew to get open a bottle of wine. She didn't know what was supposed to go with steak, but the object here wasn't to complement the food. She had chosen red. She found glasses and joined the others.

And so the charade began, Amy and Tiffany discreetly dumping their glasses into the grass, or acting so drunk that they let the alcohol dribble from their chins.

They ate steak and bread and little else, while Dustin and Mark finished the bottle of tequila. Dustin handed Tiffany a beer. She took one sip.

"Oh," Tiffany said. "I don't like this brand." She pushed it back toward Dustin after kissing the top of the bottle. "For you."

He thought it was funny, so he kissed the bottle too and took a long swig.

Tiffany looked at Dustin. "I don't want to go back tonight. Can we stay here? This place is huge."

Dustin and Mark nodded. "Of course."

"Okay with you, Amy?" Tiffany asked.

"Our moms will freak. We'll be grounded for like forever."

Tiffany waved her hand. "So life is risky."

Amy frowned. "I don't like it."

Tiffany ignored her. "Is there more where this came from?" she asked as she lifted the empty tequila bottle.

Mark headed for the kitchen. "On the way."

For the next hour Tiffany and Amy watched as the boys made serious progress on a second bottle of tequila. Tiffany started hinting to Dustin that she didn't want to sleep alone.

Amy followed her lead. "I guess that just leaves us," she said to Mark.

"Why don't you boys go lay down for a few minutes? You've been drinking so much that I don't think you'll stay awake for me," Tiffany said.

Dustin squinted in her direction, his eyes lacking focus. "Good idea," he said, wobbling his way toward the house.

Mark followed.

As soon as the boys were inside, Amy and Tiffany ran for the Jet Ski.

26

In seconds, Tiffany and Amy had untied the Jet Ski and pushed off into the cove.

Amy looked back toward the house. "They'll hear the engine."

"Well, we can't paddle home. Hang on." Tiffany started the Jet Ski and idled slowly forward until they were a hundred yards into the lake.

Then Tiffany's quick acceleration thrust Amy backward and almost off the Jet Ski. "Whoa!" She grabbed Tiffany by the shoulders.

They rushed over the glassy water, aware of the chill in the air and not just in their souls. "Someone's following us!"

Tiffany kept the Jet Ski at maximum speed. Amy crouched behind her and held on.

But whoever was following had a faster and more powerful boat. Amy risked a sideways glance. "It's Dustin!"

Tiffany cut sharply toward the left, heading for shallow water.

In moments, they found themselves in the crosshairs of a searchlight. Amy held up her hand to block the blinding glare. A loudspeaker boomed: "Virginia State Police. Stop your craft."

Police? On the water? Is it really the police? She gripped Tiffany's shoulder and felt her emotions ping-ponging from relief to fear.

Tiffany shut off the throttle, allowing the Jet Ski to idle to a stop.

The male voice on the loudspeaker sounded mechanical. "Amy Rivers? Tiffany Mitchell?"

Amy waved. "They know us!"

"They probably want to arrest us for stealing a Jet Ski."

When the white boat was a few feet away, she saw two uniformed men. One of them spoke again, this time without the aid of the loudspeaker. "Well, well, off to someplace in a hurry? You know it's a violation to be riding without floatation vests?"

Amy gasped, not having thought about it under the circumstances. "There was no time."

"Here," the man said, handing them two life vests. "Put these on and follow us. We'll sort out the details back at your place."

Fifteen minutes later, during a tearful reunion with Noah, Melissa, her mom, and her sisters, Amy cried, "I'm so sorry, Mama."

Noah draped a beach towel around Tiffany's shoulders. "We're just glad you're safe. Tell us what happened."

"It was the guys who threatened you," Tiffany said.

Melissa waved her hand in front of her nose. "Tiffany, you've been drinking!"

Amy watched as Noah took Melissa's hand. The subtle message was there: *Easy now.* Noah spoke, his voice free of tension. "How do you know, Tiff?"

"Amy found a photocopy of our pictures, probably the same ones that you saw."

An officer spoke next. "Did you bring the copy?"

Amy shook her head. "We were so scared. You have to go back there and arrest them."

An older officer with a military haircut stepped forward. "Okay," he said, "slow down and tell me about these guys. Did they force you to go with them?"

The girls shook their heads.

"Did they force you to stay against your will?"

"No."

"Did they physically assault you or sexually assault you in any way?"

Amy thought back to the kiss Mark had given her as she drifted into sleep. She looked down, unable to look at her mom. "No," she said.

"What did they do?"

Tiffany spoke. "They invited us to party with them on their boat and at their lake house. They did give us alcohol and we're minors, so that's something."

"That is something we'll discuss with them. It's called contributing to the delinquency of a minor," he said, as if reciting from a law code. "But so far, I haven't heard anything that I'd be able to get a search warrant for. Having a photocopy of two girls' pictures isn't exactly a crime."

Noah spoke. "But an exact copy of the photo that those goons showed to me in Richmond would link them to the threats. That's something."

The officer nodded. "It's probably enough for now. We don't need a warrant to talk to the boys. Most young guys break down pretty quickly, so we'll see what we get. We need to go back there soon." He paused and looked at Melissa. "I'll need Tiffany to show us which house it was."

"I need to change," Tiffany said.

The other officer handed Tiffany a yellow

paper. "This is a citation for driving a watercraft without a license."

That's when Tiffany started to cry.

Amy looked at her mom. Her expression wasn't too hard to interpret.

You're so grounded.

Tiffany's tears pushed Amy further to the edge of control. She looked at her sisters, who didn't seem too upset that she was in trouble.

Now Mom probably won't let me date until I'm twenty-one.

Becca's first awareness was of the rhythmic electronic beeping. Blip, blip, blip.

Water dripping? No, it's a truck backing up.

Where am I?

She struggled to open her eyes. Unsuccessfully. Something stopped her. *Glue?*

She needed to touch her eyes. She closed her mouth. Something was in her mouth! Gagging, she tried to reach whatever was snaking down her throat, but she couldn't lift her hands.

A calm male voice. "Okay, let's take that tube out. Hang on, Rebecca. You're just waking up after surgery."

Surgery?

Where am I?

I don't remember!

She coughed, and whatever was in her throat was expelled.

"Take deep breaths, honey." A female voice. "Whoa, this one is strong. Now he's going to take the tape off your eyelids. Hold on."

Becca pulled her hand away from someone gripping her arm. When her arm pulled free, it recoiled into her chest.

Another female voice. "Well, she's moving her right side. That's a comfort."

My right side? What kind of talk is that? Where am I?

She tried to speak. "Aaahh, ahh, ah?" *Where am I?*

The sounds coming out of her mouth didn't match the words Becca formed in her brain.

She felt her eyelids being pulled. She saw bright light. A blurry face, a poofy hat, a surgeon's mask.

I had surgery.

I made a promise to God.

"Aah aahaahh ah ah?" *What happened to me?*

"Calm down, honey. You're just waking up. You had a little surgery. You're at the University of Virginia hospital. Try not to fight."

Helpful information. Becca tried to calm

down and remember.

I remember feeling this way before. My lips felt three sizes too big, and I couldn't talk correctly. Everything I said came out funny.

My parents were standing in the corner, and they didn't know I could hear. "We've taken Noah into custody. The Peters kid is in surgery, not sure if he'll make it. He's lost a lot of blood."

Her mom spoke. "Noah's trouble, I tell you. Becca would never have been hanging out with that crowd if it wasn't for him. And now look what he's done to our baby!"

Her father's voice. "Her face. It doesn't even look like our Becca. That boy's gonna pay for this. He's facing some serious jail time."

I need to see Noah!

It was me!

He shouldn't be in jail!

Becca watched as a woman took down her mask and gently turned Becca's face toward her. "I'm Dr. Brighton. Don't be afraid. Can you tell me your name?"

"Ahaahah aahaah."

A concerned look crossed the face of the surgeon and was quickly erased. "The anesthesia is still wearing off." The woman turned her back on Becca, but she could still hear her speaking. "Let's hope she's not aphasic."

Becca found another syllable. "Ma maaa maaa!" *I can't speak!* "Maaa!" *Help!*

She managed to lift her right hand to explore. There was a bandage around her head. *Brain surgery.*

The headaches. I remember pain.

She looked at her right hand, turning it over. She remembered the seizure. *It began with my right arm jerking.* She imitated the movement several times.

"Dr. Brighton, she's seizing!" The other female voice, filled with alarm.

I'm not seizing! She didn't try to vocalize it this time. Talking was too frustrating. *I'm just remembering how my arm jerked.* She looked at the doctor and stopped the arm motion and shook her head. *I'm okay.*

Blip, blip, blip.

It's my heart rate.

She felt hands all around her. A team of people in scrubs.

"On three. One, two, three!"

Her body was lifted to a stretcher. The ceiling blurred as she was rolled out. She saw ceiling tiles, fluorescent lights, and an IV bag dangling above her. The blip, blip, blip followed along with her. She watched on a computer screen above her head. There, a bright green line danced with her heart.

A minute later, she stopped moving. A new nurse greeted her. "I'm Andrew. I'm your recovery-room nurse. You just had surgery. Here," he said, "I'm going to raise your head a bit."

She listened to an electronic hum and felt the head of the bed lift her upper body.

Better, she thought. She tried speaking again. "Ma na naaah."

Andrew lowered his face close to hers. "Say it again. Slowly."

"Ma na naaah!" *I'm in pain.* "Ma maa maaah." *My head hurts.*

"Interesting. Dr. Brighton. Take a look." He gently nodded and touched Becca's lips with a gloved hand. "Say it again for the doctor."

"Ma maa maaah." *My head hurts.* Becca twisted her head around in frustration. *Why can't I make the words sound like they do in my head?*

The doctor smiled. "Your head hurts." *She understands me.*

"That's very odd," she said. "It's as if only her lips obey, but her larynx isn't getting the brain's message from the speech center."

Andrew nodded. "We can read her lips, but her words are coming out messed up."

"For now, I want you to pass that information to the ICU nurses." Dr. Brighton got

313

close to Becca's face. "Tell me your name."

"Ahaah aaaahah." *Becca Jackson.*

"Becca Jackson. I understand."

Becca nodded. *That's weird. My lips are doing the right thing, but it sure doesn't sound right.*

As the doctor turned to walk out, she said to the nurse, "Okay, lip reading it is."

27

When the excitement of the girls' return had begun to dissipate, Noah realized that he hadn't eaten since breakfast. In fact, none of them had. They'd all been too busy and too anxious to even think about hunger. But as the relief of having the girls safely home settled in, so did the feeling of being famished.

Noah made a quick marinade of butter, garlic, and lemon juice and laid a thick slab of pink salmon on the grill. In the meantime, Mel made sweet-potato fries and a spinach salad garnished with Craisins, walnuts, feta cheese, and pumpkin seeds.

They were just setting the table when Tiffany and the police returned.

"Amy, there was no one there!" Tiffany said. "The place was locked up tight, no car in the driveway or anything."

Amy looked stunned. "Did you go in and get the copy of the photograph?"

The officer accompanying Tiffany shook his head. "We couldn't enter without a warrant. I'll talk to a magistrate and get permission to enter the residence. My partner is contacting the Lake Homeowners Association to find out who owns the house."

When the officers had gone, the group ate and talked about going home.

"Might as well," Noah said. "Whoever threatened us obviously knows where we are." He paused, remembering something. "Tiffany, did you talk to Chief Jackson since you were here?"

"Oh yeah," she replied. "He called on Mom's phone yesterday to check on us. Just wanted to know how we were getting along."

Melissa's voice was edged with tension. "Did you tell him where we were?"

"Sure," she said, shrugging and taking another helping of salad. "He said he needed to know in order to keep tabs on us. Nice to know somebody in law enforcement is taking this stuff seriously."

Noah's eyes met Mel's.

I'm sure he's taking it seriously all right. He probably hired those two college dudes to sweet-talk our girls away just to scare us into backing down . . . as if we had anything to do with threatening his daughter.

Later that night, under the banner of a

billion stars, Noah stood out on the deck and tried Becca's phone. For about the tenth time since he'd heard she was in the hospital.

Voice mail again. He looked at his watch. *Probably still in surgery.* He slipped the phone into his pocket just as Mel stepped out onto the deck to join him.

He leaned against the railing, looking out on the lake and the moon's reflection. He felt Mel's hand on his shoulder. He reached for it, taking her hand in his. He couldn't help but notice how natural it felt to take her hand in his.

But even with that simple act of kindness, he felt conflicted. His heart had balanced itself precariously on a wire. Fall back to Becca. Fall forward to Mel.

He sighed. He didn't want to hurt Mel. She was uncomplicated and honest. He could tell how she felt. "Mel, we —"

"Shh!" she said. "Just let me enjoy the silence with you."

He looked at her hand in his. It was a friendly gesture. *That's all, right?*

So why do I feel guilty for enjoying it? He cleared his throat. "We shouldn't —"

She shushed him again. "This is too perfect a night to talk about us."

She knows what I want to say before I say it.

"I've got my daughter back. And for now, that's enough," she whispered. "Just let me enjoy myself for a few minutes."

And so he relaxed.

Her face was bright in the moonlight. She smiled and gave his hand a little squeeze.

He smiled because he enjoyed it too.

Barry Jackson was nudged awake by a touch on his shoulder. He stretched and looked up to see the neurosurgeon. He tried to uncurl gracefully from the row of vinyl chairs, but his back was stiff and he almost rolled onto the floor. "Ugh," he said, sitting up. "Everything okay, doc?" He reached over and touched Rachel, who slept in the recliner next to him.

Rachel rubbed her eyes. "What time is it?"

Leslie Brighton answered, her voice quiet. "It's 2:00 a.m. We've been watching your daughter for a few hours in recovery, and I have a few concerns. She's developed a type of expressive aphasia —"

"Expressive what?"

"Aphasia," Dr. Brighton repeated. "It means she isn't able to formulate words properly."

Barry stood up. "She can't talk?"

The surgeon nodded. "Something like that. Since she didn't have this symptom before the surgery, I'm concerned that she may be experiencing a complication. We're sending her to get an emergency CT scan of the head on her way to the neuro ICU." The surgeon touched Barry's arm. "She knows who she is. Her brain is working. Her lips get the correct message, but she seems unable to voice the words that she is thinking."

Rachel stood and gripped Barry's arm. "A complication?"

"Perhaps some bleeding. We should know more after the CT scan." She took a step back. "Since you stayed, I just wanted to keep you informed."

"This is only temporary, right? I mean, she'll get over this, won't she?"

Dr. Brighton's upper lip tightened. "We don't know. We can only investigate and hope. Perhaps if we detect a problem, the shunt will have to be adjusted."

"More surgery?"

"We just don't know enough yet."

Rachel sniffed, and Barry watched the neurosurgeon walk away, leaving him to console his wife.

He didn't know what to say. In less than twenty-four hours, his daughter had gone from a brilliant pharmaceutical researcher to a brain tumor patient unable to speak. He shook his head. He felt like crying but knew he needed to be strong for his wife. *God, what is going on?*

The next morning, Noah plodded to the kitchen in search of caffeine. Mel greeted him by pouring him a cup of fresh coffee into a tall ceramic mug. He grunted his approval.

He looked around and took in the array of kitchen utensils, bowls, and ingredients on the counter. *Mel the restaurant owner strikes again.*

He reached for a large raspberry sitting in a bowl. She smiled and held up a spatula as a weapon. "Hey, I need that," she said playfully.

"What is all this?"

"I found raspberries yesterday at a roadside market. I'm making raspberry sauce and crepes."

He looked at his watch.

"Need to get to work?" she asked.

He shook his head. "I need to get over to Charlottesville." He hesitated. "Want to come?"

She turned her back, but not before he detected the disappointment on her face.

She stirred a bubbling pot of purple liquid on the stove. "Nope. I should take Tiff back to Dayton. My restaurant has seen a few too many days without me."

"I need to let my boss know about Becca's condition. He'll want me to follow up, since he set me up to try and hire her." He sipped his coffee.

"I'm sure."

"It's hard to believe she could become so ill so fast."

"I understand. You should go."

"I'm not sure how long I'll be —"

Mel turned around, her face flushed. "I said you should go. You don't have to justify seeing Becca to me." She put her hand to her mouth. "I'm sorry. That sounded so harsh."

He stepped closer and put his arms around her. It felt natural, and she didn't resist. She leaned her head toward him, and he inhaled the scent of her hair.

She looked up. "Stay for breakfast?"

He smiled. "Wouldn't miss it."

By midmorning, Becca was sitting up at a thirty-degree angle in a bed in the neurosurgical intensive care unit. The blip, blip, blip of her heart monitor was her constant friend, and she found herself able to snooze for short periods of time after the nurse gave her morphine injections to ease her headache.

She awoke in a narcotic fog, aware of a clinical odor — a mixture of iodine and alcohol with a hint of some body fluid. The smell of hospitals had a way of jarring her into the hazy memory of the night of her accident.

"Hold her still!"

Becca struggled against strong hands pressing down on her forehead.

"I'm going to be sick!"

"Stop moving! I'll never get this together properly if you —"

Becca retched.

"Oh, great," the surgeon said, cursing. "Those were my favorite running shoes."

A nurse's voice. "I can't make her hold still. Oh my, it's like one big opening between her mouth and nose."

"Get me some Pavulon and a ventilator!"

"You want to paralyze her?"

"She won't hold still. I have no choice."

Moments later, Becca lost her ability to fight back. She couldn't speak. *Hey, I can't breathe!*

Rough hands positioned her head back, her neck extended. A metal object slid into the back of her throat. She saw everything. A plastic tube. An inflated bag squeezed by a gloved hand.

A brown gauze with cold liquid touched her face. A towel covered her eyes. *Wait! I can still feel!*

Agony!

Stop! Stop! Stop!

She couldn't move. Her muscles wouldn't obey.

Searing pain in her lip and then in her nose. It felt as if the surgeon was putting a metal probe up her nostril.

Doesn't this guy know he hasn't numbed me up?

Becca felt a hand on her arm and opened her eyes. It was a gray-haired nurse wearing a pair of pink scrubs and a University of Virginia badge identifying her as Gladys. "Rebecca, you have a visitor."

Noah stood at the foot of her bed. She lifted her hand and motioned him forward.

Gladys spoke in tones reminiscent of a grade-school teacher, clearly and slowly so he could get everything. "Rebecca has a unique expressive aphasia. She is able to think the proper words, but they don't come out as she'd like. Interestingly enough, her lips seem to get the message, so even though she makes nonsense noise, you can read her lips and ignore what you hear."

Noah moved closer.

Becca felt as if she could speak, but when she did, she only vocalized crazy syllables. *Noah, I knew you'd come.*

He squinted toward her lips. He reached for her hand. "What's this? No lipstick for the patient?"

That made her smile. It was the first day in a long time she'd forgotten to even think about putting it on.

That was very weird. She'd worn lipstick every day of her life since prom night. And she always felt naked without it.

But not today.

What is different about today?

She knew. She remembered her experience on the operating-room table. She'd finally taken hold of a hand scarred by nails on her behalf. And not because she deserved it. Just because of love.

She shrugged and tried to tell him. *I don't need it.*

She had to repeat the nonsense sounds three times with Noah studying her lip movements. "Okay," he said, "I get it." He wrinkled his nose. "I'm not very good at this."

Dr. Leslie Brighton appeared at Noah's right. "I'm Dr. Brighton, Rebecca's neurosurgeon." She looked at Becca. "I'd like to discuss the results of your CT scan. Should I ask the gentleman to step outside?"

Becca shook her head and mouthed to Noah, *Stay.* She found it easier not to try to speak but to concentrate on the movement of her lips.

The doctor began. "The CT scan shows that your shunt is in good position. I'm encouraged because the size of the ventricles is already smaller. That means the shunt is working, moving the fluid away from your brain and lessening the pressure."

Becca mouthed, *Head pain.*

Hey, at least my lips obey my brain, she thought.

"Yes," Dr. Brighton said. "You might expect the pain to be better because we've lessened the pressure, but unfortunately, we also see another problem. The needle biopsy has caused two areas of fresh bleeding, one very close to your speech center. That's why you're having this problem speaking. The good news is, because it was due to bleeding and not new tumor growth, I think you have a strong chance of recovery."

Becca offered a thumbs-up.

Dr. Brighton continued. "There is so much about the brain that I find fascinating. In some cases of expressive aphasia following stroke, we see an inability to name objects that are seen. But if the patient is given the same object to hold and feel in their hand, they can name it without hesitation. So in speech therapy, we tell the patient to mentally reach out and imagine feeling the object — that makes the order to name the object follow a different neural pathway. It seems to work.

"In Rebecca's case," the doctor said, turning toward Noah, "her brain tells her voice to speak the words she is thinking, but the injury to the speech area scrambles the part of the message going to the vocal cords. Strangely enough, the lips are getting the proper message. I haven't seen this before, and I'll have to do a literature search to see if anyone has reported it. If they haven't, I think we'll have to."

Great. I'm going to contribute to medical science after all!

Dr. Brighton looked over the chart and stared at a computer screen at Becca's bedside for a few minutes.

Becca took her hand to get her attention and mouthed, *You must be tired.*

The surgeon smiled. "Yes." She sighed. "I'm going to talk to a speech pathologist. As soon as we get you out to a regular room, I'll have them start to work with you." She squeezed Becca's hand and walked away.

Becca patted the edge of her bed. Noah sat. They were quiet for a moment. Finally, Noah asked, "Why didn't you tell me?"

She mouthed, *Paper.*

He walked to the nurse's station with her request. A minute later, he came back with a clipboard and a pen.

She wrote. The tumor is bringing more oxygen to a creative part of my brain, helping me solve the artificial blood problems.

"So that's it?"

I knew that you would want me to get treatment, but if I do, I will lose the ability to figure out the problems in my research.

"But without treatment . . ." His voice sounded as though it got stuck in his throat.

No time for playing around. This thing looks like cancer. The biopsy will confirm. I could die from this.

"Becca, if you die, no one will benefit from your research."

They will if I can use the added creativity to solve the problems first.

His voice thickened. "No, Becca, you've got too much to lose. You have to get treatment." He hesitated. "Do it for me."

I can't put myself before the thousands, maybe millions who could benefit from this research.

"Let someone else discover it. Somebody

will solve the problem eventually."

Eventually is not good enough. I'm through living for myself.

"Oh yeah? Well, who are you going to live for now? You think if you lay down your life for everyone who can benefit from your research, it will soothe your soul?" He shook his head. "You think it will make up for Jimmy Peters?"

Nope, she mouthed.

"Why risk your life?" He took her hand. "I don't want to lose you again."

She pulled her hand away from his so she could write.

I need to do something for someone besides me for a change. Like you did for me.

She folded over the paper to start fresh on the next page.

You changed everything for me.

I wasn't charged. You were.

I didn't go to jail. You did.

If I had, I wouldn't have been strong and fought back. Like you did.

You went to jail a hero and came out a hero, don't you see?

I would have gone to jail a helpless nerd. I didn't have the strength to battle back like you did.

He started to protest, but she waved her hand and wrote again.

You weren't the only one to sacrifice for me.

He looked at her. She didn't try to speak. She just took his hand and nodded. When his expression changed to one of questioning, she did a simple gesture, one of the few sign-language symbols that she knew, probably some holdover from a neighbor dragging her to vacation Bible school. She took the middle finger of one hand and touched the palm of the opposite hand and then quickly repeated the move with the other hand.

He understood. "Nail prints?"

Lip movements: *Yes*.

He leaned forward, his voice edged with excitement. "What, the skeptic has taken a leap of faith?"

She nodded. Enthusiastically.

"What changed?"

She lifted the clipboard and wrote.

Afraid to die.

I remembered something that your father taught me.

As he read her words, he covered his heart with his hand and looked away, but not before she saw him brush the back of his other hand across his eye.

"That's great." She could tell he wanted to talk more, but he seemed hesitant.

She wrote.

I knew a janitor once. He shared news that I wouldn't let myself believe.

She thought for a moment and then added,

I know so little. Only one verse by memory, actually. But for now, it seems enough.

He nodded at the reference to his father. "We'll talk more. I should let you rest."

She mouthed, *Headache.*

He gently touched her cheek and lifted her fingers to his mouth, where he pressed them against his lips.

She shook her head and lifted her face. He understood the open gesture and leaned forward to meet her. It was a brief kiss. Short. A good-bye kiss, but more. A bit of a promise. That made her smile.

He turned to leave as she was writing one more thing, but he didn't pause to look back at what she had written there.

She held it up toward him anyway, the words facing his back as he walked away. She clapped her hands to make him turn and look.

Olive juice.

He laughed. It had been a standing joke between them. Mrs. Hostetler had separated Noah and Becca during their senior year English class for talking. So they developed a secret way of mouthing words to each other. Saying "I love you" seemed too mushy and intimate, so they just mouthed, *Olive juice,* a phrase that, to the lip reader, looked exactly like "I love you," but wasn't mushy and made Noah and Becca snicker behind Mrs. Hostetler's back.

Noah repeated it back, but only whispering so she had to read his lips. "Olive juice."

28

After two days in the ICU, Becca was moved to a regular room. Her headaches had lessened, and she was anxious to get to work again.

After all, time was of the essence. Clichéd, but true.

An hour after she arrived in her private room, her mother and father entered. Her father held up her satchel.

She lifted a clipboard and wrote.

Daddy, you brought my computer.

Her mother protested. "Against our better judgment. Becca, you need to rest."

I'll rest.

But I have a promise to keep.

And a problem to solve.

She opened her laptop, aware that her parents were hovering and silent. She looked up and mouthed, *What?*

Her mother sighed and looked at her father. "We talked to your neurologist. We know you didn't follow his advice."

Advice is just that, she wrote. It's not written in stone and it's not law. I can't be forced to do it.

Her father: "Becca, you're not thinking clearly."

I don't want to argue about this.

"Dr. Harrelson told us you were self-medicating." Her mother crossed her arms across her chest. "He said he thinks you have cancer and could die very soon."

I understand what I'm doing.

"We are your parents, honey. And we don't think you do. The tumor is —"

She held up her hand to cut her mother off, then wrote, The tumor is what? Causing me to act irrationally?

Her father took a deep breath. "To be blunt, that's it exactly."

Well, I appreciate your concern, but I have to make my own choices.

She watched as her parents exchanged a knowing glance. Her mother spoke next. "We've requested Dr. Harrelson to ask for a psychiatric evaluation."

Becca was stunned. She knew how this worked. Psych evaluations were followed by incompetency hearings and motions for ap-pointed guardians to make decisions for those who could not be entrusted with their own health. She held up her hands in protest and then furiously scribbled, *I'm not believing this. I hope he had the sense to laugh at your request.*

"As a matter of fact," her father said, hooking his thumb into his belt, "no one was laughing."

Her mother took a step forward. "Becca, he knows you forged his signature to get dangerous drugs to treat your own brain tumor."

What?

Her father shook his head. "Don't play innocent. A pharmacist called his office to confirm a dose that seemed high. When the doctor checked it, he saw what you'd been doing." He seemed to hesitate. "The doctors told us they saw the needle tracks on your arms."

Of course I have needle tracks. From the steroid injections.

Her father shrugged. "It looks bad, though. Like maybe you were abusing something else."

She shook her head and mouthed, *No!*

"Becca," her mother said, "he isn't going to press any charges as long as you cooperate."

As slow as our legal system works, I'll be long dead before anyone can prosecute me for trying to stay alive!

Her mother's mouth fell open. After a moment, she recovered, saying, "Honey, obtaining drugs using a forged prescription is a serious crime!"

And it will all look like more insane behavior by a judge, I'm sure!

Her father and mother agreed, nodding and standing together holding hands. Her father said, "This is really so unfortunate, but how would you really know if the tumor is causing you to act this way?"

This talk is crazy! Perhaps for the first time in my life, I'm inclined to actually do something for someone else besides me.

Her mother reached for Becca's hand. "Just talk to the psychiatrist, dear. What harm can it do?"

I won't lie, Becca resolved. *I won't tell them I'll treat the cancer. They'll have me committed against my will. I won't tell them I've put my faith in Christ and am not afraid to die. They will force me into treatment. And I'll lose my creativity.*

They will absolutely think I'm crazy.

Becca smiled sweetly at her mother and wrote, Sure, Mom, what harm could it do?

Thirty minutes later, Becca opened a new document on her laptop and wrote, "I'm pretty tired. I'd like to get some rest now." She turned the screen around for her parents to see. She was glad she had her computer now; typing was faster than writing it out by hand on the clipboard.

Her mother hugged her and said, "You're doing the right thing."

Her father kissed her on the cheek and said, "Good-bye."

She waited until they left, then took a stroll down the hallway, dragging along her IV pole. When she got to a linen closet, she slipped inside. She scanned the room for a pair of women's scrubs, then rolled them up tightly and slipped them under her arm. It took her a little longer to locate a suitable female scrub hat, but she finally selected one in generic blue with a print of small yellow daisies. Back in her bathroom a few minutes later, she yanked out her IV and held pressure with a wad of toilet tissue. She untied her patient gown, removed it, and folded it up, then carefully undid the bandage around her head and sighed. They'd shaved her head in two spots, but fortunately not so much that she couldn't rearrange her hair to cover. For now, she just settled for twisting it up and stuffing it under the scrub hat. She dressed in the blue scrubs, placed her patient gown under her pillow, lifted her satchel and phone, and went strolling down the hall toward the nursing station, where she quietly lifted a white coat from the back of a chair and walked away toward the elevators. She waited nervously for a down elevator, glancing back toward her nursing station. When the door slid open, she nodded at the doctors inside and slid to the back of the elevator, casually arranging her satchel to cover the ID badge attached to the front of the white coat.

When she exited on the first floor, she had two goals.

One: tell the truth.

Two: give the world the first successful artificial blood.

And not get caught.

But to do any of that, she had to stay alive.

29

Noah spent the first hour of the morning pounding the pavement and trails around James River Park. He needed time alone, time away from constant connectedness with Kristen, Amy, Caroline, Lizzy, Mel, Tiffany, and Becca, and time to just stop thinking about relationships, the future, and risk.

But he couldn't get Becca out of his mind. Just when it seemed she was back in his life and had made real progress on her faith journey, he couldn't even be sure she would survive to see the next full moon.

She will die if she doesn't agree to treatment.

But how can I convince her to help herself?

He tried to focus on anything except his runaway thoughts. The smell of pine, the crunch of the gravel path beneath his Nike running shoes, the glimpses of the James River between the summer leaf growth, and the sound of city commuters traveling over the bridge-arteries linking North and South Richmond would distract him for a moment or two, but eventually his thoughts returned to the first woman who'd ever had a tight grip on his heart.

He remembered going to the Rockingham County Fair, eating funnel cake and BBQ chicken with Becca and looking at Mel's blue-ribbon-winning photographs. He thought about Friday night football, of a regional and state championship, and how his mother had clipped every article from the *Daily News Record* showing him evading a tackle or making a successful pass. He remembered doing his math homework in the cafeteria, waiting for his father to finish buffing the hallways after school.

When he thought about his father, his pace quickened, as if punishing his body could push away the painful memories of a cancer that had stolen his father from him before Noah could show him he'd made good.

The doctors had found a melanoma on his father's back two weeks after Noah had been jailed on assault charges and driving under the influence of alcohol.

Six months later, his father was dead, and a county deputy accompanied Noah to his father's memorial service.

And despite all the pain, Noah's faith remained. He wondered about it sometimes. He'd had friends with far fewer reasons to shake a fist at God but who had nevertheless turned away from their faith roots. But not Noah. What turned others away just seemed to drive him further into the everlasting arms of God's comfort.

When he arrived back at his car, he noted two missed phone calls on his cell. One number he thought he recognized: the officer from the lake. He called him back, standing by his car and looking down toward the boulders at the edge of the James River.

"Officer Smith."

"Yes, officer, this is Noah Linebrink. I'm returning a missed call from my cell."

"Yes, Noah. I was just calling to follow up on our experience down at Smith Mountain Lake."

"Okay, thank you. What have you found out?"

"We checked the homeowner's record. The house where the gentlemen were reportedly entertaining your niece is owned by a pharmaceutical company. Ever heard of Jackson Pharmaceuticals?"

"Of course. Becca Jackson was the one we

were accused of threatening."

"I get that," he said. "So anyway, the link was interesting enough, so I followed up with a little visit to their CEO. He said the lake house is open to use by any of the employees, and that the records showed that the Jones family — Jones being one of his administrative assistants — had signed the house out for the week. When I asked him about the copy of the photographs of Amy and Tiffany, he explained that he had been at the house a few days before and had likely left a copy of the photographs by mistake. He claims his brother made a copy for him to show him what was going on with his niece. He said the boys were likely just friends of the Jones family and that they were just behaving like normal college guys, picking up young females to party."

"He said the photographs belonged to him?"

"That's what he said."

"That's bogus."

"He might be lying, but it covers the story so well that a magistrate will never issue a search warrant. I'm afraid we've hit the end of the road there. Have there been any new threats to Amy or Tiffany?"

"No. I've been in pretty much constant contact with my sister and Mel, Tiffany's mom, and they haven't heard anything either."

"Well, stay vigilant. Let me know if I can help you in any way."

Noah ended the call in disbelief. *The house belongs to Jackson Pharmaceuticals?* He closed his fist in anger. *JP is behind this somehow!*

Becca picked up a diet soda in the hospital cafeteria and sat at a table in the corner where she could turn her back to the crowd. She thought about her options. She couldn't exactly take a taxi all the way back to Dayton for her things. She couldn't even talk to the taxi driver in her present condition.

She opened her laptop, hoping that the other employees would see that she was busy and not try to speak to her.

The only person she trusted enough to call was Noah.

She texted his phone. Need you to come to hospital NOW to pick me up. I'll explain later. Please come NOW.

He replied. Just finished a run. Need time to clean up, then an hour on the road back to Charlottesville. Are you discharged?

Becca looked around. Could she hide here for an hour? How long would it take until the nursing staff suspected she had run away? She texted back, In effect, yes. Really need you soon.

His reply was brief but at least revealed his willingness to comply. Okay, see you soon.

She texted, Just call me and tell me when you are very close, and I'll walk out front for you to pick me up. I won't be able to speak back, but I can hear you.

She sipped her drink and decided to review the last changes she'd made in the chemical-reaction protocol to formulate the artificial hemoglobin. Quickly, she became absorbed in envisioning the molecule and was happy to see that her creative under-standing of three-dimensional structure had not been harmed during her surgery. A few critical steps remained.

I need to turn this tertiary structure into a quaternary one.

Snipping this ionic bond should do the trick if the outside environment is water loving.

For the next hour, Becca lost herself in the world of chemical bonds and molecular structure. She stared at the models on the screen and mentally moved and folded them until they matched the natural one that was perfectly designed to accept and release oxy-gen.

A young man wearing a white coat stopped by her table. "Will someone be joining you? Is it okay to take this chair?"

She smiled and nodded, lifting her head as if to say, "No problem." She avoided eye contact and stared back at her screen, feeling his eyes lingering on her. He hesitated for a moment and then said, "I'll take that as a yes," and carried the chair away to an adjacent table.

Come on, Noah, get me out of this.

A pain on the left side of her head clawed for attention. If she'd been back in her room, she could easily have asked the nurse for something to relieve it. As it was, she would have to wait until she got back to her home in Dayton.

Fifteen minutes later, her phone sounded. She pressed the accept button and listened.

"Becca? Becca? I guess you're listening. I'm almost there. Two minutes to the front of the hospital. Meet me there, okay?"

She placed her laptop in her satchel and walked out of the cafeteria into the lobby. There, she shed her white coat, hanging it in plain sight from the back of a chair. *Hopefully the owner will see it.*

She looked down at her clothing. *I can return these scrubs later.*

Then she walked outside and spotted

344

Noah's Lexus pulling to the curb. She got in and mouthed, *Thank you. Let's go!*

"Where to?"

She had already written out a response on her clipboard in preparation for his arrival. She held up one word: Home!

Back at her house, Becca studied Noah as he read the explanation she had typed out on her laptop during their trip over the mountain. She had typed out the truth: her decision to flee from the psych evaluation, her awareness that she was putting her health at risk, and her desire to put someone else's welfare before her own. He seemed troubled, but he nodded his acceptance of her right to refuse treatment.

Her priorities: money, medicine, and a place to hide. She was certain that as soon as her parents found out she was missing, she'd be in for a fight, perhaps even a defense of her sanity.

And she didn't have time for that.

She packed a modest-sized suitcase with her favorite clothing and cosmetics. Although she felt less emotionally dependent now on lipstick, she knew there might be a media date or two in her future, and she wanted to be prepared.

She changed from the scrubs, tried to fix

her hair, then decided that wearing a scrub cap with her hair tucked up wasn't the worst thing in the world for a woman who had just undergone a shunt and a brain biopsy.

She filled out a withdrawal slip from her checking account in the amount of five thousand dollars and had Noah take her to her bank. She only touched her throat and mouthed, *Laryngitis,* when the teller asked her how she was.

The next stop was Jackson Pharmaceuticals. She needed to see her uncle and make one last plea for him to pay the ransom. It would be one less thing for her to have to worry about as she prioritized her activities.

She wrote out her request on her laptop as they traveled.

She stopped in her office first. In the center of her desk sat a manila envelope that contained another revealing photograph, an acknowledgment that the account Becca had opened was acceptable, but also one more threat because the money had not yet made it into the account.

Noah waited in her office while she headed up to see the CEO.

She knocked on his door, thankful that Arlene was away from her desk for a change. Her uncle looked up and smiled. "Becca, didn't expect to see you. How are you feeling?"

She touched her throat and shook her head.

"Yes, yes," he said, "Barry told me about your problem with speech. Unfortunate." He squinted at her scrub cap. "Your parents didn't tell me you were getting out so soon."

She mouthed, *Today.*

She handed him the new manila envelope and gave him a minute to study it. Then she opened her laptop and let him read her plea:

Uncle Jimmy,
Please consider transferring the requested fifteen million into the offshore account that I've set up. Here is the paperwork needed to ensure that your name will also be on the account as a person able to move money in or out of the account without my signature.

She tapped his shoulder and handed him a banking form. He continued reading.

That way, in case I am physically unable to make the transfer, you can do it in my absence. Or if I die and you do not wish to pay the extortion, you can simply withdraw the money.

I may not have much time left. Please consider what failure to pay the fee would do to my memory as well as the harm it would do to my father's campaign. I'd like to leave as positive an impact as I can. Consider it a small gift to me, if you will, and not an extortion. And be confident that I am closing in on one of the most significant medical breakthroughs in our lifetime, one that will make JP rich beyond your wildest dreams, so this will be insignificant in the long run. Make the payment, Uncle Jimmy, so I can move on and concentrate my efforts on solving the final problems in development of an artificial blood.

He looked up.

She mouthed, *For me. Please?*

He looked at the form she had handed to him. "So if we submit this paperwork with our signatures, I will have equal access and control over the account with you?"

She nodded.

He shook his head. "The things I do to preserve your reputation." He signed the form next to her signature. He paused before handing it back. "You know how much this business means to me," he said. "But family does come first."

She nodded. *What, Uncle Jimmy with a soft spot?*

He waved his hand. "No worries — I'll have Arlene notarize this."

It seemed he was softening to the idea of putting this behind him. But she wouldn't be confident of his cooperation until she saw the transfer of money into the account.

She mouthed, *Thank you,* and scurried off to meet Noah. In her office, she took her phone out of her satchel and left it in her desk.

Noah raised his eyebrows in question.

She scribbled a note: My father will try to track my iPhone.

Follow me, she mouthed to Noah. They went straight to her lab, where she handed another printed note to David.

Of all her colleagues working on the project, David seemed the most completely loyal. He was twenty-seven, single, and OCD about his commitment to the project. He had a few outside interests, including a passion for windsurfing, something that he did on weekends at Virginia Beach. He voted Democrat and was an advocate of euthanasia rights for the terminally ill. Among her coworkers, David would likely sympathize most with her refusal to accept medical treatment. Besides, she was sure that he'd had a secret crush on her for months but had never been bold enough to act on it beyond the occasional flirting that Becca declined to reciprocate.

The note she gave him outlined her medical treatment, her reasons for deferring treatment, and her motivation to proceed quickly toward completion of the project, as well as the necessity to let Noah Linebrink in at every level. It went on to explain her need to work via email and phone from an undisclosed, hidden site, and it reiterated the reason for speed. He wanted to keep all of this confidential. Could he do this?

He looked up from his desk with moist eyes. He nodded. "I can do this, Becca." He paused. "Are you sure?"

She nodded and wrote on the bottom of the note, I'll be in touch soon.

She walked out, wishing she had taken her pain medication before unveiling her little plan.

30

From her office at the restaurant, Melissa dialed Noah's cell.

He answered after the second electronic tone. "Hey."

"Hey back. Busy day?"

"Always a challenge."

"Say, I know this is last minute, but I thought I'd see if you were heading over to Charlottesville. I could escape over the mountain and we could meet somewhere for dinner."

"Well, actually, I'm not in Charlottesville. I'm just outside Harrisonburg."

"Even better. I can cook you dinner at my place."

"Well, actually . . ."

"You're with Becca."

He hesitated. "Yeah."

"So she's out of the hospital? Doesn't exactly sound like death's-door stuff to me."

"Something's up. Her parents are trying

to force her into some sort of treatment, and she's staying away from them."

"And you're helping her hide."

"Something like that."

She hesitated. As hard as it was for her to encourage Noah to support Becca, his faithfulness made her respect him even more. "You're a good man, Noah."

"So you approve? I almost thought you might finally play the jealousy card and try to talk some sense into me."

"Jealous?" She felt her cheeks redden. "You haven't always been this intuitive about my feelings." She paused and weighed her words. "Okay, I'll admit, there is a part of me that is a little suspicious that Becca is pulling a gigantic stunt to get publicity for her book."

"Except the media knows nothing about it."

"Yet."

His voice was quiet. "You do sound a little jealous."

"I just don't want to see you hurt." She halted. "Okay, I'm jealous. I said it. I haven't exactly hidden my feelings."

"She's in trouble."

"Yeah, I can't really compete with brain cancer for your attention, can I?"

"That's pretty endearing, actually."

"Okay, I know you can't exactly speak freely, so let me do it and you can listen. I don't know why God has brought you, me, and Becca back together after all these years. Maybe it is a gift to restore your relationship with Becca. If that's what He has in mind, I'm determined not to interfere. But I'm a woman of passion too, Noah, and I get confused around you." She halted again. "Noah, I guess I'm just babbling, but I'm trying to say that I can deal with whatever God has planned. I don't always like it, but I've learned a little about trust along the way."

Melissa continued. "Just be careful with that one. I don't know why I have caution lights about her. Maybe I'm just being catty and jealous, or maybe it's the way things went down on the night that changed everything for you. She has a crisis, and you're the one who gets tangled up and hurt. I don't want to see it happen again."

She listened as he sighed into the phone. "Okay, listen, I've got to go."

Yeah, right.

He paused. "Rain check?"

"Deal," she said and ended the call.

Becca had Noah drop her off in Woodstock, Virginia, at a Holiday Inn Express. She signed in using the name Bonnie Matthews and paid for the room in cash. Before checking into the hotel, they stopped at Walmart, where she purchased a few food items, a bottle each of ibuprofen and acetaminophen, and a pay-as-you-go phone.

Noah wanted to stay and talk about her new faith, but she mouthed, *Later,* and offered him a single, no-lipsticked kiss. Lips parted, but no tongue. She wanted him but felt conflicted. She had to remain focused. If she let her feelings for Noah speed ahead, she feared she would give in to his desire for her to get treatment.

As soon as Noah left, she packed up her things and dragged her suitcase up the street to the Hampton Inn, where she checked into a second room using the name Samantha Rogers and, again, paid in advance in cash.

In her new room, she took one gram of Tylenol, eight hundred milligrams of ibuprofen, and two Dilantin capsules, gave herself a dexamethasone injection, and opened her laptop.

Four hours later, she emailed David Letchford, outlining new modifications for their hemoglobin molecule synthesis. She looked at her watch and then out the window at the night sky. *David is already gone for the day.*

Something isn't right.

What am I missing?

She rubbed the left side of her head where a dull throbbing had resumed.

She got up and went to the bathroom. It was time to wash her hair, her first time since her surgery.

It was too painful to let the water spray directly onto her head, but she stayed out of the stream and lifted the water with her hands to wash away the old blood and iodine.

After her shower, she rubbed a circle in the fog on the mirror and practiced making consonant sounds. She managed "ba ba baa," "ca ca caaa," and "da da daaa." She found that if she wasn't trying to say real words, somehow her voice and lips seemed to synchronize. It was different, but progress nonetheless.

Weird.

She dressed, ate an apple and a few crackers she'd purchased at Walmart, and opened a Gideon Bible she'd found in the nightstand. She began with the book of John, absorbed in the story of Jesus walking the dusty streets of Galilee.

Dear God, she prayed, *help me.*

Give me back my voice.

So I can tell the truth.

In the quietness of her hotel room, something occurred to her: maybe reading out loud would use a different pathway to her voice. She turned back a few pages in the Bible to the verses she knew by memory.

She began with John 3:16: "Fo fo fo faah fa faa."

Help me, Father.

"Fa gaa ga gaa ga gaaah."

She brushed away a tear and walked back into the bathroom. There, staring at herself in the mirror, she began again, concentrating on watching her lips move. One syllable at a time. She pushed her notched upper lip forward to begin forming an F sound.

"Ffff."

She sniffed. "Ffff."

She tried the G sound again, watching her lips. "Gaa."

Now the S. "Gaa." She shook her head and then gently parted her lips with her teeth closed. "Sssss." It worked!

She put the sounds together: "Ffff gaa ssss." *For God so.*

She sighed. *I don't have enough time!*

Instead, she came up with a new plan. *I can write an updated version of my memoir.*

One that tells the truth.

She walked away from the mirror and

356

opened her laptop, propping herself up in the center of the king-sized bed to begin . . .

I once called Christianity a religion for janitors. But I was drunk, spewing hateful words at someone who loved me.

It turns out I was right after all. Christianity is a religion for janitors. And maids. And pharmaceutical chemists . . .

Chief of police Barry Jackson was used to getting his own way. And even though it was late, he'd demanded that the magistrate, John Ewing, stay to see him face-to-face.

He explained the situation. He'd just gotten word that his daughter was missing from the University of Virginia hospital, where she'd been diagnosed with some sort of brain cancer.

"She'll die if she doesn't get treatment. But she's refusing."

John Ewing sighed. "That's a patient's right."

"But not if they aren't competent."

"So that's where this is going? You want to argue that she's not competent? Your daughter is one of the smartest women I've ever met, Barry."

"She isn't thinking straight. She claims this brain tumor is actually helping her think

357

more clearly, so she doesn't want to get it treated." Barry paused and paced the little office. "It's suicide. She's going to die, and that won't help anyone."

John shook his head.

Barry leaned forward. "She's got some great idea that she's on the edge of a huge medical breakthrough in her work. She refuses any treatment that may hinder her research."

"That sounds noble, not crazy."

"You don't understand. She could get treatment and still solve her problem."

"But she doesn't see it that way."

"I know my daughter. She would never sacrifice her life like this — that just shows how much this brain tumor is changing her. She isn't thinking straight."

John pushed his chair away from his desk. It appeared he was ready to leave.

"Help me out here," Barry said. "What are my options? She's incompetent. She needs urgent medical treatment. This is life and death, John."

John sighed. "She's not incompetent unless a judge says so. And no judge is going to rule that way unless a psychiatrist gives an expert opinion that the judge believes."

"But she ran away from the hospital. She *ran away* from the psychiatric evaluation because she knows she's crazy. She needs to be committed."

"Look," John said, "I'm not sure you're right about this. Rebecca has a right as an adult to refuse medical treatment. But if you *are* right, and she is mentally incompetent — and I'm saying *if* — then the only way to prove it is to force a mandatory three-day evaluation at a state mental hospital. She can be held for three days against her will. If the state psychiatrist feels that she's incompetent, then and only then will a judge agree to have your daughter committed against her will and force her to undergo treatment."

"Please," Barry pleaded, "I'm begging you. Issue the order for a three-day evaluation. You'll be saving her life."

John shook his head and turned his attention to his desktop computer screen. "Come back in an hour. You'll have your order. Then you can have your guys pick her up and take her to Western State." He paused, locking eyes with the chief of police. "But I sure hope you know what you're doing. She's not going to like this."

"I know what I'm doing," Barry said. "I'm saving my daughter's life."

31

The next day, Barry Jackson barged into his brother's executive office at Jackson Pharmaceuticals to find his brother's administrative assistant at his side, sweetening his coffee. Barry didn't smile. "I'm looking for Becca."

"Good morning to you, too, candidate. Coffee?" James touched his assistant's well-manicured hand. "Arlene, could you get my brother a cup of coffee. Black?"

Barry lifted his head in acknowledgment. "Thanks."

"Becca was by yesterday," James said. "Pitiful sight, really. And too bad. I only hope she can come through and finish her project."

"My daughter's dying. Show a little compassion."

"Her project is worth billions. Show a little practicality." James paused, and his voice softened. "Hey, that sounded too harsh. I know what this is doing to you. And her. She is desperate to finish her project."

"She needs treatment. I've been authorized by the magistrate to pick her up. Is she in her office?"

"I haven't seen her."

"If you do, I need to be the first to know."

"Tell me — what exactly is her prognosis? Did the doctors actually give you a timeline?"

"The neurologist painted a very bleak picture. He said that without treatment, it could be as little as a few weeks."

"She came by to plead with me to make the payment to prevent the photographs from getting to the media. Can you believe that? The woman is facing death, and she's still concerned about you."

Barry felt his face reddening. "It's humbling. I've acted like a jerk to one of the few men she's shown an interest in, and she still looks out for her father."

"You know, if I drag my heels for a few weeks, it won't make any difference to her if I make the extortion payment or not."

"We're talking about my daughter, Jimmy. You can't be so callous as to be thinking about money when Becca is dying."

James held up his hands. "I'm kidding, bro. I'm not going to leave you hanging out to dry." He took a deep breath. "You think people would really blame you?"

"Of course. I was her father. My deputies overlooked the obvious, and I let them get away with it."

James chuckled. "Daddy's little girl."

"Is it really such a difficult thing for you to part with a few dollars?"

"Fifteen million is hardly a few dollars."

"Pocket change for you, especially considering what her project will be worth to the company. Maybe you owe her."

"It's the principle. People shouldn't be allowed to get away with this sort of bribery."

"Isn't there a way you can set up a trace? Follow the money back to the person making the demands."

"I don't have enough information yet. There are so many layers that I can't be sure. Becca wants me to transfer the money into an account that only she and I can control. After that, we're supposed to move the money according to instructions we get later."

"There are things more important than money."

Jimmy nodded slowly and muttered, "Family first."

Barry smiled. "That's what Mama taught us."

■ ■ ■ ■

A few minutes later, Becca heard an electronic chirp signaling she'd received an email.

She opened it and read.

Becca,
What's going on?!!

I just came from your office, where I went to upload the latest synthesis run onto your desktop, and your father was there, going through your stuff. He found your phone in the desk, so he knows you are hiding. He asked me whether you'd spoken to me, and since you really didn't "speak," I said no.

He has some order from a magistrate to pick you up and force you into a three-day psych evaluation at Western State Mental Hospital, so unless you want to do that, I'd suggest being careful. When I went out for lunch, I saw a deputy parked at the entrance, so I think they've staked things out to see if you show up here.

I can handle the synthesis changes as long as you are very specific. The last modification you made is closer, but we still haven't matched the molecular profile of natural hemoglobin. Everything is good up to level 5300. After that, the strands keep wanting to curl instead of folding like they should.

How are you holding up? Anything I can do?

Your father acts like you could be dead somewhere for all he knows. Is that true? Are you really that bad off? Maybe you should get help.

If you need ANYTHING just email or call if you have a new phone.

David

No, David, I can't get treatment yet. You said it yourself — we still haven't matched the molecular profile of natural hemoglobin.

She spent the next thirty minutes practicing vocalizing syllables. She added a P sound, a T sound, and an F sound but couldn't seem to make her vocal cords make an R. For whatever reason, her voice seemed to be returning, albeit too slowly for her schedule. *Maybe the bleeding from the biopsy is being reabsorbed.*

She reread the email. *He has a magistrate's order to have me evaluated?*

I don't have time for this!

Noah spent the afternoon corresponding with David Letchford. They decided that even if the hemoglobin molecule wasn't perfect, they would go ahead and try using the gel microspheres to carry it and see if the micropores could be opened and closed by manipulation of the pH.

David needed another day to have enough product synthesized for a trial run. Noah agreed to come to Jackson Pharmaceuticals the following day to pick up the solution.

For most of the afternoon, as Noah mulled over the synthesis of an artificial blood, he found himself thinking about Becca . . .

Teaching Becca to pass a football.

Becca "borrowing" Noah's father's keys to the school to decorate Noah's locker for his birthday.

Giving Becca a ring from a Cracker Jack box. She wore it every day for a month.

Becca "synthesizing" her own version of Gatorade for Noah to use at football practice — a mixture of water, fresh lemon, a crushed-up children's vitamin tablet, sugar, and salt.

Becca decorating an empty Wheaties cereal box with a photograph that Mel had taken of Noah in his football jersey and then filling the box with Cap'n Crunch, since that was his favorite.

That gave him an idea.

Since he had to be in the valley the following day anyway, why not surprise Becca with a little carry-in supper?

He started by googling Rebecca Jackson images. He selected the author shot on the back of *Pusher,* the one of her standing in a white lab coat. He printed it off and headed out to buy some cereal.

Rachel Jackson always baked when she was nervous. Cooling on the counter were two tins of lemon poppyseed muffins, an apple cake with a caramel glaze, and two loaves of oatmeal bread. In the oven was a casserole dish of Barry's favorite mac and cheese that she doctored by adding ricotta cheese and spicy Italian sausage crumbles.

When Barry came in, he smiled despite the stress. He inhaled deeply and leaned in to give his wife a kiss. She offered him a cheek and wiped her hands on a kitchen towel.

"I ran into Deputy Franks," she began. "He told me that you got an order to pick up Becca."

He nodded and opened the refrigerator.

He popped the top from a bottle of Blue Moon beer. "That's right."

Rachel tried to catch her husband's eye, but he turned and walked toward the den. She trailed after him. "Barry, I'm having second thoughts. What if Becca doesn't survive? We don't want her to be angry with us right before . . ."

Barry sighed. "I just feel so useless standing on the sidelines, watching her. I can't help thinking that she isn't acting rationally." He picked up the TV remote. "WHSV covered my speech at the Rotary Club today."

"That's nice," she said, her voice laced with sarcasm. "Becca will be humiliated, honey." She reached for his shoulder but saw him stiffen before she could lay her hand down, so she halted the movement and closed her hand in the air.

Barry shook his head slowly. "Well, we don't have many options here. According to that doctor, Becca's nearly out of time. She'll just have to realize that we didn't have any choice — that we did it out of love."

"I know her. She won't cooperate."

"She will if she wants to get on with her research."

"Couldn't you just bring her in for us to talk to? We could convince her."

"You just said that you know her. If that was true, you'd realize how futile it is trying to talk sense into someone so headstrong."

The kitchen timer sounded. Rachel walked away mumbling, "I wonder where she got that."

"I heard that, Rachel!"

She heard his footsteps behind her. He opened the refrigerator again. He was going for his second beer in less than two minutes.

She looked at him with disgust. *This is why you weigh two hundred seventy pounds.*

"Look," he said, his voice softening as he wiped his mouth with the back of his hand. "In a few weeks, after Becca has gotten a course of chemo and some radiation and she realizes she's alive because of us, don't you think her attitude will change?"

Rachel shrugged and lifted the bubbly casserole from the oven. "I'm not sure."

"We'll, that's the chance we have to take if we want to save her life. The neurologist even said that if the tumor shrank enough, the surgeons might be willing to operate."

"Great," she said. "So our daughter will live on, hating her parents. How delightful."

"She'll be *alive,* Rachel. That's all that's important." He walked over to the cupboard and took out a plate. He didn't wait for the mac and cheese to cool before filling his plate and walking back to the den to watch the news.

She smiled sweetly at his back. *Maybe I can warn Becca.*

But how? If I email her, he'll see it. And she won't answer her phone.

She worked a large muffin free from the tin and sat at the kitchen table with a diet Coke. *Maybe I could call Noah. I'll bet he knows where she is.*

David Letchford stared at the readout in front of him and shook his head in amazement. It was as if Becca could make predictions about molecular structural changes with an accuracy that bested his computer programs.

She wanted additional changes to the bonds at 6320 and 1774.

How does she do this?

Could this really be the result of a tumor?

Or some sort of divine gift?

He opened his desk drawer and looked at a small framed photograph taken of him and Becca at last year's Christmas party. She didn't know he had it. He didn't keep it on top of his desk for others to see.

He liked the image. She'd laid her arm around his shoulders. It looked so natural there. And that smile . . . those perfect lips!

If I don't tell her how I feel soon, I may never get the chance.

Oh God, don't let her die!

Becca opened a Word document titled *Pusher: Revisions* and started a new chapter.

I once heard that if you do a good job for someone, they tell two others about it; if you do a bad job, they tell seven.

Isn't that just human nature? To focus on the bad instead of the good? Or maybe it's just a matter of personality. But I know what was true for me.

From the day of my accident until now, I haven't been able to look at myself in a mirror without seeing the flaws. A millimeter offset in the vermillion border of my lip. A faint scar extending up to the center of my nose.

I ignore my long, straight blonde hair.

I ignore my high cheekbones and the straightness of my nose and the way it gently turns upward, something that plastic surgeons try to re-create for their patients. (I read that in *Cosmo,* so it may not be entirely accurate, but I do have a nice nose, nonetheless.)

I ignore my natural olive-tan complexion.

I ignore my blue-green eyes and my long lashes.

All I've seen until recently is the flaw.

So I've spent my adult life covering it up.

My mother always asked me why I didn't have it fixed. A good surgeon would have been able to correct the error.

It's funny, I never really spent much time wondering why I avoided corrective surgery. I just kept supporting the lipstick industry.

I think it's because I felt I deserved to look this way.

I *was* flawed. Still am.

And though I believe I deserve it, I'm starting to understand how destructive guilt has been for me all these years.

Sure, I'm flawed.

Who isn't?

A wise hospital chaplain told me that my flaws were my ticket in. As long as we feel perfect, we'll never realize our desperate need for help.

So yeah, I doubt I'll ever get my lip fixed.

'Cause now it reminds me that I'm a pretty needy gal. And for some reason, that feels okay.

Note to the mortician: NO LIPSTICK.

32

That afternoon, Becca pushed through a two-hour sensation of buzzing in the left side of her head. The whole time, she kept the image of their current hemoglobin prototype in front of her, visualizing, rotating, and testing the structural results of subtle changes in outside pH.

She typed like a crazy woman.

But she wasn't crazy.

At least not if it meant she didn't understand the consequences of her actions.

By late afternoon, she emailed a new set of instructions to David.

She stood and stretched, then showered, letting the noise of the water cover the quiet way she practiced saying simple words. She dried her hair and dressed, selecting a throwback seventies-style blouse and jeans.

She texted Noah. She needed to know her pathology result. She needed to know for sure.

■ ■ ■ ■

Noah called from his car. "Could I speak to Dr. Brighton? I'm calling for her patient, Rebecca Jackson, who is unable to speak. She'd like the pathology report from her biopsy."

The office assistant promised that the neurosurgeon would call as soon as she was out of the OR.

Twenty minutes later, his phone rang.

"Hello."

"This is Leslie Brighton."

"Actually, this is Noah Linebrink. I'm a close friend of Becca's, and she asked me to call on her behalf. As you know, she has aphasia and can't exactly ask you these things herself."

"I see. So I take it you're in touch with my patient? I was shocked she left the hospital so soon."

"Well, I hope you can understand. Her parents had arranged a psychiatric interview. They are hoping to have Becca declared incompetent so that she can be forced into treatment."

"I see." Her voice sounded so matter-of-fact. "Well, this is highly irregular. I'm not supposed to give out information except to the patient."

"These are crazy circumstances. I'm sure she'd tell you to tell me if she was able."

"Well," the surgeon said, "I guess there is little risk. Rebecca is going to die before she can sue me if she does nothing to treat this thing."

Noah's first thought was a sarcastic *That's encouraging!*

"The pathologist has confirmed that Rebecca has a glioblastoma multiforme. It is a very immature tumor. That's bad news, but not entirely bad news."

"What do you mean?"

"I've been experimenting with a new protocol to fight these cancers. We take a few cells from the biopsy, grow them in tissue culture, then incubate them with Rebecca's white blood cells to allow the lymphocytes to react to the cancer and form antibodies. Then we send the antibodies through an amplification and give them back to Rebecca to target just the tumor."

"Kind of like her own personal chemotherapy."

"Exactly. It uses the principle of a vaccine."

"How quickly does it work?"

"Because it targets only the cancer cells, we have seen some dramatic responses within days, even hours."

"Thanks, Dr. Brighton. I'll encourage her to come in."

He ended the call and dialed Becca.

The phone rang. Becca recognized Noah's number on the display.

"Ha haa." *Hello.*

He explained what the neurosurgeon had said. "You don't have much time, Becca." He paused. She could tell he was frustrated by the one-sided conversation. "Think about it, okay?"

First things first, Becca thought. *I'll let you know.* She ended the call.

I'm so close to the finish with my research. Could I finish this phase, then get treatment, then pursue a life with Noah again?

With her index finger, she traced her lips, remembering the tender way Noah had kissed her.

God, help me.

I want another chance at love.

Amy wasn't allowed to return to summer school. Her mother insisted it wasn't a punishment. She only wanted Amy to be safe and stay close to home. She had taken away her phone privileges, stating flatly that there had to be consequences for her immature behavior at the lake. The crazy thing was, even though Amy wasn't allowed to use her phone, her mother made her carry it at all times in case she needed to call Amy or in case Amy needed to make an emergency call for help.

Thinking through her experience with Tiffany, Amy was conflicted. She had been scared . . . but she'd also felt so *mature.* She knew she'd developed a lot in the last year. She'd had her period for six months and had outgrown two cup sizes during that time. But the boys in her class didn't look at her the way Mark had. He looked at her like she was an equal, attractive even, and not just a little-girl tagalong. The boys in her class were immature dweebs. All they cared about was stupid professional wrestling that everyone knew was fake, farting, and the latest singing sensation.

But with Tiffany, Dustin, and Mark, she hadn't felt like a tagalong. Yes, she knew it had been set up, but Mark hadn't just been acting, had he? He liked her. She could tell.

But he was dishonest. I can't trust him.

Still, she couldn't help her runaway fantasies of what could have been.

She remembered how it felt, the warmth of his thigh as it brushed against hers under the beach towel. And she found herself dreaming of that surprise kiss.

She found herself dreaming of how things might have been if she'd met Mark under different circumstances. They could hang out. Eat out together. Hold hands and laugh. He could help her with math. She hated math, but her mom insisted she stay on track to take calculus in high school.

She was bored. Her sisters were watching Animal Planet. Her mother was in a bad mood because her father was late on his child support. Again.

She googled "how to kiss." A wikiHow article came up. She moved her lips and tongue to match the instructions.

"What are you doing?" Her mother's voice!

She closed the laptop a little too fast and a little too loudly. "Just checking my email," she said, glaring at her mother. "You haven't taken that away from me."

Her mother sighed. "I need a few things at the store for dinner. Can you watch Caroline and Lizzy? Just for a few minutes."

"Sure." She waited until she heard her mother's car in the driveway, then opened the laptop. *Where do you put your hands when you kiss?* She looked at the drawings on the screen.

Hmm. I wonder if Mark would like that?

■ ■ ■ ■

Becca wasn't very hungry, but she knew she had to eat. She grabbed her satchel and walked through the lobby with plans to grab some fast food near the hotel, but just as she stepped out under the covered entrance-way, she saw a rose-colored Lexus heading toward the Holiday Inn Express next door.

Noah?

He came to surprise me!

She decided to walk down and see him in the lobby. He undoubtedly thought she was still checked in there.

But she hadn't gone twenty feet across the parking lot when she saw an unmarked police car pass by. It was easy for her, as a cop's daughter, to identify the telltale markings: the adjustable spotlight and the extra radio antennae.

He's following Noah, hoping he'll lead him to me.

She didn't think the policeman had seen her. She scurried back inside the lobby and watched out the windows facing the neighboring hotel.

She took out her cell and texted Noah.

U R being followed by an unmarked police cruiser. I am watching from Hampton Inn. Do not lead him to me!

She watched as Noah's car pulled into the Holiday Inn Express parking lot. *He must be reading my text.* She quickly sent another.

I'll take a cab to the Walmart parking lot. You can drive there. Park on the west side and go in the main entrance. Stay ten minutes. Exit through the lawn and garden center. I'll be in the Chinese restaurant across the parking lot.

She walked back out under the covered entrance and waved to a yellow cab. When she got in, she touched her throat and mouthed, *Laryngitis.*

The driver nodded. "Okay, where to?"

She mouthed, *Walmart.*

He punched the meter and pulled out as she twisted around to look toward the neighboring hotel.

Fifteen minutes later, Becca's heart quickened as she watched Noah half-jogging across the parking lot, holding a picnic basket. For some reason, he reminded her of the ranger in the old Yogi Bear cartoons. *So much for acting discreet.*

He entered, appearing breathless. She offered a little wave and peered out over a laminated menu. He sat and kept his voice low. "Okay, this is a little crazy, but I think I saw the cop. Why are they following me?"

Her laptop was already open and she'd anticipated his first question, so she'd written, "My father got a magistrate to sign off on a three-day forced commitment for a psychiatric evaluation to see if I can legally refuse medical treatment. They were hoping you would lead them to me."

"This is wild," he whispered. "Your father would do that to you?"

She nodded and typed, "In his own little way, it's kind of sweet."

"Wow," he said, "you're suddenly into giving grace."

More typing: "I didn't say I was compliant. But I think I understand." She let him read that before writing, "I still have a bit of a headache, but my voice is returning slowly. I can vocalize most of the alphabet if all I want to do is make syllable sounds. It's weird."

A waitress came, and Becca pointed to number fourteen, shrimp lo mein. Noah ordered spicy cashew chicken.

He leaned forward. "I'm stopping at JP in the morning. David Letchford is working around the clock to get me some synthesized product to combine with my latest crop of gel microspheres from PRINT."

She mouthed, *Great.*

They sat in silence for a moment before Noah spoke again. "If this works, will you go in for treatment?"

She wrote, "It has to work first."

"Can't you trust us to figure out the last steps?"

Typing again, she wrote, "I know this sounds crazy, but I know there are still problems to solve, and the way I was approaching them before would have taken me years to overcome them. It's like I was blind to the answers."

"Then hurry," he said. "I'll help you." He halted before adding, "I don't want to lose you."

She felt her eyes beginning to tear. She attempted speaking but covered her mouth when she only managed, "Aaa." *Again.*

Watching her mouth, he seemed to understand. Either he'd read her lips or understood her broken vocalization.

She tried another simple sentence without much success. *Me neither.*

He sniffed. Then he lifted the picnic basket. "I was bringing you supper."

He lifted a box of Wheaties and handed it to her.

She smiled at the way he'd plastered her image on the front. She knew what was inside. She opened it anyway. *Cap'n Crunch!*

She typed. "Funny. Even after all these years, I can't pass a cereal aisle in the grocery store without thinking about Cereal Sundays."

She had come to his house every Sunday evening. His family ate a traditional big Sunday midday dinner, so evenings were whatever they could scrounge. Noah always joked about fixing her supper, but what he really meant was pouring cereal out of a box.

His favorite was Cap'n Crunch. She was a consummate mixer. She would start with something good for her in the bottom of the bowl, invariably something with bran. In the middle, she'd transition to a sweet granola. On the top, her selection was either Cocoa Krispies or Lucky Charms.

"Cereal Sundays," he muttered. "Come to think of it, I still eat cereal every Sunday evening."

She smiled and wrote, "Americans consume 160 bowls every year. Fact."

He laughed. "You're such a nerd. How do you know these things?"

She ignored him and wrote, "There are almost three billion cereal boxes sold each year. If you laid them end-to-end, they would stretch around the earth thirteen times."

She enjoyed watching him laugh. It was one of the things she had always liked about him. He laughed so freely and heartily, not like some people who were too self-conscious to let themselves go.

And it made her laugh back at him. After she'd laughed along with him about her nerdy facts, she realized that she'd been vocalizing a "ha ha ha" without thinking. *Hmm. Laughter vocals must follow a different brain path. It bypasses the injured part.*

She watched out the front window as a young couple passed, hand in hand. She typed something she'd been wanting to know. "Why didn't you ever marry?"

He looked out across the Walmart parking lot. "I dated some. Even had a fiancée for a while after college." He smiled. "But she didn't like cereal. I knew it would never work."

She laughed again and mouthed, *I'm serious.*

"Okay. Fact. I was engaged once. But she was the one who broke it off. Said she could never measure up to some ideal woman I had in my head." He reached over and touched her chin. "Maybe she was right." He paused. "You're back to wearing lipstick?"

She gave him a little pucker and wrote, "I

like the way it makes my lips feel."

"I don't need to tell you this, but I will." He said it slowly, as if each word were its own sentence. "You. Are. Beautiful." He touched her lips. "With or without this stuff."

She took a deep breath and began to type. "Do you think God honors deathbed commitments? I mean, when I was about to go into surgery, I prayed for God to save me. I was afraid, Noah."

He nodded. "God knows your heart, Becca."

She nodded and wrote, "You are just like your father."

He whispered, "I miss him." He paused. "I think about him every day."

She understood that. She wrote, "I've thought about two people every day for the last twenty years. Jimmy Peters."

He nodded. "Me too."

She smiled and then mouthed, *And you.*

He turned her question around. "And what about you? Why didn't you get married?"

She typed. "Oh, I did. I married my research. Every date I ever had, I bored to death talking about molecules, oxygen delivery, and my goal of changing the world."

"You know, you use that stuff to intimidate everyone and keep them at a distance." He hesitated. "You never did that with me."

She nodded and typed, "That's because you looked at me differently. The men I dated weren't interested in dating a smart blonde. Blonde, they wanted. Perfect pouty lips, they liked. But they wouldn't have liked what I was covering up."

"So you kept them at a distance with a cold coat of intellect."

She mouthed, *Guilty.*

They ate quietly after the food came, since Becca didn't want to get anything on her keyboard. Occasionally, she just let her eyes linger on Noah's face and pondered the fortune of a woman he'd call his.

When she finished, she typed, "Stay with me tonight."

He looked surprised.

She shook her head and typed some more. "Not like that, stupid. I have two beds in my room. We can stay up and talk."

"It may be too tempting."

She typed, "Noah, I just had brain surgery. I have an inoperable brain cancer. If we tried anything, I'd probably stroke out and die."

He laughed. "That would be a real turn-off." Before she could type again, he said,

"How do we get there without being seen?"

She thought for a moment. "I'll take a cab back. I have the phone number to text when I'm ready. You should park somewhere close, like a restaurant or the Holiday Inn Express. Then just come to the Hampton Inn. Room 311."

"Okay, text your cab. Maybe he can drop me next to my car so I don't have to walk across the lot."

33

Thirty minutes later, as the sun colored the sky in the west, Becca heard a gentle knock on the door.

She looked out through the peephole.

Noah was holding up a carton of milk and some plastic bowls. "To go with the cereal," he said to the door. "In case I want a snack."

She opened the door and rolled her eyes.

After he put the milk in the little refrigerator, Becca showed him all the details of her latest efforts at hemoglobin synthesis.

After an hour, Noah yawned. "So is this going to be all business?"

She shook her head. "Look what I discovered," she mouthed. "I can sort of whisper."

It was faint and sounded a little spooky because she was trying to phonate without using her voice box, making word sounds by blowing air through her lips.

"I had an interesting conversation with Mel about you," he said. "You know she thinks you don't understand grace."

Becca nodded and whispered, "She has been telling me that for a long time, trying to get me to see why I feel I have to perform."

"It sounds like you're finally getting it," he said, taking her hand. "But it's not a onetime thing. I have to continually remind myself why I'm okay with God. I may have days where I think I've done well and therefore He must be more pleased with me, but that's wages, not grace. So I go back over the by-grace-alone verses all the time."

She nestled her head against his shoulder and let her hand rest on his chest. *God, how I wish things had been different. I wish I hadn't run away from You and this man for so long.*

She lifted her head. "I need to take some pills before bed." She paused. "And a shot."

"Still running your own little medical show, huh?"

She nodded. "Have to."

She went to the bathroom, took four ibuprofen tablets, two Dilantin capsules, and two Tylenol caplets, and gave herself an eight-milligram injection of dexamethasone. *That ought to hold the old brain swelling at bay.*

She dressed for bed in the bathroom and brushed her teeth. She wore a pair of silky but modest pajamas and quickly inserted herself beneath the covers of the bed opposite where Noah sat.

Only when he bent over her and gave her a tender kiss did the tears start. She fought the urge to sob and sucked his lower lip in between hers to keep her own lips from quivering.

She pulled away. "This can't end well," she whispered. "I'm afraid I'll break your heart."

In the morning, Becca awoke to the sound of the shower. While Noah was busy in the bathroom, she dressed and brushed her hair. When he finished, she slipped past him and finished her morning preparation.

When she came out, she tried to say, "Breakfast in the lobby." Unsuccessfully. She frowned and mouthed the words. Her speech was coming back, but not at the rate she wanted.

Noah wore a pair of khakis, a polo shirt, and Sperry topsider deck shoes. He looked as if he'd just stepped off the University of Virginia campus. "We could stay and have cereal."

She shook her head and whispered, "Need coffee."

"Okay," he said, "lead the way."

They took the elevator down two floors. As soon as she stepped off, a Dayton cop jumped up from his chair opposite the elevator. She looked frantically down the hall, but the cop took her elbow in his meaty hand before she could even think of running.

"Easy," Noah said.

The man wore a name tag that said Mike Raines. He spoke into a radio. "I've got her. Repeat, Jackson in custody."

So that's what I am now? In custody?

The officer spoke forcefully. "Dr. Jackson, I've been ordered by the magistrate of Rockingham County to take you in for a mandatory three-day evaluation."

She nodded, thinking, *I don't have three days.* She looked at Noah and whispered, "Need my meds."

Noah held up his hands. "Hey, she's on a lot of medication. Give us a chance to collect her things."

"They've got medicines where we're going," he said. "And some nice patient gowns too."

"How'd you find her?"

"We followed you. When your car didn't leave the parking lot overnight, we staked out all three motels on this strip." Raines offered a plastic smile and nudged Becca toward the door. *So much for coffee.*

She grabbed Noah's hand and locked onto his face. "Collect my things. Take them in your car and check out for me."

He nodded.

She took a step away with the officer, then fought free just enough to throw herself back into Noah's arms. At the rate her cancer was progressing, she didn't know whether she'd last another three days to be with him again.

She pressed her lips against his and lingered until the officer interrupted.

"Okay, okay, enough with the good-byes. Let's go, Dr. Jackson."

He escorted her to the back of his unmarked police car. Once in the backseat, she saw there were no inside door handles, and there was a metal grate separating her from Officer Raines.

The police car pulled away from the hotel. She tried to think. There would be no escape once she was in a locked ward at Western State. She would have to make a move before they arrived. But what would make him stop?

She could ask to use the bathroom, but she didn't have anything to write a message on.

She tapped on the metal grate. "Baaa

raaa!" *Bathroom!*

He shook his head — he didn't understand. He wouldn't take his eyes off the road long enough to look at her to read her lips.

She repeated it a few times without improved clarity. "Baa raa, baa raa."

That's when she decided that a good old-fashioned grand mal seizure would get his attention.

She started by gathering saliva in her mouth for a few minutes. She wanted to work up a good crazy-looking foam. She unbuckled her seat belt so she could fall off the bench seat.

She started by jerking her right arm, flailing it against the metal screen a few times for good measure. Then she threw her head back and moaned and foamed until saliva ran from her chin. She jerked her arms and legs wildly and stared through the ceiling of the car.

"Dr. Jackson?" Officer Raines had twisted around to watch.

She heard him curse.

"Dr. Jackson!"

She kept flailing and added a few guttural noises and some heavy breathing, complete with spraying her spit around the car.

The car pulled over and stopped.

She jerked her arms and legs.

The officer repeated her name a few more times.

Becca stole glances at him but wouldn't allow her eyes to focus. She knew that a real seizure involved incontinence, but she wasn't about to pee in her pants and doubted whether it would add anything convincing to her act. The officer's face was already etched with fear.

Finally, after watching her flail for another thirty seconds or so, he flipped on the siren and accelerated down the road.

Becca eventually stopped flailing but kept up the heavy breathing and spit running down her chin. She stared off, eyes open and unfocused. *Local hospital, here I come!*

Five minutes later, they pulled to a stop.

Officer Raines turned around. "Dr. Jackson? Dr. Jackson? We're at a hospital. I'm going to get help."

If only I could get out of this car!

Soon he returned and opened the door. Two strong men dressed in green scrubs lifted her to a stretcher and pushed her through a set of automatic doors. She watched the ceiling pass rapidly, finally coming to a halt in a cubicle separated from its neighbors by curtains. She heard the deputy explain: "This lady was being transported in the back of my car when she started jerking, like having a seizure or something. I know she's got something bad, 'cause her father says she's been diagnosed with some sort of brain tumor and she needs treatment."

Another male voice, much calmer than the officer's: "She is known to have a brain tumor? Is she on any medicines?"

"Yes, but I don't know what."

"Okay, sir, you'll have to stay in the lobby. We'll take good care of . . ."

"Rebecca. She's Rebecca Jackson."

A nurse started an IV. "She's got a ton of needle tracks over here," she said. "Drug abuse, I'd bet."

The doctor leaned over her. "She's been in some sort of treatment for a brain tumor, so maybe it's just from blood draws.

Becca remained as unresponsive as she could during the physician's exam, but because he wanted to test her level of consciousness, he had to access her reaction to a painful stimulus. He twisted the skin beneath her right collarbone. Only the fact that she was aphasic kept her from screaming. She reached for his hand.

"Hmm. Localizes to pain," he mumbled.

The nurse, a woman of about sixty, wiped Becca's chin with a moist rag. "Dear me. A brain tumor? And so young, too."

Just then, Becca heard the oscillating sound of an ambulancc sircn. It first grew, then stopped.

She listened to the swish of the mechanical doors. Her nurse and doctor disappeared toward the sound. A moment later, the nurse yanked a curtain across the foot of Becca's stretcher.

"Seventy-two-year-old male with new onset crushing chest pain, pressure seventy over palp. Monitor showing sinus tach, rate 144."

Becca sat up, yanked out the IV, and grabbed a gauze from a small table by her stretcher. She peered around the curtain. Everyone had gathered around the old guy having a heart attack.

She slipped off the stretcher, turned, and briskly walked through a set of double doors and into a hospital hallway. Two left turns, down a long hall and then right, down a flight of stairs, out into another hallway and out the back door. It seemed humid, even for Virginia. She looked across the parking lot filled with employee vehicles. Beyond the lot was a grove of trees. Beyond that, she wasn't sure, but it wouldn't take her long to find out.

34

Becca moved quickly through a grove of trees and across a grassy area, then crossed a road and headed into a thick forest. She could see a road to her right, so she tried to stay at least one hundred feet into the trees, traveling parallel to the road.

When it appeared she was coming up on a yard behind a house, she slowed and moved over to the road so she could read a street sign.

She texted Noah.

Come now. I'm in the woods at the corner of Jefferson St. and Stonecrest Dr. behind Shenandoah Memorial Hospital in Woodstock. I'll explain later.

Noah was sitting in the parking lot at McDonald's, unwrapping an Egg McMuffin — a far cry from his normal flatbread, pumpkin seed, and oatmeal breakfast, but he was stressing over Becca's quick departure with

the deputy and in search of comfort carbo-
hydrates. The sound of an incoming text
distracted him. He laid aside the wrapper,
stared at his phone, and read the message.

What? Becca's on the run? Again?

He activated his GPS and entered
Stonecrest Drive. He was six minutes away.

Becca, this is insane!

A few minutes later, he drove slowly down
Stonecrest Drive and turned right on Jefferson Street. Becca emerged from the trees,
waving madly.

He unlocked the door, and she got into
the backseat and immediately lay down. He
turned and stared at her face. "Go north on
11," she whispered. "Stay off I-81."

Melissa rounded the counter at her diner
and topped off Barry's mug of fresh coffee.
"Not out on the campaign trail today, boss?"

He shook his head. "I'm sure you've heard
about Becca."

"Some," she said. "I heard she was sick."

He sighed. "She's so darned independent,
that one." He looked up at her, and for the
first time ever, she thought she detected
moisture in the lawman's eyes. "You know
she's refusing treatment and she's likely to
die if she doesn't get it?"

Melissa sat across from him.

Barry shook his head. "And get this, I have an order by the magistrate to take her in, so she can be evaluated to see if she's actually competent to refuse treatment, and my boys track her to a motel up in Woodstock where she's shacked up with that Linebrink guy —"

Melissa coughed, interrupting him. When she made eye contact with Barry, he continued after sipping his coffee. "My guy picked her up and was taking her to Western State when she had some kind of seizure. He had to divert and take her to a local hospital up in Woodstock." He shook his head slowly and wiped at the corner of his eye. "Becca's dying, Mel, and there doesn't seem to be anything I can do about it."

"If she's in a hospital, they'll treat her. They have to, right?"

"Only if she'll consent," he said, "and apparently, she's out of time."

She found herself reaching over and patting his hands, a gesture that came to her naturally. A week ago, she couldn't have imagined herself sympathizing with the man she was sure had manipulated her so cruelly.

Noah will be crushed.

"I asked my deputy to be sure they move her back to the University of Virginia. At least they know her case. Maybe if she's still unconscious, she won't be able to refuse treatment."

His cell phone vibrated. She released his hands so he could retrieve it. "It's my deputy," he said. He punched a button with his thumb. "Chief Jackson."

Melissa watched his face redden.

"What? When?" He cursed. "Call unit two and do a search in the neighborhoods around the hospital. Now!" he yelled.

She thought he was going to throw his phone. "Idiots! She was wheeled into the emergency room and apparently just walked away while the doctors were attending someone else." He slapped the table. "She's obviously gone mad!"

Twenty minutes later, Noah pulled into a gas station. Becca got out and sat in the front seat.

"Where to?" He paused. "I need to go to Jackson Pharmaceuticals to meet with David Letchford. Obviously, I can't take you with me." He hesitated. "And I'm sure I'll pick up a tail again when I leave JP."

She nodded and shrugged.

"How'd you get away from the deputy?"

She demonstrated by jerking her arms and legs and hanging her tongue out.

"You faked a seizure?"

She smiled. Then she whispered, "They took me to the hospital. I ran away when they were busy with someone else."

"Okay," he said, sighing. "Who can we trust?"

She raised her eyebrows at him as if in question. *Don't know.*

"How about Mel? I can ask her to take you down to Smith Mountain Lake. I signed out the house for ten days when I took Amy and Tiffany there to hide. You should be safe there, and it has Internet access so you can work."

She mouthed, *Okay.*

He picked up his cell and called Mel.

"Noah, what's going on?" Mel said, then hesitated. When she spoke again, he could hear the disappointment in her voice. "You spent the night with Becca?"

"It's not what you think." *Why do I feel I need to explain?* "We had separate beds. She's sick, Mel."

"Well, you told me you were helping her hide."

"Yes. Her parents want to have her committed and force her into treatment."

"Have you considered that that might be a good idea, Noah?"

"She just needs a few more days to work on her research."

He listened as Mel sighed into the phone. "What do you need me to do?"

"She'll be at a gas station with a small Taco Bob's restaurant attached, about fifteen miles north of Woodstock on Route 11. Can you pick her up and take her to the Bradshaw Pharmaceuticals lake house?"

"Can I leave her there?"

"Sure."

"And where will you be?"

"I need to go to Jackson Pharmaceuticals."

"I'll do it. *For you.* Because you ask, not because I think it's right."

"Thanks, Mel. I owe you."

"We'll talk about that later."

"I'm going to leave her here now. She can't really speak much because of some problem she developed after her biopsy."

"It will take me forty-five minutes. Will she be okay?"

"I think so."

After hanging up, Noah caught Becca's eye and nodded toward the entrance to Taco Bob's. "Sit in there at a table. Order a taco or something. Mel will be along in about forty-five minutes."

He left her there with her suitcase and satchel and headed south on Route 11. When he got to Woodstock, he circled the parking lots of the Holiday Inn Express and the Hampton Inn, hoping to pick up a tail and lead them off in the wrong direction.

Melissa asked Mary Heatwole, a longtime waitress at Melissa's BBQ, to watch the restaurant. Then she drove through town, cut over to I-81, and traveled north toward Woodstock. While she drove, she silently prayed: *God, help Noah. Give him wisdom. I don't want him to get hurt.*

She passed gentle rolling hills of green corn and a few dozen long poultry houses that overlooked the highway. She watched the oncoming traffic for a red Lexus but must have missed it when the median was wide and wooded.

She thought about Becca. She'd been her friend for — well, since forever. They'd never been part of the popular crowd, although Becca had ridden into the limelight as the quarterback's girlfriend during their senior year of high school. And once Becca started dating Noah, their friendship waned, probably because of a mutual jealousy over Noah's attention. After Becca left for college, they saw each other less frequently, since Becca had headed off to the University of Virginia while Melissa went to Virginia Tech.

After Becca came back to the area to work

for Jackson Pharmaceuticals, Mel had seen her more often. When Becca would stop in with her father at Melissa's BBQ place, she and Mel would reminisce about old times. Their relationship was pleasant. They talked about everything . . . except Noah.

It was midmorning and nearly ninety degrees by the time Melissa saw Taco Bob's and the attached BP station.

She could see Becca through the window, sitting alone, sipping a fountain drink.

Mel sent a quick text message and got out of the car. Becca waved. She mouthed, *Thank you.*

Melissa didn't really know much about Becca's aphasia, but fortunately, Becca had written out a paragraph explaining a few things. Becca turned the screen of her laptop around so Mel could read:

I have a glioblastoma multiforme. Sounds scary. It is. It is a deadly brain cancer, but there is a silver lining. The tumor is supplied by a rich network of blood vessels that are not only feeding the tumor with oxygen, but bringing extra oxygen to an area of my brain that is helping to solve some of my critical research problems in the creation of an artificial blood. I fear that if I am treated before I solve my research problems, I won't be able to figure out just what I've been doing wrong for the past six years on this project, because the extra oxygen that it brings to my brain is making me very creative. That's why I'm refusing therapy until I can solve the problem. My parents certainly don't like me gambling with my life, so they are out to have me committed to Western State Hospital for a psychiatric evaluation. If they can prove I'm incompetent, they can force me into getting treatment. That's why I'm running. And that's why I need your help. I thought you had a right to know.

My brain biopsy caused some bleeding, which has resulted in a weird expressive aphasia. When I try to talk, it comes out in a jumble of syllables, but my lips are getting the proper message, so if you can read lips, we'll communicate fine. Just don't listen if I try to vocalize because I sound like a baby!

Mel read the note slowly. "So how long will you live if you don't get treatment?"

She shrugged, motioned Mel close, and whispered, "Not long. Weeks maybe. I'm hoping I can quickly finish my project and then think about treatment."

Mel shook her head. "Becca, what if it's too late? You dying isn't going to help anyone." *And Noah will be crushed. Again.*

Becca whispered, "It's a risk I have to take."

Mel doubted that. "Are you sure you're in this for the right reasons? Are you really in it for all the people your research can help, or are you still looking for validation?"

Becca started to protest, but Mel turned away. She didn't want to lip read any more of Becca's explanation.

Becca began to type.

"Let's go," Mel said.

Becca shook her head and turned the screen around for Mel to read:

I'm finally doing something for someone other than me. I don't have to do this to be right anymore. I know God loves me. Period. Independent of performance. That's grace, remember?

Mel read it and looked back at Becca. *Really? Have you really changed?* "Becca, you're risking your life. Do you really want to put your parents through losing a child? Do you really want to put Noah through this?"

Becca held up her hands in surrender.

Mel turned toward the door of the little

restaurant. "Let's go."

They headed south on I-81.

As they neared the Mount Crawford exit, Mel picked up her phone, punched a number, and waited. When the other party answered, she simply said, "Be there in five."

She took the exit. Becca touched her arm and shook her head vehemently, but Mel didn't want to look at her.

She pulled into the Exxon station. Becca's father and two deputies were waiting.

Becca pounded the dashboard. She looked at Mel, her eyes glaring, and tried unsuccessfully to talk.

Mel smiled. "Sorry, Becca, but I couldn't let you do this to Noah. He cares for you. And you were just going to break his heart."

A deputy opened Mel's passenger door while Barry Jackson waited, leaning against his Dayton Police SUV. When the deputy led Becca past, her father said, "It's for your own good."

She looked at him and shook her head.

The deputy ushered her into the backseat of a second police cruiser.

Mel sighed. *Noah's gonna kill me. But I did this for him.*

35

David Letchford met Noah at the front of Jackson Pharmaceuticals and ushered him through the security checks to the lab. David could hardly contain his excitement. He handed Noah the readout of the nuclear magnetic resonance data on their synthesized hemoglobin. "Compare this," he said, "with this." He handed him the NMR of a natural hemoglobin.

"Amazing," Noah said. "I'd say ninety-nine percent."

David smiled. "Nope. Ninety-nine-point-nine percent."

"And she figures this out how?"

"I've watched her. She just draws out a sketch of the molecule and starts mentally breaking the bonds to create the right fold. It's genius."

Noah texted Becca.

Progress! I'm at JP and will combine your molecule with my gel spheres tomorrow. We are almost there. Pray this works.

The reply from Becca came quickly.

Checking in at Western State now. Mel turned me over to my father!

"No," Noah said.

"What's wrong?"

"Becca says that our friend who went to pick her up turned her over to her father. She's at Western State."

"No way!"

Noah rubbed the back of his neck. *What was Mel thinking?* He looked back at David. "How quickly can you get me a solution of your product?"

"Been here all night making the changes Becca suggested," he said. "Give me an hour." He shook his head. "Do you really think we can do this without Becca's input?"

"We have no choice."

David's eyes darted beyond Noah toward the entrance to the lab. "Uh-oh, boss alert."

Noah turned to see James Jackson approaching. He stood and shook his hand.

"Noah, what brings you to our fine laboratory?" The CEO rested his hand on David's shoulder. "Selling our secrets to the enemy, David?"

Noah stepped forward. "Becca and I have been cooperating on an important project. I assumed you'd been briefed."

"Briefed, yes, but there's no signed agreement. So why is it that you two seem to be running forward without a contract?"

"Special circumstances surrounding Dr. Jackson's illness," David said. "She may not have long to live, and she enlisted Noah's help to push the project forward. We understood that the contract was just a formality."

The CEO frowned. "Let me ask you something, Noah. If I have one of the most brilliant minds working on this project, why would I want to bring in outside help?"

"The project will have worldwide impact. I think laying aside our concerns about compensation and competition would be noble for such a beneficial cause. Besides, Becca pursued one side of the problem, and I, another. Together, we can have a product ready for testing in months, if not weeks."

"Sounds naive."

"Becca's dying," Noah said. "She wants to leave this one last significant mark. I'd like to help her do it."

"And you'd like Bradshaw to share in the revenue."

"Of course."

James Jackson touched the shoulder of a passing man wearing a white lab coat. "Call security. I want someone to escort Mr. Linebrink out of this facility."

"But, sir. Becca asked —"

James held up his hand. "As you have said, Becca is dying, so she might not have long to protest my decision." He looked over at a uniformed security guard who now stood at Noah's side. "Escort him out. And search his briefcase. Use our top security-breach protocol. Run his laptop through the zero-tolerance theft program. Erase anything that has a JP tag on the identification."

With that, the guard gripped Noah's elbow and started urging him toward the door.

Becca gripped her leather satchel tightly and stared across the table at Dr. Keith Lee, her evaluating psychiatrist. He was of short stature, with jet-black hair and Asian features.

She'd already had to surrender her belt on check-in. They cited "the rules" and said that all incoming patients were put on suicide precautions for twenty-four hours and that those precautions included removal of anything that could be used for hanging.

A nurse, a twentysomething woman who appeared barely old enough to be out of college, told Dr. Lee, "She refuses to give up her laptop."

Lee nodded and said in a soft voice, "This is an unusual case. I've been briefed on her medical condition by reading the magistrate's ruling. So, because of her expressive aphasia, I think we need to allow her to keep the laptop." He looked across the wooden table at Becca. "But I'm afraid we'll have to remove the shoulder strap from the bag.

Resisting the urge to roll her eyes, Becca unclipped the leather strap and handed it to the young nurse. "Heee hee ha," she said, demonstrating her aphasia. She slipped the laptop from a sleeve in the satchel and opened a new Word file. The first thing she wrote was, "I'm concerned about my medication. Everything was taken from me during the intake. I am on several important medicines to keep down brain swelling due to my cancer."

Dr. Lee read the communication. He turned to the nurse. "Casey, I want you to pull up the list of medications that Dr. Brighton prescribed during her last admission." To Becca, he added, "Since we are both state institutions, we share a database. It shouldn't be a problem getting you the medications."

She tried to hide her alarm. *Except that I got these medicines myself!*

She nodded, attempting to show compliance. She didn't want to reveal anything that would reinforce their bias that she was incompetent.

Dr. Lee led Becca down the hall to his office, where he said she would be more at ease. He was right. Beside the desk and bookshelves, there was a comfortable grouping of stuffed leather furniture that surrounded a coffee table. The table appeared to be made of old stressed wood and had a glass top over a drawer in which the doctor had placed items for display through the glass. She paused momentarily, looking at the items. An old parchment with Chinese lettering, an ornate sword, a carved wooden box, and a collection of what appeared to be metal utensils were carefully arranged.

Dr. Lee smiled. "It's my collection of antique Chinese medical artifacts. Except for the sword," he said. "That's just for looks. Samurai."

They sat on the same couch to facilitate his reading of her computer screen.

Dr. Lee clasped his small hands in his lap. "Dr. Jackson," he began, "it is my job to render an opinion of your mental competence." He spoke with little accent, more New York than Chinese. "I've been briefed by the magistrate's report. I know all about the fraudulent prescriptions and your colorful escape from the police, as well as how you lcft a hospital against medical advice."

She listened but felt an uncomfortable churning in her stomach. *He's biased against me, and we haven't even begun!*

He began with a series of questions, taking Becca through something she guessed was routine. A test of her memory. He gave her three words to remember. Mouse. Tree. Ballet slippers. Five minutes later, he asked for the words. He asked about orientation to time, place, person.

So far, so good.

"Who is the president?"

She typed the correct response.

He went on to questions a bit more bizarre, asking her whether anyone was controlling her thoughts or inserting thoughts into her mind.

He asked about paranoia.

She smiled and decided to go for honesty. "If you mean," she typed, "that I think others are getting in the way of my goals, then yes. My parents and this county magistrate don't understand the urgency of my research and the way that the brain tumor has allowed me to make amazing progress." She turned the screen for him to read.

He started taking notes on a yellow legal pad.

She glanced over but couldn't read his handwriting.

He asked her about grand and magnificent ideas.

She wrote about the billions in health-care savings and the millions of patients every year that she would be able to help if her project was completed. She needed him to understand that her current situation was all about her research.

She tried to interpret his facial expressions, but he was unreadable beyond his fascination with her answers.

He leaned toward her laptop screen. "And you feel uniquely qualified to complete this work, above everyone else?"

Again, she opted to write an honest response. *God, help him understand. This does sound a bit crazy.*

She wrote about her experience on the plane, where she'd first realized her new ability to solve and understand a three-dimensional puzzle. She wrote about the times of near-genius revelations that advanced her understanding of how to create an artificial hemoglobin.

She watched his eyebrows rise as he read. *He's skeptical.*

"So you would call this fatal brain cancer a gift?" he asked.

She typed. "In a way. I know it is threatening my life, but it is also advancing a medical breakthrough."

"A potential medical breakthrough," he corrected.

She shook her head and typed. "You must understand. The implications of my research are huge. No more risk of blood-transfusion reactions or viral transmission, hundreds of millions in savings for blood banks and donation centers, thousands of patients who can be optimized essentially risk free."

He leaned back. "What motivated you to get into this work?"

She briefly typed out the story of her accident.

He read it and crossed his arms. "Dr. Jackson, I have read your memoir, and what you are telling me is different. Is it possible that your brain tumor is affecting your memory?"

She shook her head and typed. "I simply shared the version that I'd been told over the years. I guess I wanted to believe it so badly that I was willing to tell the story that way. But in my heart, I knew what had really happened."

"So you lied."

She pursed her lips. They felt dry. *I need lipstick,* she thought. She nodded.

"And now, your tumor is prompting you to tell the truth?"

She typed. "Something like that." She turned the screen and let him read, but then turned it back and began typing again before he could respond. "Facing death does something to you, Dr. Lee. I want to do the right thing before I die."

"You seem to be motivated by guilt. Guilt can be powerful, Dr. Jackson, but also very disruptive to our personal well-being."

She typed, "Guilt motivated me for a long time. But I think I've come to a peace about what I've done. Now I just want to do what I've been gifted to do. More 'get to' than 'have to.' Understand?"

"So you know what you are doing will result in your death?"

More typing. "I know it's a possibility."

"Do you want to die, Dr. Jackson?"

She shook her head. *No!*

"Do you think about harming yourself?"

No!

"Do you obsess about harming others?"

Only crazy people who stand in the way of my goals, she thought. She hid her thoughts behind a smile and mouthed, *No.*

He shifted in his seat. "Let me ask something else. Do you believe that God is leading you? Does He want you to sacrifice

416

yourself for the good of mankind?"

She thought about that. She wrote, "Not exactly. Possibly."

His phone sounded. He laid the legal pad on the table to read a text message. While his attention was turned to answering the message, she stole a glance at his notes.

He'd circled several phrases: *Grandiose thinking. Paranoid. Guilt-ridden. Death wish. Uh-oh.*

The last one caught her eye.

Savior complex.

Becca looked away. *This is not going well!*

David Letchford headed out of Jackson Pharmaceuticals for a late lunch. When he got to security, he attempted to bypass the security screen — his usual habit. Typically, they would more carefully screen people coming in.

But not today.

"Sorry, Dr. Letchford. I'll need to search your bag. Put your keys and phone here and walk through the detector, please."

David unloaded his pockets into a plastic tray and walked through the metal detector.

He waited while the muscular security guard searched his briefcase and a small cooler. He inspected a ziplock bag containing a peanut butter and jelly sandwich, an apple, and a bag of chips. He didn't bother opening the thermos.

In David's briefcase were two metal bottles marked "Biohazard."

The security guard eyed the bottles and lifted them as if they contained something infectious. "What's in here?"

"Nothing. Just empties," David said.

The guard unscrewed the lid and held it upside down. Nothing. He sniffed it and closed it back up. Then he inclined his head toward the door.

David collected his things and, whistling, headed through the doors into the Virginia humidity.

Five miles down the road, he pulled off into a private drive. He opened his briefcase and the cooler and transferred the contents of his thermos into the two metal biohazard bottles and, after removing his food, placed them in the cooler.

He unwrapped the peanut butter and jelly sandwich and sent a text to Noah Line-brink.

I'm out. Fifteen minutes away.

36

The next morning, Becca spent hours taking a long test known as the MMPI, the Minnesota Multiphasic Personality Inventory. She tried to be honest but found herself irritated at some of the true-or-false questions that seemed to have no adequate answer that cast her in a favorable light.

"Once in a while I think of things too bad to talk about."

True. Doesn't everybody?

"I have never been in trouble because of my sexual behavior."

I was caught in a lip-lock with Noah Linebrink while sitting in the front of my father's police cruiser.

"I have had very peculiar and strange experiences."

This is a peculiar experience, so yes.

"Everything is turning out like the prophets of the Bible said it would."

True. But will they think I'm crazy if I answer

419

this way?

"Parts of my body often have feelings like burning, tingling, or crawling, or like 'going to sleep.' "

Yes, but that's my brain tumor.

She rubbed the back of her neck. She needed pain medication and some steroids.

I'm answering these questions honestly, God, but my answers sound crazy, even to me.

She got up and knocked on the window of the locked door to the little room where she had been left alone to complete the test. The young female nurse opened the door.

"Could I get something for pain?" she whispered.

"We checked your medication records. It seems that when you left against medical advice, the medications were automatically voided."

"I need something for pain. And I'm soon due for my anticonvulsant. I could have a seizure if I don't get something soon."

"I'm authorized to give out Tylenol," she said. "Otherwise, I'll have to check with Dr. Lee."

"But he's a psychiatrist. Does he know how to handle a neurosurgery patient?"

The nurse put her hands on her hips. "Dr. Lee has an MD from Johns Hopkins. I think

420

he's competent to prescribe meds," she said.

Becca sighed. Arguing wouldn't help her cause. "Okay," she said, "I'll take the Tylenol." She tilted her head toward the door. "I'll be in there."

She sat back down to take the test, but a buzzing in the left side of her head distracted her.

She tried to focus, but the words seemed to blur.

Great, she thought. *All I need now is a migraine to make it seem like I'm noncompliant.*

Noah hadn't pulled an all-nighter in the lab since he was a PhD candidate.

But it had been a long, long time since he'd been this excited about a result. A half-empty pizza box sat on the counter. Two empty cans of a caffeinated java energy drink lay in a trash can nearby.

He was using the absorption of light to measure the percent of saturation of his artificial blood with oxygen and carbon dioxide.

He held up the data comparing natural blood to their artificial product.

Amazing.

She's done it.

We've done it.

It is nearly identical.

He could think of only one metaphor that came close to capturing how he felt about what he and Becca had accomplished.

Noah Linebrink is back to pass, flushed out of the pocket. Becca Jackson cuts left, right, and then straight down the field, outsprinting the pass protection! Linebrink unloads a bomb. Jackson is in the open. The throw is long . . . but wait, Jackson makes an unbelievable one-handed grab in the end zone! Touchdown!

During the second day of Becca's psychiatric evaluation, Dr. Keith Lee shook his head. "I'll be honest with you, Dr. Jackson, I have some serious questions about your behavior." He slapped a folder on the desk in front of him. "But your MMPI clearly shows that you have a grip on reality."

She smiled. *Nice to know.*

"But," he said, "the most basic natural instinct is self-preservation. And you seem to have lost it."

She shook her head in frustration. She opened her laptop and wrote, "So are you going to have me committed for therapy against my will?"

He shifted in his seat. "I want you to live, Dr. Jackson. I'm not sure why you seem so intent on dying."

She held up her hand and wrote, "I am not intent on dying. I'm just more intent on helping millions than I am in treating my cancer." She added, "You didn't answer my question."

"You'll know at the end of our three-day evaluation."

At 3:00 p.m., Becca was sitting in a common lounge and trying to avoid frustrating attempts at conversation by the other inpatients. She leafed through a *National Geographic* dated May 2011.

A young female nurse approached. "It's time for visiting hours, Dr. Jackson. You have a visitor."

Becca lifted her leather satchel and followed the nurse into a smaller public area inside two sets of locked doors. Noah sat in the center of a red vinyl couch, appearing as if he'd slept in his clothes. His hair looked like he'd been wearing a baseball cap for a few hours. He smiled when she came in.

She waved and took out her laptop.

"How are you?" he asked.

"Headache," she whispered. "They won't give me enough medicine." She opened her laptop and wrote, "I've got to get out of here. The people are crazy. See that guy in the red sweater? He thinks he's Bill Clinton. He thinks I'm a Republican, so he doesn't like me."

"You want him to like you? Tell him your name is Monica."

She let him read her lips: *Shut up!*

He shoved a folder into her lap. "Look."

She looked at the NMR profiles and put her hand to her mouth.

She flipped through a dozen more pages — data from oxygen uptake and delivery curves generated from Noah's work last night after infusing the gel microspheres with the artificial hemoglobin.

She raised her eyebrows in a question. She typed, "It works?"

He smiled. "Beautifully. We just need to test it. That will take some approval, but we're on our way." He paused. "Don't you get it? Now you can get treatment without compromising our chances of success."

She took another look at the papers in her lap. Suddenly, she couldn't stop the tears.

This is what I've been working for.

This is for Jimmy Peters.

She stood up and wiped her tears.

She motioned for the young nurse. Becca typed a message and turned the screen for her to see. "Please get Dr. Lee. I want to go to the University of Virginia and submit to treatment for my brain cancer."

The nurse walked away. Becca sat on the couch next to Noah and gripped his hand. A few minutes later, Dr. Lee came in and sat across from them. "I understand you've had a change of heart?"

She nodded and pointed at the screen where she'd written. "Please transfer me to the University of Virginia hospital under the care of Dr. Leslie Brighton."

"Well, it seems someone may be trying to get by without an involuntary commitment on their record." He paused and leaned back in his chair. "You thought I was going to rule that you were incompetent, didn't you? Scared you into saying you'll get treatment."

She shook her head and began to type. Frantically. "That's not it at all! Noah here is one of my co-researchers, and he's just brought me some great news about our project. It seems we are so near the finish line that I don't need the advantage that this crazy brain tumor has been giving me."

Dr. Lee read the screen. "I see." He paused. "But this three-day evaluation is mandated by your local government. I can't release you to another hospital until the time is up."

She wrote, "I may not have that much

time. I need to get started on chemotherapy as soon as I can."

"Unless the magistrate overturns his own injunction, my hands are tied. You'll be released at the end of three days."

"Wait," Noah said. "If I talk to your father, maybe he can convince the magistrate to overturn his order."

She whispered, "Do it!"

Dr. Lee shrugged and stood. "Have fun. I've never seen one of these things overturned."

Becca reached over and tapped Noah's shirt pocket. He handed her his cell. She entered her father's number and handed the phone back to Noah.

After a conversation that lasted only minutes, Noah turned back to her. "He said he'll talk to John Ewing. It was his order that sent you here."

Ten minutes later, Dr. Lee walked in carrying a fax from the magistrate. "Looks like we can send you to the University of Virginia," he said.

He turned to leave the room but stopped halfway. "By the way, Dr. Jackson — I may not have agreed that your behavior was exactly rational, but I do admire what you were trying to do." He tilted his head to the side. "It's nice to see someone doing something noble for a change."

She mouthed, *Thank you,* before he turned and left. Then, to Noah, she wrote, "I'm going to get my things. Can you give me a ride to UVa?"

"Sure."

She walked back toward her room, but as she entered the long hallway, she began to stumble. Her vision blurred, and she felt a stabbing pain in her head. *I'm going to vomit.*

She put her hand to her mouth and rushed toward the door to her room. The floor felt uneven. Her arm began to jerk. She managed to open the door, then collapsed onto her hands and knees. She wretched violently, purging herself of the institutional breakfast and lunch. Her last thought was that she was going to fall into her own puke.

Ten minutes later, Noah asked the nurse to check on Becca. "She said she was just going to collect her things."

"She probably just got held up with her discharge paperwork. You can't just walk out of here, you know."

Just then, another patient ran up the hallway toward the front nurses' station. "Hey, somebody — help! There's a woman back here on the floor. I think she's dead."

37

Noah ran down the hallway with a nurse behind him yelling, "You can't go back there! It's a patient living area!" He ran into the room he saw staff rushing into.

He stopped at the door, his worst fears confirmed: Becca was on the floor, looking lifeless.

A man wearing a pair of scrubs asked for space. "Get her on her side," he said. "She's breathing."

Noah pushed past a woman in the doorway and said, "She has a brain tumor. She's been having seizures."

"Call Dr. Lee," the nurse yelled. "And get an ambulance! We'll have to get her over to a general hospital."

"She was being transferred to UVa," Noah said. "Please take her there."

He surveyed the room. Something smelled awful. *Vomit.*

Noah knelt over her.

A young female nurse touched his arm. "You'll have to give her some space, sir."

Becca didn't respond to her name. She remained comatose with her eyes open and glazed. The paramedics arrived, quickly placed her on a stretcher, and started an IV. Then they wheeled her away down the hall.

Noah glanced around the room, pulled open the drawers in a small dresser, and dumped the contents onto the bed. He rolled a few toiletry items up inside her clothes, gathered them into his arms, grabbed her laptop, and sprinted for the front lobby.

At the University of Virginia hospital, Noah found that Becca had been taken straight to the neuro ICU. He peered through a set of automatic double doors at the activity inside. He spotted Dr. Brighton, Becca's neurosurgeon, and wanted to ask her about Becca.

He didn't have to wait long. Dr. Brighton came out with a handful of other white-coated staff.

"Dr. Brighton? I'm Noah Linebrink. I'm with Rebecca Jackson."

"Yes, Noah," she said.

"How is she?" He halted. "You know she's

wanting the special chemo treatment now, right?"

"So I heard. I just got off the phone with the psychiatrist from Western State." She took a deep breath. "But we've got other problems to sort out first. She's had three witnessed seizures since leaving the other hospital. If we can't control this, I'll have to think about an induced coma. I'm afraid if she keeps seizing, there may be permanent damage."

"Permanent damage . . ."

"Brain damage. I'm concerned about the oxygen levels in the brain during the seizures."

"But if you start treating the cancer, won't that stop the seizures?"

"It will help, but it won't stop them quickly enough."

He nodded and felt a lump rise in his throat. "Do whatever you can. I know she wants to live." He pointed down the hall. "I'll be in the waiting room if she has any changes."

He walked down the hall, sat in a vinyl recliner, and stared at the faces of the families who had loved ones in the ICU. The neuro ICU wasn't where you went if you had a cold or even a broken arm. You went there only if you had a brain aneurysm, brain surgery, a stroke, or some other neurologic catastrophe like a broken neck. He could see the fear in the hollow eyes of the families.

He pulled Becca's laptop from the padded sleeve. He wanted to review their last conversation. He just needed something to hold on to.

He read her comment about the patient who thought he was Bill Clinton. That made him smile. He read the few remaining comments and closed the file.

On her desktop he saw a folder entitled, "Instructions for Noah." Inside was a document by the same name. At the top was the heading: *In case I die or am incapacitated by this crazy cancer.*

Beneath it, she had written:

1. Never loved a guy so much as Noah Linebrink.
2. Never hurt a guy so much as Noah Linebrink.
3. Open the file called "Revisions" and send the new manuscript to my publisher. I'm committed to telling the truth. About all of it. Send it to eddirector@putnambooks .com.

Noah shook his head. *Oh, no you don't. It's*

431

history, and you don't need to trash yourself on my account.

He searched for the "Revisions" file and dragged it into the trash. Then he pulled down the menu and held the cursor over "Empty Secure Trash."

But he couldn't do it. *It's Becca's choice,* he thought reluctantly.

He dragged the file out of the trash, closed her laptop, and slid it back into the sleeve. As he did, he noticed two more manila envelopes tucked in behind the laptop sleeve. He pulled them out. More photos and more demands.

Wow, Noah thought. *Even though she has been getting more threatening letters, she has somehow remained focused on getting the job done. Or maybe because she's so committed to telling the truth now, she doesn't care that someone else is threatening to do exactly that.*

Noah went to the cafeteria's salad bar and selected spinach leaves, garnishing them with black beans, mushrooms, a sprinkle of Parmesan cheese, and sunflower seeds. He used the light ranch dressing and ate at a corner table where he could watch all the white coats hurrying about. Twenty minutes later, as he was finishing up, Dr. Brighton stopped at his table.

"Noah."

He looked up.

"Becca seized again. The routine meds wouldn't break it, so we induced a medical coma. The seizures are now controlled."

"How long will you need to keep her like this?"

"We'll use an EEG monitor to assess for new seizures. Once she's been seizure free for forty-eight hours, we'll lighten the sedation and reverse the coma. In the meantime, my lab is preparing a tumor-directed, antibody-type chemotherapy. As soon as I've had a chance to amplify an antibody response to her tumor, we'll give it back to her so that it can attack the tumor."

"Best-case scenario?"

"She wakes up and knows you." She paused and put her hand on his shoulder. "But there is always a worst-case scenario too."

He didn't ask, but she plowed ahead anyway. "It's possible the seizures and growth of the cancer have already done their damage and she never wakes up even after we lift the medical coma."

He nodded and watched her walk away.

He sniffed and pressed his napkin against his trembling lips. *Please God, let it be door number one: best-case scenario.*

■ ■ ■

That afternoon, Noah looked up from where he was catnapping in a recliner in the intensive-care waiting room to see Barry and Rachel Jackson enter.

Barry nodded but did not speak.

Rachel walked over just as he was struggling to his feet. "Noah, we just saw her." Her lips started to tremble. "She's paralyzed."

"It's the effects of the coma. The doctors have placed her in a coma to stop the seizures and hopefully allow her brain to heal."

Rachel's expression was one of concern. "How are you?"

He could tell she was inspecting his current wardrobe. He lifted his baseball cap, aware that she probably wouldn't approve of him wearing it inside. He ran his fingers through his hair, an attempt to restore a little body to the smashed, oily strands. He glanced down at his wrinkled shirt, a polo with a Bradshaw Pharmaceuticals logo. "Sorry for this," he said, gesturing toward his hair, his clothes. "I worked all night on Becca's project. The good news is that —"

Barry stepped forward and cut him off.

"You're the whole reason she's obsessed with this crazy idea of fake blood, aren't you? If you hadn't come back and stirred up her feelings about this, she'd have gotten treatment weeks ago."

Noah felt like stepping back, but his calves were already pinned against his chair. Barry was large, but certainly no larger than the defensive ends Noah had faced as a quarterback, so he stood his ground and even edged a little closer to the lawman. "Actually, Becca's fascination with this project was the reason I came back. She was obsessed with this long before I came on the scene."

Barry pointed a finger at Noah's chest. "Yeah, well, we all know where this notion that she needed to save the world came from."

Noah had had enough. Becca's illness, the dangling love relationship that remained just out of reach, and the lack of sleep all pushed him toward a snapping point. He was reaching for Barry's stumpy index finger, imagining how it would feel to snap it back over Barry's hand, when a woman's sob interrupted.

"Oh, Rachel," Trish Jackson cried. "This is just horrible!"

Trish was Barry's sister-in-law, a woman

with a trailer-park background who'd assumed the role of wealthy socialite with more grace than anyone had thought possible. She was a force to be reckoned with, and many knew that behind the CEO, Trish was one tough ruling woman.

But today, she looked off-center. She carried a bouquet of roses. She brushed back a tear. "I can't believe this is happening."

Rachel opened her arms to receive her, and Trish responded by offering her a cheek for a close-but-no-skin air kiss. "We're all in a bit of shock," Rachel said.

Trish sniffed. "I brought flowers."

"They're beautiful," Rachel said.

Noah thought that red roses would have been more appropriate for an anniversary, but he kept quiet.

The group sat and fell into an awkward silence. Noah felt like the odd man out, although he was pretty sure that he was the only one Becca would have really wanted to keep vigil.

Barry broke the silence. "James is working, I suppose?"

Trish's eyes misted over again. She dropped the bouquet on the chair beside her. "I suppose. I asked him not to come."

Rachel leaned forward. "It's not his fault, Trish. Becca just let this research project take over. James didn't make her . . ."

Barry grumbled. "It was Noah who —"

Trish melted down and cried, leaving the others uncomfortable and wondering. Rachel handed her a tissue.

"I went to pick up some flowers at the Blue Ridge Florist." Trish sniffed. "As it turned out, there was an order for Jackson Pharmaceuticals already. I thought James was being sweet." She paused. "A bit out of character, but sweet. I took the flowers to the car before I read the little card. 'For Arlene, with love, Jimmy.' "

Rachel shook her head. "Oh, that could mean anything, Trish. Jimmy's always been good as gold. He probably sends flowers to all the employees for their birthday."

"They're red roses!"

Noah looked at Barry. He was looking down, avoiding Trish's eyes.

He knows something.

"I'm going to get some air," Noah said, deciding to walk the hallways.

Anything was better than sitting with a scorned woman and a couple who blamed him for their daughter's critical illness. As he was leaving, he heard Trish's voice.

"He'd never divorce me. I'd get half of everything, even JP."

He took the elevator to the lobby and

strolled through the cafeteria, looking for comfort carbs. He selected an energy bar and walked out through the massive foyer and past the gift shop, nearly bumping into Mel as she hurried into the building.

"Noah." She gasped. "When I heard the news, I came as soon as I could."

"Yeah, things are pretty crazy up there right now, so I thought I'd get some air. Becca's parents and her aunt Trish are up there. Becca's been put into some sort of medical coma to let her brain rest and keep her from seizing."

"Barry and Rachel stopped in at the diner to let me know what was going on. They wanted to thank me for helping."

Noah let the comment pass.

Mel continued. "I guess Barry has finally figured out that I didn't have anything to do with sending Becca those pictures."

She looked up into his face, squinting as she studied him. He saw the discouragement set in. "What, now *you* doubt me?" She touched his arm gently. "Noah, I'm so sorry."

He pulled away. "Mel, I just saw two more manila envelopes with more of your pictures and threats. I guess Becca has been too absorbed in her research to even tell me that she'd gotten more."

"Noah, I didn't —"

Noah interrupted, looking away. "I don't know what to think. I never would have suspected you. But then you turned her in."

"For her own good, Noah."

He looked back at her, trying to read her. "Well, then, who? Who else would have all of your pictures?"

She seemed exasperated. If it was an act, it was a good one. "Noah, everything I did was for her . . . and for you." She took a step forward. "And why would I threaten her?"

He held up his hands. "Jealousy?"

She shook her head. "This was a mistake. I came over here thinking you might need some support. I guess I was wrong."

"Why did you turn her in, then? It's like you were working against us."

"Is that what this is about? You think I turned her over for her evaluation because of jealousy? I did it for you, Noah. I knew if she delayed much longer, she could die, and I knew what that would do to you." She shook her head at him, frowning. "Someone had to force Becca to get treatment, and I figured it might as well be me."

"Mel, I —"

"And to think I was —" She started to sob.

He touched her arm, but she wrenched away and ran out of the hospital.

Noah took two steps toward the exit and stopped. He was bone weary. He had no energy to chase Mel, nor any to return upstairs to face Becca, paralyzed in the ICU, or the drama in the waiting room.

Instead, sighing, he plodded toward the parking garage.

That night, Noah tossed fitfully despite his exhaustion. He dreamed of high school, of a Halloween party where he'd dressed as Superman, Mel as Lois Lane, and Becca as Princess Leia.

"You told me you were coming as Luke Skywalker." Becca wasn't smiling.

"I couldn't find my lightsaber. So I went with plan B."

"Including your very own Lois Lane?"

"It was her idea. Cool, huh?"

The dream morphed.

Becca stood in her lab, stirring a large pot of boiling blood. "It's not real," she said, "it's artificial."

She came close and pulled him into an embrace. "Don't worry, my father's deputy won't find us." She kissed him passionately. When he finally broke free, he was running his fingers through her blonde hair. He pulled it to his face, but it was auburn! He looked into the face of Mel.

"What do you say, cowboy? Do I kiss better than I cook?"

The scene changed. He was being taken to jail.

A police officer. "You hit a kid. I hope he lives. Looks like he lost a lot of blood to me."

A hospital emergency room. An injured child in the middle of a tangle of tubes and IVs.

"Give him the artificial blood. It's safe. He won't get HIV!"

But no one listened. Everyone kept working, talking about how horrible it was. "Did you know that the guy who did this was drinking?"

"And underage!"

Becca's face. "Kiss me, Noah."

Mel's face. "I kiss better than I cook." She winked at him. "And you know I can cook."

38

The next morning, Noah rose early so that he could catch Dr. Brighton on morning rounds. Besides, it was less likely that he would see Barry and Rachel if he could get in and out before morning visiting hours.

He found her exiting the unit, leading ten others, an assortment of residents, interns, and medical students. "Dr. Brighton," he said, stepping forward. "How is Rebecca Jackson?"

She stepped close to him so she could keep her voice low. "Some signs of improvement. No seizures last night. We gave her an injection of anti-tumor vaccine this morning." She paused. "So we'll see."

"Thanks."

The team trailed away.

Noah thought of his options. Stay and face the drama of Barry and Rachel or head over to Dayton to see if he could make peace with Mel. He wasn't entirely convinced Mel hadn't sent the pictures, but he had to admit, it would have been out of character for her. She'd been a strong Christian ever since he'd known her.

Still, he thought, *jealousy can make people crazy.*

Regardless of how he felt toward Mel at the moment, he knew he hadn't handled their encounter well. He'd come across as accusing and hurt. And in the process, he'd messed up their friendship. So he decided to skip the waiting-room drama and head to Dayton.

Melissa had always enjoyed the morning crowd. The breakfast menu required a good short-order cook, and Mary Heatwole fit the bill perfectly, allowing Melissa to mingle with the patrons and catch up on Valley news.

She carried the coffeepot over to Ralph Peters and leaned against the counter. She refreshed his mug. "Guess you heard about Becca Jackson?"

He nodded and looked up with a blank expression. "And why, exactly, should I care?"

Mel shrugged. "She's local, that's all."

"I guess you read her book like the rest of Dayton, huh?"

"Parts. Can't say I'm a huge fan of her slant."

"Everyone acts like the fateful Halloween accident traumatized her and Noah Linebrink so much. But what about me? I lost my only son as a result of that accident. Then she goes off and tells *my* story in her memoir and makes the big bucks off of it. And what do I get?"

He looked down at his plate of eggs and shook his head slowly.

Mel reached over and touched his arm. "Mr. Peters, what did you ever do with those pictures I sent you after your son's memorial service?"

"Oh, I knew what you were doing, Mel. You wanted to vindicate Noah. But I didn't really care who was responsible. I had a dead son, and nothing could bring him back."

Again, she prompted, softer. "But what did you do with the photos?"

He sipped his coffee. "I burned 'em. Didn't want 'em around." He nodded and repeated, "I burned them."

She looked up as the bell on the door jingled. In walked Noah Linebrink. *Oh no.* She watched Mr. Peters look over his shoulder.

"No worries," he said, pushing his mug

across the counter. He pitched a ten-dollar bill on the counter. "I was just leavin'."

"I'll get your change," she said.

"Forget it. Looks like you could use the tip."

He walked out, avoiding contact with Noah.

Noah sat at the booth in the corner. It was the one where Barry Jackson usually sat so he could see everyone come and go.

She placed a mug of black coffee on his table. "Didn't expect to see you."

"I owe you an apology."

She waited.

"I've known you a long time. I shouldn't have doubted you."

She softened. "It's been a stressful time for all of us."

"Stress isn't a good reason to lash out. I'm sorry."

"I remember that about you."

"What?"

"Every time you and I would have any kind of fight, you'd always come over the next morning and apologize."

"And your mom would feed me."

"Mostly cereal."

"Hey, I like cereal."

She lifted her order pad. "Is that what you'd like?"

"Cheese omelet. Side of grits. Whole wheat toast."

"Wow," she said. "I thought you'd gone all oatmeal and fruit on me. Barry and Rachel must really be stressing you out."

He chuckled. "You wouldn't have believed them last night." He lowered his voice. "Trish brought in these flowers that James bought for his secretary . . ."

Rachel and Trish were on their third cup of coffee, sitting at a green metal table under an umbrella in a courtyard just outside the UVa hospital cafeteria, when Barry walked up.

Rachel stood and gave him a peck on the cheek. "How'd the rally go?"

"Great," he said. "I asked the crowd to keep Becca in their prayers, said she was fighting for her life, suffering from a brain cancer." He shrugged. "The press didn't ask any hard questions after that."

"Wow," Rachel said sarcastically. "Glad that's working out for you."

"Rachel, I didn't mean it like that."

They sat down at the table.

Trish changed the subject. "I'm going to ask James to make that payment Becca was concerned about. That will be one thing less for her to worry about."

Barry leaned forward. "Do you think he'll go for it?"

"I think I have the leverage to influence him."

Barry sighed. "That's a relief. I don't like that threat hanging over my head."

"Your head?"

"Sure. My department would be blamed for messing up the investigation. Everyone would think I covered for my daughter, even if I was kept out of the loop."

Rachel reached for his hand. "But you did cover for her."

He kept his voice quiet. "I just looked the other way, that's all."

Trish fidgeted with a ring on her finger. "Any decent father would have done the same thing. I think we should tell Becca about James's decision to pay when we visit."

"She's in a coma."

"You never know what she can understand. I've heard you're supposed to talk to people who are in a coma. I read it in *Cosmo.*"

Rachel hesitated. "Did you confront Jimmy last night?"

She shook her head. "He was asleep when I got home and out to the golf course before I got up this morning." She smiled. "I'm waiting until the right time."

Rachel sipped her coffee. "The right time?"

Trish shrugged. "I'll make his favorite meal, massage his shoulders . . . and remind him that I get half if he ever leaves."

Rachel covered her mouth. She couldn't believe this was the same woman who had seemed so broken up about the flowers the day before.

Barry looked sad. "That secretary doesn't hold a candle to you, Trish. Jimmy knows that."

She smiled. "I know," she said. "I know."

Two days later, Noah called Mel. "Just got off the phone with Becca's neurosurgeon. She's going to remove the coma drugs in the morning."

"That's great, right?"

Noah sighed. "She isn't the most optimistic doctor around. She said only time will tell. Becca might wake up and be better . . . or she might not wake up at all."

"She probably has to say that, Noah. She doesn't want to give you false hope."

"Maybe."

"You scared?"

"Yeah."

"Want me to be there?"

He nodded, then caught himself and spoke. "That would be great."

"What time?"

"The neurosurgery team rounds at six. I think they'll turn off the drugs on rounds."

"I'll be there, Noah."

He smiled. "See you." He paused. "Pray," he said, but the connection had already been closed.

39

At ten the next morning, Becca opened her eyes. She heard the blip, blip, blip of her own cardiac monitor and understood. A tube was in her throat, and her chest lifted and fell with each breath forced into her lungs. She blinked and looked to the side. Noah sat in a chair, looking tired. Melissa touched his shoulder and handed him a cup of coffee. "You'll be no good for Becca if you're asleep," she said. "You'll need to be strong for her."

Becca understood. *Mel is taking care of Noah.*

She lifted her hand. *Is something restraining me?*

She managed to wiggle a few fingers.

Noah looked over. "Her eyes are open!"

He stood and reached for her hand. "Squeeze my hand, Becca."

She tried.

"She squeezed it. She understands me."

He looked at her. "Blink if you understand."

Becca blinked.

"Nurse, she's waking up."

Over the next thirty minutes, Becca was able to lift her hand, then her arm, wiggle her foot, and finally raise her head.

A man dressed in blue scrubs said, "That's good enough for me." He teased loose the tape holding the tube to Becca's cheek. "Now cough."

She did, and he pulled the tube. He slipped an oxygen mask over her face. She motioned for Noah. He and Melissa stood next to her bed.

She worked her right hand, imitating a writing utensil.

"She wants to write something."

The nurse, a man who appeared forty-something, brought a small clipboard-sized erasable whiteboard. Evidently things like that were used frequently in the neuro ICU.

Becca wrote, "Hemo$_2$car." She wrote it just like that, with the two in the subscript after the *O* to indicate oxygen.

Noah read it. "Hemo$_2$car?"

"It's the name of our new artificial blood. It's short for hemoglobin oxygen carrier."

Noah and Mel looked at each other. Noah spoke first. "Becca, you talked!"

"I did," she said, realizing it was true.

"Hemo$_2$car," Noah repeated. "I like it. When did you come up with that?"

"It came to me while I was sleeping."

"Becca, this is amazing. They gave you the tumor antibody while you were in a coma. If you can talk, it must be working. How do you feel?"

"I have a little headache."

The nurse smiled. "Can you rate your pain on a scale of one to ten?"

Becca shrugged. "Two, maybe three."

"We can deal with that."

"Yes," Becca said, "we can."

"I'm calling Dr. Brighton." The nurse walked away. A few minutes later, he returned. "Dr. Brighton has ordered a new CT scan. She wants to see why Becca has regained her speech."

Becca looked at her two friends. "You wouldn't believe how badly I want to brush my teeth. How long have I been out?"

"This is going on the fourth day."

She ran her tongue over her teeth. "This feels so gross. Do not get close to me."

The nurse promised to get her a toothbrush. "But first, off to the CT scanner."

"Noah, I need my laptop. I need to work on some manuscript revisions."

She watched as his face seemed to tense. "Something wrong?"

"You need to rest. You can work later."

Thirty minutes later, as Mel and Noah waited for Becca to return from CT, Mel slipped her leather Bible into her handbag. "I really should get back to Dayton. The restaurant suffers if I don't pay attention to it."

Noah understood. With Becca awake, Mel didn't want to interfere with his reunion. "Okay," he said, standing with her. "Thanks for being here for me."

He went with her to the hospital exit, gave her hand a squeeze, and watched her go, auburn hair dancing on her shoulders as she walked. She glanced back one time as the door closed, and he glimpsed her wiping her eyes as she turned away again.

Noah returned to the ICU to find Becca already settled in.

She looked up and smiled. "Noah. Noah," she repeated, like she was trying it out. "I like being able to talk again."

"Well?"

"The CT confirms that the bleeding from my biopsy is resolving. That's why I can talk."

He leaned forward and celebrated with a kiss, but it seemed more mechanical than emotional, Noah thought. *Must be the set-*

ting. How romantic can a hospital bed be, anyway?

He lingered close to her face. "Don't you get what this means? A new start for us," he said.

"Oh, Noah." She gathered his hand into hers and drew it up under her chin.

But when he pulled back, he saw the tears. "Hey, what's wrong? This is good news."

She tilted her head to the side and sniffed. "Tears don't always mean sadness."

Late that afternoon, after Noah and her parents had left her to rest, Becca opened her laptop.

She began to type.

Can anyone really believe that a deathbed conversion is valid? Until recently, I would have led the charge of the skeptics.

But then it happened to me.

It wasn't like the ground wasn't fertile. My life was ripe for change. I'd spent my life living for myself, striving to make a name for myself and, in a way, atone for the accident. I had everything a professional could want. Money? Check. Big house with a view and a pool? Check. Successful research? Check. A bestselling memoir? Check.

454

But I didn't have peace. I knew from my time with Noah and his family that there was more to life than I was experiencing.

Then came Africa.

It's a place of dust, sweat, beauty, and blood. I found people with overwhelming need. Orphans. Millions of them.

I found malnutrition. Poverty.

And the very rich, often with the poor begging at their well-guarded gates.

I found hope in the midst of profound illness.

Superstition. Witchcraft. Suspicion of Western medicine and pharmaceuticals.

Government corruption from the top to the bottom.

But most of all I found people with stories. Individuals with children, hopes, dreams. I saw the devastation of those stories by HIV and the lack of knowledge, money, and care that could help them find the dreams that they'd long abandoned.

I was healthy. Driven. And, some would argue, beautiful (but I confess, I would have never described myself that way).

Then came cancer and the threat of death.

I remember clearly, on the eve of my emergency brain biopsy and shunt to relieve the pressure on my brain, how I desperately wanted to live, but how afraid I was that I wouldn't be able to finish my research. But more than anything, when the neurosurgeon told me in black and white about the extreme risks I was about to take, I feared *death.* I thought about my life and how empty my house, car, and career was without love. I was transported back to a night spent laying out in the African wilderness, fearing for my life . . . and my main regret was that I'd failed at love.

I remembered the advice of my high school janitor and the verse he'd shared with me.

And so, as I was wheeled into surgery and the mask was over my face while I drifted off under anesthesia, I quoted the only verse most baby Christians know, something so common that it has become an "oh yeah" without people grasping the meaning. John 3:16. It's been plastered on posters at NFL games and on T-shirts. But to me, it hadn't tarnished, hadn't become ho-hum or routine. So as I went to sleep, I wrapped myself in the comfort of that verse, and I just *knew* I believed it was true.

I quoted it as the anesthesiologist fed me oxygen through the mask. Sadly, it was the only verse I knew by memory except for "Jesus wept," and that one wasn't going to do it for me. I didn't even know I was moving my lips until the gas passer lifted my mask and told everyone that I was quoting the Bible.

I didn't care. I knew it was true, and I needed to tell my soul the truth before I faced surgery and the possibility of the Grim Reaper.

For God so loved the world that He gave His only Son, that whoever believes in Him will not perish but have eternal life.

I believe God gave it to me. Belief. Eternal life.

So yes, I believe in deathbed conversion.

Becca pulled down the menu and selected save. Then she closed her laptop. She'd written enough for now.

The following evening, Becca started working on a to-do list, mainly people she needed to talk to about facilitating a joint effort between Jackson and Bradshaw.

She listed the major players, and the players behind the players who had the power to influence the decision:

Uncle Jimmy, CEO JP.

Greg Thatcher, CEO BP.
Noah, David Letchford, Jessica Choy.
Aunt Trish.

She looked up to see Noah walking in with Melissa. "Hey, guys."

Noah took her hand and gave it a squeeze.

Becca smiled. *What, no kiss in front of Melissa?* "Good news. They're moving me to a regular room."

"How are the headaches?"

"Believe it or not, my old standby, Imitrex, works the best."

They chatted about the weather and other surface issues. "I like your lipstick," Melissa said. "What is it?"

"Clinique Almost Lipstick. It's basically not lipstick, and not a gloss either, but something in between."

Noah groaned. "You ladies don't need it at all in my opinion." He caught Becca's eye. "I thought you were over covering up."

She offered a coy smile. "This isn't about covering up. It's about embellishing."

A nurse came in. "Your new room is ready. Think you can sit in a wheelchair?"

"I can manage." She took Mel's hand. "Take this guy out somewhere nice and bring me some takeout, would you? I'm getting tired of hospital food."

She watched as Mel and Noah exchanged a look.

"Okay," Mel said.

"And no fast food. I want something good. Go to the downtown mall and eat outside. I'm going to live vicariously through you, so have a good time."

They followed the nurse pushing Becca's wheelchair and got into the elevator with them. Becca and the nurse exited on the fourth floor, and Noah and Mel headed for the lobby level.

They followed instructions and settled on Zocalo. They sat at an umbrella-covered table outside and ordered a house white wine for Mel and a Newcastle Brown Ale for Noah. The place was perfect.

Mel ordered grilled salmon with green-chili-and-goat-cheese couscous and smoked pico with a cascabel cream. Noah ordered a grilled pork tenderloin with corn cake, chorizo-braised collards, and apricot chutney. For Becca's takeout, they ordered chili-dusted sea scallops.

The evening was warm and carried a feeling of expectation for Noah. There was hope for Becca's recovery and excitement over the research.

"You know," he said quietly, "I haven't let

this sink in. If this product is successful, a Nobel Prize is almost a given."

Mel sipped her wine and stayed quiet.

Noah enjoyed watching the people strolling the mall. He leaned back in his chair and focused on really relaxing. He'd been so consumed with the research and Becca's illness that he hadn't really had any recent chances to just be. He looked over at Mel. The late evening sun caught her hair just right, giving her orange highlights. "You know what this reminds me of?"

She shook her head.

"When my family used to eat with yours after church on Sunday, at your picnic table in the backyard."

"What, you smell a poultry house?"

"Your place didn't smell like a chicken house."

"If the wind blew from the west, it did."

"I was thinking of the outside table, Dad drinking Newcastle, your father trying to get the charcoal just right —"

"And me whipping your butt at lawn darts."

"You were so bad at lawn darts," he said, laughing. "Your dog would hide under the picnic table."

"Your father always made us discuss the sermon."

Noah held up his beer and imitated his father. "And how is this applicable to your life, son? How will you think or behave differently if you apply this to your life?"

They fell into a comfortable silence until Mel spoke again. "You know, this feels like a setup."

"A setup?"

Mel shrugged. "A date. Like Becca wanted us to go out."

Noah downplayed the idea. "She was hungry for some good food, that's all."

Mel raised her eyebrows. "Feels like a date."

He set down his mug. "Mel, we're friends. Becca and I are getting another chance."

"I know." She looked at him over the wineglass held beneath her chin, her hair sparkling in the evening sunlight. "I'm just saying, it *feels* like a date."

40

Three days later, in her husband's plush work office, Trish Jackson unlocked the screen on James's cell phone and scrolled through his sent messages. Then she plopped down in his leather chair to wait.

She looked up from behind his desk when she heard the door.

"Trish, honey, I didn't expect to see you here."

Calmly, she set the phone on a large rustic coffee table in front of a leather couch. "When were you going to tell me about Arlene?"

"Trish, I —"

"No excuses, James."

"She means nothing to me."

"Flowers, texts, phone calls. Nothing?"

"She was lonely. Her husband left her. She trapped me, honey. I should have seen it coming. I —"

"I want out. I'll have Skyler and Sons

draw up the papers."

"Don't do this," he pleaded. "I'll cut things off with Arlene. Really. She means nothing."

"You've said this before."

"And we've always pulled through. We're good together."

She paused to keep him hanging. Then: "Two conditions."

"I'm listening."

"Retire. You need to pay attention to me and your grandchildren."

"You said two conditions."

"Marriage counseling."

She watched his face harden.

"I like work," he protested. "What will I do?"

"Concentrate on me."

She studied him for a moment. *Maybe he's not worth it. But I still love him.*

"Couldn't I just scale back?"

"Been there, done that. Ain't happening. You quit, or I leave. It's long overdue." She paused. "Oh, dear, did I say only two conditions?"

James sighed.

Trish didn't flinch. "Fire Arlene today."

Becca was about to knock on her uncle's office door when it opened and she nearly bumped into her aunt Trish.

"Becca," she said. "I didn't know you were out of the hospital."

"Just discharged today. I talked my parents into stopping here before heading home. There are some things I need to discuss with Uncle Jimmy."

Trish raised a perfectly plucked eyebrow. "This wouldn't have anything to do with fifteen million dollars, would it?"

"So you know about that?"

"Of course. Jimmy shared it with me."

"Yeah, about the money — there are a few things I need to tell him."

Trish didn't seem to want to hang around for the details. She just smiled and said, "If you need something from him, just ask. I think he's primed." She paused, placing a hand on Becca's arm. "Let's just say if he gives you any trouble, then he's in trouble."

With that, Trish winked and walked on, leaving Becca alone.

She took a deep breath and pushed open the door to her uncle's office.

Time for the truth.

Two days later, Noah got his first chance to see Becca since her discharge. He'd talked to her on the phone quite a bit, but research had dominated their conversations and left

464

him feeling a little out of sorts about their relationship. And he was even more unhappy that their first face-to-face meeting turned out to be all business with his boss, Gregory Thatcher, at their facility in Richmond.

As the meeting concluded, Becca looked at her watch and said she had time for a quick lunch before her driver took her back to Richmond. Although she had not had a seizure since her last admission to the hospital, her doctors still wouldn't allow her to drive.

Noah shrugged. "It's too early for lunch."

"Brunch then."

He smiled. He took her to Mabel's Trailer and asked for the oatmeal special.

A few minutes later, Mabel set down two steaming bowls in front of them. Becca tried it out and then lifted a bite on her spoon. "What exactly is this?"

"Caramelized bacon and green apple."

She nodded and took another bite. Her speech was muffled. "Amazing." Then: "How soon can you get me another round of product? I want five liters."

He sighed. Work talk again. "I'll talk to David. Probably three, maybe four days."

"Okay," she said.

She continued eating in silence. When she finished teasing the last clump of sweet bacon onto her spoon, she said, "I've scheduled a news conference for Friday afternoon."

"You're anxious to report how things between Bradshaw and Jackson are progressing."

"You might say so."

He pushed his chair away from the table a few inches. "Becca, what's going on? I thought you and I had embraced this new chance for us, but it seems you're just pushing me away."

She seemed to study him for a moment. "Do you think this can really succeed with us working so closely together?"

"I can't imagine anyone else I'd rather work with."

"I've had a lot on my mind with this joint venture. Don't read too much into it, Noah."

On Friday afternoon, Amy called Noah and asked if she could hang out with him for a while.

"I'm sick of Thing One and Thing Two," she said, pacing, waiting impatiently for his answer.

She listened to him sigh. "I need to go to the Valley. Big news conference at Jackson Pharmaceuticals."

"Can I go with you? I like your car."

"Suit yourself."

He picked her up an hour later. "Wow," he said. "You're back to wearing lipstick? Your mother is letting you grow up?"

Amy shrugged and put on her seat belt and inhaled the scent of leather. "I like the way your car smells."

"We were talking about your mother."

"She feels guilty for making me quit my summer school class, so I think she let me use lipstick to make up for it."

Amy promptly plugged in her iPod earbuds and looked out the window. She listened to Katy Perry.

She was still staring out the window when Noah pulled through the security gate at Jackson Pharmaceuticals. While he talked to the guard, Amy's gaze wandered to a guy operating a weed whacker near the entrance sign. *Mark!*

Her mind raced. She knew that the house where Mark and Dustin took her and Tiffany was owned by Jackson Pharmaceuticals, so it actually made sense to her that she'd see him here. She twisted her body around to watch him. It *was* him.

Did Dustin force him to leave?

Maybe he really wanted to see me again.

Noah parked.

She hesitated. "Do I have to go to this news thing? Can't I just stay here and listen to music?"

"It may take an hour, Amy."

"Leave me the keys so I can lower the windows."

"Wow. How about, 'Would you be so kind as to leave me your keys so I can lower the windows oh favorite uncle of mine?'"

She stuck out her tongue. He handed her the keys.

She watched him walk away. Once he disappeared into a bank of glass doors at the front of the building, she unbuckled her seat belt and opened the door.

She walked to the end of the parking lot and then across the grass toward the noise of lawn maintenance. She walked over a little rise and found him there, shirtless, with beads of sweat glistening on his tanned chest.

He looked up, and his eyes shot open wide. He snapped off the weed whacker and pulled a protective headset from his ears. "Uh — Amy, what are you doing here?" He took a step back and laid down his equipment. He reached for a white T-shirt on the ground a few feet away.

"I'm not here to get you in trouble."

He didn't meet her eyes. Maybe he was

looking around for his supervisor. "Hey — we didn't do anything wrong."

"I just want to ask a question."

He put on his shirt. "Okay."

"I just want to know why. What were we, some side job or something? Did someone pay you to party with us?"

"Look, it's not like that." He hesitated. "Well, it's kind of like that. But it's not what you think. Some guy, a cop, comes up and asks me if I want to spend a few days at a lake house for free. All I need to do is find you and Trish and occupy you for a night. The guy just wanted to scare your parents or something."

She tried to decide if he was telling the truth.

"Seriously, Amy, I told the guy no way. But then he showed me your picture and offered to buy food and drinks. I thought, a free vacation with girls like you and Tiffany? I thought I'd be a fool to turn down an offer like that."

"So what, you and Dustin just decided to split Tiffany and me up, like possessions?"

"I asked if I could bring a friend since there were two of you. The guy said sure."

"So Dustin gets Tiffany and you get stuck with the short straw?"

His mouth dropped open. "What, you're

kidding me, right?"

She just stared at him.

"Amy, it was *my* deal. I got to pick first. Dustin got the short straw."

She liked the sound of that. *Maybe under different circumstances.*

"Look, I'm sorry if you were hurt, but when you and Tiffany left, we kinda freaked and thought we might get in trouble, so we split." He picked up a water bottle and took a long swig. "We really didn't do anything wrong."

"The officer said you" — she gestured with quotation marks using her fingers — "contributed to the delinquency of a minor."

"About that — just how much of a minor are you?"

She didn't want to say.

He waited.

"I'll be fourteen next month."

"Holy —" He stopped himself. "No way."

She smiled sweetly. "Yes way."

He shook his head and mumbled something about jailbait. "Do me a favor," he said. "Remember me and call me in about five years."

She laughed. "I just might do that."

Inside a spacious conference room at JP,

Becca left her leather satchel with Noah and approached a podium with six microphones. She looked great. Perfect blonde hair styled to cover any signs of her recent surgery, and perfect lipstick. *To embellish, not to cover up,* Noah thought.

Becca cleared her throat, surveyed the dozen or so reporters who had gathered, and began after the crowd's excited murmuring ceased. "Thank you for coming. As many of you know, I'm Dr. Rebecca Jackson, vice president in charge of research and development here at Jackson Pharmaceuticals.

"I've asked you to come today to celebrate several milestones. The first is something I'm particularly proud of."

Noah beamed. *She's going to announce the success we've had in developing an artificial blood.*

"Jackson Pharmaceuticals has established a fifteen-million-dollar endowment for assisting the Maasai people living in an area of Kenya known as Loita Hills. These gracious people participated in the clinical trials of our antiretroviral drug, Mopividine, and this is partial compensation for their participation. The endowment will cover ongoing costs of HIV therapy, the cost of infant formula for all mothers with HIV choosing not to breast-feed, education costs for their children, a new well, and a new clinic."

Noah shifted in his seat. *Fifteen million? The same amount demanded in the letters blackmailing Becca.*

Is the amount a coincidence?

He thought back to the last time he'd seen the manila envelopes demanding follow-through. He couldn't quite place his finger on what had bothered him about those letters, from the first. Something wasn't right.

While Becca talked on about the mothers she'd met in Loita Hills, Noah lifted her leather satchel. He opened the laptop compartment and ran his hand behind her computer. The manila envelopes were still there.

He lifted the first envelope and stared at the front. That's when it hit him. The envelopes weren't postmarked!

Unlike the first ones, these threats hadn't been mailed.

Noah slid the envelopes back behind the laptop and looked up at Becca. *Did you do this?*

Were you extorting your own company for money to pay the Kenyans?

"Finally," Becca said, "I have a significant announcement about the future."

Here it comes. Our artificial blood that will change medicine forever.

"Bradshaw Pharmaceuticals and Jackson Pharmaceuticals have reached an agreement to cooperate on a joint venture to pursue an artificial blood product."

Hands shot up.

She pointed to a gentleman in the front row.

"How close to success are you?" he asked.

"Closer than ever. We have yet to conduct human trials, but we will keep you updated." She paused and looked right at Noah. "But we are making significant strides, particularly due to the work of Dr. Linebrink, one of the researchers at Bradshaw."

Tell them about your brilliance! Tell them what you've done.

Instead, Becca held up her hands to signal an end to the questioning, turned, and walked into a back room.

41

Noah found Becca sitting at her desk. "Okay, just what was that?"

"What?"

He leaned against the door frame and looked at the beaded Maasai necklace hanging on the wall behind her desk. "So, fifteen million given to the Maasai residents of Loita Hills just happens to be the same amount that someone was blackmailing JP for?"

"Yep," she said, not looking up. "Say, I'm putting together an oversight board for how to invest and distribute funds from the endowment. Dr. Jacob Opondo will be chairing the effort. Would you help?"

"I, uh, sure. But fifteen million?"

She nodded and stared at her computer screen, avoiding his eyes.

"Becca, when you were in a coma, I saw the envelopes demanding the money." He hesitated. "The ones that hadn't been mailed yet."

"Yeah, about that . . ."

"You were blackmailing your own company?"

She looked up at him. "I'm not proud of what I did. But I'm not the same woman who launched that scheme."

"Becca, that was crazy! Not to mention the fact that you put a lot of people in danger, including me."

"I had no idea my father would react that way. I knew he was bullish, but —" She halted. "Noah, I'm so, so sorry."

"But you got the money, nonetheless."

"I got the money, but I also told my uncle what I'd done." She pushed her chair away from her desk. "He refused to help them, so I did what I thought I had to do to help the families we hurt by our research."

"You told your uncle?"

She nodded. "After I got out of the hospital. I knew what I'd done was wrong and that I couldn't go through with it." She smiled. "But Trish helped me. Evidently she has some leverage with him that I don't."

Noah remembered the waiting-room drama. "I can only imagine."

"So yes, it was me all along. I owe you and Melissa an apology, but I really had no idea that my dad and Uncle Jimmy would go all vicious on you guys, thinking you were the ones threatening me."

"I ought to go. Amy's waiting for me."

She called to him before he could leave. "So about a fresh batch of our product . . ."

Noah sighed. "Special courier to Jackson Pharmaceuticals, refrigerated, Monday morning. What's the rush?"

She didn't answer.

He walked back and leaned over her. "I'm proud of you." She didn't look up. He wanted a kiss, but she didn't offer him her face. Instead, he kissed the top of her head. "Love you for your looks."

With that, he left her staring into her computer screen.

Noah found Amy sitting in the car, quietly singing along with her iPod. "Hey, gorgeous."

She pulled an earbud. "Come again?"

"Want to grab some grub?"

"Sure. I'm starving."

He backed the red Lexus out of its parking spot. "I know this dynamite little barbecue place over in Dayton."

She laughed. "Do they barbecue tofu and sprouts or something?"

"Shut up."

■ ■ ■

James Jackson walked past the empty desk where Arlene used to work and sighed. He took a seat at his large mahogany desk, opened a new Word document on his computer, and began a letter addressed to the JP Board of Overseers.

After the salutation, he began:

Effective immediately, I am tendering my resignation from Jackson Pharmaceuticals . . .

In the IV preparation area where Jackson Pharmaceuticals manufactured and tested the administration of IV drugs, Becca found the technician she needed. "I have a shipment of sterile fluid coming in on Monday that I need packaged for IV administration."

The young man wore a white lab coat over a T-shirt bearing *The Big Bang Theory* logo. "A sterile fluid?"

"Artificial hemoglobin packaged in gel microspheres in a normal saline carrier."

He smiled. "Artificial blood?"

"Yep," she said, smiling. "It's sort of spooky, because it's clear."

"Maybe you can dye it red so people will

trust it."

"No way."

"But just think," he said. "A pale anemic patient will get transfused and turn into a pale patient who isn't anemic."

"It's not like we're going to replace their whole blood volume. There will be limits. But you're right. The patients who receive the artificial blood will not be anemic, but they will still be pale."

"Monday, huh? I'll get right to it."

42

Tuesday morning, Becca briefed David Letchford and swore him to secrecy.

Then David established an IV line in Becca's right forearm and took a set of initial vital signs.

Heart rate 76, BP 124/80, oxygen saturation 98 percent.

She then donated one unit of blood.

Repeat vitals:

HR 86, BP 120/80, oxygen saturation 98 percent, all essentially unchanged.

She then donated a second unit of blood with a slight increase in heart rate, but no change in blood pressure or oxygen saturation.

David looked at her with concern. "Are you sure?"

"Absolutely. This information will be the tipping point in getting FDA approval for further trials."

She donated a third unit. Now her heart

rate jumped to 122 and her blood pressure began to sag, 90/50. Her oxygen saturation remained normal.

She felt slightly winded. "Okay, draw a hemoglobin level."

David drew off another two milliliters of blood and injected it into the analyzer. A minute later, the readout revealed a hemoglobin level of 7.6.

"You look pale."

"Yeah, well, you look scared."

"I am. Scared of your father if something happens to you and he finds out I helped you."

"Time for Hemo$_2$car."

David set up the transfusion and began to drip in a unit of the artificial blood. After one unit, Becca's heart rate slowed to 90, and her blood pressure normalized, back to 110/75.

David drew off another sample for the analyzer. He looked at the readout. "Hemoglobin 8.4. It can't tell the difference in your natural hemoglobin and the artificial one."

"I want to donate another unit."

"But now you'll be donating some artificial blood."

"Not very much."

She gave another unit. Heart rate sped up again — 116. Blood pressure 100/65. Hemoglobin 7.4.

David transfused her another unit of $Hemo_2car$.

Blood pressure and heart rate normalized; hemoglobin measured 8.5.

She motioned toward a bag of artificial hemoglobin. "Another one."

"Becca, you've proved that it works."

"One more."

They repeated the process. At this point, she'd given a total of five units of blood. Hemoglobin back down to 7.3.

She received a third unit of $Hemo_2car$. Hemoglobin rose again to 8.4.

To make up for the other two units, David gave her two more units of $Hemo_2car$. Her hemoglobin rose to 11.0.

"That's my baseline."

"You're looking pretty pale."

"I'll reapply my lipstick. No one will notice."

She felt a tingling in the left side of her head.

"That's enough for today," she said. "I think I'll call my driver."

David looked at the data sheet in his hand. "This is huge, Becca. Huge!" He paused. "Why don't we go celebrate? Dinner? My treat."

"David, that's sweet, but I think I'll just

head home."

"Drinks?"

She smiled. "I've got a headache. Rain check?"

He nodded. "You sure you're okay?"

"I've got normal hemoglobin."

"That you do."

He touched her shoulder gently, lingering a bit more than he'd ever done in the past. "See you tomorrow."

Becca walked to her executive bathroom and injected her right thigh with Imitrex.

Instead of the normal brief sting, her skin began to swell and bruise. She held pressure on the injection site. *What happened? Did I hit an artery?*

She held pressure for a few minutes, then called her driver. At the front entrance, he let her into the back of a JP limo.

She texted Noah: It works. Hemocar works. She stared at her phone, trying to figure out how to put in the small "2" subscript after the O, and then decided her phone wouldn't do it. She pushed send.

Noah called right back. "Becca, what do you mean?"

"Let's just say I know it works."

"Becca? What did you do?"

She didn't answer.

"You took it yourself, didn't you? That's

why you wanted the product."

"I had to know."

"Why didn't you wait for approval?"

"Some things just can't wait." She paused. "Listen, I'm on my way home. Can you come tomorrow? We'll celebrate. I'll show you the data."

"How much did you take?"

"Five units out. Five units in."

"That's insane."

"No, that's confidence based on years of research. And get this, Noah: we measured my hemoglobin after getting the Hemo$_2$car, and it was the same as before I donated my own blood. It works, Noah. Perfectly."

"I'm coming over. You need to be watched."

"I'm fine. Really. I'm pretty pale. I have a little headache, but that's nothing new."

"No arguments. I'm coming over."

She didn't want to argue. "I don't guess I can stop you." She heard him sigh. She shook her head. "You're hopeless."

"Good-bye."

"I love you for your brains," she said and terminated the call.

Five seconds later, her phone signaled an incoming call. She looked at the phone. *Noah. Now what?*

She accepted the call. "Yes."

"You didn't let me respond." ·

She sniffed. *Don't say it. Not now.*

"I love you, Becca Jackson."

Why did he have to choose to tell me now? "Noah," she said, her voice starting to thicken, "you know how I feel." She paused. "I've loved you forever." She ended the call and brushed away a tear.

She dropped the phone into a small pocket on the side of her satchel. The pain in her temple seemed to be intensifying. She opened a compact mirror and flipped on a ceiling light. She studied her pale image and gasped.

She opened a tube of lipstick. Estee Lauder's Pure Colour in Wild Blossom. *If anyone ever needed color . . .*

She pursed her lips to receive the stick.

Her hand froze just in front of her lips as pain knifed its way from the left side of her head through the back of her eyes. Her hand pitched forward, striping the lipstick across her cheek.

Electricity in her head. A flash of light. And then blackness.

Rebecca Jackson was seen briefly in Rockingham Memorial Hospital, where a breathing tube was inserted into her trachea to protect her airway. She was given a dose of

IV steroid and flown by Pegasus to the University of Virginia.

After Rebecca's arrival in the emergency room, Dr. Leslie Brighton surveyed the activity from the foot of the stretcher. A respiratory therapist turned a dial on a ventilator. An intern plunged a needle just below the inguinal crease to draw blood, and a nurse wiped a stream of pale red fluid oozing from the patient's nose. Dr. Brighton shouted, "I want a complete lab profile. Electrolytes, complete blood count, and call the scanner. I want a head CT stat!"

"This is odd," a nurse said, holding up a tube of blood for Dr. Brighton to see. "It doesn't even look like blood."

Leslie held the tube up toward the light. "This is the blood you drew?" She shook her head. "It looks diluted."

"It looks like watery Kool-Aid."

"You must have drawn it above the IV line."

"No. Joel did a femoral stick because her arm veins are so used up."

"Then she must be profoundly anemic." Leslie massaged the side of her head. "Maybe she's GI bleeding. Or maybe the chemo has suppressed her bone marrow. Have the lab type and cross her for four units."

Joel Evanston, the intern on neurosurgery, motioned for Leslie's attention. "Dr. Brighton, look at this. It's like she has a huge hematoma in her thigh."

She examined Rebecca's right leg. "It's swollen like a hematoma, but it's not purple like most blood collections." *What am I missing?* "Let's get this patient up to the scanner!"

43

In Kenya, Dr. Jacob Opondo wiped the sweat from his brow and adjusted the IV fluid running into a scalp vein of the infant in front of him. The Maasai child had been brought in the day before by a mother in Loita Hills. The baby was severely dehydrated from a battle with diarrhea and typhoid fever.

He pumped up the small blood-pressure cuff and slipped his stethoscope into his ears. A few moments later, he moved the stethoscope to the chest and frowned. "There's no recordable pressure."

His nurse rushed to his side.

The child gasped and stopped breathing.

"Shall I start compressions?" the nurse asked.

"No," he said. "There is no use."

He threw his stethoscope to the floor in disgust. "Look at this place. I don't even have enough money to pay the light bill. We have one sink for six examining rooms." He looked back at the still infant as the nurse replaced the top in the makeshift incubator. "What's our tally this month, Margaret? Six deaths?"

"Seven," she said softly.

Just then, the door flew open, and a young doctor waved a piece of paper. "An email came for you, Dr. Opondo."

"Can it wait? I'm not in the mood for more bad news."

"No, Daktari, you must read this."

Jacob took the paper and held it under a gas lantern. As he read, his hand began to tremble.

Margaret looked up. "What is it?"

"Dr. Rebecca Jackson has done it. We've been given a —" He halted, squinting at the paper before continuing. "Fi-fi-fifteen-million-dollar grant!"

Noah sang along to a Josh Turner song, tapping the steering wheel. Unlike many singers, whose tenor vocals were out of Noah's range, Josh Turner's bass range was perfect for him.

Things were finally gelling between him and Becca, and he was impatient to get back to her side.

She actually said it this time. And not just in

a rush at the end of a phone conversation like she always has.

He remembered the last words she'd spoken.

I've loved you forever.

The music was so loud he almost didn't hear his phone. He hurriedly turned down the volume and picked up his cell. He didn't recognize the number. "Hello."

"Noah, Barry Jackson here. I hope I didn't wake you."

"No," he said, his gut tightening. "I'm driving."

"We're at the hospital. Becca was brought back in." His voice cracked. "It doesn't look good. I wanted you to know."

"What happened? I just talked to her a few hours ago."

"Not sure. Her driver said she just passed out in the back of the limo on the way home. The doctor says she's had some sort of bleeding in her head."

"Is she awake? Can she talk?"

Noah listened as Barry cleared his throat. "No," he said. "I think you'd better come."

Two hours later, Noah stood in a small circle with Becca's parents and Dr. Brighton. The neurosurgeon talked calmly and didn't mince words.

"She's had an intracranial bleed around the cancer. At this point we are keeping her alive with the ventilator. We'll need to do a few more tests in the morning, but she isn't responding as if there is any brain function."

No brain function! Noah shook his head. "But she said the last CT showed her bleeding was resolving. I thought the cancer was shrinking from the treatment. She had her voice back. She was getting better!"

Dr. Brighton shook her head. "The last CT did show that the bleeding from her biopsy was improved, but I told Rebecca clearly that the tumor was not responding as we had hoped. I advised her to get her affairs in order."

What? She didn't say that!

Noah studied the faces of Becca's parents. "All she told me was that the scan showed the bleeding was improved. That's why her voice was better."

"The tumor hadn't responded?" Rachel covered her mouth and spoke through her fist. "That's why she kept working at such a crazy pace. I told her to slow down."

Dr. Brighton spoke in a quiet voice. "There are a few things that we are investigating, things I don't understand. There may have been some complications from my chemotherapy, something we've not seen before."

Barry straightened his sagging posture. "Complications?"

"When she came in, her blood looked very dilute, almost pink. I thought she must be profoundly anemic, but her hemoglobin levels measure near the normal range, the same as during her last admission." She shook her head. "There's something else. Her platelet count was low. When the platelet count is low, bleeding is more likely because the platelets help form clots to stop bleeding." She reached for Barry's hand. "My chemotherapy efforts may have caused the platelet count to drop. I haven't seen this before, but I will investigate it, I promise."

Noah gestured with his hands as he talked. "Could the platelet count have been low if another IV fluid had been given?"

Dr. Brighton wrinkled her forehead as if she didn't understand. "Like causing a drop because of dilution? That's possible, but we don't know that she'd had any fluids other than a little saline during the helicopter flight to our facility."

"This wasn't because of your chemotherapy, Dr. Brighton," Noah said.

Barry stared at him. "What do you know about this?"

"She called me this afternoon. She'd done an experiment on herself to prove that our artificial blood could work."

Rachel clutched her husband's arm. "No."

Noah nodded. "Becca donated five units of her own blood and had them replaced with our product that she named $Hemo_2car$. That's why her hemoglobin was normal and her platelet count was low."

Dr. Brighton held the edge of her white coat lapel. "But the blood looked so dilute."

"$Hemo_2car$ is clear — producing dilute-looking blood, but normal hemoglobin."

Dr. Brighton nodded slowly. "She knew she didn't have long. She wanted to make one last contribution. What a lady."

Late the next afternoon Noah gathered with Becca's parents and Mel around Becca's bed in the neuro ICU. They had just been told that Becca's tests showed no brain activity. She was brain dead. The only thing currently mimicking life was the rise and fall of her chest with the mechanical breaths of the ventilator. The medical team asked for permission to remove the life support.

Noah looked at Barry and lifted a Bible. "Is it all right if I read something?"

Barry nodded.

"I'd like to read a verse that she read to

me over the phone just a few days ago."

Noah ran his finger down the page. "Here, in John 11:25 and 26. 'Jesus said to her, "I am the resurrection and the life. Whoever believes in me, though he die, yet shall he live, and everyone who lives and believes in me shall never die." ' "

Melissa brushed tears from her cheeks.

Rachel cried softly. Barry kept his arm around his wife, supporting her quietly.

Noah continued, "So now we know that she lives."

Barry nodded at a nurse standing by, who switched off the monitor and the mechanical ventilator. Becca's chest was still.

Noah let the tears roll unhindered.

The quartet stood without speaking, their tears a bond between them that laughter could never rival.

Barry gripped his daughter's hand. Rachel leaned forward and kissed her daughter's cheek.

Mel leaned against Noah, holding him up even as he supported her.

Noah watched Barry tenderly caressing his daughter's hand. He'd spent most of his life resenting the way Barry had tossed him aside, but in that moment their loss linked them, and Noah saw a gentleness that he admired.

Barry moved aside as Noah stepped forward. He leaned down and kissed Becca's forehead and paused to whisper in her ear, "Love you for your looks."

He could not stay. He turned and fled from the room.

The following morning found Noah sitting on a stool at Melissa's BBQ. When he'd left the hospital the night before, it hadn't seemed right to go back to Richmond, so he'd followed his heart back to Dayton. After a night in a Harrisonburg Holiday Inn Express, he drove over to Dayton for breakfast.

Mel wasn't in. He gave Mary an order for scrambled eggs and sausage and sipped a mug of hot black coffee. Alone, he contemplated the whirlwind of his life. Becca had blown in and out again, scraping the edges of his heart and leaving the wounds open. The first time, it had taken him years to come to peace with the idea of a life without Becca. He prayed as he sipped. *God, how long will the raw hurt remain fresh?*

He looked up when the bell on the door jingled. He winced a little when he saw Barry's large frame. Noah looked down at his coffee, hoping Barry would pass and sit in his regular booth.

Instead, Barry collapsed onto the bar stool beside Noah. There was no ignoring him.

"Noah," he said, inflecting his name as a greeting.

"Morning, Barry." Noah cleared his throat. "I couldn't seem to go anywhere else after last night." It was more of a confession than an explanation.

Barry nodded at the waitress, who set a mug of steaming coffee in front of the lawman without speaking.

"I need to say some things," Barry began.

Noah shifted in his seat and looked around. They were alone at the bar.

"I've done a lot of things I'm ashamed of, Noah. Not least how I've treated you. I owed you a debt of thanks for protecting my daughter. Instead, I pushed you away."

"I did what I did by my own choice," Noah said. "Nobody made me take the fall for Becca."

"But I shouldn't have let you. I didn't realize what you'd done right away. But when I looked at the evidence, it was pretty obvious that my deputies had misinterpreted things. Then, instead of coming forward and straightening them out, I decided it must be what you wanted. So I just looked the other way. Later, when I thought you might squeal the truth, I tried to keep you away from Becca."

Noah studied him for a moment. Barry's shoulders were pitched forward in defeat.

"People are complicated, Barry," Noah said, placing a hand on the other man's shoulder. "You did what you did for Becca's sake. I know that."

"I owe you an apology, probably a ton of them. For thinking you were threatening Becca, for sending those guys to scare you, for arranging for your niece to go missing, all that in addition to how I treated you after the Halloween accident so many years ago."

"Hey, I made my peace with my decision a long time ago. Truthfully, I wasn't sure you knew what I'd done. I thought you looked at me as the drunken teen I was that night, so I didn't blame you for wanting me out of Becca's life." He took a sip of his coffee. "But for the record, you're forgiven. For all of it."

He watched as Barry brushed at the corner of his eye. He didn't seem able to speak, and when he did, his words came out as a choked whisper: "That means a lot."

After Barry had collected himself, he spoke again. "I've withdrawn from the race. Officially, it's because of Becca's death and needing to pay attention to my family. Well, that part's true. I do need to spend more time with Rachel. But the real reason is that I've been a power-hungry jerk. The last thing Dayton needs is another politician looking out only for himself."

"Gosh, Barry," Noah said, "that's almost enough to make me want to vote for you."

Barry smiled.

Mary set a breakfast plate in front of Noah and looked at the police chief. "Your regular, Barry?"

He nodded. "Yes indeed."

"Will you be moving to your regular table?"

He made eye contact with Noah. "No, Mary, I think I'll be sitting right here with my daughter's good friend."

Noah smiled. *God, the world has gone crazy.*

Two days later, Noah sat on a leather couch in Mel's living room in Dayton. Mel was busy in the kitchen after promising to help cater a meal that would follow a memorial service at the Dayton Baptist Church.

He was holding Becca's satchel, which Barry had given him because Becca had left instructions that Noah was to get anything related to their research. He unzipped the front section, which was divided up for filing papers. He lifted out a yellow legal pad and glanced at her notes.

She'd sketched diagrams of the hemoglobin molecule. On several, she'd taken a red marker and crossed through certain chemical bonds, then drawn an arrow to show how the molecule would fold as a result of the broken bond.

He paged through several more and halted, staring at another doodle that Becca had sketched. This diagram wasn't a drawing of a molecule; it was a people diagram, with bonds linking them together. Becca. Noah. Kristen. Amy. Uncle Jimmy. Mel. Barry. Rachel.

She'd drawn bonds between herself and a half-dozen friends and family.

Lower on the page, she'd drawn a similar diagram but had crossed out the bond between her and Noah and drawn an arrow showing the way the relationship diagram would fold as a result. She drew an arching arrow bringing Noah and Mel together.

Noah stared at the page. *Becca was pushing me away, breaking the bond between us because she knew she was going to die.*

He smiled. *And it appears she thought she could predict the outcome of broken bonds.*

Mel called from the next room. He looked

up to see her staring at him from across a large kitchen island. "What's so interesting?"

He shoved the pad back into the satchel. "Becca's research diagrams, that's all."

He opened Becca's laptop and clicked to open the folder entitled "Revisions." He selected the document and started to read, then invited Mel to sit with him so they could read the account together.

There are individual events in a person's life that change everything in seconds. Happiness is stolen. Injury leads to death. And love finds a way to shine through in the midst of darkness.

For me, the event that changed everything was a fateful Halloween night when I was seventeen years old. Almost every day since then, I have thought about that night, knowing that I would give anything to erase it, but lately I've understood. God used the worst day in my life to set my feet on a path that will, I hope, result in a benefit for millions.

Noah invited me to a party of the popular kids. You know the type. The football jocks, the cheerleaders, and those kids who always got the leading roles in school plays and sang the solos at the Christmas concert. There were a few of us in orbit around Noah, and he brought us along as if we fit, but I think that without Noah, Mel and I would have been more comfortable at a Scrabble convention.

Mel giggled at that. They kept reading.

The point was, he invited *me*. We were supposed to go as Luke Skywalker and Princess Leia, but when he showed up with Mel, he was Superman and she was Lois Lane. I was the odd man out, wearing a Star Wars costume. He'd lost his lightsaber, he said, and his costume didn't work without it.

I was inexperienced. I was mad. I was jealous. A bad combination made worse when I started drinking the punch someone had spiked with vodka.

I lashed out at Noah and Melissa. He had come and put his arm around me while I sat on the couch, nursing my third glass of punch. I think Noah had been drinking too, but probably only a beer. I chided him, "Why don't you just go sit with her, your little church buddy?"

Mel was taking pictures and asked us to smile. She wanted to take my picture with Noah, but I could see she had eyes only for him and she'd been photographing him half the night.

Noah tried to kiss my ear and whisper for me to calm down, but I exploded. The alcohol was my excuse, but I knew, down deep, that in my insecurity I was jealous of the bond he had with Mel. They had always had this church thing in common, while I couldn't seem to believe. I cursed him and told him that Christianity was just a religion for janitors, a slam I used hoping to hurt Noah, because his father was the custodian at our school and always had a Bible handy to share with the students who cared to listen.

I don't remember everything I said in that argument, only that I was abusive and loud and that I demanded to leave. Noah cautioned me not to drive, but I rushed out when he went to the bathroom and sped off in my car, away from that party and my embarrassing behavior.

Noah ran after me on foot. Unfortunately, he didn't have to run far. I heard him yelling behind me to stop. I looked in the rearview mirror at him waving his hands, and I looked back at the road just in time to see a small child in a ninja outfit. I swerved, clipped the boy, and ran off the road into a tree.

When I came to, Noah was yelling for

someone to call 911. He checked the boy first and told me the boy was Jimmy Peters and that he was breathing. I heard a siren. Noah knew he didn't have much time. He checked on me, then pushed me across the front seat onto the passenger side and sat behind the wheel. He ripped his cape, the one to his stupid Superman costume, and shoved it up against my face. I was vaguely aware of what he was doing. I watched in half horror as he took my blood and smeared it on his forehead.

When the officer opened the driver's side door a few minutes later, Noah looked up and asked, "What happened?"

An ambulance crew took Jimmy first, and I waited for a second emergency vehicle. Noah was on his feet walking around. An officer made him blow his breath into a machine. I remember Noah telling someone not to let me look in a mirror, because evidently I kept asking everyone over and over to let me see. All the while, Mel kept snapping photos, documenting the night my life went to hell. Pictures of Noah without a scratch. Pictures of me behind the wheel and Noah pushing me aside.

I've gone over the events that took place after that a thousand times.

Noah took the rap for me and went to jail. My father saw to that.

I should have spoken up. I wanted to. A million times. But I'd been told the story differently by so many that I longed to believe the other version. After all, I was drunk. Did I really remember? Had Noah refused to let me drive and left the party to take me home? I reported *that* version, the one that had been reported in the papers and in the first edition of *Pusher.* But if you reread my account, you'll notice that I told it in third person, just as the newspaper did. I told it so many times that I started to believe it myself.

But under the surface, I felt such shame, such guilt for letting Noah take my punishment. I would go to jail now and accept my penalty — except that if you're reading this, I'm probably already dead.

Noah was Jesus to me. I didn't see it then, the way I see it now. It was Noah and his father, the janitor I thought I was *above,* who taught me what true love is. Noah, like Jesus, took my penalty, took my place, and never once stopped loving me.

The events of that day changed me. Jimmy Peters was saved by a blood transfusion but was infected with HIV, developed AIDS, and was kicked out of school by a well-meaning but misguided school board. (It was the '80s, and we didn't understand AIDS.) And I was set on a pathway to find a safe way to transfuse blood.

Why not manufacture a blood substitute that can do what normal blood does, but without the risks associated with transfusion?

It became the obsession of my professional life.

Funny thing was, it became Noah's, too.

Noah closed the laptop. He'd read enough for now.

"Are you okay with the story she wants to tell?" Mel asked.

"She wanted this to be told, and the way she tells it, I think it's okay. It's her chance to reach out and do what she thought was right. For herself and for God." He paused. "I'm going to send it to her editor."

Mel squeezed his arm and got up from the leather couch. "I need your help with something," she said.

He followed her to her little study, where she'd spread out old photographs. Mel touched the top of a framed picture. "I thought I'd put up a display at Becca's memorial. Help me pick out two or three, would you?"

He lifted the photos one by one. "This one," he said, handing her a shot of Becca laughing and carrying her calculus book. "And this one." It was Becca sitting on the bleachers, reading. In the background, out of focus, was the football team in their practice jerseys. Her blonde hair glistened in the sunlight. Her lips were pursed as if she was concentrating or memorizing something for school.

Mel held up another one. "I'm biased toward this one." She smiled at him, and he could see that her eyes were glistening. "But it's not for the memorial. It's for me."

Noah looked at the picture. She'd had someone else take it. Noah stood as Superman with his arm around a grinning Lois Lane.

A natural fit. Happy.

He looked down at Mel as the light caught her auburn hair. Sans lipstick. She didn't have anything to hide.

"You know what?" he said, lifting the picture from her hand. "I love this one too."

■ ■ ■ ■

AFTER
WORDS

. . . A LITTLE MORE . . .

■ ■ ■ ■

When a delightful concert comes to an
end, the orchestra might offer an encore.
When a fine meal comes to an end, it's
always nice to savor a bit of dessert.
When a great story comes to an end, we
think you may want to linger.
And so, we offer . . .

AfterWords — just a little something
more after you have finished a
David C Cook novel.

We invite you to stay awhile in the story.
Thanks for reading!

Turn the page for . . .

**• An Interview with
Harry Lee Kraus, MD**

AN INTERVIEW WITH HARRY LEE KRAUS, MD

Q: How does *Lip Reading* typify a Harry Kraus novel?

A: Readers have come to expect several things when they decide to invest in one of my books. The first — and probably my "signature" and something that I'll never fully get away from — is the medical flavor. Each one of my novels, *Lip Reading* included, contains authentic medical elements. The medical field will likely provide the setting for the story. The protagonist, or main character, is likely a career medical insider or a patient. In the case of *Lip Reading,* my protagonist, Becca Jackson, PhD, is both! She is both a pharmaceutical researcher and a patient.

Kraus novels always contain people in desperate need for a grace encounter. That means that my protagonists may or may not be Christians, but faith elements will be integral parts, not add-ons. Without the faith element in a typical Kraus novel, the story unravels.

Q: That means you are dealing with evil, front and center, in your stories. How do you approach this without offending Christians who want an escape from evil?

A: Well, first, if a person wants a cozy, everything-is-rosy "Christian" novel, they should look elsewhere. My characters are flawed. They are sinners. And — no surprise — sinners sin! A story about sinners in need of grace that has no sin would be a boring story indeed. That said, I am careful not to glorify sinful behavior or to show sin without consequence. Sexual sin, while not something that I avoid, is not depicted in a way that titillates the reader.

Alcohol use in "Christian" novels always stirs controversy. I have decided that I will show non-Christians drinking, as to avoid it would not be real. I have also allowed my Christian characters to drink as this is modern-day reality for many Christians, but I have avoided drunkenness in my Christian characters — not because it is not a real problem for Christians, but because it is a concession I have made so as not to offend sensitive church attendees.

Language is another challenge for Christian writers. I have decided not to use the actual words when a character curses. My characters do occasionally use bad language (again, sinners sin and I think real life needs to be authentic), but I usually handle this by simply saying something like, "He cursed."

I'd also like to address the issue you've raised of readers wanting an escape. Readers do seek entertainment and escape. But what readers hate (conflict!) in their private lives, they love in their fiction! Conflict in real life is miserable; conflict in fiction is essential and foundational. As we read, we experience the conflict vicariously and can identify with the characters as they deal (or fail to deal) with the conflict successfully. Hopefully, in the process, my reader is challenged with fresh ideas about how to deal with problems in his or her own life.

Q: How is your own life reflected in *Lip Reading*?

A: Again, the medical "fingerprints" are all over this book. My life as a general surgeon provides the ideas for stories like this one. My work as a surgeon has brought me into many situations where blood transfusions are needed, and I have often wished for a suitable substitute for transfusion that would be safe and effective. That's where the whole research angle for this novel, the development of an artificial blood, came from. I've practiced for years as a missionary surgeon in East Africa, and I have seen the devastation of the AIDS crisis there up close. Having an effective blood substitute is not just a fiction-writer's dream; it is a real-life dream of many physicians dealing with the expense and risk of blood transfusion.

In addition, my life in Kenya and my love for the "dark continent" is reflected in the backstory in *Lip Reading.* The novel opens in Kibera, a slum where I have personally worked, and gives glimpses into the Maasai people, one of the dominant tribes in Kenya. They have held fast to their primitive lifestyle and their colorful dress and culture, and their rugged living conditions provided a fascinating backdrop for my story.

Q: Your novels often contain inspirational themes. What comes first, message or story?

A: Story always comes first. I'm not saying that an underlying message isn't important, but without an entertaining story, the reader loses interest — and fast! I always try to dish up a generous portion of what the reader desires: suspense (whether it is a life in jeopardy or a relationship on the rocks or the tension of a potential romance developing) and tension. A good novel is always about a great character with a problem. The character can't be perfect; there will be flaws with which the reader can identify. And then the problem looms. How the character deals with the problem and changes as a result is the essence of the novel. And for a Kraus novel, faith is usually one of the elements that helps the protagonist overcome the problem or is a by-product of successfully conquering the difficulty. That's where the message comes in. But the message can't be tacked on; it must be naturally woven into the story so that as the protagonist encounters a faith challenge, the reader will also be forced to think about the necessity of faith.

ABOUT THE AUTHOR

Dr. **Harry Kraus**, MD, is a board-certified general surgeon. He has divided his professional life between the USA and Africa. He is an accomplished writer of both nonfiction and fiction, the author of over fifteen books, including *An Open Heart* and *A Heartbeat Away.* Medical realism and gripping plotlines distinguish his writing, as he gets most of his ideas with a scalpel in hand. Harry resides in Virginia with his wife, Kris, and the youngest of their three sons.

The employees of Thorndike Press hope you have enjoyed this Large Print book. All our Thorndike, Wheeler, and Kennebec Large Print titles are designed for easy reading, and all our books are made to last. Other Thorndike Press Large Print books are available at your library, through selected bookstores, or directly from us.

For information about titles, please call:
(800) 223-1244

or visit our Web site at:
http://gale.cengage.com/thorndike

To share your comments, please write:
Publisher
Thorndike Press
10 Water St., Suite 310
Waterville, ME 04901